CHAPEL LAUNCHED HIMSELF OFF THE LANDING, INTO THE AIR. . . .

He came crashing down hard on top of the security guard, whose body broke his fall. The man cried out, something in Russian Chapel didn't understand. Chapel grabbed the baton out of the man's hand and hit him a couple of times with it, hit him until he stopped protesting.

Then he was off again. Down another flight. Another. Up ahead the stairs ended at a short corridor. At the end of that corridor was a sign covered in warnings and writing he couldn't read. The door had a push bar and it looked like an alarm would sound if it was opened. It had to be an emergency exit to the street.

He hit the push bar at full speed, expecting the door to crash open, expecting to spill out into sunlight and chill morning air and freedom, and—

The door didn't open.

Chapel hit the door with his shoulder, hit it again and again until he felt like he was going to break the bones in his one good arm. Still it wouldn't open.

He could hear people coming up behind him, hear them getting closer, and there was nowhere to go except back, right into their path. He hit the door with his left shoulder.

A needle sank deep into his neck. He whirled around, as ferocious as a tiger . . . but suddenly . . . felt very . . . woozy. Very . . . weak.

By David Wellington

JIM CHAPEL MISSIONS

THE HYDRA PROTOCOL
CHIMERA
"MINOTAUR"
"MYRMIDON"

DAVID WELLINGTON

THE HYDRA PROTOCOL

A JIM CHAPEL MISSION

HARPER

An Imprint of HarperCollinsPublishers

This book is a work of fiction. The characters, incidents, and dialogue are drawn from the author's imagination and are not to be construed as real. Any resemblance to actual events or persons, living or dead, is entirely coincidental.

HARPER

An Imprint of HarperCollins*Publishers*
195 Broadway
New York, New York 10007

Copyright © 2014 by David Wellington
Excerpt from *The Cyclops Initiative* copyright © 2016
by David Wellington
ISBN 978-0-06-224881-7

First Harper premium printing: April 2015
First William Morrow hardcover printing: May 2014

Printed in the United States of America

Visit Harper paperbacks on the World Wide Web at
www.harpercollins.com

10 9 8 7 6 5 4 3 2 1

For those who served, and those who still do

Acknowledgments

This book would not have been possible without Russ Galen, my agent, and Diana Gill, my editor. I've thanked them both often enough that I hope they're getting the point by now. I would also like to thank the people at HarperCollins who made the last year so much fun, in marketing, publicity, in library outreach (though we seriously need to release that blooper reel), in getting me to the conventions and public appearances and arranging for me to meet my readers (who definitely deserve some gratitude as well). Specifically I'd like to thank Danielle Bartlett, who worked tirelessly on my behalf even though she'd just had a baby and was a bit busy with other things. It was a great summer—I got to go to San Diego Comic-Con for the first time, among many other highlights—and it wouldn't have happened without Danielle. I am truly grateful.

THE HYDRA
PROTOCOL

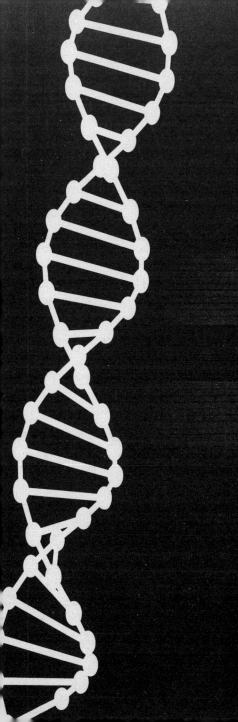

PART I

RIKORD ISLAND, EASTERN SIBERIA: MARCH 2, 07:14 (VLAT)

Dust motes hung in the early light streaming down through the archive's overgrown windows, twisting slowly in the dead air. A card catalog cabinet lay overturned on the cracked linoleum, its contents gutted and spilled onto the floor so the fine handwriting on the cards was bleached to sepia by years of sun exposure. One wall of the main room was lined with stacks of periodicals held together by fraying twine—old party literature from discredited regimes, outdated factbooks and bound analyses from long-dead KGB agents, all marked STATE SECRET, all still forbidden long after the Cold War had ended.

She stooped down in the dust and picked up a photograph of Brezhnev that had been filed in with the rest. It was just a standard portrait, the kind that might have hung in every office building in Russia forty years ago. Still it had been stamped as secret, with a warning indicating the penalties for unauthorized access. Most likely the librarians here had gotten in the habit of stamping everything that came across their desks.

The Soviet Union had never had time to come to trust computers. Right up until the end hard copy had been the rule—all secret information must be printed, bound, and filed, even if by 1991 no one wanted it anymore. What she was looking for had to be here, in this old archive building on an uninhabited island on the wrong side of Russia. For years she had tracked down the information, the last piece she needed to complete her mission. Her life's work, she thought, with a little grim humor.

So much had been lost when the coup failed and Yeltsin took the reins of the country. In the first flush of liberty the country had gone mad, like a dog chewing at its own paw. KGB installations across the country had been ransacked and set aflame, people who knew vital things had been taken away and quietly killed before they could be debriefed, computers had been smashed, archives razed. Of the seven KGB libraries in Russia that had once housed the information she needed, six had been pulled down and their records burned. This one had survived only because no one remembered it was here. Even the librarians who once worked here had disappeared, some crawling into bottles to drink themselves to death—the traditional suicide method for ex-KGB—some emigrating to breakaway republics or even nearby Japan.

Here was the last repository of the records the KGB had kept on dissidents, on foreign spies, on people who simply could not be trusted. Here was the institutional memory of a police state.

Here—

Here it was.

One of the twine-bound stacks held theater asset reports, dry technical papers listing every rifle, tank, and canteen the army possessed in a given region. Hidden among them was one marked with the sigil of the Strategic Rocket Forces. It was not only marked secret but sealed with a red band and actual wax. One glance at the title and she knew she'd found it:

STROGO SEKRETNO/OSOVAR PAPKA
SYSTEMA PERIMETR PROJEKT 1991

After so long she could hardly believe she held the report in her hands. The last copy on Earth, and the only piece of paper that could make the world safe again. She placed it inside her coat, close to her heart, and then pulled up her zipper to keep it in place.

Hurrying to the door she almost missed the sound. A crackling, the sound of someone stepping on broken glass outside. She stopped in the doorway and tried not to breathe. She heard a man speaking, though she could not make out the words. Then someone else laughed in response. It was not a kindly sounding laugh.

She didn't know what to do. She'd known they would follow her, that they would chase her to the ends of the world. She'd accepted the risk. But here, in this lonely place where only seabirds lived now, she'd thought she would be safe.

Evidently not.

"Will you make us come in, little friend?" someone called out, in Russian. "There is no other exit. You must come this way eventually. And we will not wait for long."

She closed her eyes, trying to get an idea of where the voice came from. To the left of the door, she believed. But there were two of them. If they'd been trained by the KGB, one would stand directly before the doorway, the other to the side. If they were Spetsnaz—much worse—they would flank both sides, because they would expect her to come out shooting.

She was unarmed. She had not even thought to bring a gun to the island. After all, there were no people on it.

There was no solution except to march forward, into the sunny doorway. Outside, the larch trees that covered most of the island fell away to form what looked like a natural clearing, just large enough for them to land their helicopter. She saw it first, a small late Soviet model that could not be hiding too many men. At least there was that.

Next she saw the man who had called out to her. He was in front of her and a little to the left. He wore a turtleneck under a well-tailored blazer and had the dead fish eyes of a man who had killed before. He had a knife in his hand, the kind one might use to pry open an oyster. His much larger partner, who wore a denim jacket, was off to the right a little ways, watching her. His hands were in his pockets. Perhaps he wanted her to think he had a gun, but if he did, he would have already shot her.

Just knives, then.

Konyechno, she thought. Okay.

The man in the blazer came toward her, his knife held low by his thigh. He spoke softly, as if he wanted to persuade her to come quietly, though she knew his orders were to make sure she never left the island. "Did you find it?" he asked. "The thing you came to steal? It will not—"

He didn't get to finish his sentence. She moved in fast, sweeping her leg across the back of his calf to bring him off balance. She brought her right arm across her body, protecting her torso while delivering a strong blow to his forearm. It was not enough to knock the knife out of his hand, but it left him unable to strike, his knife arm stretched out to his side. He tried to recover by shifting his footing, but her foot was already behind his leg and she kept him balancing on the other foot. With his free hand he tried to grab for her throat but she twisted away, shooting out her left hand to grab his wrist. She dug her thumb deep into the tendons there and his hand released, dropping the knife.

He had been trained in fighting, she could tell. He did not panic or try to break free—he knew she had locked his leg. Instead he brought his hands up to punch at her face and her throat. He had the advantage of mass and arm strength and one good blow to her trachea could put her down, but she was faster and managed to take his strike on the side of her head. Her ear burned with pain but she ignored it. She had too much to do, yet.

She threw her arms around his waist and pushed her head under his armpit. He was already off balance so she threw her own weight backward, letting herself fall onto her posterior. His own weight carried him over her back, head first, and she both heard and felt the moment when his skull struck the ground behind her.

KGB, she thought. He'd been trained by the KGB.

She'd been trained by Spetsnaz.

She threw his dead weight off her back and twisted around, her toes digging into the hard ground. One arm pushed up from the dirt and she was half standing, half crouching and facing the second man.

He looked surprised.

"When I was a little girl," she told him, "I wanted to be Ecaterina Szabo. You know, the gymnast?"

He seemed to remember then that he'd been sent to kill her. He moved quickly, his hands coming out of his pockets, and both holding knives. As he came closer she saw just how big he was. The moves she'd used on his partner would be useless on such a bear—his inertia would be too great for her to counteract.

So instead she snatched up the fallen knife from the ground and threw it into his stomach.

He grunted in pain but kept coming, his eyes wild.

There was no time to get out of his way, so she didn't. Just before he fell on her she lanced out with her foot. Her heel struck the pommel of the knife she'd lodged in his belly, driving it in deep until she felt it touch his spine. She rolled to the side as he collapsed on where she'd been, and she scuttled away as he began to scream.

"I was too tall to be a gymnast."

For a second, no more, she let herself breathe. She let herself feel the panic she had suppressed before. Her breath made a little mist in the cold morning air.

She touched her jacket and felt the paper folder inside it. Made sure it was safe.

Then she got up and dusted herself off. Went over to their helicopter and found no one else inside. In a few minutes she was airborne, headed for Sakhalin Island. From there she could find her way into Japan, and then on to America. Where the real work would begin.

SOUTH OF MIAMI, FLORIDA: JUNE 10, 18:16 (EDT)

Jim Chapel leaned on the prow of the yacht and peered down into the water that foamed and churned beneath him. Ever since he'd been a kid, growing up not far from here, he'd loved the ocean. He knew no more peaceful feeling than looking out over its incredible blue expanse, watching it roll in from the far horizon. What human problem could mean anything measured against that blue infinity? Whatever was waiting for him back in New York, whatever Julia was going to tell him, for the moment, at least, he could put it in the back of his mind, tuck it neatly away and think about—

Behind him a vast rolling thump of noise shattered the peace, followed quickly by a squeal of feedback and another squeal, less loud but far more human, the sound of a woman screaming. Chapel spun around just as the beat dropped in and the DJ really got the party jumping.

The yacht was rated for fifty people—it had that many life jackets on board, anyway. Nearly two hundred men and women were crowded onto its main deck, leaping and swaying and throwing their fists in the air as the DJ asked if they were ready to tear it up and burn it down. More squeals and screams came as men in surfer shorts grabbed women and hoisted them up in the air, tossed them into the on-deck pool, poured liquor down their bodies to suck it out of their navels. Chapel had to smile and shake his head as he watched the bacchanalia unfold.

"Jimmy! Jimmy, goddamnit!" someone shouted, and a man ten years Chapel's junior came running across the deck. "Jimmy, get away from there; can't you see you're in the wrong place? The party's over heeeere!"

Chapel laughed and braced himself as Donny Melvin came rushing at him like a linebacker. The younger man barreled into him and wrapped his arms around Chapel's torso, and for a second Chapel thought Donny was going to pick him up and bodily carry him over to the party. Donny could have done it, too—Chapel had a couple inches of height on Donny, but Donny had nearly twice his mass, and the vast majority of it was muscle.

Donny had always been a big guy. He and Chapel had gone through Ranger school together and bonded over the fact they'd both grown up in Florida. Back then, Donny had constantly complained that the life of a soldier interfered with his ability to lift weights and that he was running to flab. That had regularly elicited nothing but groans from the other grunts, who wanted to bitch about how heavy their packs were—some of them suggested Donny could carry their packs for them. When Chapel went off to Afghanistan, Donny had gone to Iraq. Flabby or not, after one particularly nasty firefight in Fallujah, Donny had ended up carrying two wounded soldiers off the battlefield, one under each arm. He'd gotten a medal for that.

Since his discharge Donny had clearly returned

to working out almost full-time. Nor was he particularly modest about his body. He wore nothing but a pair of white-rimmed sunglasses, some floral print board shorts, and a neon pink pair of flip-flops. One of his massive biceps had been tattooed with a banner reading 75 RANGER RGT, while his other arm had been decorated with a multicolored banner showing he'd fought in the war on terror. Neither of those tattoos was regulation, though now that Donny was a civilian again, he was allowed to do with his skin as he pleased.

"How many times did I invite you down for a cruise, and you always said no? I don't know how you did it, but you picked the perfect time to say yes. There is some serious action over there," Donny told Chapel as he released him from the bear hug. "I'm talking *talent*, Jimmy. Normally, I call one of these boat rides, I'm looking at five or six girls I would do bad things for. Today there's at least a dozen. At least come take a look, huh?"

"Maybe *just* for a look," Chapel told Donny.

"I promise, your redhead girlfriend will not mind if you look," Donny told him, smiling. "And anything else that happens, well, we *are* in international waters."

"That doesn't give me a get-out-of-monogamy-free card. And stop calling me Jimmy. Only my elementary school teachers and my mother ever called me that."

"Sure thing, Jimbo," Donny said, grabbing Chapel's arm and pulling him back toward the deck.

Chapel couldn't help but grin. Donny Melvin deserved a little fun after what he'd done in Iraq. If he was a little raucous about it, where was the harm?

Back on the deck a group of girls in bikinis shouted and squealed as Donny burst into their midst. One of them threw her arms around his neck and kissed him on the cheek. She had a plastic cup of beer in one hand and she spilled half of it down Donny's back by accident, but Donny just whooped at the icy touch and hugged the girl. "This is Sheila," he shouted over the thumping music. "She's a student at—what school was it?"

"Shelly!" she shouted back.

"What?" Donny asked her.

"My name is Shelly!" she shouted. "Shelly!"

"Seriously?" Donny spun her around and squatted to take a look at the tattoo that rode just above the top of her bikini bottom. "Oh, man! King James, meet Shelly," he said. "You can recognize her by the butterfly back here."

Shelly spun around with a mock scowl on her face, which prompted Donny to get a shoulder under her stomach and lift her up into the air. She screamed and giggled and spilled the rest of her beer as he carried her through the crowd toward the open air bar. Dancers and drinkers alike moved out of his way, some of them raising cups in salute as he barged through their midst. This was, after all, Donny's party. And Donny's boat.

Donny had not exactly signed up with the army for the GI bill. His father owned half the orange trees in Florida. One day Donny was going to have to learn how to take care of orange trees himself. But clearly that day was not today.

"Shots!" Donny shouted, and a hundred people all around him shouted it back. The two bartenders grabbed for bottles with both hands and started lining up waxed paper shot glasses on the marble top of the bar, which was already strewn with empty cups and discarded pieces of swimwear. Donny laid Shelly down on her back across the bar, and one of the bartenders poured a good measure of liquor right into her open mouth. Two other girls had already come rushing up to hang on Donny's arms. It didn't seem to be slowing him down any.

"Who's your friend?" one of them asked, a blonde with elaborately plucked eyebrows. She gave Chapel a look that might have melted him on the spot if he was ten years younger. It threatened to melt him anyway, old as he was.

"A fellow soldier, I think," another woman said, from Chapel's right. She had a slight accent he couldn't place, and when he turned to look at her, he saw she wasn't like any of the bikini-clad coeds surrounding Donny. "He has the bearing. And the quiet that hides behind the eyes. Yes?"

The woman was significantly older than the coeds. Early thirties, Chapel thought. Short dark hair surrounded vaguely Asian features and instead of the orangish tan of the girls, her skin was a rich, warm shade that looked like it actually came from spending time in the sun. Shelly and the blonde and all the others were beautiful, in a sort of mass-produced girl-next-door kind of way, but this newcomer was striking, the kind of woman you would take a second look at wherever you saw her. She wasn't wearing a bikini, either—instead she had on a short sundress that tied at the back of her neck. The dress gave just the subtlest sense of the athletic body underneath and somehow seemed more scandalous than a bikini would, since it left so much to the imagination.

"He's got soldier hair," the blonde said, reaching around Donny to run her fingers across the stubble on the back of Chapel's neck. "I love that feeling! It tickles," she said, laughing.

It did more for Chapel than just tickle. Still, he found himself turning to look at the older woman. He found he wanted to look at her very much. Nothing more, of course, not with Julia waiting back in New York. But like Donny had said, there was no harm in looking.

"Quite a lot hidden back there, I think," she said, as if the blonde didn't exist. "Jim here could tell us all a few things, if he let himself."

Chapel's mouth started to curve into a frown. How had she known his name? Nobody had introduced them. But it seemed the mystery would have to wait.

"In the pool, now," Donny called out, lifting a pair of plastic cups over his head.

"You go ahead," Chapel told him, smiling at his friend.

But Donny wasn't having it. "My party, my rules. I'm getting hot and I want to cool down. With you," he said to the blonde, "and you," to a brunette who looked up with the wide eyes of someone who had just won the lottery, "and Sheila, of course."

"Shelly!" the girl yelled from the bar, sitting up and knocking over the paper shot cups the bartender had been arranging on her stomach. Nobody seemed to mind. Shelly jumped off the bar onto

Donny's back and howled in laughter as he ran with her over to the pool, only a few feet away. He jumped in with Shelly still clinging to his neck, sending up a great wave of chlorinated water that splashed half a dozen dancers nearby. A general roar of excitement went up and the DJ switched to a new track, one with an even faster beat. One by one girls and men jumped in the pool after Donny, until the deck was awash with their splashing.

"Jim-meeee!" Donny shouted. "Where's my Jim Dog? Jim-Jam, you get in here right now or I'll have the captain throw you overboard!"

Raising his hands in protest, Chapel tried to laugh off the invitation.

Donny wouldn't hear it. "In. The. Pool. Now!" He lunged out of the pool and grabbed Chapel's leg. "Now!"

"Hold on," Chapel said, suddenly alarmed. If Donny pulled him into the pool just then, it was going to be a problem. "Let me just—"

"Get that shirt off him," Donny shouted, and a couple of coeds came giggling up to do just that. Despite his best efforts, they managed to pull Chapel's polo shirt over his head.

Chapel knew exactly what would happen then.

The girls in the pool stopped laughing. One of them wiped hair from her eyes and stared at his left arm, and especially his left shoulder. It took a second for others to notice, but he could tell when they did because their eyes went wide too. Nobody said anything, of course. But it looked as if the water in the pool had suddenly turned twenty degrees cooler.

"Damn it, Donny," Chapel said, under his breath.

Under the polo shirt, Chapel's left arm looked just like his right one. It had the same skin tone and the same amount of hair. The illusion ended at the shoulder, though, where the arm flared out into a wide clamp that held it secured to his torso.

There was no point in trying to hide it anymore. Chapel reached up with his right hand and flipped back the catches to release the arm. It was a prosthesis, an exceptionally clever and well-designed replacement for the arm he'd lost in Afghanistan. When he took it off and laid it down carefully on a deck chair, it looked like something torn off a mannequin. He worried about just leaving it there, but he doubted anyone would get too close. None of these people would want to touch the thing.

The DJ didn't scratch a record. Most of the partygoers saw nothing, and their roaring clamor of excitement didn't drop by so much as a decibel. But around the pool the whole atmosphere of the party had changed, grown more subdued. The party was ruined.

Chapel stepped down into the pool and submerged himself until only his head was above the water. He looked over at Donny with half a grimace on his face. He wanted very much to duck his head under as well, and just disappear.

"Does it hurt?" Shelly asked.

"No," he told her. "Not anymore."

"How did . . . I mean, how—"

Donny swam over to stand next to Chapel. "Shelly," he said, "do you remember 9/11?"

"Of course I do!" she squeaked. "I was in fifth grade when it happened. We got to go home from school for, like, three whole days."

Donny's face squirmed as he tried to contain a braying laugh, but he couldn't quite manage it. Eventually he just gave in and let the laughter boom all around the pool, until somebody else picked up on it, and then everyone was laughing. Even Chapel. "This man here," Donny said, "is an American hero!," and he grabbed Chapel's right hand under the water and dragged it up into the air, making Chapel stand up and show his ruined left shoulder again.

The pool erupted in one huge roaring cheer, as cups everywhere lifted in the air and pointed in Chapel's direction. The dancers jumped up and down and the bartenders grabbed new bottles and the party lurched back into full-on mode, back to exactly where it had been before Chapel's shirt came off.

Good old Donny, he thought.

SOUTH OF MIAMI, FLORIDA: JUNE 10, 21:04

The party never really ended, but the level of alcohol consumed on board meant that by the time the sun set, a lot more people were sitting down than dancing. Dinner—catered by one of Miami's best authentic Cuban restaurants—was served at eight o'clock and that helped alleviate the chaos a little, too.

Chapel found he had to be careful where he walked on the deck, which was strewn with abandoned cups and greasy paper plates. It would be very easy to slip and fall overboard, and he was a little surprised nobody had done so yet. He found Donny holding court in a lifeboat that hung off the starboard side. Nestled in there with him on a canvas tarp were Shelly and a couple of girls Chapel hadn't been introduced to. A guy who looked like a surfer, maybe half Chapel's age, was tuning an acoustic guitar while he puffed on a joint. As Chapel leaned over the side of the boat the surfer tried to hand it to him, but Chapel politely waved it away.

"Permission to come aboard?" Chapel asked.

Donny smiled. His eyes were a little hooded, and he looked like he was ready for a nap. Shelly was stroking his arms as if she couldn't believe how muscular they were. "Granted," he said. "Jim . . . Jim . . . I need another stupid name to call you."

"Keep going, you'll get there," Chapel said, climbing into the lifeboat. It swayed a little and he mostly fell inside, right on top of a woman he hadn't seen. Everyone seemed to think this was hysterically funny, including the woman he'd fallen on.

"Sailor Jim," Donny said, finally. "Is that something? Is there a Sailor Jim? Lord Jim, maybe. Isn't that a book?"

"There's a Slim Jim," Shelly pointed out.

"I was saving that one for later." Donny reached over and steadied Chapel as he tried to find a seat in the crowded lifeboat.

Once Chapel was safely ensconced he turned to apologize to the woman he'd fallen on. It turned out to be the dark-haired Asian woman he'd met earlier at the bar, the one who'd pegged him as a soldier. She acknowledged his apology by closing her eyes for a second and giving him a vampish shrug.

"I've had worse things fall upon me," she said. "So Donny has told us all about you."

"He has?" Chapel asked, a little alarmed.

"Is it so strange? You are the honored guest of this voyage. And a very interesting man to hear him tell it. A man of many accomplishments. You fought in Afghanistan, he says?"

Chapel frowned. What had Donny been saying about him? Donny didn't know anything too secret—most of Chapel's military career was classified—but he valued his privacy. "I don't much like to talk about the past."

"Me either," Donny announced. He struggled to sit up, pulling Shelly with him until she was sitting on his lap. "Especially when the present is so much more interesting. In all the years I've been sailing on this yacht, this is the very first time Jim Chapel has agreed to grace us with his presence. I want to know why now, after all this time."

Chapel sighed. "I had some things I needed to think through. I thought I would get away for a few days, give myself some quiet time."

"Exactly what you should expect from one of my world-famous party cruises. Peace and quiet!" The girls in the lifeboat all cheered and shouted at the idea. "C'mon, Jimster. Spill the beans. You said it was something to do with that girlfriend of yours. The sexy redhead."

Chapel laughed. "You've never met Julia. How do you know she's sexy?"

"Red hair. Likes soldiers. Sounds like a good start," Donny pointed out.

"She's . . . amazing. Julia." Chapel found himself

smiling without meaning to. "And she is. Very sexy, I mean. More than that, she's beautiful. And smart. Very sharp. She and I went through some things together, tough things, and it just brought us closer together."

"The good start is turning into a good thing. But you didn't come all this way to tell me you think you like somebody. You've got a decision to make—I can see it in your face. A *big* decision."

Chapel was not a man given to giggling or outward signs of joy. But he came pretty close just then. "Yeah."

Donny nodded. A lot of people assumed when they saw him that he was just some dumb meathead, but Donny had been an Army Ranger, and you didn't get into Ranger school without something between your ears. "Well, I accept, of course."

Chapel's eyes went wide. "You—what?"

"I accept the position as your best man. Because that's obviously why you're here. To ask me to be your best man."

"Best . . . wait a minute," Shelly said, and put a hand over her mouth.

"Hold on!" Chapel protested. "I haven't asked her yet—maybe I should before I go looking for someone to—to—"

Donny moved Shelly next to him, then lunged across the lifeboat and grabbed Chapel up into a rib-cage-crushing bear hug. Chapel laughed and slapped his friend's back until the big ranger released him.

"Oh my God, oh my God, oh my God," Shelly said, tears starting to form in her eyes. Despite the fact she'd never met Julia and had met Chapel only a few hours ago, it seemed she was pretty excited by the prospect of a wedding. Any wedding.

Chapel had to admit he was pretty excited himself. The idea to propose to Julia had come to him in a sudden flash of inspiration a week earlier. The two of them had been going through a rough patch, fighting a lot, and it had taken him a long time to realize why. Julia didn't think he was serious about her, that he was just stringing her along. She needed to know that he was committed to their relationship. As soon as he'd thought of it, a proposal had seemed like a great idea. There was no hesitation in him, no doubt. He was ready to spend the rest of his life with Julia. Why not formalize it?

"It may be too early for congratulations," the Asian woman said. Her eyes searched his for a moment though he couldn't figure out why. "But all the same. How wonderful."

"Wonderful? It's awesome! Oh my God, Donny, can I be your date at the wedding?" Shelly asked.

"Hold on," Chapel said, laughing. "Nothing's official yet, I still—"

He stopped because he'd seen something out of the corner of his eye. He made a point of not turning to actually look but, yes, it was there. Up in the wheelhouse of the yacht, high over the deck, someone had switched on a blue light.

"I was serious about that best man thing, if you want me," Donny said. "I know you've probably got someone else in mind, but let me just point out— if you go with me, your bachelor party is going to be sick. And I mean epic. I will get every stripper in South Florida together and they will march in a parade in your honor, Jam Master Jim. You know nobody throws a party like me—"

"Uh, sorry," Chapel said. Up in the wheelhouse the blue light switched off. He heard a chain rattle somewhere up in the bows and knew the yacht had dropped its anchor. "Listen, I—"

"Most guys would go with a limo to take you to and from this bachelor party," Donny went on. "I'm thinking helicopters. Multiple helos."

"I, uh," Chapel said. He hadn't expected this to come so soon. "Talking about this," he said. "It's making me a little queasy."

"Try this," the surfer with the guitar said, and he tried to pass Chapel his joint. "It's good for seasickness."

"I think what our new friend is trying to say is that he's getting an attack of cold feet," the Asian woman said. "Perhaps he should go lie down in his cabin."

He wanted to thank her for that—it was the perfect out—but he was too busy doing his best impression of someone about to throw up. "I'd better get out of this boat," he said.

Donny helped him climb back down onto the deck. "You okay?" he asked, suddenly serious.

"Fine," Chapel told him. "I just need to lie down for a second." He patted one of Donny's giant biceps in thanks and then headed forward, making sure to stagger a little. Behind him he heard some of the girls laughing, probably making fun of the poor guy who'd had too much to drink or who maybe was a little too afraid of commitment.

As soon as he was out of their sight, Chapel dropped the act and hurried down a ladder to the cabins in the next deck down. He passed by a few partially opened doors, beyond which revelers had broken down into smaller more private parties, then found his own cabin. The door was still locked. Good—he'd worried that some couple in need of a bed would stumble into his cabin uninvited. That would have been a problem, since all his gear was in there.

His bag was still sitting on his bed where he'd left it. He made sure the door was locked, then took off his clothes. He unzipped the bag and pulled out the drysuit and his other gear.

The blue light had been a signal meant just for him. It was time to get to work.

OFF CAY SAL BANK: JUNE 10, 21:43

The first thing Chapel did was put on a hands-free radio headset. He switched it on and whispered, "Angel? Are you receiving me?"

The voice that answered him was sexy and warm, and like every time he heard it he felt his stomach do a little flip. "I've got you, sugar. Are you all geared up?"

"Putting on my drysuit now," he told her. Angel was his operator, his direct connection to his boss and any information he might need to complete his mission. She had saved his life more times than he liked to think about—certainly more times than he could ever thank her for. He had never met her in person, though, only ever heard her voice—which was how it had to be. Angel knew enough secrets that if she ever fell into the wrong hands, she could devastate national security. Chapel didn't even know where she was calling from, or anything really about her except that she was a civilian and that his boss trusted her completely, just as he did.

As he zipped up the drysuit—a form-fitting neoprene bodysuit designed for technical diving—he listened while she read off the local water temperature, the weather forecast for the next twelve hours, and the names and headings of every seagoing vessel in the local area. He adjusted a strap on his headset to make it secure, then zipped up the coif of the suit, covering most of his head. He would leave the mask and flippers for just before he went in the water. The suit was heavy and he started overheating as soon as it was on, but it was necessary. He couldn't get his artificial arm wet, which meant he needed a closed suit. Where he was going it was going to be a lot colder, too, and he imagined he would be very glad for the suit's insulation in a few minutes.

The suit came with a compact rebreather system that was just a little better than anything a civilian could buy. Chapel was an experienced diver, which made it feel just plain weird that there was no air tank hanging off his back. Instead the rebreather had him breathe constantly into a bag across his chest that looked like a collapsed life vest. He checked the system with ten normal breaths, in and out, in and out, just like he'd been trained. Everything about the rebreather was different from the SCUBA gear he was used to, right down to how you breathed through it. The system used a full face mask so he didn't have to hold a regulator in his mouth. Instead of giving him a steady stream of gas from a tank, the rebreather took in his exhalations and scrubbed out the carbon dioxide, then returned the air to him rich in oxygen. A small tank of helium mounted on his stomach would be mixed in with his own oxygen and nitrogen to prevent some of the nastier physiological effects of a deep dive. The system was finicky and hard to use—you had to constantly monitor the partial pressures of the three gases, while also managing the pressurization of the drysuit—but it definitely had its advantages. Most important, it produced almost no bubbles, which was good for covert work.

He strapped on a buoyancy compensator and a dive computer and he was ready to go. "Angel, do you see anyone up on the deck right now?"

She looked down on the yacht with orbiting satellites good enough to make out what the partyers on board were drinking and told him it looked clear. "You're good, sweetie. They're all back around the pool. Don't forget my transponder."

"Got it right here." Chapel grabbed the transponder, his mask, and his flippers and slipped out the door of his cabin. Down a short corridor he opened a door and stepped out onto to a swimming balcony built into the bows of the yacht, riding just above the waterline. He put on his mask and flippers and stepped down into the water, trying not to make too noisy a splash.

Chapel had grown up in Florida, which meant he'd spent what felt like half his youth in these waters. It felt good to be back in the ocean, like he was some kind of amphibian that had spent way too long on dry land.

Well, he thought, *technically* these weren't Floridian waters. *Technically* they belonged to Cuba, which was why he had to go to such lengths to keep his dive a secret. The captain of the yacht had anchored in a place he wasn't supposed to. *Technically* what Chapel was about to do was illegal under the law of the sea and two sovereign nations. *Technically* if he was caught doing it, he could be arrested, given a quick trial, and then executed.

Hopefully it wouldn't come to that.

Before he went under completely, he kicked himself around the side of the swimming balcony and over to where the yacht's thick anchor cable slanted down into the water. He clipped the transponder unit onto the cable and switched it on. The unit carried Angel's signal and relayed it through the metal cable. Wires embedded in his gloves could pick up that signal when he touched the cable, allowing him to talk to Angel no matter how far below the water he went.

"How's it work?" Angel asked.

"Pretty good," he told her. "Your voice is a little distorted, but I can understand you just fine."

"Do I still sound all breathless and sultry?" she asked.

"That comes through, no problem," he told her.

There were benefits to working for the world's most technologically advanced military.

He tested the mask to make sure it wouldn't fog up with his breath. Then he ducked his head under the water, bled some air from his buoyancy compensator, and dropped down into the dark ocean like a stone.

OFF CAY SAL BANK: JUNE 10, 22:24

For a second he flailed around in the dark, looking for the anchor cable. His good hand grasped it, and he pulled himself over to hug it. He waited a moment for his body to adjust to the weightlessness of the water. Then he started his descent.

There wasn't much swimming involved. He turned himself upside down and started climbing down the cable, hand over hand. A little moonlight streamed down around him, shafts of it spearing down into the dark and occasionally lighting up the flickering shape of a passing fish. The local wildlife kept its distance, scared of this big weird shape that had invaded their domain. Sharks would be less wary, but probably wouldn't attack him on principle—or so he hoped.

After a minute or two, the light went away, and he could see nothing through his mask but black water. There was no sound anywhere except for his own breathing and the rhythmic slap of his hands on the cable.

Down. Put one hand forward, grab the cable. Release the other hand. Move that hand down, grab the cable. Down. Nothing to see. Nothing to hear. Nothing to smell but the rubber mask. He could barely feel the cable through the thick gloves. Down.

It was funny—well, not ha-ha funny—how fast the total lack of light affected him.

He couldn't remember the last time he'd been in darkness this profound. Where he lived now, in New York, it never really got dark. There were streetlights outside his apartment's windows, and the city itself gave off so much light it painted the sky no matter how cloudy it got.

This was like being at the bottom of a coal mine. This was like floating, weightless and lost, in the depths of space. This was like being blind.

Down. One hand after another. Down. He kept repeating the word to himself in his head, reminding himself that he was moving in a particular direction. He had no referents other than the cable. His body didn't feel like it was upside down. If he let go of the cable now, if he swam away, he wouldn't even know which direction was up, or how to get back to the surface.

Better not let go, then. Down. He checked the luminous readouts on his dive computer, made sure his oxygen mix was at the right partial pressure. If it was off, if the various safeguards and fail-safes built into the rebreather all went off-line at the same time, he could flood his lungs with oxygen and give himself oxygen toxicity. Supposedly that felt like being pleasantly drunk, but it was a great way to die underwater. Especially if you were diving alone. The first symptoms would be disorientation and giddiness.

He definitely felt disoriented. He double-checked the readouts.

His oxygen levels were fine.

Down. Release with one hand, clutch with the other. Down.

When Angel spoke in his ear, he was absurdly grateful. "You're making good time," she told him. "It's going to feel longer than it actually is. Can you still hear me okay?"

"Loud and clear. Everything okay topside?"

"Yeah. So. Now that we can talk in private . . ."

Chapel stopped climbing down the cable for a second. "Yes?" he asked. "Something on your mind?"

"I just wondered—have you got the ring yet?"

Chapel wanted to laugh. Never a great idea on a dive, of course. Laughing used up a lot of air. He forced himself to merely grin through the plastic mask. If any fish were watching with better eyes than he had, maybe they would see the scary monster from above the surface bare its teeth.

"Yeah," he told her. "It's waiting for me back in New York. I just have to pick it up." He pulled himself down another meter. Down.

"Is it nice? Julia deserves something nice."

"I agree." Down. One hand over the other. "It's nice. A gold band with a single diamond. Nothing showy—you know that's not her style. Not too big."

"I think if it were me you were proposing to," Angel told him, with just a trace of jealousy in her voice, "I'd be perfectly happy with something showy. And big."

"Stop trying to make me laugh." Down. Release with the left hand, clutch with the right. Release with the right hand, hold on with the left. Down.

"You know I'm happy for you," Angel said. "You know that."

"I do," he told her. When he'd first told Angel

that he was going to propose, it had felt distinctly weird. He was confiding in a woman he'd never met. He didn't even know what Angel looked like. But it didn't feel weird for long. She'd been whispering in his ear for so long he felt like they were old, close friends.

"I mean, I'm happy for you now. I wasn't . . . convinced. At first."

"I know," Chapel said. Down. Angel had suggested he take his time and think about what he was doing. He and Julia had been fighting a lot, and they had both said things they couldn't take back. Angel had suggested that maybe that wasn't the best time to make things official. But Chapel was certain he was making the right decision.

Down. One hand. The other hand. Down.

He checked his depth gauge. Thirty meters. This was the farthest he'd ever dived before, and he was only a fifth of the way to the bottom. It had felt like no time at all. Or like he'd been doing this for hours.

"How long until I can turn my lights on?" he asked.

"A little ways, yet. I just wanted to tell you something. I know you can make her happy. You've never failed at a mission yet, Jim. I think if you put your mind to this, you'll be a great husband."

Down. He wished he could kick his way down. It would be so much faster. But he had to stay with the cable. Down.

He thought about what Angel had just said. "Is there a 'but' somewhere in that statement?"

Angel was quiet for a while. He started to worry there was a problem with the transponder. But apparently she was just thinking about what to say next.

"Not so much a 'but,'" she said.

Down. Hand over hand. Down.

"More," she said, "oh, I don't know. A hope. I wanted to say that I hope she can make you just as happy. That you're sure you're making the right choice for yourself."

He stopped again. He told himself he was resting, conserving his energy. In truth, what she'd said had just distracted him so much he couldn't concentrate on his descent. When he realized that, he forced himself to focus. He adjusted the pressurization of the drysuit and checked over his dive computer. Then he started down again.

Angel couldn't really be jealous, could she? Admittedly she was the woman he was closest to in the world other than Julia. And Angel flirted with him all the time—and he definitely reciprocated. But that was just the way they were, wasn't it? It was just banter. Harmless.

At least, he'd always thought it was.

Down. Suddenly concentrating on climbing down the cable was a great distraction.

"I am sure," he told Angel. "I definitely am."

"Good. As long as you're sure. Then I guess you have my blessing, though I notice you didn't ask for it."

He smiled inside his mask. Down. One hand, then the other. Down. "Can I turn my lights on yet?"

"Give it another ten meters."

Down. One hand, the other. Left hand, right hand. Down.

Seventy-five meters down. Halfway to the bottom. He tapped a button on his dive computer screen. A halogen lamp the size of his pinkie finger mounted on either side of his mask flicked on, spearing light out into the darkness.

There was nothing to see, of course, not even any fish at this level. But he'd never been so glad to see anything as the cable he held in his hands. He looked down and then up along its length. It stood as straight as a pillar in the middle of the ocean.

He looked at his gloves. Put a hand to the cable. Then the other.

Down.

OFF CAY SAL BANK: JUNE 10, 22:37

Lying between the Florida Keys and Cuba, the Cay Sal Bank was one of the world's largest coral atolls. From the surface it was almost invisible, merely a handful of tiny cays—rocks too small to be called islands. Just below the waves, however, more than three thousand square miles of ground rose up from the ocean floor, in most places coming within twenty feet of the surface. Unsurprisingly it was a graveyard for shipping—dozens of oceangoing vessels had run aground there, and most lay where they'd fallen, barely covered by the lapping blue water of the Caribbean.

If you could remove all that water and look at the bank in open air, it would resemble an enormous and ludicrously high plateau, with a flat top and—almost—sheer sides. If you stepped off that hypothetical plateau, you could fall two thousand feet before hitting the ground.

But that "almost" was important. Though from a distance the sides of the bank would look sheer, up close they were rough and slightly tapered, interrupted everywhere by promontories and narrow ledges that would stop your fall long before you hit the bottom. Donny's yacht had dropped its anchor onto one of those ledges about eighty fathoms—a hundred and fifty meters, as Chapel's dive computer reckoned—down.

That was still very deep. It was far, far deeper than Chapel had ever dived before, even though he'd been SCUBA diving since he was old enough to get his certification. It was deeper than most professional divers went. A hundred meters down, still pulling himself along hand over hand, he could feel the water above him pressing down on him, squeezing him inside his drysuit like a tube of toothpaste. He was getting cold, too, which was always a bad thing on a dive when you couldn't afford clumsy fingers. He'd passed through the thermocline where the water dropped fifteen degrees in the space of a couple of meters of depth. Up on the surface he'd sweated inside his suit, and now he felt like he was slicked down with a layer of clammy water.

He concentrated on breathing normally, on regularly checking the gas levels on his dive computer. On sticking to a steady pace.

At a hundred and twenty meters down he saw the rocky wall of the slope as a looming shadow, a patch of darkness that cut off his lights. A little farther he started to see towers of coral rise up around him like the fingers of some enormous beast reaching up to snatch at him. The wall of the slope kept getting closer, which perversely enough made him feel claustrophobic—he'd gotten used to the sense of floating in limitless space, so any indication that there was solid ground nearby made him worry about falling and smashing into the ground below.

Of course that was an illusion. All he had to do was turn one knob on his belt and he would fall upward instead, dragged up by his own buoyancy. His body didn't want to be down here, and only constant effort and high-tech engineering made it possible to fight his way down through the dense ocean at all.

The water down there was murky and thick with marine snow—a constant cascade of organic debris, the bodies of dead plankton settling slowly to the seafloor. There were fish down there who lived on that snow, but he saw few of them. They had evolved to live in an environment of perfect darkness, and his lights probably confused the hell out of them.

A hundred and forty meters down he saw what he'd come for, a long, tapered shadow at the very limit of his light.

"I've got it," he told Angel. They had agreed in advance not to talk about the mission during his descent, except in the vaguest of terms. The odds of anyone listening in to their frequency were remote, but you couldn't be too careful when you were working an illegal operation. "Right where we expected."

The yacht's anchor had fallen not half a dozen yards away from the wreck. The satellite data was spot-on. Now that his light touched the seafloor, it was safe for him to let go of the cable, but he found himself reluctant to do so. Once he let go, he would be out of communication with Angel, for one thing. But he knew his hesitation was more psychological than practical.

He indulged himself for a few seconds, under the pretense that he was scoping out the wreck before proceeding.

What lay before him was a wrecked submarine about two hundred and twenty feet long and thirty feet wide. It lay on its side, its long sail pointing away from him, its underslung tail fin sticking up in his general direction. A Kilo class sub, one of the old workhorses of the Russian navy.

For twenty years it had rested down here undisturbed by the world above. Coral had begun to grow over its tail and up its sides, while countless barnacles broke up the curve of the hull. Mud and drifts of marine snow obscured much of its skin, but he could still see the rivets that held the hull plates together.

He couldn't see any names or designator numbers painted on its side, but he knew what he was looking at: the B-307 *Kurchatov*. Maybe the last submarine in history to fly the flag of the Soviet Union.

OFF CAY SAL BANK: JUNE 10, 22:48

The *Kurchatov* had been built in the early 1980s as an attack sub, designed to search out and destroy enemy shipping. As far as anyone knew, it had never fired one of its torpedoes, though, or seen any kind of real action. Like most of the world's military submarines, it was more important as a deterrent than an actual weapon. It did possess one claim to fame, though—or rather, it would have if anyone had ever been allowed to know about its final mission.

In August 1991, when it became clear the Soviet Union wasn't going to last, a bunch of Kremlin hardliners attempted a coup d'état against Gorbachev in a last-gasp effort to hold on to power. After months of planning, they flooded Moscow with tanks and paratroopers and the world held its breath, but after only two days the coup failed. All the plotters were either arrested or committed suicide, and it was clear that the old USSR was finished.

The plotters must have known there was a chance they would fail, because they had given very special orders to the captain of the *Kurchatov*. He was to put in at the closest convenient port to Moscow and take on passengers, specifically the wives and children of some of the coup plotters, who might become victims of mob retribution during the coup. Originally the captain's orders had simply been to take that human cargo out to sea and keep them safe until the coup succeeded and they could come home.

Chapel had learned all this from his boss, Rupert Hollingshead, who had it from the CIA. The information the American government possessed did not indicate what the *Kurchatov*'s captain was supposed to do if the coup failed. It was known that the captain was fanatically loyal to his superiors in the Kremlin, a member of the Communist Party, and a personal believer in state socialism. Perhaps when he realized that his homeland failed to share his beliefs, he decided to go somewhere where people still did. So he'd set course for Cuba, a voyage that would have strained his overcrowded vessel to the very limits of its fuel and supplies.

The captain signaled ahead of his intentions and had received an offer of asylum from the government of Fidel Castro. He'd been ordered to bring his vessel into the port of Havana where he would be welcomed as a hero of the socialist revolution. Why he failed to obey those instructions was unknown— maybe he didn't trust Castro as much as he'd trusted his Soviet superiors, or maybe he was simply out of fuel. For one reason or another, just after Christmas in 1991, he had come to a dead stop in the water twenty miles from Cuba and ordered everyone to abandon ship.

The sub's crew had intentionally scuttled their boat, opening all its hatches and letting it sink gracefully while they fled in lifeboats. Most likely the captain had intended for the submarine to sink to the very bottom of the ocean, but instead it had come to ground on the sloped side of the Cay Sal Bank. The crew and passengers had all disappeared into the Cuban population. And that was the last anyone had heard, or probably thought, about the *Kurchatov* until now.

Until Jim Chapel was ordered to disturb its decades-long sleep.

Through the murky water Chapel could only get a rough idea of how the submarine had fared after being scuttled, but it was obvious right away that it hadn't come through unscathed. It must have struck the rocks several times as it sank, judging by the massive dents on the hull. Worse, it had been torn open toward its rear half where it had scraped up against a long spar of hard coral. A boat like the *Kurchatov* was built with two concentric hulls to withstand oceanic pressures. Both hulls were made of thick reinforced steel, but the coral had cut through them like a ceramic knife through a tin can, leaving the whole interior of the sub open to the seawater. That might actually be a good thing. Chapel hadn't relished the prospect of trying to muscle open the heavy pressure hatches in the sail, normally the only way inside. The tear in the hulls might give him a better access point.

"Angel," he said, "I'm going off radio now. Everything good up top?"

"There's a little movement about twenty miles from you. Looks like a fishing boat. Nothing to worry about."

"Okay. Talk to you in a few."

"Be careful, sweetie," she said. "I'll be here, waiting."

Chapel let go of the anchor cable and kicked away from it, using just his flippers to propel him toward the sub. He swam down toward the crack in its side and reached out to touch the place where the hulls had been cut through. The tear was pretty rough, and when it first happened the edges of the opening might have been razor sharp, but time and salt water had smoothed them down until he was pretty sure he wouldn't rip his drysuit crawling through. He peered in through the rent, letting his lights play over the big boxy shape of the engines, then pushed inside.

THE WRECK OF THE *KURCHATOV*: JUNE 10, 22:53

Tiny fish darted away from Chapel's lights as he pushed his way through the cramped engine compartment, gingerly crawling along using his hands to keep from colliding with any sharp or rusted surface. It wasn't easy. Submarines were cramped by design, cluttered by nature, and the crushing, tearing impact that tore the *Kurchatov* open had crumpled much of its hull, reducing further the room he had to maneuver. It felt more like he was spelunking than diving as he had to consider each move, work out in advance where his legs and arms would fit. Everything around him was pitch-black until he looked directly at it. But this wasn't like the darkness outside, when he'd felt like he was drifting through outer space. Chapel was constantly aware that he was surrounded on every side by metal, by ton after ton of Soviet-era military equipment, and the thought of pushing himself deeper inside the crumpled tin can was daunting.

It didn't help that the only sound he could hear, the only noise in the world, it seemed, was a deep, rumbling groaning sound that never quite stopped. It was just the sound of the submarine settling around him, straining against its own weight as it must have been doing for twenty years. But it was distorted by the water around him and amplified by the otherwise ubiquitous silence until it sounded alien and wrong, a sustained symphony of grinding, roaring moans.

At least he didn't have to worry about radiation. The *Kurchatov*, like all Kilo class submarines, ran on diesel fuel, not a nuclear reactor, and there had never been any nuclear missiles on board. There were plenty of nasty chemicals around him—the lead-based batteries that filled the lower third of the sub had probably been leaking poison into the water for twenty years—but his drysuit would protect him from the worst of that.

The biggest danger he faced was ripping his suit or hitting his head on the low ceiling. If he stunned himself down here or if he lost visibility, he could be in real trouble. But he doubted it would come to that. He'd done his homework. Chapel had trained for this mission for weeks before coming down to Miami. He'd studied every known schematic of a Kilo class sub, memorized where everything was inside, thought himself through each motion he needed to make, every inch of the submarine's interior he would have to traverse.

Of course, the interior of the sunken boat looked nothing like the photographs he'd studied. The interior would have been painted a drab, uniform tan when the sub was operational. It had gone through a real sea change since. Every surface inside was coated in organic muck, drifts of marine snow mixed with mud and the skeletons of coral and other invertebrates. A colony of tiny white-shelled clams had taken over one of the engine housings, looking like shelf fungus on a fallen tree. Brain coral had wrapped itself around one of the big fuel pumps. He thought he saw an octopus slither underneath an oil trap as he approached, though it was gone before he could be sure.

At the fore of the engine compartment stood a

massive pressure hatch with a wheel mounted on its front. It lay on its side now, and for the first time Chapel realized that the entire submarine was heeled over on its port side and that what he'd been thinking of up and down were actually port and starboard. Added to the virtual weightlessness he felt while diving he had to force himself to remember what direction was up—something he definitely needed to keep in mind if he wanted to get back out of the wreck.

The door was closed, but he searched around its edges with his fingers until he found that it had either been left open by the crew—the better to scuttle the sub—or had been knocked out of its frame by the impact with the coral spar. It swung open with just a little elbow grease and let him into the engineering decks.

The semiclosed hatch had kept most of the marine life out of the middle of the submarine, so it didn't look quite as alien to his trained eyes. The engineering decks were just as he'd expected to find them, tight corridors where every wall was lined with electrical boxes and stowed equipment. All tilted ninety degrees from the schematics he'd pored over. Strange ropy growths hung from both walls—now the ceiling and the floor—and at first he tried to identify what animal had left them behind, but then he realized they weren't growths at all. They were the remains of string hammocks. The VIP passengers on board must have found any space they could to bunk down in, even the hot, noisy engineering areas that would normally have been unlivable. Chapel imagined just how desperate they must have been to cram inside the submarine with the fifty men of the *Kurchatov*'s crew, living shoulder to shoulder for long weeks as the sub inched its way across the Atlantic. They must have been terrified, he thought—afraid to surface in case a vengeful Russian proletariat was looking for them, constantly worried about being detected by American antisubmarine patrols. And all for nothing. Though every one of the coup plotters had been arrested and sent to prison, from what Chapel had read there had been no serious retribution against the families that stayed behind. The people who made the desperate journey in the *Kurchatov* had suffered in the tin can in vain.

Who knew, though? Maybe they were happier now in Cuba. Winter in Havana had to have Moscow beat.

The boat was less damaged through the engineering decks, and Chapel made a little better time crawling along until he reached another pressure hatch, this one leading to the crew and command areas underneath the sail. The door opened as easily as the one in the engine room and Chapel slipped inside, letting his lights play over what had once been the *Kurchatov*'s bridge. There were more hammocks here, though most were stowed carefully out of the way of the sonar screens and computer stations. Chapel pulled himself over the long silver pipe of a periscope stalk and found the narrow stairway leading down to the bunkrooms and officers' cabins below.

He was getting close. Ahead of him, in the submarine's bows, lay the enormous torpedo tubes, but those were of no interest to him. What he needed would be in the captain's cabin if it was there at all.

Chapel ignored the groaning roar of the submarine and pulled himself along the stair rail, resisting the urge to kick for speed. The crew deck was one of the tightest spots in the whole boat, with four tiny rooms crammed together in a space half the size of a school bus. He saw the wardroom first, little more than a closet where the crew could have taken their meals or what little leisure time they got. It comprised a single narrow table with a bench behind it and a twelve-inch television set mounted to what had been its ceiling. The crew's bunks lay beyond, with room for maybe twenty men at a time if they were very friendly. The crew would have had to sleep in shifts, taking turns using the same bunks, catching what sleep they could under blankets that smelled like the men who'd had them before.

The captain's cabin had its own pressure hatch, which was closed. It lay on what had become the floor of the submarine, originally its port side, so it was beneath him. Chapel expected the hatch to open like the others, but his fingers couldn't seem to get any purchase around its seals. He tried the wheel and found that it turned freely, but when he tried to pull it open it was like attempting to lift the entire submarine with his bare hands.

Chapel tugged and pulled for a while but that made him breathe heavier, and he couldn't afford that with the amount of breathing gas he was carrying. He forced himself to take shallower breaths and relax.

He closed his eyes. Tried to block out for a

moment the sustained painful groan of the dead submarine. Tried to think about why the door wouldn't open.

Was the damned thing jammed? Maybe the impact that tore open the engine compartment had warped the door in its seals. Chapel felt around the edges of the metal door, looking for any sign that it had crumpled or fused in place, but he found nothing. He tried the wheel again. Looked for any kind of mechanism that might have locked the door shut—nothing.

In his frustration he smacked at the door with his hand, though that was worse than useless, since in the thick water he couldn't get much leverage, and—

"Huh," he said to himself.

He slapped the hatch again, and this time he listened to the sound it made.

Again. Yes, definitely. It didn't make the clanging sound he would have expected. It sounded more like he was striking a drum.

It seemed impossible, but it had to be right. The door wasn't jammed or locked. It was being held shut by the pressure of the water on top of it, because the cabin beyond was still full of air. This one hatch must have remained sealed when the sub went down, unlike all the others. Even after twenty years it hadn't been breached.

Chapel knew there was no way he would ever get the hatch open by main strength. He would have had to fight the entire ocean to do it. Luckily he'd come prepared. In a pouch at his belt he had a small lump of plastic explosive and an electronic detonator. He worked the plastique carefully, rolling it into a thick rope, then pressed it into place along the hatch seals. Then he swam away from the door, moving into the tiny wardroom. It had a folding door that he shut behind him. He put one arm over his mask and hit the detonator.

The explosion made a lot of noise and a huge shock wave that buffeted Chapel even through the wardroom door. He hated to think what would happen to any nearby fish. When it had passed, he shoved open the wardroom door and swam back out.

The crew deck was full of bubbles and disturbed sediment that made his lights nearly useless. A thick torrent of silver bubbles rushed up out of the place where the cabin hatch had been, the trapped air of twenty years screaming out and upward. Chapel fought through the curtain of roiling air and heard it hiss against his suit, felt it push back against him as it tried desperately to escape. He reached for the wheel to open the hatch—the pressures would equalize soon, and it would open easily once—

Then a grinning skull came flying at him and smacked him right in his mask.

THE WRECK OF THE *KURCHATOV*: JUNE 10, 23:49

Chapel sucked in a deep breath and shoved himself backward, out of the storm of bubbles, but the skull kept after him, bouncing against his face again and again. He collided painfully with something behind him and one of his flippers broke loose, and for a second he could only spin around, desperately grabbing for it as the disturbed muck of the submarine rose up around him, filling up the cone of his lights, making him half blind—and still the skull kept bobbing after him, bumping against the ceiling, its teeth lunging right for his mask.

It took all his self-control to stop thrashing and try to calm down.

It wasn't some long dead sailor's ghost that was after him. Just the remains of a man who had sealed himself in his cabin when the submarine went down. Chapel forced himself to reach out and take hold of it, one thumb in an eye socket. The skull wanted to float out of his hand—there must still be a bubble of air inside it, a bubble that had lifted it out of the ruptured hatch. When he had shot backward, away from the cabin hatch, he had created an eddy in the water that had sucked the skull after him. That was all.

The skull looked a lot less imposing when it wasn't attacking him. It was just a normal human skull, fleshless and yellow. It was missing its lower jaw. There was a big ragged hole in the back of it that looked like the exit wound of a gunshot.

He got his flipper back on. The muck had started to settle again, and he could see a little better. The bubbles had all but stopped streaming from the breached door. Still holding the skull, he used the fingers of his free hand to lift the cabin door, releasing a last trapped pocket of air.

Around him the hissing roar of the escaping air slowly subsided, and once again he could hear the long, drawn-out death knell of the submarine. He ignored the noise and slipped inside the captain's cabin.

This room hadn't changed at all in twenty years. It had been sealed shut and full of air, not seawater, until Chapel came along. The tan paint on the walls was intact, and the captain's meager furnishings were still in good shape—hardwood gleamed where it had been polished, brass shone in Chapel's lights. It was a ridiculous mess now, though. Chapel had done far more to disturb the cabin than the ocean could. Letting in the seawater had sent papers floating like two-dimensional fish that swirled around him. The blankets on the single narrow bunk fluttered and frayed as he watched, stirred up by the water that had rushed inside.

Curled up in one corner of the floor—what had been the portside wall of the cabin—was most of the captain's body minus the skull. The body was still dressed in a Soviet naval uniform. Clutched in one skeletal hand was a pistol that must have fired the fatal shot, the one that left the exit wound Chapel had found in the skull.

He could guess what had happened. His briefing hadn't mentioned what became of the *Kurchatov*'s captain. At the time Chapel assumed he had just gone ashore with the rest of his crew and his passengers. Apparently not. Instead the man had elected to go down with his ship.

He must have sealed himself in his cabin and waited for the end as the submarine sank to the bottom. He must have listened to that horrible groaning, just as Chapel was now. How long had he waited until he took his own life? Had he used up all the oxygen in the room and chosen not to let himself asphyxiate? Or had it happened long before then, when he realized that his beloved nation was no more? Maybe—

Maybe, Chapel thought, he should stop trying to imagine the captain's last moments and focus on the mission at hand.

He realized he was still holding the skull. He turned it upside down to let a last wavering silver bubble of air out of its cavity, then gently put it down with the rest of the skeleton. Then he turned and looked for the captain's desk. It was a tiny ledge that folded up into the cabin's wall. He pulled it down on its hinges and some of its contents drifted out—more papers, a pair of brass calipers that settled quickly to the floor. It had a compartment that could be locked but hadn't been. He opened the compartment and found a couple of neatly folded charts inside and an envelope that probably held the captain's orders for what to do when the coup failed.

Not what he was looking for.

Chapel turned around and found the captain's personal locker under the bunk. He pulled open its door and reached inside to search the contents.

He drew out the contents of the locker. A spare uniform. A wooden box containing a couple of Soviet medals. A box of ammunition for the captain's pistol. Some old photographs.

None of that was helpful to him. But he was out of places to look. The cabin was tiny, with very little in the way of storage space—the desk and the locker were pretty much it. He supposed that what he was looking for could be hidden somewhere, underneath the thin carpeting that lined the floor, maybe, or in a secret compartment built into the walls, but—

Think, Chapel, he told himself. What he was looking for wouldn't be hidden in a secret compartment that was difficult to access. The captain would have needed it every time he used the sub's radio. It had to be close by, and easy to get to, but secure . . .

Chapel spun around and looked at the skeleton. At the uniform jacket it wore. He kicked over and looked down at the skull, saying a silent apology. Then he pulled at the jacket until its buttons came loose. The rib cage underneath collapsed under his hands as he rummaged in the captain's pockets.

There! A little book with a black leatherette cover, just as it had been described to him. It looked like an address book, but when Chapel opened it to a random page, he saw columns of numbers and Cyrillic characters in a grid. The pages had all been laminated to protect them from the water. This was what he needed.

He stowed it in a pouch at his belt and took one last look at the captain's skeleton. He wished he could take the medals, too, or some token of the man's passing so he could send it to the captain's family. So they would have something of the man. But no—no one could ever know that Chapel had been inside the submarine, that *anyone* had touched it since it sank.

He could only offer the respectful moment of silence that one military man owed another. The recognition, something like a prayer, of those who served in secret. He saluted the skeleton, then turned to leave the cabin that would forever be the captain's tomb.

Out on the crew deck he stopped and checked his

partial pressures, then took a second to get his bearings. His head felt a little light, but not enough so to make him giddy. The long dive and the scare he'd gotten when the captain's skull came at him had left him exhausted and sore, as if he'd been working hard for hours.

It was time for Chapel to get out of there. To head back to the surface. He knew he wouldn't feel right again until he could take off his mask and breathe the clean air above the waves. Time to start his ascent.

OFF CAY SAL BANK: JUNE 11, 00:43

Moving carefully, Chapel retraced his path and emerged from the broken tail of the submarine, back out into open water.

It was going to take a lot longer to go up than it had to come down. Diving to these kinds of depths was always a risky proposition, and he'd gone down a lot farther than anyone ever should. His tissues were suffused with gaseous nitrogen from breathing the Trimix provided by his rebreather. He was going to need hours of decompression time before he was back in real air again, to prevent the bends. The rebreather would help shorten that time, especially with the helium he'd added to his mix, but it was dangerous to breathe too much helium during an ascent as well, so he was going to need to take his time.

So he took his time looking for the cable. He swam around in circles for a bit until he found the ledge, a darker patch of shadow to one side of him. He made his way slowly up that slope, pausing for a few minutes every ten feet, paying very close attention to his depth gauge because it was the only way to tell that he was, in fact, ascending and not diving deeper into the cold water.

When he reached the ledge, he stuck close to it, reinforcing in his mind the idea that it was down, a floor from which he could make his ascent. He stumbled on the anchor almost by mistake, banging his artificial hand on one of its flukes. He yanked the hand back in surprise, then cursed himself and patted around himself carefully to find it again in the murk. Then he did something he really, really didn't want to do—he turned off his lights. That left him blind, but at least he didn't have to stay deaf anymore.

Groping his way up he reached for the anchor cable. The conductive wires in his glove made contact with the metal cable and he heard a very welcome hiss in his earphones. He was back in communication with Angel.

"It's done," he told her. "I'm starting my ascent. Should take—about two hours, now." Saying it made his heart sink. He was more than ready for this dive to be over.

His frustration didn't last long.

"Chapel? I've got you—can you hear me all right?" she asked. She sounded nervous. That was never, ever a good sign.

"You're coming through just fine. There were some hiccups, but I've managed to—"

"Chapel, you need to be up top *now*," she said.

"What?" He didn't understand. "No, Angel, I need to decompress—"

"There's no time. I wish I could have kept you apprised, but you were out of communication for so long. Chapel, start your ascent now, *please*."

Chapel reached for the cable with his free hand and started hauling himself slowly upward, hand over hand. "I can reduce the number of decompression stops," he told her. "I'm supposed to stop every ten feet and pause, but I can make it twenty—"

"No, Chapel—you don't have that kind of time. The Cubans found the boat."

Oh no, he thought. That was bad. That was very bad.

The *Kurchatov* had sunk in disputed waters, claimed by both the Bahamas and by Cuba, which made them off-limits to American vessels. When Chapel had spoken with the yacht's captain and asked him to drop anchor here, he'd known there was a risk they would be spotted by the Cuban coast guard. The risk was low—Cuba wasn't known to have a large number of vessels patrolling these waters—but they had tried to prepare for it anyway. Angel had been watching for any approaching vessels, and one must have appeared while he was down in the wreck.

"How much time do I have before they arrive?" Chapel asked. There was no question in his mind that the Cubans would approach and board Donny's yacht as soon as they spotted it.

"None. They've already signaled the yacht that they're coming aboard. In a few minutes they'll be boarding and they'll probably search the whole boat. You need to be topside right now."

Chapel grunted in frustration. "What if I just stay down here until they're gone?" he asked. "That'll give me plenty of decompression time. If I come up now, I'm at real risk for decompression sickness."

"You're going to have to chance it. Chapel, your name is on the passenger list."

Crap, Chapel thought. He hadn't thought of that. When he came aboard Donny's yacht, Donny had insisted he sign in. He would have preferred to come aboard incognito, but it hadn't seemed like a big deal at the time.

"If you're not present when they board the yacht, they'll have way too many questions and they'll be able to claim the yacht is evidence in an ongoing investigation," Angel told him. "They'll impound it and tow it back to Cuba to try to figure out what's going on. You can stay down and wait for them to leave with the yacht, but then you'll be surfacing in twenty miles of open water with no way home but to swim there."

Worse than that, Donny and all his party guests would be arrested and thrown in a Cuban jail until they could explain what had happened to the missing man on the guest list. He couldn't let that happen to his friends.

"All right, Angel. I'm going to have to go back into radio silence for a minute. I'll contact you when I hit the surface."

"Understood. The Cubans are coming in from behind and slightly to starboard of the yacht. If you're going to make bubbles or a splash, try to use the bulk of the yacht to cover your ascent."

"Got it." Chapel let go of the cable and swam

backward for a second. *This is going to hurt*, he thought. Coming up from this depth without decompression stops made it inevitable that he was going to get the bends, rebreather or no.

It couldn't be helped. He unbuckled his weight belt and let it fall away into the murk. He shed as many of his pouches and pieces of equipment as he could, even the dive computer, then he started kicking toward the surface. His natural buoyancy started lifting him up immediately, straight toward the waves above, but even that wasn't fast enough. He unclipped the helium tank from his abdomen and pointed its nozzle downward, then threw open its valve and used it like a miniature rocket booster.

Up. Straight up. A hell of a lot faster than he'd gone down.

OFF CAY SAL BANK: JUNE 11, 01:12

As Chapel approached the surface his eyes started working again. A little moonlight was coming down to meet him, and it turned the surface of the waves into a vast rolling mirror, obscured by a large dark mass. As he got closer he saw that shadow split into two. One part was the yacht, big and square and right over his head. The other must be the Cuban coast guard ship. It was only about half the size of the yacht, but it had the sleek, streamlined curves of a warship and looked like a shark nuzzling up against a bloated sunfish.

As he got even closer he could make out a few details. The Cuban ship had tied up to the side of the yacht, which had to mean the Cubans had already boarded. Chapel was going to have to sneak back on board and hope he could mix in with the partygoers so no one noticed he hadn't been there the whole time.

Angel could help him get a feel for how things were up there. As he neared the surface he reached for the anchor cable again. "Angel?" he asked. "What can you tell me? Am I too late?"

There was no answer except the steady hiss that meant his earphones were working. They just weren't picking anything up.

Chapel poked his head above the water and studied the cable. The transponder unit he'd clipped to it was gone. Someone must have found it.

That could be very, very bad.

Once he'd broken the surface, though, his headset could patch into the cellular network and he could at least make contact. "Angel," he whispered, "are you receiving me?"

"I sure am, honey," she said back. "You've just got time, if you hurry."

The mystery of the missing transponder would have to wait. Chapel climbed up onto the swimming balcony at the bow of the yacht and started tearing off his gear. The mask came first and suddenly he was breathing real, fresh air again, not his own recycled breath. It burned his lungs—there was a lot more oxygen up here than he'd been getting below—but it tasted so sweet he didn't care. He wriggled out of the drysuit as fast as he could, careful not to get his artificial arm wet. He opened the pouch that held the little laminated book he'd salvaged from the *Kurchatov*, then bundled up all the rest of his gear, drysuit, rebreather, headset, all of it, and tossed it over the side. It floated for a second and then disappeared without so much as a gurgle. It was a real shame to just throw away all that expensive equipment, but Chapel knew if he was caught with technical diving gear, the Cubans would ask a lot of questions he was in no position to answer. Worst of all, it meant losing his connection to Angel as well—but that was another thing he would have a hard time explaining.

Wearing nothing but a thin pair of trunks, Chapel ran hands through his sweaty hair and stepped through the balcony's door, into the lower deck of the yacht. He could hear someone shouting in Spanish over his head, but no one saw him as he moved quickly toward the stairs that led to the main deck.

Halfway up, a brick wall came out of nowhere and hit him full on.

At least, it felt that way. Every muscle in his body just shut down at once. A wave of fatigue and dizziness passed through him, and he felt a desperate, unbearable desire to sit down, to lean his head against the wall. To go to sleep right then and there and not even bother finding a comfortable place to lie down.

"Shit," he breathed, because he knew where that came from. It could take hours for the first symptoms of decompression sickness to set in, he knew, or just minutes. The faster it came on, the worse it was going to get.

In all his time diving, Chapel had never gotten

the bends before. He'd always been careful to decompress in stages, to read dive charts more carefully than some people read the Bible, to know his limits. He'd managed to stay clear of every diver's worst nightmare—until now.

But he'd seen other divers go through it. It wasn't pretty. He remembered one guy down in Mexico, off the Yucatán, curled up in the bottom of a rowboat, screaming and crying as his joints shook and spasmed. If that was what awaited him—

He couldn't let it. He couldn't give in to the nitrogen in his blood. Chapel forced himself to stand upright, to keep moving. He climbed the stairs one at a time, forcing himself to lift each foot, to keep himself steady.

Just a little farther. Just up a few more steps. Up ahead the main deck opened up around the pool. Chapel could just see what was going on out there. The partygoers were lined up around the edge, none of them talking. Most were looking at their feet or up at the sky, anywhere but at the soldiers who had boarded the yacht.

There were a dozen of them, all of them carrying carbines slung around their necks. They wore the green uniforms and flat-topped hats that Chapel always associated with Fidel Castro. That was strange. Those were Cuban army uniforms, not the white sailor suits that naval personnel wore.

Another mystery. Chapel had no time for mysteries. It was taking everything he had to keep climbing the stairs.

The soldiers were looking every partygoer up and down, checking names against a list. They didn't leer at the young women in their bikinis, didn't try to outmacho the muscle-bound guys in their Speedos. The soldiers had a job to do, and they were being consummate professionals. Not what Chapel had expected at all.

He came up to a broad archway that led to the main deck. He would walk out there, he thought, walk out calling his own name and apologizing profusely. He would claim that he'd been stuck in the head and couldn't get up top until just now. Maybe, just maybe, the Cubans would buy it.

He took a step toward the deck, but his foot never came down.

Instead a bright blossom of pure red agony burst inside his knee, and his leg bent under him until he was standing like a flamingo. A flamingo that very much wanted to die.

"Christ," Chapel said, biting off the word so he didn't shout it. The pain was incredible. He'd been shot before, several times in fact, but even that didn't hurt like this. Nothing ever had.

At least, not until his good shoulder started up, too. It felt like his arm was being cut off, like he was going to lose that one too. Like there was a knife inside his arm, ripping away at his muscles, grating against his bones. He reached over with the artificial arm to grab the flesh there, to squeeze it even though he knew that wouldn't help at all.

Standing on one foot, suddenly off balance, he couldn't stay upright anymore. He crashed to the floor, his head thudding on the polished wood of the deck. He could only hope the Cubans hadn't heard him fall.

Out by the pool they were nearly done with their inspection. One of the Cubans, a young guy wearing round glasses, looked down at a piece of paper in his hand. He smacked it with the back of his fingers, and it made a noise like a snare drum.

Chapel brought his head up so he could watch. He didn't need to—he knew what was going to happen next. The young guy was clearly the commanding officer of the Cuban patrol. He strode up to Donny and got way too close to his face.

"*¿Dónde está* Chapel, James?" the Cuban demanded.

OFF CAY SAL BANK: JUNE 11, 01:21

Chapel curled up into a ball on the carpeted floor of the stairway landing. He couldn't get up, could barely breathe. The pain had spread to every joint in his body, and it was only getting worse. He could hear people moving out on the deck, but his eyes were clamped tightly shut and he knew he wouldn't be able to get away, wouldn't be able to move from the spot where he lay. At any moment the Cubans would start searching the yacht and they would find him—there was no chance of his even rolling into the shadows, must less finding a place to hide.

Once they found him the questions would begin. They would want to know what was wrong with him. It wouldn't take long for them to figure out that he was suffering from decompression sickness, and then they would want to know why he was diving in Cuban waters. They would find the little black book and he would be arrested, dragged back to Cuba, and thrown into a bottomless pit of a jail and never heard from again.

And there was nothing he could do to stop them. He couldn't fight like this, and he couldn't run. He tried desperately to move, to use his artificial arm—which at least didn't hurt—to drag himself farther down the corridor, back to the top of the stairs. If he could push himself down those steps, and if he didn't break his neck, maybe, just maybe—

Soft hands touched his head and shoulders. Fingers slipped under his chin and took his pulse. "You smell of brine," a woman said. "We have to fix that somehow. Can you walk?"

He tried to open his eyes. Found he could just barely crack one eyelid. He saw dark hair and nothing else—he couldn't turn his head to get a better look.

"I take it that means no," the woman said.

The voice—he remembered it, the accent he couldn't place. The woman in the sundress, the Asian woman he'd met with Donny and Shelly and the rest. She must have found him there on the carpet. But why? Why wasn't she out with the rest of the partygoers, out on the main deck?

"I can't lift you on my own, and there's no one else to help. You have to get on your feet," she whispered. "Please. So much depends on this."

He had no idea what she was talking about. But he knew if he didn't get up and get moving, he was doomed. Chapel reached down with his artificial arm and grabbed one of his ankles. His leg was curled up underneath him, his knee and ankle both on fire, but he could push the leg out straight if he didn't mind some searing agony.

Well, he minded. He minded a lot. But he managed not to scream.

"Good," she said. "You're a strong guy, yes? A powerful guy. You can do this. You have to."

He reached down and straightened out his other leg. He could just twist sideways until he was sitting up, though it felt like he was being torn in half. With his back against the wall he pushed upward from his knees. His feet slid away from him on the wet carpet, but he recovered before he fell again. Using every shred of willpower in his possession, Chapel was just able to push himself up until he was leaning against the wall, as little weight as possible on his feet.

"Here, on my shoulders," she said, and pulled his good arm around her neck. Straightening out those muscles made Chapel want to pass out, but he forced himself to stay conscious. *Just a little longer. Just a couple more seconds*, he promised himself. "Donny's cabin is just here," she told him. "Move your left foot forward."

Chapel fought to open his eyes, to see what was happening. He didn't know this woman. Why was she helping him? Just because he was a friend of Donny's? "You'll get in trouble," he said, his voice sounding weak and small even to his own ears. "Just leave me," he told her.

"I don't think so. Come, now, move your left foot forward. I know you can. Good. Very, very good. Now your right foot."

She didn't exactly carry him, but she took a lot

more of his weight than he thought she could. Together they set off at a snail's pace down the corridor.

Behind Chapel, out on the deck, someone started shouting in Spanish. Someone else shrieked in fright.

Chapel must have glanced backward.

"You're thinking this isn't a normal patrol, that they didn't find us by accident, and you are right. But they don't know who you are, only that you were missing when they demanded to see everyone on board. You can't let them find out who you are."

He felt his eyes widen—mostly because it hurt so much. What did she know about him? His mission was utterly secret—nobody on board even knew who he worked for, much less what he was doing here.

Questions were going to have to wait. He focused on moving his feet.

A door opened in front of him—she must have opened it. He could still barely keep his eyes open, barely see where he was. Beyond the door lay a sizable cabin, bigger than the one he had on the deck below. It had room for a little table and a couple of chairs and a widescreen television on the wall. It also had a private bathroom with a big shower stall. The Asian woman shoved Chapel into the stall and ran the water, which came out icy cold at first. Chapel shivered as the water poured down over his aching face and chest. He tried to keep his left arm out of the spray, but the rest of him was quickly soaked.

"For the salt smell," she told him, adjusting the water temperature. "Get your trunks off. Don't worry about modesty now. This is not the time. Get them off!"

If he hesitated, it wasn't because he was afraid of letting her see him naked. It was because the little black book was jammed down the side of his shorts. It was the only hiding place he had.

"It hurts too much, I know," she said. She bent down and pulled down his trunks. The little black book fell out before he could stop her. She didn't seem surprised. Instead she shoved it into a pocket of her sundress. She wadded up his shorts and put them in a laundry hamper that was already full of wet bathing suits and towels.

"Wait," he said. "That book—"

"Shh," she told him. "I can hear them outside, be quiet!"

It was no use. Chapel had to focus on holding himself up and not collapsing inside the shower stall. He felt so weak that just the water pouring down on him could knock him over. He heard the Cubans out in the hall as well—he could hear them shouting, even over the roar of the blood in his ears. He heard them pounding on the door, demanding to be let in.

Then he heard the sound of wood splintering, and he knew they were breaking their way in.

The Asian woman did something then he could not have expected. She reached up and undid the strap of her sundress, then let it fall away from her body until she wore nothing but a pair of black lace panties. She balled up the dress and threw it in the laundry hamper. Then she pushed her way into the shower, sliding in under Chapel's body, her bare breasts pressing up against his sternum.

"Put your arms around me," she whispered.

That was when the door flew open, knocked half off its hinges. Cuban soldiers came rushing in, their guns in their hands, ready for anything. They spread out around the cabin, covering every part of it, ready to shoot anyone who moved.

Underneath Chapel, the Asian woman moaned as if she were in the throes of passion. Chapel stared at her face and saw her looking back, cool and dispassionate. She didn't even close her eyes as she moaned again, nodding at him.

Message received. Chapel forced his arms around her, fighting the pain in his elbow and his wrist. His artificial arm wrapped around her waist, and he pulled her close. Water streamed over his silicone skin, which was bad—he was supposed to keep the arm as dry as possible—but there was nothing for it. He tried to grunt out a cry of arousal but only managed a whimper.

The door of the shower stall banged open, and a Cuban soldier stared in at them. A mischievous smile started to crack on his face, but he fought it down—the man was a professional, all right.

Behind him the young soldier with the glasses, the one in charge, peered in at the two of them. He didn't so much as blink when he saw them like that.

For a second Chapel worried that the ruse would fail, that the man would realize the two of them were only acting as if they were aroused. But then the Asian woman turned her head to look at the Cubans and she let out a whooping screech of embarrassment that was enough to make the two soldiers step back. The Asian woman brought a hand up to her face, and her eyes went wide as saucers. And then she started giggling.

It was not a sound Chapel ever expected this woman to make. It was the sort of giggle someone like Shelly might let out if she were caught in this situation.

"Oh my God," the Asian woman said, and her accent was gone. She sounded exactly like one of the coeds up on the deck. "Oh my God oh my God, Jimmy, there are . . . people here! Oh my God!"

The Cuban soldier who had discovered them turned beet red and turned his face away. The commanding officer still stared at them, and Chapel could see he wasn't quite convinced.

"Did you two not hear us when we called everyone up to the main deck?" the officer asked, in perfect if accented English.

"I thought I did," the Asian woman said. "Jimmy, didn't I say something, I was like, like—"

"Hey, buddy," Chapel said, forcing himself to sound normal despite the pain and weakness. "Can we at least finish before we get the third degree?"

The officer frowned. Then he addressed his soldier. "No need to search these two, I think," he said, in Spanish. "Get their names and check their papers, that's all." He glanced back at Chapel and shook his head. "*Borracho pendejo*," he muttered, and then he walked away.

The soldier, still blushing, gave them an embarrassed shrug. "May I see your passports, please?" he asked.

SOUTH OF MIAMI, FLORIDA: JUNE 11, 02:32

It was another hour at least before the Cubans finished their search of the yacht. Chapel would very much have liked to know what they were looking for, and why they had devoted so much manpower and time to investigating what was clearly just a party boat that strayed accidentally into disputed waters. He had no way of finding out, though.

It was all he could do to curl up on a bunk and try to breathe through the pain.

He only knew the Cubans had gone because Donny came into the cabin and told as much to the Asian woman. She had put her sundress back on but had sat with Chapel the whole time, stroking his back and telling him how strong he was. He appreciated the effort, but it didn't help much. Donny came in with the news that they were headed back to Miami and that the Cubans had left them with just a stern warning. When he saw Chapel curled up on his bed, though, his eyes went wide and he grabbed the door frame as if he was having trouble balancing.

"What's wrong with him?" Donny asked. "He didn't drink that much."

"He has the raptures of the deep," the Asian woman said. "We need to get him treatment right away."

"The raptures . . . you mean the bends? He's got the bends? Jimmy, what the hell have you been up to?"

"Please," the Asian woman said. "He's in great pain. He may die!"

"Shit," Donny said, and he ran over to kneel next to the bed. "Jim. Jim, come on, man, look at me.

Look at me—you're a ranger, man. You can get through this."

"Oxygen," Chapel managed to croak. The pain came in waves, and just then it was hitting a peak. He could barely move his lungs.

"He needs a hyperbaric chamber," the Asian woman said. "There's one in Miami. Call ahead and have it made ready. But in the meantime—"

"Oxygen," Chapel said again.

"He's right," the Asian woman said. "He needs to breathe pure oxygen, to flush the nitrogen from his system."

"We have some SCUBA tanks onboard," Donny suggested. "I can get one up here right away."

"That won't work," the Asian woman told him. "Those tanks hold only normal air, and that'll just put more nitrogen in his blood."

"There's . . . there might be an oxygen tank in the medical kit—I think—"

"Go now," the woman told Donny. "Please."

Donny nodded and rubbed at his mouth with one hand. Then he ran off to get the tank.

Chapel turned his head to the side, to look at her face. She looked scared. He wondered just how bad he looked to make everybody so scared. "Why are you helping me?" he asked. She didn't answer, just rubbed at his arms. "I don't even know your name."

"Nadezhda," she told him. "Nadia, to my family and friends."

A Russian name. Who was this woman? "After . . ." Chapel paused to let the pain in his joints reach a fiery crescendo. It got so bad he couldn't see for a moment. "After that shower we took together—"

"Yes," she said, and smiled at him. "You can call me Nadia."

Chapel closed his eyes. When he opened them, she was gone. He must have blacked out for a while. Donny came running into the room and put a mask over Chapel's face, and that was the last thing he remembered for a while. When he woke up again, he was on a stretcher being wheeled down the yacht's gangplank. The sky was red with dawn. He heard seagulls and smelled diesel fuel and knew he must be in Miami. Donny was walking alongside the stretcher, holding Chapel's hand.

The pain was just a shadow of what it had been. The oxygen must have done its job. The relief of it, of not hurting so much he wanted to die, washed through Chapel and was better than any surge of endorphins.

"You're awake," Donny said. "You had us pretty worried there, for a while."

"Sorry about that." Chapel could move his head again without crippling pain. He turned as far as he could and looked back at the yacht. The deck was lined with blond girls in bikinis, and they were all watching him with concerned looks on their faces.

"Listen, Jim, I have a feeling about . . . about what happened back there. I have a feeling my captain didn't just accidentally wander too far south."

"Maybe not," Chapel said.

"I have a feeling you didn't just come on my boat for a chance to relax and think things through."

"Maybe that was part of the reason," Chapel said.

"I'm starting to get another feeling. A feeling that maybe I'm not supposed to ask you too many questions."

Chapel sighed. He would love to explain to Donny everything that had happened—why the yacht dropped anchor where it did, why he had gone diving in the middle of the night. It didn't work that way, though. "I'd trust that feeling."

Donny just nodded. He'd been a good soldier. He knew that good soldiers didn't get all the answers they might want; they just got orders and followed them whether or not they understood them. Donny had never worked for military intelligence, and he'd never had to deal with real secrets, but he knew the drill.

"You saved my life," Chapel told him. "I'm never going to forget that."

"It was Nadia who knew what to do," Donny said.

Nadia.

The Asian woman had saved him from the Cubans, too.

Chapel thought of something then. He got a feeling of his own—a bad one. "Where is she?" he asked.

"She went ahead to the hospital, to get things ready. Practically jumped off the boat before we reached the dock. Why? You want to thank her in person?"

"Something like that," Chapel said. What he really wanted to know, what he was suddenly very afraid of, was whether when she left the yacht Nadia had been carrying a little black book. She hadn't said anything about it, but she hadn't looked surprised when she found it, either. And it was awfully convenient that when the Cubans boarded the yacht and made everybody line up on the deck, Nadia had stayed behind exactly where she needed to be to get Chapel into the shower.

But Chapel couldn't ask Donny about the little black book. Maybe he could learn a little something, though. "Who is she?" he asked.

Donny shrugged. "Just some Miami party girl. I don't think she's American."

"I kind of guessed that myself—but what was she doing on the yacht?"

Donny looked confused. "I met her in a club in Miami a couple of weeks ago. I was there with Sheila, and the two of them hit it off. I meet a lot of girls in clubs—they know about my boat, and they all want an invite on one of my cruises. Sheila said Nadia looked like fun, so we asked her to come along. I don't think I said twenty words to her since I met her."

Chapel had more questions—a lot more—but he didn't get to ask them. Paramedics took him away then and drove him straight to a hospital. Nobody wasted any time. Soon they had Chapel in the hyperbaric chamber, a steel tube little bigger than a coffin with one window over his face. Doctors came and tried to talk to him, but he couldn't communicate very well—once the chamber was sealed, its compressors made such a racket he couldn't hear anything.

They left him alone while the chamber worked its magic, subjecting him to pressures that would scrub all the nitrogen bubbles out of his bloodstream. It took the pain away almost immediately, which was great, but the doctors managed to let him know he would have to stay in the chamber for at least twenty-four hours.

He couldn't move around in the chamber, couldn't make any phone calls, couldn't do anything but lie there and think.

Think about a little black book. A little black book he'd been willing to dive to the bottom of the sea to retrieve. A little black book he'd been willing to die for.

A little black book that was probably in Nadia's hands now.

He knew nothing about the Asian woman with the Russian name. Nobody else seemed able to help. The doctors told Chapel she had, indeed, come to them and told them what kind of treatment he needed—she'd even been able to tell them what depth he'd dived to, which was crucial information for his therapy. The doctors were quite clear that she had saved his life.

But as soon as she'd told them what they needed to know, she had disappeared. No one had seen her since.

Chapel knew when he'd been played.

Who was she? A foreign agent? His mission had been secret, the details known only to three people—Chapel, Angel, and his boss in the Defense Intelligence Agency, Rupert Hollingshead. A leak was next to impossible—but somehow Nadia must have discovered what he was up to. Had she been sent to make sure his mission failed?

A dozen scenarios ran through his head as he tried to make sense of it. None of them came up the way he'd want them to. He was sure she had known what he was after, and she had used his decompression sickness to get the book away from him. Maybe she had called in the Cubans to destabilize the situation, or maybe she had just used them to further her cause.

Even Chapel had no idea why the book was so important. Hollingshead had never told him, and he had known better than to ask. But he bet Nadia had that information. He was going to have to track her down. Find her and make her give him the book back. That, or explain to Hollingshead that he had failed.

When they let him out of the hyperbaric chamber, the first thing he did was ask for his clothes and his cell phone. The doctors told him to take it easy, and that they wanted him to stay for another twenty-four hours for observation, but he knew he wouldn't have time for that. He turned on the phone and called Angel as soon as he was alone.

"We've got a problem," he told her.

"Sugar, it sounds like you've had nothing but," she replied. "I'm just so glad you made it, that you're feeling better—"

"There's no time, Angel," he said, as apologetically as he could manage, given how keyed up he was. He tucked the phone into the crook of his shoulder and started pulling on his jacket. "I need you to find somebody for me, and she's not going to make it easy. All I have is her first name, Nadezhda, but she was on Donny's boat and she should be on the passenger list, the same one that got me in trouble. I can give you a physical description and—"

He stopped because when he put his artificial arm through the sleeve of the jacket, something hard in the inside pocket tapped against his chest.

He couldn't think of what it was—he'd had nothing in there when he went aboard the yacht.

"Chapel?" Angel asked. "Everything okay?"

"Hold on," he told her. He reached carefully inside the pocket. Felt leatherette and laminated pages.

It was the little black book.

Nadia must have put it there. She must have put it in his jacket before she left the hospital, knowing he would find it there.

"Uh," he said, because he couldn't think of anything more appropriate. "Huh. Angel—never mind. I made a mistake."

THE PENTAGON: JUNE 13, 09:13

They wouldn't let Chapel fly. There was still some nitrogen dissolved in his fatty tissues, the doctors told him. Spending any length of time in the pressurized cabin of an airplane would put him at risk of forming new bubbles and suffering a total relapse. He needed to stay at sea level for a month, just to be safe. But he had to get back to work, and back to Julia, so he took the train.

The whole way up the East Coast he kept the little black book in his jacket pocket. He didn't risk letting anybody see it, though he very much wanted to study it and try to make sense of what he'd risked so much to salvage.

He arrived in Virginia first thing in the morning. He stopped off at Fort Belvoir, the headquarters of INSCOM and the Defense Contracts Audit

Agency—two groups he'd worked for before starting his present life as a covert operative. To maintain some kind of cover identity, he still kept an office at the fort. He visited it every few months for appearances' sake. He kept a change of clothes, there, too, and it gave him a chance to shower and clean up before meeting with his boss.

From Fort Belvoir it was a short drive and a long stretch of traffic before he could reach the Pentagon. Once there he walked through security, which was actually a nice change of pace because it went so smoothly. Chapel always had a problem with metal detectors since his left arm set off alarms in every airport in the world, but the Pentagon was accustomed to being visited by amputees and they had an officer on duty trained in clearing prostheses. Chapel was inside the building in minutes. He headed back to an unexceptional office deep inside C Ring and then called for an elevator that shouldn't be there. The armed guard whose job was to ride that elevator all day smiled when he saw Chapel and hit the button for H Ring without being asked.

The Pentagon wasn't supposed to have an H Ring. Very few people knew that it did. The elevator dropped through two underground levels and opened on a long corridor of unmarked doors. People cleared for entrance to those doors would know which one they wanted—signs were unnecessary.

Chapel opened the door to his boss's office without being announced. Again, it was unnecessary—Rupert Hollingshead would have known Chapel was coming as soon as he walked in the Pentagon's front door.

As usual, the transition from the drably painted corridor to Hollingshead's office was jarring. The door was just simple metal painted an institutional green. The office behind it, by way of contrast, was lined with immaculately polished hardwood and featured a full wet bar with brass accoutrements, overstuffed leather armchairs, and a working fountain that filled the air with a musical sound. The office looked like nothing so much as a gentlemen's club straight out of nineteenth-century London.

When it was constructed, the office had been a common room for a suite of fallout shelters meant to be used by the Joint Chiefs of Staff during a nuclear war. The intention had been to give the Chiefs some measure of comfort in a stressful time. Now it had been appropriated as office space for a man whose life was one constant bout of stress.

Not that the man would ever let it show.

"Bit, ah, early for a drink," Rupert Hollingshead said, coming out from behind the bar. "But if you'd like some coffee, son, it can be arranged."

Chapel smiled. "Admiral," he said. "It's good to be back."

Hollingshead's eyes twinkled merrily behind round spectacles. The man looked like he belonged in this room. He wore a tweed jacket and a bow tie—the sort almost no one wore anymore, the kind that actually had to be tied instead of clipped on. He looked like an absentminded Ivy League academic more than anything. He even had long sideburns that were far from regulation.

The look—right down to the facial hair—was designed to put people at ease and make them think this man was a harmless old eccentric who wouldn't hurt a fly. It completely belied the fact that Hollingshead had been a rear admiral in the navy during the first Gulf War, or that since then he had become one of the most powerful spymasters in the American intelligence apparatus. He was the director of a directorate that did not officially exist, a man who could whisper in the ear of a president in the morning and start a war by dinnertime.

Hollingshead came over and grasped Chapel's hands. He always took the left hand as well, as if to acknowledge the artificial arm without being too obvious about it. "So very sorry, son, to hear about the, ah, bends and all that. Won't you take a seat?"

"Yes, sir, though I don't intend to stay very long. I have an appointment in Brooklyn to keep."

Hollingshead's face broke into a beaming smile that would have lit up any fallout shelter. He knew all about Julia, of course, and what Chapel hadn't told him personally he would have heard from Angel. "You are a very lucky man, Captain Chapel. You couldn't have picked a better helpmeet."

"I am blessed, sir, it's true. I know it's premature, but I hope you'll come to the wedding."

"Wouldn't miss it, son, not for rubies or pearls."

Chapel grinned. "Just talking about it out loud like that, like it's something that I need to put on my schedule . . . it still feels weird. But it should be official by tonight." He shook his head in disbelief. "I admit, I'm a little nervous. What if she says no?"

"Then my intelligence estimates will have been proven wrong."

Chapel started in surprise. "You didn't—I mean, you haven't—"

"Just a small joke, son. No, I haven't had DIA analysts working out the likelihood of Julia Taggart becoming Mrs. Julia Chapel. Call it an intuition. Or rather, let's say that I couldn't think of two people I hold in higher regard, and better suited to a life of shared bliss. Maybe we should have that drink after all, to celebrate."

"Thank you, sir," Chapel said, his grin returning, "but I'd just as soon get this debriefing over with and get on the train to New York." He reached in his pocket and took out the little black book. He riffled through it, seeing once more the grids of numbers and Cyrillic characters that filled each page. Then he handed it over. "I hope it's worth the trouble it took to secure it."

Hollingshead took the book and tucked it into a pocket of his jacket. "It's worth more than its weight in diamonds, believe me. You know what it is, of course."

That was a question, and maybe some kind of test. Chapel nodded. "It's a one-time pad." A code-book, in other words, containing the key to a cipher that theoretically couldn't be cracked. The captain of the *Kurchatov* would have consulted those grids when sending secret messages back to his superiors in Russia. Each character in his plaintext message was transposed with a character from one of those grids, using basic modular addition. On the other end of the transmission, in a Kremlin basement perhaps, someone else would have an identical pad and be able to decrypt the message. If the characters in the grids were truly random, and if nobody else had access to the pad, the message could never be decrypted since the cipher was unique to that particular message.

One-time pads had been used by both sides throughout the Cold War. They had only been replaced by the advent of computer cryptography. The Kremlin and the Pentagon had relied on them for decades, but unfortunately they weren't very practical. One problem was that the receiver of the message needed to know which page of his own pad to use when deciphering the message, or even which pad to use if more than one existed. In real-world use, the KGB had ended up using what were essentially one-day pads—the same cipher matrix being used for every coded transmission sent in a twenty-four-hour window. There was also the difficulty of making sure every submarine commander, say, received a new pad every month—a tricky bit of logistics when some submarines went on six-month-long cruises and rarely called in at friendly ports.

Because of these issues, one-time pads had fallen out of use—as far as Chapel knew, no major intelligence operation had used them in years.

Which raised the question of why Hollingshead wanted this pad.

"Completely useless, of course," Chapel said.

"Of course," Hollingshead said, though a mischievous grin threatened to crack his face in half.

"Even if codebooks like that were still in use— even if the Russian Federation used the same sort of codes as the Soviet Union used to, which they don't—this pad would still be obsolete. The codes in there haven't been used for twenty years."

"Indeed." Hollingshead took off his glasses and started polishing them with a silk handkerchief. "Hardly seems worth putting the life of my best agent at, um, risk, wouldn't you say?"

"I follow my orders, sir," Chapel replied. "I don't question them. Usually."

Hollingshead nodded in excitement. "I've got quite the plan for this little book, son. It's a shame I can't tell you what it is."

Chapel smiled at his boss. "The suspense might kill me," he joked. But he understood. The one-time pad was meant for some incredibly secret mission, something truly vital to national security. He desperately, desperately wanted to know why Hollingshead thought it was good for something.

But he was never going to find out.

Chapel wasn't going on the next mission. He was going to get married instead. He'd already asked for, and received, a leave of absence while he went home and proposed to his girlfriend. Hollingshead had been overjoyed when he heard the news.

"She's a lovely girl, and you're a very lucky man," Hollingshead said, standing up to come shake Chapel's hands again. "I couldn't be happier for you. Well, ah, that's not strictly true."

"Oh?" Chapel asked, surprised.

"Well. I have a, ah, well, not a reservation. Call it my one regret. It's simply that I wish I could use you for this mission. It's perfect for you. But that doesn't matter. Nothing else matters but the joy you're going to deliver to that wonderful woman.

Have you thought about where you're going to honeymoon? I'm partial to Barbados."

"It's a little premature to think about that, sir."

"Of course, of course," Hollingshead said. He beamed from ear to ear. "Well, take all the time you need. I'll see you when you get back."

"Thank you, sir," Chapel said. He stood up and saluted.

The director saluted back. "If anyone deserves a little time off, it's you, son. Enjoy it. Enjoy it as much as you possibly can."

"I will," Chapel said. He couldn't help but burst into a smiling laugh. "I really will."

BROOKLYN, NEW YORK: JUNE 13, 15:46

Chapel drove to Manhattan, where he stopped off at the jeweler's and picked up the ring. It was beautiful, gleaming in its little box. He paid the man and headed south, across the Manhattan bridge, into the heart of Brooklyn. Toward home.

Toward Julia.

He parked the car outside their little apartment building and looked up at their windows. They shared one floor of a brownstone, just a couple of rooms, tiny by the standards of anyone who'd never lived in a New York apartment. There had been some very good times in those little rooms.

He caught a flash of movement behind one of the windows. A glimpse of red hair as Julia walked past. She was up there. Good.

He realized he'd been sitting in the car for ten

minutes. Was he nervous? He didn't feel nervous. Mostly he felt a little numb.

He headed up the stairs with his good hand clutched tightly around the ring box in his pocket. He had to force himself to let go so he didn't crush it. When he got to the door, he tried the knob and found that it was unlocked. That was a little weird— Julia, like most New Yorkers, kept her doors locked when she was home. But it didn't mean anything. He needed to stop thinking like a spy. He turned the knob and stepped inside. There was a little end table next to the door, a place to put keys or plug in a phone. He took the ring box out of his pocket and laid it there, so that he wasn't holding it when he first saw her. "Julia?" he called.

For a second, only silence answered him. Then he heard her call back, "In here."

We walked back to the bedroom, where she waited for him in the doorway.

She had never looked more beautiful. Her red hair fell around her shoulders and down the back of the thin black sweater she wore. Her eyes were clear and bright. She smiled at him, though it looked like a tentative kind of smile. Well, they hadn't left things very well when he headed down to Miami. In fact, he'd had to walk out in the middle of a pretty nasty fight. Maybe she was still angry.

"I'm back," he said.

"I can see that. I didn't expect you back so soon. Normally you're gone a lot longer."

The fight they'd had—all the fights they'd had— were about the same thing. Chapel couldn't tell her what he did when he went to work. He couldn't even tell her when he was leaving, or when he was coming back. He would just disappear, usually before she woke up in the morning, and reappear when everything was done. Typically he showed up with a new scar or two.

Every single time he left her sitting in this apartment, wondering if he was ever going to come back, or if he was already dead and she would never get to hear about it. He could never promise her he would be alive from one day to the next. For someone like Julia, it was unbearable. She wanted children. She wanted to grow old with him. He couldn't promise her anything like that.

But maybe he could give her something else.

"I needed to be back here." He took a step closer and she moved sideways, blocking the doorway to the bedroom, as if she was hiding something. He could see around her, though. He could see a suitcase lying on the bed.

She wouldn't meet his gaze.

"Were you going out? Damn," he said. "I was really hoping to get some time with you. There's something I want to talk about."

"I'm headed out, yeah." She did look at him then, and her face fell. "Jim, you look terrible. You're pale and your eyes are bloodshot. Are you all right?"

"Fine," he said. The bends had left him a little weak, but the doctors had said he would make a full recovery in a few days. "Listen, I need to say—"

"No," she said. "No, stop. I can't do this."

He was confused. "Do what?"

"Pretend like everything's normal."

Chapel's heart sank in his chest. What was going on?

"I thought it would be easier if I just left. If I wasn't here when you got back. I thought maybe we could do this on the phone, or . . . I don't know. By e-mail."

"Do what?"

She sighed and shrank in the doorway. "I'm going to stay with a friend for a while. Please don't ask me which one. I need to get away. I need—"

She couldn't seem to finish her sentence. She shook her head and ducked into the bedroom. Grabbing the handle of the suitcase, she dragged it off the bed. It looked like it was too heavy for her.

"Let me help you," he told her. "The car's just downstairs."

Her eyes went wide, and she reached out to put a hand on his chest.

"Jim," she said. "Jim." Tears filled her eyes. "Jim, don't you get it? I'm leaving you."

Blood rushed in his ears. For a second the world's worst headache burst through his skull. When he could see again, he realized she'd moved past him, dragging her suitcase into the front room.

He chased after her. "No, no, I know we were fighting, I know it was worse than usual, but—"

"I can't do it!" she shouted at him. "I can't talk about this. I have to go!" She turned around and stared at him as if she were daring him to say something.

"We can figure this out," he promised. "I can—I can talk to my boss—"

"No," she said. "Please don't."

"Just hear me out! I can quit my job." When she said nothing, he nodded, eager, because he knew this would fix things. "I can quit. I can stop doing this."

"No, you can't," Julia said, wiping at her tears. "You shouldn't."

"I can. I really can. I can go back to my old position. My desk job. Don't you see? I'll be home every night. You'll always know where I am. And nobody will be shooting at me, ever again. I did this for—"

"You hated that job. You said they gave it to you because they felt bad about how you lost your arm. You said that job was killing you."

He closed his eyes. "For you, it would be worth it," he told her.

She stood there and wept for a while. Let big racking sobs climb up through her chest and out of her eyes and her throat. He reached for her but she pushed him away.

Eventually, when she'd recovered a little, she wiped clots of mascara off her cheeks with the balls of her thumbs. And then she shook her head.

A silence followed, as if all the air in Brooklyn had turned to ice and nothing, anywhere, moved or made a sound. Chapel thought his heart even stopped beating. He wanted to go to her, to hold her in his arms and tell her everything was going to be okay, but he didn't dare.

"You would resent me for the rest of your life," she said. "No. I won't let you."

"It's my decision."

"No, it isn't. It shouldn't be." She grabbed the handle of the suitcase. "I called a taxi—you can keep our car, at least, for now. We'll . . . we'll talk, and figure out who gets what. But let me call you first. Okay? Don't call me until I call you first."

Chapel shook his head in confusion. "Are you saying you don't love me anymore?"

Julia laughed, a thick noise with all the mucus in her throat. "If I didn't love you, it wouldn't destroy me when you went away. But it does, and I can't take it anymore. I have to go." She turned toward the doorway, the suitcase's wheels rumbling on the hardwood floor. She put her hand on the door-knob. Turned it. Pulled the suitcase closer to her and picked it up with both hands to get it over the threshold.

He tried to think of something to say, but there was nothing. Nothing anywhere inside of him that could change her mind, and he knew it.

Before she left she glanced down at the end table by the door. He saw the moment when she saw the ring box sitting there.

She turned to look at him.

"Oh, Jim, you didn't . . . you didn't think I would . . ."

She made a noise then like she was gagging, like she might throw up from choking on tears. It was a horrible painful noise, and he couldn't bear it; it made him want to curl up and die because he'd made her feel that way. He couldn't stand up anymore but he couldn't fall down—his knees were locked and he felt like he was nailed to the floor.

He didn't see her close the door behind her. He only heard the doorknob turn and the latch inside it catch as it clicked shut.

BROOKLYN, NEW YORK: JUNE 13, 21:06

Eventually it got dark.

The light on the apartment walls turned briefly orange, then blue, then faded away. It never truly got dark in Brooklyn, but with the curtains drawn the room grew dim. It was almost a relief. But Chapel got up anyway and found the lamp. It was lying on the floor, where he'd knocked it down. He switched it on where it lay, and a cone of yellow light spread across the bedroom. It lit up the sheets and pillows where he'd torn them off the bed and thrown them on the floor.

He'd used his left arm, his artificial arm. He'd felt like some kind of machine, tearing up his home, but that was exactly how he'd wanted to feel. A destructive machine that didn't think, didn't feel.

The light lit up the bottle of bourbon lying on the floor, making it glow with its own amber light. The bottle he'd fetched from the kitchen and then never opened because he knew it wouldn't help. The light glinted dully from the white backs of the pictures he'd grabbed and flipped through and then turned facedown on the floor like cards because he couldn't stand to look at what they showed. Even a hint of red hair or a corner of a lip or a single eye looking back at him from those pictures would have been too much.

The light showed him where his phone lay, after he'd thrown it at the wall. He reached out and picked it up. The screen had cracked right across, but it still lit up when he entered the passcode.

Her number was there in his contacts. He'd

opened up that contact and stared at it a dozen times, come very close to pressing the call button, and then stopped himself. She'd said not to call.

Maybe that had been a trick. Maybe she expected him to call anyway, and if he did, he would pass the test and she would know she'd been wrong, that it could work, that he still loved her enough to chase after her . . .

Or maybe she'd been completely honest with him, which was much more like the woman he knew. Maybe if he tried calling her that would be it, the last straw. Maybe there was still a possibility of her coming back but only if he played by her rules . . .

Or maybe she wouldn't even pick up. Maybe his call would go through to her voice mail, and he would have to listen to her recorded greeting, the one where she was laughing because when she recorded it he was kissing her neck . . .

By the time he'd finished thinking through those possibilities—for the dozenth time—the screen went black again.

She was gone. She was really gone.

Repeating that to himself didn't make it real, no matter how many times he thought it in his head.

BROOKLYN, NEW YORK: JUNE 13, 23:39

He tried to sleep. He didn't bother getting up, he just grabbed a sheet from the floor and pulled it over himself.

It smelled like her.

Like Julia.

He balled up the sheet and threw it across the room. It opened up in the air like a parachute and fell slowly to the floor. It made the whole room smell like her.

He went in the kitchen and curled up on the tiles, which just smelled like floor wax.

He couldn't sleep there, either.

BROOKLYN, NEW YORK: JUNE 14, 03:12

He entered the passcode on the phone. The screen lit up and told him the phone was down to reserve power. It didn't matter.

He opened the phone app and his thumb hovered over the button that would bring up all his contacts. He shook his head and pressed the button for the keypad instead. He dialed a number he knew by heart, one that he wasn't permitted to enter into his contacts. The phone picked up before he'd entered the final digit. She must have been waiting, monitoring his phone in case he called.

"Good news, I hope," she said.

That struck him so hard it made him want to laugh. Except it wasn't funny at all.

"Chapel? Baby? Are you all right?"

He ground the ball of his living thumb into his eye socket, trying to push away what he was feeling. This call didn't require the use of his emotions. "Angel," he said. "Tell the boss that I'm available. I'll report for duty first thing in the morning."

"Honey, do you know what time it is? Maybe you should—"

"Just . . . please, Angel. Just tell him that. Okay?"

"Chapel, tell me what's wrong," she said.

He shook his head, even if she couldn't see him. Then he pressed the power switch on the phone and made the screen go dark again.

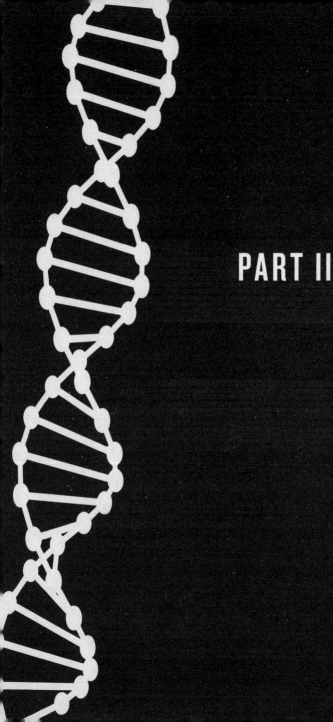

PART II

Even as Chapel made his way through security at the Pentagon, he could tell there would be something unusual about this mission. Rupert Hollingshead was waiting for him just inside the checkpoint. The director looked completely out of place, surrounded as he was by men and women in the uniforms of the various armed forces. No one gave him a second glance, though—he was a fixture here, and even though the vast majority of people working in the aboveground rings of the Pentagon would have no idea what his job was, they knew enough to salute him as he passed by.

"Son," Hollingshead said, when Chapel approached him. "Son, you look terrible. Are you unwell? Do you need to sit down?"

"I'm just tired, sir," Chapel lied. "Maybe I'm not fully recovered from Miami."

"I can imagine," Hollingshead replied, steering Chapel toward a door that led into one of the inner rings. It was not the way Chapel would have gone to get to the elevator that took one down to H Ring, but he didn't ask where they were headed. "When Angel told me you were, ah, coming back so soon, I . . . well. I didn't know what to think. I can guess a little of it. Your homecoming yesterday didn't go as we expected, did it?"

"No, sir. Sir, if I can ask for a favor—"

"Anything. Absolutely anything you need," Hollingshead told him, a grave look on his face.

"I'd like to not talk about my personal life right now. If that's all right."

Hollingshead's face fell, and Chapel felt bad instantly. But the last thing he could handle at that moment was talking about what had happened in Brooklyn. He suppressed a sigh. "It's just—I'd like to get to work as quickly as possible."

Hollingshead nodded. "Keep your mind off things, I'd imagine. Well. I suppose that's fine for now. But, son—I'm going to need you at the very pinnacle of your game today. If you're going to be distracted or you're going to be on the phone all day, well, ah—"

"No, sir," Chapel promised. "I'm ready to focus on something else."

Hollingshead nodded again. "Then we'll say no more. Now—as to business. We can't meet in the usual place for a reason that will soon become apparent. I've reserved a briefing room for us and had it swept for listening devices. Sadly, that does not mean we'll be able to speak with complete candor. Again, for a reason soon to be made manifest. The same reason we're meeting in a new spot, actually. So before we go in, I need to tell you something."

"Sir."

Hollingshead lowered his voice. "What you're going to hear is all true. I've had it verified to the best of our considerable abilities. Everything checks out. It may also be the most vital matter my office has ever concerned itself with. Furthermore, it's one of the most sensitive. I must say, I'm glad you're here, even if I'm not pleased with the reason you were able to come in." The director raised his hands in protest. "Never mind, we're not talking about that." He walked briskly up to an unremarkable door and put his hand on the knob. "You think you're ready for this. I'm not, and I don't mind telling you." He turned the knob and opened the door.

Beyond lay a small windowless conference room with a table and a dozen chairs and not much else. The walls were bare concrete—they weren't even painted. The lighting fixtures were just uncovered fluorescent tubes, and the table was made of glass. That was probably to make it harder to plant a bug underneath it. There was no television screen available, nor any computers—not even a telephone. The back of the door was lined with noise-absorbing egg crate foam and the door itself had a rubber seal around its edges.

Chapel took out his cell phone and turned it on. It got no reception, not even a single bar, and no wireless signals were available either.

Hollingshead went to the end of the table and took a seat. When he spoke, his voice sounded oddly flat in the shielded room. "I imagine this all looks quite primitive," he said, grinning a little.

"It looks safe," Chapel said, putting away his phone.

Hollingshead took the little black book—the one-time pad—from his coat pocket and set it down on the glass table. Even from across the room Chapel thought it still reeked of seawater. That was probably an effect of how odorless the rest of the room was. He ran a finger along the floor and brought it up to his eyes and found no dust at all. When Hollingshead had said the room had been swept, Chapel hadn't considered that he might have been using the term literally. "Exactly how small can they make a bug these days?" Chapel asked.

"The size of a grain of rice," Hollingshead told him. "Even here in the Pentagon we can't completely eliminate the possibility of being overheard. But this room is, ah, the very best we can do. Needless to say, nothing we discuss here can be spoken of outside these walls."

"Of course," Chapel agreed.

Hollingshead nodded. Then he glanced at his watch. "We're waiting on a third. Someone with information we need. They'll be here in a few minutes, but first—I need you to tell me something. Tell me everything you know about the Dead Hand."

Chapel opened his mouth to speak, then closed it again. He sat down at the table. "Well, two things, I suppose. I know what it is."

"Go on."

Chapel shrugged. "A computer system. The Soviets built it back in the eighties in a secret location south of Moscow. It was supposed to be one of the biggest and most complex computers in the world, at least for the time. It was wired into their nuclear arsenal, with links to every missile silo they had."

"And its purpose?" Hollingshead asked.

Chapel nodded. "It was called the Dead Hand because it was supposed to be similar to the dead man's switch on a train—a switch the train's driver has to keep constantly touching or the train won't go. If the driver has a heart attack or something, he'll let go of that switch and the train will automatically stop. Except the Dead Hand was designed for the opposite purpose. It was designed to constantly monitor the region around Moscow. If the Kremlin were destroyed—say, by an American nuclear attack—the Dead Hand would turn itself on. And then it would launch every missile the Soviets had at the United States. It was designed so that even if we successfully decapitated the Soviet command structure, they could still have their revenge and make sure we didn't survive World War III. A completely automated retaliation system."

Hollingshead fiddled with the one-time pad on the table in front of him. "Like the Lernaean Hydra, wouldn't you say? You cut off the head, and a new one grows back—it only gets more dangerous. The ultimate deterrent. We wouldn't dare attack Moscow, knowing the price we would pay."

"That was the theory," Chapel said.

"You said you knew two things," Hollingshead prompted. "What was the other?"

"I know it doesn't really exist." Chapel sat up straight in his chair. "It was a ruse. Nobody sane would ever build something like that—a machine that could destroy an entire country with no human input. The possibility of a computer error could never be ruled out. The Soviets floated the story of the Dead Hand as a kind of engineered urban legend. They wanted us to think it existed. But of course after the fall of the Soviet Union, when Russia became our ally, the story wasn't necessary anymore. A number of Russian officials have denied categorically that the Dead Hand was ever more than a thought experiment—they claim it was never built, and never got past the drawing board."

Hollingshead nodded. He wasn't meeting Chapel's eye, which was a bad thing, usually. "You know two things," he said. "One of them is correct."

"You don't mean—"

"Son, this may come as a surprise to you, but when you say nobody sane would ever create such a thing, well, that group doesn't include the leadership of the Soviet Union in the 1980s. They were paranoid enough to build the damn thing. It is very real, and it was designed for exactly the purpose you describe. It went online in 1983."

Chapel felt like the temperature in the room had just dropped twenty degrees. "And if we're sitting here talking about it—"

"It went online in 1983, and it has been functional ever since. It's still there, still doing its job. Ready to launch every missile in the Russian arsenal at the United States, at a moment's notice. Nobody ever turned it off."

THE PENTAGON: JUNE 14, 08:28

"You're kidding me. This thing is still active? It's a loaded gun pointed right at our heads, and it's still active?"

"Yes," Hollingshead said. "Even though the politics have changed, the launch codes have not." The director sighed deeply. "It's an existential threat to the United States, to the, ah, well, the entire world, actually." He gave a wan smile. "If that many nuclear warheads exploded all at once, it really wouldn't matter where they landed. The resulting fallout and nuclear winter would mean the end of the world."

Chapel couldn't speak.

Hollingshead pushed the one-time pad away from him, into the middle of the table. "Now you know everything I know about the Dead Hand. Fortunately, we have another source of intelligence available to us." He glanced at his watch again. "She should be waiting out in the hall, if you would be good enough to get the door."

Chapel stood up and reached for the doorknob. "She?" he asked. "It's a woman? You don't mean—"

He turned the knob and opened the door and there she was.

Nadia.

The Asian woman from the party yacht. The one who had saved his life.

"Jim," she said, and gave him a warm smile. "You're looking much better than the last time I saw you. I'm so glad."

She held out a hand. It took him a second to collect himself enough to shake it. "Please," he said, "come in."

She walked into the room, and Chapel closed the door behind her.

She didn't look exactly like he remembered her. For one thing, she wasn't wearing a thin sundress and basically nothing else. Instead she had put on a black business suit over a white blouse. The skirt was maybe two inches shorter than would be considered conservative, but she would have passed for a civilian staffer outside in the halls of the Pentagon. She had cut her hair a little shorter. On the boat she had worn subtle but elaborate makeup, but now she had on only a dark red shade of lipstick and maybe a touch of eye shadow.

She was, though, every bit as striking as she had been the last time he saw her, when she was wearing nothing but panties and sharing a cramped shower stall with him.

She was empty-handed. No briefcase, no purse. The director indicated with a gesture that she should take a seat. That meant she had to walk past Chapel. Her perfume—very light, very clean—trailed through the air after her.

"The two of you have met, of course," Hollingshead said. "Though I imagine you were not, ah, properly introduced."

Chapel realized he was still standing by the door, and the two of them were looking at him expectantly. Hollingshead gestured at a chair across from Nadia, and Chapel took it. He hadn't realized how exhausted he was until he sat down.

"Captain James Chapel, United States Military Intelligence," Hollingshead said, "please meet Nadezhda Yaroslavovna Asimova, Federal Service for Technic and Export Control of the Russian Federation."

"Nadia to friends," she said, with a smile. "Which I hope already includes the both of you."

Chapel tried to smile back. He was worried if he moved his mouth too much, his jaw might drop and hit the floor.

He forced himself to recover a little professionalism. "FSTEK," he said. "Technic and Export

Control—that's the group that oversees information security and technology transfer. Part of the Russian intelligence community." He sat up straighter in his chair. "Forgive me for using a loaded term—but we don't get a lot of Russian spies here in the Pentagon."

Nadia laughed to show she hadn't taken offense and rolled her eyes. "You make us sound so glamorous! Boring stuff, of no interest, truly. We make sure all the Kremlin's computers have proper antivirus software and oversee sales of Russian information technology to other countries. I am little more than a glorified file clerk back home."

Chapel shook his head. He turned to stare at Hollingshead for a while. "Sir," he said, "are you telling me that you had a Russian agent shadowing me on my last mission?" He couldn't believe it.

"A Russian agent who saved your life," Hollingshead pointed out.

"I did what I could to help, that is all," Nadia said.

Chapel stood up out of his chair and paced around the room. "I'm sorry, I seem to have missed something here. You two are acting like this is all perfectly normal. That an agent of a foreign power was sent—without my knowledge—to accompany me on a top secret mission." He almost asked if Angel had known—but maybe Nadia still didn't know about Angel. Maybe that one fact had been kept from her.

On the boat she had known his name. She had known how deep he was diving, and she had known how important the one-time pad was. It seemed she'd been better informed than he was.

"Son," Hollingshead said, his eyes flashing a warning, "please sit down."

Chapel went to his chair, but he didn't sit. He rested his hands on the back of the chair because he felt like he might fall down. "This is not how we do things—"

"It is today," Hollingshead said, and the warning in his eyes was very close to turning into flinty anger. "Agent Asimova has vital intelligence to share with us. And that mission you were on—I wasn't the one who planned it."

Chapel was definitely about to fall down. He sat before that could happen.

"It was Agent Asimova who told us where to find that one-time pad. And why we would want to recover it."

"Nadia, please," she said. "Call me Nadia."

Hollingshead was silent for a second. Then he turned to face Nadia and gave her his warmest, most grandfatherly look. It was a good one—he'd cultivated it for years. "Nadia, thank you. I believe you're here today to brief us on the Dead Hand system. If Captain Chapel is done with his outburst, maybe you could begin."

"Of course," she said. "Jim?"

Chapel rested his head on one hand. "I'm listening," he said.

THE PENTAGON: JUNE 14, 08:37

Nadia fidgeted as she spoke. Chapel couldn't really blame her for being nervous—how would he feel, after all, if he were invited to give a speech at the Kremlin? He could sense from her body language that it was more than that, however. She was excited to give this presentation. Clearly it was something she'd been involved with for a long time.

"There are three principal components of the Perimeter system. That is, what you call the Dead Hand. The Russian name for it is 'Perimetr,' because it guards the entire border of what was the Soviet Union."

She got up from her chair and paced behind the table. "I was hoping I would have a whiteboard, or perhaps I could give you a PowerPoint slideshow . . ."

Hollingshead gave her an apologetic smile. "For security reasons we need to keep this as an oral briefing," he said.

"*Konyechno*. I mean—of course," she said. She took a deep breath and launched in.

"As I said, three parts. The first is a shortwave radio station located just outside of Moscow. Station UVB-76, or MDZhB, as it is called now. You may have heard of this station, I believe it is called 'the Russian Buzzer' in amateur radio circles. It broadcasts a continuous buzz tone, at a rate of twenty-five tones per minute, and it does so twenty-four hours a day, every day, as it has since the 1980s. This is in effect an 'all-clear' signal. Its meaning is simple: Moscow still stands. As long as this signal is broadcast, Perimeter remains dormant and is completely safe.

"The second component is an array of sensors buried throughout Russian territory. There are approximately one hundred and fifty acoustic pickups, seventy-five air pressure monitoring scoops, and fifty electric eye sensors spread across the various republics that formerly comprised the Union. They are all dedicated to one function, which is to register the particular signature of a nuclear explosion anywhere inside the former borders."

"That sounds like some pretty delicate equipment," Hollingshead asked. "If it was installed thirty years ago, are you sure it's still functional?"

"The numbers I listed," Nadia explained, "are our best estimate of how many of the sensors remain intact. Approximately ten times as many were originally built."

"Just an estimate?" Chapel asked. "You don't know for sure?"

A flash of deep worry passed across Nadia's eyes. "I will . . . elaborate in a moment. First, I need to tell you about the third, and most vital, component of the system. This is a computer complex located in a hardened bunker south of Moscow. The computer is one hundred percent automatic, requiring no operators or maintenance to keep it running. It has its own dedicated radiothermic power plant and multiple redundancies in its circuits in case any of them ever burn out or are damaged. The system exists at a sort of minimal state, performing only self-diagnostic functions on a daily basis, as long as the shortwave signal is continuous. Only if that signal stops will Perimeter awaken. If it does, its first action will be to query the array of sensors. If there is no result, Perimeter takes no action. If, however, it detects the signature of a nuclear blast, it will automatically send a signal to every nuclear weapon in the Russian arsenal. Our weapons are hardwired to receive this signal—upon reception they can and will arm and launch themselves without human action and despite any attempt at human interference. The system was designed to resist tampering or sabotage and eliminate human error from the decision to launch."

Hollingshead pushed his glasses up onto his forehead and rubbed at his eyes. "You can imagine how we must feel about this."

"I imagine," Nadia said, "that you feel frightened by it. That was the intention of its designers."

"I think 'outraged' is the more, ah, appropriate term. Ms. Asimova, your leaders have built a veritable sword of Damocles and dangled it over our heads. Though it sounds like there are some basic fail-safes built in, thank God. The shortwave signal from Moscow keeps the whole thing asleep."

Nadia sat down hard in her chair. "Except when it fails." She put both her hands on the glass tabletop and pressed down on them, as if she were trying to keep them from shaking. "It has happened twice. Both times in 2010. Once for a full twenty-four hours, and then again for only a few minutes, the buzz tone fell silent. The cause—"

"Wait a minute," Chapel said. "Your people let this thing lapse, the one thing preventing the end of—"

"Please," Nadia said, holding up her hands to implore for peace. "The signal has remained active ever since that time. The failure was a human error. The problem here is that the men in charge of this buzz tone do not understand what it is they guard. They do not know about Perimeter. They did not know that when they were derelict in their duty, they put the whole world at risk."

Chapel could feel his jaw fall open. "Nobody told them?"

Nadia looked sheepish. "It is a secret. Secrets in my country are . . . like a sacred thing."

Hollingshead cleared his throat. "The sensor, ah, array," he pointed out. "Another fail-safe there. It detects what, again?"

"Sound, light, and atmospheric overpressure," Nadia said.

"It looks for an atomic explosion, yes," Hollingshead said, nodding vigorously. "No real worries there, are there? No one is about to detonate a nuclear device on Russian soil. Your country doesn't even do nuclear tests anymore, as I understand."

Nadia bit her lip. "We cannot rule out the possibility that a rogue state would detonate a bomb inside Russia. Though the sensors are looking for a megaton-scale blast, not just the much smaller explosion of, say, a dirty bomb. We believed until recently, in fact, that an event on the scale that would trigger Perimeter was of negligible threat."

"Something changed that?" Chapel asked. The look on her face definitely suggested as much.

She looked down at her hands. "In February of 2013, a meteor exploded in the air over the city of Chelyabinsk."

"I remember that," Chapel said. "The YouTube videos were pretty incredible."

Nadia inhaled sharply. "As it burned up in the atmosphere, the meteor was large enough to light up the sky like a second sun. When it exploded, its sonic blast created an air overpressure wave that shattered windows across the city." She looked from one man to the other. "Heat, light, overpressure."

Chapel fell back in his chair. Looking over at Hollingshead, he saw the director's mouth moving as if he were trying to speak but the words wouldn't come.

"My government has wanted to take Perimeter offline for some time. We thought we had time, time enough at least to . . . to fix things," Nadia said. "The last few years have convinced us otherwise. If the shortwave signal had faltered at the same time the meteor hit Chelyabinsk—if these two conditions ever happened again at the same time . . ." She pushed down on the table until her hands turned white. "It would be the end of the world."

The silence in the briefing room had felt flat before, all the ambient sound soaked up by the hard concrete walls. Now it felt like it buzzed with an angry energy. Chapel knew the effect was purely psychological, but it didn't matter. He felt a nasty headache coming on when he thought about what Nadia had just said.

"You need to turn this thing off now," he told her. "You need to shut it down."

Hollingshead nodded. "We've been asking for that for years. Every time, the Russian government has brushed us off. Most often they simply tell us that the Dead Hand—Perimeter—never existed, that it was only ever a thought experiment and it was never built. Sometimes they contradict themselves and say it was switched off years ago, before the fall of the Union. Most often they just say they won't discuss matters of state security. But clearly the time has come, Ms. Asimova. Clearly the time has come."

Nadia looked over at the director with a sad smile. "This feeling is one shared by my superiors. We are not insane. We know that a Perimeter launch would be the end of our country, as well. The reason it has not been done, the reason I am here today, is a matter of great national . . . embarrassment. I can think of no better term."

Something occurred to Chapel. "You said earlier you could only estimate the number of functional sensors in the network," he said.

She nodded. "That's correct. We don't know how many of them are still active, because we do not know exactly where they are. Until recently, we didn't know where the Perimeter computer was located, either."

"I beg your pardon?" Hollingshead asked.

Nadia turned to look at him directly. "On 25 December, 1991, Mikhail Gorbachev officially ceded power to Boris Yeltsin. Famously, on that day he handed over the nuclear launch codes, effectively surrendering the Soviet military to what was then called the Commonwealth of Independent States, the precursor of the Russian Federation. It is unclear to my office whether Gorbachev even knew about Perimeter—it was considered then of utmost secrecy, and even Gorbachev was kept in the dark on some things by the KGB. What is known is that Gorbachev never mentioned Perimeter to Yeltsin. He did not tell him where it was, or how to turn it off.

"You must understand how strenuously they kept

their secrets in the Soviet Union. No one was given information they did not immediately require. Even now the men who work at MDZhB, the shortwave station, have no idea why it is so important that the buzz tone is played night and day. The technicians who work on our nuclear missiles do not know that they can be activated without warning. Even my office, which is in charge of maintaining security around the nuclear arsenal, had no confirmation that Perimeter existed until a few years ago."

"This keeps getting worse and worse," Chapel said.

Nadia did not disagree. "It took me years to track down the Perimeter computer. Between August and December of 1991, the KGB knew that the Union was going to fall. They used that time to destroy every bit of secret material they could—they thought that the new regime would seek to prosecute them for their atrocities, and they wished to destroy all evidence of their crimes. There were seven secret KGB libraries in the Union at one time. Six of them were burned to the ground that year. A seventh, on an uninhabited island south of Vladivostok, was spared, but even its existence was nearly lost. I had to go there personally to find the information I needed. To find out where Perimeter is located, and how to stop it."

"So you do have a plan," Chapel said.

"That's why I'm here," she told him. "And why I am speaking to you two. It is my intention to personally end the Perimeter project. But I need your help."

THE PENTAGON: JUNE 14, 09:12

Chapel frowned. "Why?" he asked.

Hollingshead cleared his throat. "Son, we're being given an extraordinary opportunity here. A chance to eliminate a grave threat. Let's not, ah, examine our gift horses altogether too closely."

Chapel shook his head. "I'm sorry, sir. I don't mean any disrespect. I just don't see why the Russians would bring us in on this. It seems like their problem—and one I'd think they'd be happy to take care of internally, and quietly."

"Quietly, yes," Nadia said. "We will have no official support from my country, not even any contact with my organization once we begin. This must be done in absolute secrecy. If the world never finds out that we lost control of Perimeter, it is for the best. For the operation to be conducted internally, well, that is not possible in any case."

Chapel raised an eyebrow.

"Most reports of the system describe it only as being located south of Moscow. When Perimeter was constructed," Nadia said, "the designers looked for a place unlikely to be attacked in a war, conventional or nuclear. A spot of limited strategic value, and a place they knew their enemies would never occupy. Unfortunately, they did not take into account that the real threat to their power would come from within. The place is no longer inside Russian borders. It is now in foreign territory."

"Where?" Hollingshead asked.

"Kazakhstan. Near the Aral Sea."

"That certainly adds a, to put it mildly, wrinkle to things," the director said. "I assume the Kazakhs don't know what they have. And that you'd like to keep it that way."

"Correct," Nadia said. "It will not be easy, but we must enter the country unknown, take down Perimeter, and exfiltrate before they know we were there. Diplomatic relations between Kazakhstan and Russia are good, right now. We want to keep it that way."

"I can think of another reason, besides diplomatic relations," Chapel said.

Hollingshead shot him a nasty glance—but then nodded for him to continue.

Chapel's eyes narrowed. "If you make this an American op, and something goes wrong, you won't take the blame."

Nadia shrugged. "If you wish to see it that way, fine. Though I imagine if the Kazakhs capture me, it will not take long for them to determine who I work for. I am not asking you to take this risk alone."

"There's another reason for our involvement," Hollingshead said. He reached out and tapped the one-time pad where it sat on the table. "When Ms. Asimova first came to me, she said this was what she was after. She knew where it was and how to use it. We had the ability to retrieve it."

"Russia does not possess the resources it once did, not in the Western theater," Nadia explained. "Getting a Russian frogman into Cuban waters would have proved difficult. We knew you had the capacity."

"But what do you even want that thing for? The codes in it are twenty years out of date," Chapel said.

"So are the codes Perimeter uses," Nadia told him. "Perimeter was given daily ciphers by the KGB. When they were driven from power, they stopped updating its clearances."

"You mean it's still running off that pad," Chapel said.

"As far as Perimeter is concerned, it is still 25 December 1991, because no one told it otherwise."

Chapel couldn't help but grin. He nodded at this pad. "You needed this thing pretty badly, I guess."

"Simply to enter the Perimeter bunker, one needs a code sequence. If it is entered incorrectly, the system automatically arms itself and cannot be reset locally."

"We'd better make sure we enter the right code, then," Chapel said.

Nadia's eyes flashed as if she'd just caught Chapel in something. "So you agree to come with me? To do this together?"

Chapel grinned. "Wouldn't miss it. Though I'm still not clear on why this is a joint operation. You have the one-time pad—we would give it to you even if you said you wanted to run the rest of this mission yourself. So I'll ask again. Why do you need us? Why me?"

"As a *svidetel*. A . . . witness, if nothing else," Nadia told him.

"A witness?"

"If I am successful, if I deactivate Perimeter, there will be no visible sign. Nothing overt will happen. I could turn it off tomorrow, but if I then came back here and told you it was done—"

"We wouldn't believe you," Hollingshead said.

"Exactly right. The president would have to assume you were lying. Attempting to deceive us so that we would relax our guard."

"Indeed. Trust, but verify, yes? That is the policy. Once Perimeter is defeated, Agent Chapel can vouch that it was done, and our two countries can start talking about disarmament again. We are going to make the world a safer place," Nadia said. "Even if only the three of us in this room ever know about it."

"When do we leave?" Chapel asked.

THE PENTAGON: JUNE 14, 09:36

Nadia was escorted out of the Pentagon by a pair of marine sergeants who weren't told who she was. On her way out, she turned and glanced back at Chapel. She gave him a hopeful smile that he tried to return. Once she'd turned a corner, he closed the door again and turned to look at Hollingshead.

"You trust her?" he asked.

"I wasn't without my doubts when she first came to me," the director said. He laid a hand on Chapel's artificial shoulder. "I vetted her personally. She's definitely an agent of FSTEK, though like you she doesn't show up on their official payroll. Her direct superior, Marshal Bulgachenko, gave a message to our ambassador in Moscow vouching for her. Beyond that she's a mystery."

"Is that good enough?"

"In this business if she wasn't mysterious, I would worry. It's the best we're going to get, son."

Chapel nodded. "Yes, sir."

"Of course, I don't want you to think I'm selling her the shop, either. Just because the Russians are our allies now doesn't mean we don't spy on each other. Even if, as I suspect, she's completely on the level, she's got perfectly functional ears. She'll take any chance she can get to learn things she isn't supposed to know. It's vital you don't give anything away—for instance, she can't learn about Angel. I know you're used to relying on our friend while you're in the field. That won't fly this time. If she sees you talking to an invisible helper, she's going to get curious."

"So I'm going in blind?" Chapel asked. He relied on Angel for *everything* during a field operation—for intelligence, for insights, just for someone watching his back. Working without her would be a severe handicap.

"No. You'll be able to contact her. You'll just have to be discreet about it. As in all things."

"I am a silent warrior," Chapel said, quoting the motto of the intelligence service.

"I know you are, son. Fair enough. Are you all right with taking Asimova's lead? This is going to be her operation. You'll be playing second fiddle, I'm afraid."

"Understood."

Hollingshead nodded and turned to go. But then he stopped. He looked back at Chapel with a questioning eye. "There's just one more thing. It's, ah. I suppose this isn't my place. But if it affects your operational efficiency—"

"Sir?"

Hollingshead frowned. "Back there, in the briefing. You seemed . . . angry. That's not like you. A couple of times there, you got downright confrontational."

"You have my apologies, sir."

Hollingshead nodded. "Chapel. Son. I said I wasn't going to talk about your personal life, and I'll stick to that. But I need to know you're truly ready for this. That if I send you into the field right now, your head will be squarely in the game. I expected to find you distracted and a little dazed, given the circumstances."

"May I ask how I seem right now, sir?"

"Focused. Maybe a little too focused. You're blocking out everything else but your work. If that becomes a problem—"

"It won't," Chapel said. He sounded curt even to his own ears. He hadn't intended that.

Hollingshead flinched a little. He blinked. Straightened his cuffs. "It's not too late," he said. "I can still send someone else on this."

It wasn't a threat. Hollingshead was asking a question, Chapel knew. He was offering a lifeline.

Maybe he wasn't in the perfect head space for a mission like this. But he thought he could get there. And the alternative—going back to an empty apartment in New York, checking his phone every thirty seconds for a call that wasn't going to come—was unacceptable.

"I can do the job, sir," he said, forcing a measure of calm into his voice. "I can do it right."

"Hmm." Hollingshead looked him right in the eye for an uncomfortably long time. Chapel made sure not to look away. Then the director shook his head as if clearing it of unpleasant thoughts and said, "Very well. Let's talk about how we get you to Kazakhstan."

WASHINGTON, DC: JUNE 14, 13:24

Chapel would have left for the mission then and there, if he could. Unfortunately, the doctors had grounded him for a month after his bout with decompression sickness, and Hollingshead wouldn't let him fly until it was safe. The intervening time wouldn't be wasted. Papers had to be readied, cover stories established, travel arrangements made. The hardest part was that Chapel could do so little of it himself. Most of the preparations were made by low-level functionaries in the State Department who had no idea what they were working on, only that credentials for certain people had to be readied at the shortest possible notice. Chapel would never even meet the people working on his behalf.

Chapel's official orders were to get some sleep. The best therapy for the bends was sleep and fluids. Chapel tried to maximize the latter, keeping a water bottle with him at all times, but he knew he couldn't just sleep away the remaining time. He checked into a hotel in Washington—it was far too tempting to go back to New York, to try to find Julia and talk to her—and spent his days haunting various military archives.

A long couple of weeks at the Military Intelligence records center, huddled over computer screens and microfiche terminals, left him with a stiff back but little wiser. He looked for anything the DoD had on the Dead Hand system and came up with nothing of consequence. The best intelligence analysts of the Cold War had determined that, yes, the system existed and, yes, it was functional, but that was it—two things he hadn't doubted since Hollingshead told him as much at the start of his briefing. U2 spy planes, reconnaissance satellites, even human intelligence—spies on the ground—had failed for thirty years to turn up anything concrete beyond those two facts. He did discover one thing new. In the 1970s, Project Azorian had recovered part of a Soviet nuclear submarine from the bottom of the Pacific Ocean. The Project's findings had been limited—the sub broke into pieces while it was being hauled up—and as far as the public knew, nothing significant had been learned. In a top secret file, though, Chapel found out that Azorian had recovered the warhead from a Soviet ICBM and that for years afterward it had been carefully dismantled and every aspect of its hardware and software studied in secret American labs. There was a great deal of technical data there that Chapel couldn't begin to comprehend, but one piece of paper near the back of the file indicated that an unexpected module was found inside the warhead's control bus, little more than a single computer chip designed to accept commands received by shortwave radio. The module was completely isolated from the rest of the warhead's electronics and had the capacity to arm, direct, and launch the missile by remote command. The scientists who found it believed it was there because the Soviet leadership didn't trust their own people to launch the missiles when the time came. To Chapel, though, the presence of that module meant something else. It meant that Nadia's story was true. That the Dead Hand—Perimeter, as he increasingly called it in his head—was completely capable of launching a nuclear strike, even now.

Everything Nadia had said in her briefing checked out, as far as it was possible to verify such things. He'd had no reason to suspect she was lying, but he was glad to have some confirmation.

That evening he took dinner at his hotel and then retired to his room. He switched on the television, not even really caring what was on. Eventually he fell asleep.

The next day he spent talking with Angel, on his phone, asking her to look into a few things for him. She said she would get back to him as soon as possible, but that the answers he wanted would take time. He went for a very long swim, something he always did when there were too many thoughts in his head.

He ate lunch, and then dinner, lingering over the meals.

He checked his phone a couple of hundred times. Nobody was calling him.

The next day he started again, looking at records that had been stamped secret and sealed for decades—whether or not there was any new information in them.

And the day after that he did it again.

The month he spent in Washington was hell. It was unbearable. He needed to be out in the field, away from memories and regrets. Away from any place Julia had ever been.

One day he went in for a medical examination. The doctors cleared him to fly. He did not waste any more time—there was a flight from Ronald Reagan International leaving that evening.

Hollingshead bought him a beer at a bar downtown, but he didn't even finish it. He was too keyed up. It was time to go.

IN TRANSIT: JULY 15, 20:04

Forty thousand feet above the Atlantic, in the business class section of a 777, the lights had been turned down and all was quiet. Chapel couldn't sleep. He'd never been good at sleeping on planes, and now he had enough on his mind to keep him awake anyway. He pulled on his headphones and switched on his tablet. Launched an audio player and loaded a language file. He was never going to get fluent in another language in the time frame of this operation, but he could at least pick up a few essentials.

"*Qos keldiñiz!* Welcome." The voice on the recording was flat, unaccented. He'd hoped to use the excellent audio files the army used to train its translators, but Hollingshead had nixed that. Chapel and Nadia were undercover, posing as an American businessman and his Russian assistant. If customs officials checked Chapel's tablet and found military software on it, there would be questions, and that was unacceptable.

"*Tanisqanimizğa qwaniştimin!* I am pleased to meet you." So Chapel had been limited to commercially available language products, and finding one for Kazakh in a hurry had been difficult. He was forced to make do with a digitized version of an old language tape that was mostly just a list of common phrases and their English equivalents.

"*Men tüsinbeymin.* Sorry, I didn't get that." Chapel smiled to himself. He was going to need that one a lot. He remembered when he'd had to learn Pashto, back when he was first shipping out to Afghanistan. He'd thrown himself into that language, immersed himself in it night and day. "I don't understand" had quickly become his most commonly used phrase.

"*Osini jazip bere alasiz ba?* Can you write that down for me?" He'd been a different person back then. So committed to his job. So desperate for a chance to head overseas and do his part, to track down Osama bin Laden and bring him to justice after 9/11. He hadn't been a real soldier then, not quite. Years in Ranger school and then at Fort Huachuca in Arizona, where they trained him in intelligence work, had left him feeling more like a student than a warrior. He'd had both arms back then, too.

"*Keşiriñiz!* I beg your pardon." For a brief while he'd gotten to be a real soldier. A silent warrior. It hadn't lasted long enough. What was he now? He sometimes wondered. The jobs Hollingshead found for him weren't classical intelligence work—no dead drops or clandestine meetings in parking garages, no miniaturized cameras up his sleeves. His work didn't follow the comfortable pattern of military life, either. He didn't report to a commanding officer. He didn't get direct orders from anyone wearing a uniform. Now he was an invisible warrior, not just a silent one. Now he was flying to Bucharest in preparation for sneaking into a foreign country and carrying out illegal sabotage. Now he was the kind of person Julia couldn't love anymore—

"*Sizben bilewge bola ma?* Would you care to dance?"

Chapel flinched in his seat. That wasn't the same voice he'd been listening to. It was sultry and velvety and sent a chill down his neck.

"Sorry to break in on the lesson, sweetie," Angel said. "I just figured now would be a good time to check up on you. Don't say anything; just lie back and listen, okay?"

Chapel glanced over at Nadia. She was curled up in her seat with the back reclined as far as it would go. Sleeping like a baby. She was even snoring—if she was faking it, she was doing an excellent job.

"Nobody can hear me," Angel told him. "You hear that faint hiss in the background? That's not just because the recording quality on your language file is so cruddy. I'm pumping some pink noise into this connection so that even the little bit of sound that leaks from your headphones won't make sense to anyone listening. We're safe, communicating like this. The director told me how important it was that we keep things on the quiet side."

Chapel reached for the tablet. He tapped a few keys. As he'd expected, nothing appeared on the screen. He typed SHE'S ASLEEP and hit the enter key.

"You should be, too," Angel told him. "Still, I don't want to take any chances. I've got a preliminary report on those questions you asked me, in case you're . . . curious. Don't bother answering, baby—I know you are."

Chapel tried not to grin. Good old Angel. She could make even a dry intelligence briefing sound like a naughty innuendo. He suspected she did it just to make sure he was paying attention, but he'd never complained.

"Nadia Asimova," Angel said, "never mind the patronymic. Russian citizenship, born in Yakutia— Siberia, in other words, the exact geographic center of nowheresville. Daughter of a metallurgist and a doctor. Age thirty-one, a little on the young side for you but not ickily so."

I'M NOT LOOKING TO DATE HER, Chapel typed.

"If men spent more time doing background checks on the women they chased," Angel said, ignoring Chapel's words, "they wouldn't get in trouble so often. Anyway, it looks like she had a pretty normal childhood, except she showed an early talent for gymnastics, which is something they take very seriously in Russia. Got her name in the paper a few times for winning competitions. But she wasn't just a jock. She did *very* well in school. Top of her class every year, and she even skipped two grades. At sixteen they whisked her away to the Bauman school in Moscow, which is the Russian equivalent of MIT. She started a six-year course in nuclear engineering."

DIDN'T FINISH?

"Disappeared off the face of the earth," Angel told him. "There are no black marks on her record—I mean, at all. Her faculty adviser was already looking to place her in a high-powered job during her second year, which means she wasn't exactly struggling with her course load. But then the records just stop. No incomplete credits, no notice that she had dropped out, but no degree awarded, either. I think you know what that means. Somebody in the intelligence community over there took an interest and recruited her before she could finish her studies."

FSTEK?

"Yes. FSTEK. Though I had a heck of time proving it. She isn't on the books with any intelligence group, which is unusual even in Russia. No payroll records, no tax forms, no health insurance forms. The only mention of her anywhere since college is when she received a medal."

A MEDAL?

"'For Distinction in the Protection of the State Borders.' It's a medal usually reserved for members of the FSB—the organization formerly known as KGB—but it can be given to anyone in intelligence, or even a private citizen. There's no indication why she got it. She's too young for it to be a lifetime achievement award, though. She must have done something really valuable to the Fatherland. Something nobody wants to talk about, but they're real glad it got done. There was a brief private ceremony at FSTEK headquarters in 2011 and then . . . she disappears again. Nothing since."

NOTHING AT ALL?

"Not that I can find. It wasn't easy getting what I have," Angel said. "It's not exactly like I can just call up the Kremlin and ask them for the personnel dossier on one of their secret agents."

Chapel frowned to himself. You didn't expect to turn up much on a spy—the Russian government would go to great lengths to keep Nadia's operations secret, of course. But there should be something more if she was what she said she was—a "glorified file clerk." The absence of evidence in this case suggested that Nadia was something like him. Invisible, and vital to Russian state security. THANKS FOR CHECKING, he typed.

"No problem, sugar. You know I'd do anything for you. I'll be in touch," Angel said.

"*Joliñiz bolsin*. Bon voyage." It was the same flat voice from before, the voice of the language file. Chapel shut down his tablet and took the headphones off his ears.

Without the light of the screen, the dimness of the airplane cabin felt oppressive and chilly. Chapel huddled down in his seat. Then he turned and looked at Nadia where she was curled up and snoring, still.

She had pulled a blanket up over herself minutes after takeoff, but now it had slipped down off one shoulder and fallen partially to the floor. She was still dressed for July in New York, and the scarf she wore was just a thin scrap of silk. He saw her hugging herself for warmth.

He felt a sudden wave of tenderness toward this woman. She had saved his life in Miami, which was enough to make him feel something for her, but it wasn't just that. She really was like him, wasn't she? Sucked up into the black hole of intelligence before she even knew there were options. A brilliant childhood and then she just fell off the map. No. She'd been intentionally vanished. Taken away from her life because she was too valuable to waste on normal things like having a family, a career, a life.

He wondered if there had been someone waiting at home for her, someone who had dreaded every second she was away, not knowing if she was alive or dead. Someone who couldn't handle it after a while and walked away from her.

Or maybe not. Maybe she'd never had anybody. Maybe there'd been no time.

Reaching over her, he lifted the blanket and pulled it back up to her chin. He'd been very careful not to touch her, but as he sat back down in his own seat he saw one of her eyes open and peer up at him. Like any good intelligence operative she had the ability to wake very quickly from sleep.

"Sorry," he whispered. "You looked cold."

She smiled at him and wriggled around for a second, pulling the blanket closer around herself. A moment later she was fast asleep again.

Damn.

He couldn't believe he'd let himself get carried away like that. It had been inappropriate, for one thing, and, worse, he'd let his emotions rule him. Always a dangerous thing on an operation.

He sighed and sat back. Tried closing his eyes for a while.

It occurred him only hours later that Angel hadn't told him the one thing he truly wanted to know— something that had nothing to do with Russian spies. She hadn't told him whether Julia had called his phone or not.

Which meant she hadn't.

Angel would have told him, otherwise.

BUCHAREST, ROMANIA: JULY 15, 10:06 (EET)

Nadia's plan was to travel to Uzbekistan, where she knew some people who could get them across the border into Kazakhstan. First, though, they had to make a quick stop in Romania to pick up the third and last member of the team.

At the customs desk in Bucharest, Chapel handed over their fake passports—the best the U.S. military could supply. He had to remove his artificial arm and let the officials x-ray it, even though it was clear they had no idea what they were looking at. A woman in a leather jacket frowned at the arm as it lay in a plastic bin, the lifeless hand dangling over the side. She pulled on latex gloves and then took out a pocket knife. Chapel protested as she extended the blade, but she said she had to stab the arm for security reasons. "What exactly would that prove?" he demanded, but that just made the woman look more stern than before.

Nadia pulled out a hundred-dollar bill and pushed it across the desk.

The customs woman put her knife away. "Welcome to Romania, Mr. Carlson," she said, with a very warm smile.

As they walked toward the taxi rank, Chapel whispered to Nadia, "If I'd known it was that easy, I would have brought my gun, too."

"Oh, no," Nadia said. "There are very strict laws here about firearms. That bribe would have been ten times as much." She pointed at the restrooms. "I need a moment," she said. "Can you wait here with the luggage?"

Chapel nodded and sat down on a plastic bench marred by old cigarette burns. He watched the people flow by while he sat with their two small suitcases. Nadia didn't return for ten minutes. When she did, she had completely changed.

She had ratted out her hair and put on a lot more makeup—far more than she'd worn on the party boat. She had kept her business slacks but rolled up the cuffs to show the pair of cheap sandals she'd slipped on. Her blouse was gone in favor of a halter top and a thin gold necklace with a crucifix. She looked ten years younger.

Chapel must have been staring wide-eyed, because she laughed when she came up to him. "Where we're going," she said, "we need to look the part."

"Should I change?" he asked.

"No, you'll be fine in that jacket. Just don't smile, whatever you do." She smirked at him again. "Come on. We have an appointment to keep."

They took a bus to a nearby train station, one that had lockers big enough to hold their bags. Once those were secure, they went outside and stood in a long line for private transportation. As they waited for a taxi Chapel argued again that they didn't need to be here. "This computer tech you want to hire— he's just a security risk," Chapel said.

"You don't know him yet. He's adorable. You want to just give him a hug, he mopes so," Nadia told him.

"I'll buy him a stuffed animal and we'll leave him here." He tried to think of a way of explaining to her they didn't need a computer tech when he had access to Angel. There was no way her guy could beat Angel's abilities. But how to say that without giving away Angel's existence? "I know enough about computers for this job," he said.

"Really. You know how to reprogram a Soviet legacy system from the eighties? In the Cyrillic alphabet? Don't worry so, Jim. I've worked with this man before. He can be trusted. And anyway, I'm lead on this mission, am I not?"

"Yes, ma'am," Chapel said. He had a feeling he wouldn't have any trouble remembering not to smile. Between the jet lag and this security risk and the fact he hadn't gotten much sleep on the plane, he was already in a foul mood.

Bucharest didn't help.

He'd read it was called the Paris of the East, but the city Chapel saw wasn't exactly a glittering metropolis. Every building seemed to be the same gray-yellow color—maybe the structures had been white once, but the million cars that puffed black exhaust had stained them like a coffee drinker's teeth. Half the buildings were enormous brutalist office blocks; the other half sprawling palaces that looked like they were about to fall down. Some of them looked like they'd been built from cardboard and then sprayed with quick-setting concrete, they were in such bad shape. Construction cranes and scaffolding covered half the façades, apparently fixing up the buildings as fast as they could fall down.

Chapel couldn't make sense of the place. There had to be money here—all that construction was costing somebody. But on the street level the city looked depressed and decrepit. He saw piles of trash on street corners, where mangy dogs fought over choice pieces of refuse. The people didn't seem to take much notice. There were also a lot more Western Union offices than he thought a city like this probably needed. "What's with all the wire transfer places?" he asked.

"Cybercrime," Nadia said. "Romania's principal export."

Chapel turned to stare at her.

She shrugged. "Perhaps I overstate the case. But this is the European headquarters for e-mail scams and identity theft. There are little towns out in Transylvania—that's northwest of here—where half the population is made up of arrows."

"Arrows?"

"People who accept money in a scam, otherwise innocent people who sign for wire transfers and then hand over the money to gangsters. It makes it difficult to trace the money to the actual criminals. Cutouts, as we might say."

Chapel glanced at the cabdriver, but he seemed oblivious. "Cutout" was an espionage term for the people who transferred information from one party to another without knowing anything themselves. It wasn't the kind of term you should bandy about when you were working undercover on an espionage mission.

"Relax," Nadia said. "Are you always so nervous on business?"

"It keeps me in one piece. Well, technically, two."

She laughed. A lot of people got uncomfortable when he joked about his artificial arm, but not Nadia. Yet another reason to like her, even if he thought her attitude was far too relaxed for the serious work they were doing. Maybe, he thought, he *should* relax a little.

Maybe when Perimeter was shut down and he was home again.

"You're tired," she told him. "You didn't sleep."

"Yeah," he admitted. He would very much like, he thought, to go lie down somewhere.

"Why don't you head back to the airport and rest?" Nadia asked him. "I'll collect our friend and bring him to you. It's something I can do easily on my own."

Chapel shook his head. "No," he told her. "You wanted a *svidetel*, an American witness." He gritted his teeth. Was she trying to shake him off her trail? "That means I see everything you do. When this is done, when I vouch for you, I need to be able to say I was part of everything."

He was blatantly saying he didn't totally trust her, but her reaction wasn't what he expected. "Good," she said, smiling. "I'll be glad to have you along."

The taxi took them through the various sectors of Bucharest, circling around toward the Strada Lipscani, the street Nadia had asked for. Chapel thought for a second the driver was taking them on a scenic route but Nadia explained they were just avoiding a sort of perpetual traffic jam that clogged the center of town. The route took them past the old princely court of Vlad the Impaler, though Chapel couldn't see much of it from his window. Eventually the taxi dropped them off on a long street lined with big gray-yellow buildings that Chapel did have to admit looked a little like Parisian houses. One of them had a huge mural on its side of a blue sky full of birds.

They got out and Nadia paid the driver in leis, the local currency. Nadia must have brought them with her—he hadn't seen her exchange any money at the airport. They headed down the block, passing an endless series of bars and nightclubs that were shuttered up for the morning. Half the places seemed to have English names—the Gin Factory, the Bastards Club—and the rest had names so strewn with accent marks and diacritics that he couldn't even guess how they were pronounced. "Here," Nadia said, outside of what looked like an unexceptional coffee bar. They stepped through the glass doors into blaring hip-hop so loud it made the air pulse. A dozen or so patrons were lounging on couches and low chairs, while a bored-looking attendant stood behind a counter lined with samovars. Nadia went up and grabbed a cup of tea without asking or paying. She spoke to the attendant, but the girl just sneered and went back to looking out the windows.

Nadia didn't seem bothered by the attitude. She headed for a chair and plunked herself down, throwing one long leg over an arm of the chair. She left the teacup sitting on the other arm and pulled out her phone and started texting.

Chapel saw immediately why she thought he didn't need to change his clothes. Half the patrons in the shop looked like her, or like male equivalents in T-shirts, American jeans, and flip-flops. They lounged across the chairs like sitting up had gone out of style. Standing near or behind each of them was a guy in a suit with the same haircut Chapel wore—short and vaguely military. The men in the suits flashed gold chains and big, chunky rings, but otherwise Chapel fit right in.

Bodyguards, he thought. The men in the suits were there to protect the casually dressed kids. Some of the bodyguards drank tea. One was smoking a very nasty cigar. None of them spoke to anyone else. Instead they traded tough-guy looks that never went anywhere, while the kids ignored them, too busy working their phones.

Chapel very much wanted to sit down, but he had to maintain his cover. Maybe one of the other bodyguards would sit, he thought. Maybe that would make it okay.

"This guy knows we're coming?" he asked.

"*Konyechno*," Nadia said, her voice almost drowned out by the blaring music. "Be still. Nobody talks here."

"I noticed. Was he supposed to be here to meet us?"

"Yes. But that's never how things work out, is it? Just hold your horses, as you say. And be quiet."

Chapel frowned. He stared at the posters on the walls, advertising various music events. One showed Barack Obama wearing Kanye West's trademark louvered sunglasses. He couldn't read the names of the bands.

As tired as he was, he came very close to falling asleep on his feet. He barely noticed when a long car pulled up in front of the tea shop and two blond men got out. When they came in through the door, he stiffened, but so did all the other bodyguards.

The two newcomers were dressed in suits, but they weren't wearing any jewelry. One wore horn-rimmed glasses so smudged Chapel wondered if he could see anything. The other one had a neatly groomed mustache with just a hint of silver in it. He looked around the room, sizing everyone up, then came to stand in front of Nadia and Chapel. Without even glancing at her, he spoke to Chapel.

"You ask for Bogdan?" he asked. "Yes? Yes?"

Nadia sat up and smiled. "He sent you?"

"Yes, yes, he sent me, and my friend. We take him to you now, okay? Yes?"

There were a lot of things Chapel didn't like about the situation, but he looked around for cues before he did anything. This could just be the way business was done in Bucharest. Nadia didn't seem too concerned. But one of the bodyguards, a big guy with a dollar sign hanging from a golden chain, was watching the two blonds very carefully. His hands kept squeezing into fists, and then releasing. He knew who these newcomers were.

Chapel caught the bodyguard's eye. Maybe he could call on professional courtesy. He raised an eyebrow.

The bodyguard shrugged and started to look away. Then he shook his head in a gesture Chapel understood immediately. These two were bad news, the kind you definitely did not want to get involved with.

Nadia was standing up, reaching for her purse. Chapel took a step out from behind her chair, and the blond with glasses moved like he was Chapel's reflection in a mirror, curving in to intercept him. As he did so his jacket swung open just a little, just enough for Chapel to see what was underneath.

"Is okay, yes. We take you," Mustache said. "We go now. Yes?"

"Gun," Chapel said.

Nadia reached into her purse, but Mustache grabbed her arm. She had just been trying to put her phone away. Now it chimed and everyone froze.

Mustache tried to keep Nadia from looking at the phone, but he failed. "This is from Bogdan. He says he's on his way."

"Yes, is fine, he says is fine, yes," Mustache said.

But Chapel was already moving.

BUCHAREST, ROMANIA: JULY 15, 11:44

In Ranger school, Chapel had an instructor named Bigelow who taught him everything he knew about unarmed fighting. For months he had trained daily, learning all the special reversals and inversions and strikes, until he thought he could take anybody alive in a fight. Then one day Bigelow showed up with a paintball gun. He'd stood at the far end of the training room and told Chapel to use everything he knew, to come right at Bigelow with every deadly technique he'd been taught, but to stop the second he was hit by a paintball.

Chapel tried twelve different techniques. He tried feints and dodges and sweeps, tried to use the room's furniture for cover or as improvised missile weapons, tried to trick Bigelow by pretending to surrender so he could grab the paint gun away after Bigelow lowered his guard.

Each and every time, Chapel had come away with

a painful blue splotch on his uniform. "We've got a problem," Bigelow said, when he finally called an end to the session. "There's no way you're going to win this. The lesson I'm supposed to teach you today is that up against a man with a gun, you can't win if you're unarmed. You have to put your hands up and surrender."

Chapel, breathing hard and itchy with sweat, was pissed off enough at that point not to say "sir" and leave it at that. "How many shots does it take most people to learn that lesson?"

"Three. And that's the problem. You're a smart guy, Chapel. But for some reason when you're beat, you get dumb. You get too dumb to just give up."

In the tea shop in Bucharest, Chapel watched the gun swing at the hip of the blond guy with the glasses and he got real dumb, real fast.

Mustache already had Nadia by the arm. He was going to force her out into the street, into his car. Chapel could worry about that later. He saw Glasses start reaching for his pistol and knew what he had to do. Glasses was reaching across his body, using his right arm to go for the pistol on his left hip. Chapel grabbed the right arm with both of his hands and forced it downward, past the gun, and at the same time he lashed out with one foot to sweep Glasses's legs.

The blond guy was fast enough to see the sweep coming and he took a step backward, but that was exactly what Chapel wanted. It put Glasses off balance, even as Chapel was still yanking downward on his arm. Glasses had no choice but to bend at the waist, while trying to get his arm free from Chapel's grip. Eventually he figured out he could reach for the pistol with his left hand, which was still free.

Chapel couldn't let him do that. He danced backward, pulling Glasses with him, and the guy went down on his face, down on the floor using his left hand to try to catch himself. He recovered quickly and reached for the pistol again with his left hand, so Chapel had to stomp on his left wrist, pinning it to the floor. That left Chapel in a bad position, though, his hands and one of his legs committed to keeping Glasses from moving. There was still Mustache to contend with—if Mustache let go of Nadia, he could come at Chapel with anything, any kind of attack, and it would connect. Holding Glasses's right arm up in the air and pinning his left arm with his foot, Chapel looked up, expecting to see a fist—or maybe a knife—come at him from the side. If Mustache had a gun, too, this was all over.

It turned out he didn't need to worry.

Nadia had one hand on the floor, pressing down to add leverage to the kick she'd aimed at Mustache's chin. In that position she looked like a Cossack dancer, which might have made Chapel smile if he wasn't so busy holding Glasses down. With just a sandal on her foot her attack couldn't do much damage—Bigelow had never thought much of kicking attacks under any circumstances—but it did have one effect, which was to make Mustache rear back, his face pointed at the ceiling, his arms out at his sides for balance.

Nadia dropped to the floor and spun around—like a break dancer now—her legs stretched out to sweep Mustache off his feet. He went backward into the chair she'd been sitting in a minute before as if he just wanted to take a seat and watch her move.

Chapel wouldn't have blamed him. He'd never seen anyone move like Nadia just had, not outside of a Kung Fu movie.

She spun around on her shoulder and then twisted herself up into a kneeling position in front of the chair. With both hands she reached under the bottom of the chair and tilted it backward until it slammed into the floor, leaving Mustache staring at the ceiling. She vaulted over the chair and landed with one shin across Mustache's throat. Even over the blaring hip-hop music Chapel could hear Mustache gurgle out a scream.

It had been about two seconds since Chapel saw Glasses's gun. He was panting like a horse and he had no idea what to do next. Nadia's hair hadn't even moved. She gave Chapel a wicked smile.

He glanced down at the gun, still hanging on Glasses's hip. Nadia dashed over and grabbed the gun out of its holster. She took one quick look at Mustache—who was not moving—and ran for the door.

"Crap," Chapel said. He had no choice but to follow her. He stomped on Glasses one last time and dashed out of the shop. Behind him he heard someone scream—maybe the girl who ran the counter. He didn't turn around to look.

Outside was bright sunlight and air that stank of diesel fumes and movement in the street. Chapel forced himself to focus, to see what was going on. A car was roaring up the street toward him, a black sedan full of men in suits. Most of them were blond.

Not that way, then. He turned to look down the street—

And saw an almost identical car coming from that direction.

BUCHAREST, ROMANIA: JULY 15, 11:46

"There," Nadia said, pointing across the street. She started running again, and Chapel headed after her. The far side of the street was one long stretch of gray-yellow architecture, columns and windows and doorways but strangely no signs or glass storefronts. The building there must have been standing since before the big construction boom. Chapel saw one doorway lit up by sunlight in a way that seemed wrong, as if the sun were coming from behind the door. Nadia raced through it and disappeared. Chapel hurtled after her, having no idea if he was about to slam into a piece of plateglass or a locked door or what.

Instead, he found himself emerging into a vast open pit of reddish dirt topped by blue sky. He glanced around and saw that the building he'd passed through was nothing but a façade, a thin veneer of bricks that must have once been the front wall of a palatial building. Now it was just a free-standing wall, held up by wooden props, a mask to hide the giant construction site beyond.

Ahead of him he saw the base of a multistory crane, a couple of green construction vehicles, a row of portable toilets. The far side of the lot was dominated by a massive pile of tailings and broken bricks, whatever remained of the demolished building. Thick sections of pipe, each a yard wide, were stacked in a pyramid near the far wall.

Behind him he heard shouting and knew that the blonds were in hot pursuit. He raced after Nadia, only to collide with her as she stopped and turned to look back as well. She put one arm across Chapel's chest to hold him back and shouted, "Get down!"

Chapel knew an order when he heard it. He dropped to a crouch and she leaned over his back, firing her pistol three times at the doorway they'd come through. Chapel twisted his head around and saw plumes of dust lift from the back of the façade, her three shots catching the empty door frame. He thought he saw someone peering through the doorway, but if he did, they were smart enough to pull back, out of view.

"I'm a crap shot," Nadia told him. "You want this?"

He grabbed the pistol out of her hand. Slipped on the safety and shoved it in his pocket. "A shootout back here is the wrong play," he told her, keeping his eyes on the doorway. Nobody was dumb enough to show themselves there. "If we kill someone here, even in self-defense, there's no way we get out of Romania with the mission intact."

"*Konyechno*," she said.

"We have to move," he told her. He straightened up and ran toward the back of the lot, hoping there would be some exit back there. There was, but it was useless. A big gate large enough to drive a truck through, chain link twenty feet high and topped with razor wire. It was also locked up tight with a massive padlock. No way he could break through there. It seemed the only way in or out of the lot was through the empty doorway back on the Strada Lipscani. Back where the entire blond suit gang was gathered, waiting for them to show themselves.

They could try to hide—but to what point? The blonds would just come into the lot and search for them, and even if Chapel was willing to shoot his way out, he would run out of bullets before they ran out of men.

"Come on," Nadia told him, grabbing at his hand.

Well, she was the lead on this operation. He followed her as she ran toward the green construction vehicles. He ran faster when a bullet tore up the red dirt near his feet.

Apparently the suits had grown tired of waiting.

"Cover me," Nadia called.

Chapel spun around until he was running backward—dangerous over the broken ground of the construction pit, but at least it meant he was facing the doorway. He saw a flash of blond hair and snapped off a shot that hit the base of the doorway. The blond hair disappeared again.

Behind him he heard electrical sparks jumping and then the growl of a heavy-duty diesel engine. He glanced back over his shoulder.

"Get on," Nadia said.

She had hot-wired one of the construction vehicles, a miniature bulldozer. Chapel ran over and jumped onto the back of the thing, sitting down on its propane fuel tank and holding on to the roll cage. He fired another shot back at the doorway, barely even aiming, just to keep the men at bay.

With a lurch and a roar the bulldozer started forward, its blade coming up in front until Chapel doubted that Nadia could even see where she was going. She punched the throttle and he was nearly thrown clear, but he managed to hang on as she rolled toward the stack of giant pipes against the far wall of the lot.

"Wait, Nadia—" he had time to shout. If she heard him, she didn't show any sign. She definitely didn't slow down.

The dozer's blade crashed into the pipes, the impact nearly throwing Chapel off. He did drop the gun, though he managed to grab it before he lost it completely. The pipes rang like bells and grated together.

Nadia threw the machine into reverse, backed up, and rammed the pipes again.

The pipes were held together in their stack by a thick plastic strap. It snapped with the second impact, and suddenly nothing was holding them back. They rattled and crashed together, rolling over one another, right into the gate. The gate wobbled and twisted under its own weight and started to open.

A coil of razor wire at the top of the gate came loose, then, and started to unravel and fall. Chapel looked up and saw one end come spearing toward him, the head of a silver snake striking right at his face. He rolled over to one side as the wire slashed down across his jacket sleeve, one barb tearing deep into the silicone flesh on his artificial arm.

With a great *whoomp* of displaced air the gate fell outward, off its posts. It crashed into the street beyond, burying parked cars. Chapel didn't hear any screams—hopefully there'd been no pedestrians back there.

Nadia didn't let up on the gas. She rumbled up over the fallen gate and into the street beyond, where horns blared and Chapel heard the distinctive crump of metal colliding with metal. The little bulldozer hit a curb or a buried car or who knew what. It started to turn over, capsizing in slow motion. The two of them just had time to jump clear.

BUCHAREST, ROMANIA: JULY 15, 11:51

Behind him, the blonds were spilling into the construction lot. A couple of them had guns up and at the ready.

"Come on," Nadia shouted, and Chapel looked over to see her standing on the roof of a wrecked car parked by the sidewalk. The bulldozer blade was imbedded—nearly fused—with the car's doors.

The big pipes had kept rolling into the street, knocking aside anything they touched. They had piled up against the row of shops on the far side, smashing windows and decapitating parking meters.

Already a crowd was gathering in the street. Chapel hoped the owners of the wrecked cars and shops weren't among them. He raced after Nadia as she wove her way between cars stopped in the street, dozens of them crammed into a narrow little lane. Drivers slammed their horns and shook their fists and threw their hands in the air in impotent rage.

"Our enemies will not bring a car through this," she said, grabbing for Chapel's hand. "Nor will they dare shoot with so many witnesses."

That last part sounded like wishful thinking. Chapel let her lead him down the street and around a corner. He couldn't see their pursuers, but he was sure they were still coming. "This way," Nadia whispered, and slipped down an alleyway between two buildings. She took a left on the next street, a right on yet another. She came to a flight of stairs and hurried down, nearly jumping onto the landing below.

In the dark of the stairs, she grabbed Chapel and pushed him through a door, then slipped in behind him and closed the door behind her. The space they were in was nothing more than a custodial closet, a narrow space lined with shelves. It was so small he could feel her pressed up against him. He was glad to see she was finally breathing hard.

"Two minutes," she whispered. "If there's no sign of them—"

"Who?" Chapel asked. "Who were those guys?"

"I have no idea," Nadia said. In the dark closet he couldn't see her face. "Bogdan is . . . involved with some people, some criminals, but—"

"Hold on," Chapel said. "You said he was a computer expert. Then you said this was the capital of cybercrime. Are we hiring a crook?"

"I do not know that word," she said, her Russian accent suddenly much thicker. It wasn't much of a dodge. Maybe she thought she was being funny. "Please be quiet. Am listening for enemies."

He shook his head and let it go.

"One minute," she said. He kept quiet. "Now."

She opened the closet door and Chapel followed her out, down another flight of stairs into what he realized was a subway station. She bought a pair of tickets from a machine and handed him one. They headed through the turnstiles and down to a platform, where a train was just coming in. Nadia stopped and watched the windows of the train cars as they rocketed by.

"Third car, second door," she told him, and ran toward the train as it slowed to a stop. The doors pulled open and people started flooding out, swarming around them in their haste to reach the exit. Chapel saw a very tall, very thin man wearing clunky headphones start to step out of the car. Nadia pushed toward him and said something Chapel couldn't hear, and the two of them stepped into the car.

Chapel fought his way through the people and managed to get on the train before the doors closed again. He pushed through the commuters until he found Nadia and the tall guy sitting down, whispering back and forth.

They looked up at Chapel as he approached.

"Meet Bogdan Vlaicu," Nadia said, as Chapel leaned over them. "Our third."

BUCHAREST, ROMANIA: JULY 15, 12:12

Bogdan looked like a bundle of sticks in an old gray coat. Long, mousy hair fell down over his eyes and hid much of his face. The headphones he wore were hooked up to a tiny MP3 player wrapped in layers of ancient duct tape. Over one shoulder he carried a canvas satchel.

He barely glanced at Chapel during the long subway ride, acknowledging him with a nod of his head and then turning back to his whispered conversation with Nadia.

When they reached their destination, Nadia led them out of the subway and to the train station where they'd stowed their bags. They found an empty waiting room and hunkered down. "The plan," she said, "was to fly to Tashkent from here. But our plane tickets aren't for another six hours. I suggest we get out of Romania as soon as possible."

"Agreed," Chapel said. "We drew a lot of attention back there. The police will want us for questioning, at the very least. So we go by train?"

Nadia agreed. "A train to Istanbul, in Turkey. That puts a fair amount of distance between us and this trouble, and we can get a flight to Uzbekistan from there. Bogdan," she said, "are you ready? You made the preparations I asked you to make?"

"Yes, it is done. Yes," Bogdan said. He sat down on a bench and stared straight ahead, one hand clicking the buttons of his MP3 player repeatedly, as if it were a nervous habit.

Chapel pulled the headphones out of Bogdan's ears to get his attention. "Do you have a passport?" he asked.

"Some," Bogdan replied. He reached inside his satchel and took out a handful of them. "Do you want I am Croatian, Latvian, or Czech?"

Chapel took the passports and riffled through

each of them. "This one looks the most authentic. Latvian," he said, handing the rest of them back to the Romanian. Then he unzipped his own bag and took out a bag full of shampoos and travel-sized soap. The bag had a hidden compartment where he'd put two fresh passports, one for him and one for Nadia. He leafed through them. "Your name is Svetlana Shulkina now," he said.

Nadia wrinkled her nose. "That is the name of a mail-order bride."

"I'm Jeff Chambers," he said, ignoring her. He zipped the old passports, the ones they'd used entering Romania, into the hidden compartment. "I'll go get our train tickets—in a minute. First I want to talk about what the hell just happened."

Nadia smiled at him. "We got away," she said.

Chapel shook his head. "There was no reason for us to draw so much attention, not this early in the mission. You think they were looking for Bogdan?" He turned to the Romanian hacker. The man had his headphones back on. Chapel removed them again, expecting Bogdan to protest, but he didn't. "Bogdan, who's looking for you?"

The Romanian just shrugged.

Chapel wanted to grab him by the lapels and throw him up against the wall until he gave a proper answer. He fought back that urge. "Are you in some kind of trouble?" he asked.

Bogdan shrugged again. "Usually."

Chapel turned to Nadia with a skeptical look. "You're sure this is the guy we want?"

"Absolutely. He and I worked together once before. Didn't we, Bogdan?"

"Yes," the Romanian said. He was putting his headphones back on.

"Ignore all of . . . this," she said, waving at Bogdan to indicate what Chapel was looking at. "The first computers Bogdan ever saw—that a lot of Romanian kids ever saw—were looted from Soviet-era office buildings here, old Vector-06Cs and East German U880s. They were usually broken and outdated, so the kids had to teach themselves to rebuild them from parts. Bogdan was always a prodigy. He made a name for himself back in the early nineties by upgrading computers to run pirated copies of Western games. Now people hire him to port their old business software over to Western operating systems. He can write code for the ES EVM standard in his sleep."

Chapel didn't understand much of that, but it sounded appropriately technical. There was one problem, though. "I take it most of his clients are people who don't want their data uploaded to Facebook."

"*Konyechno*," Nadia said. "He works for gangsters and thieves, yes. They hire him because he is very good, and because he does not talk." She laughed. "He's exactly who we want, 'Jeff.' The kind of man who will fly halfway across the world to do some computer work with no questions asked for fifty thousand U.S. dollars in cash—and never tell a soul about his adventure. Did you think I hadn't thought this through? I've been planning this operation for years."

"I'm sorry," Chapel said. "I didn't mean to suggest—"

He stopped because Nadia had turned her back and was pulling her halter top over her head. She grabbed a fresh shirt from her luggage and pulled it on, stuffing the halter top back inside. She ran her fingers through her hair to try to straighten it back out and then used an alcohol wipe to remove most of her makeup.

"Impressive," Chapel said. "You look completely different, now."

"I'm Siberian. Most people think I look Mongolian, or maybe Korean," she said. "Around here I stand out, so I need to work the accessories. The farther east we get on this trip, the less conspicuous I'll be and I won't need all the costume changes." She smiled at Chapel. "A gentleman might have turned his back."

Chapel felt his cheeks grow hot. "I'm sorry, I, I forgot, I just—"

She gave him a forgiving smile. "Nothing you haven't seen before, I think. Now, I believe you were going to go buy us some tickets?"

"Yeah. Yeah . . . I'll do that," Chapel said. He headed for the door of the waiting room but stopped before he went through. "By the way," he said. "You were really something back there. Using that bulldozer to escape was inspired." He thought about the way she'd taken down Mustache, as well. "Pretty good for a glorified file clerk."

"There's more than one way to deal with bureaucracy," she told him. She reached around her neck and unhooked the crucifix she'd been wearing.

Bogdan looked up, suddenly coming back to life. "Can I have this, if you don't want anymore?" he asked.

"Sure," she said, handing the necklace to him.

"Are you a Christian, Bogdan?" Chapel asked.

"No," he said. "I just want all help I can get."

Nadia had said she'd worked with Bogdan before. Judging by what Chapel had seen so far, maybe he knew what he was getting into. Chapel was pretty sure *he* didn't.

IN TRANSIT: JULY 15, 19:44

The toilet on the train to Istanbul—the first train they'd been able to catch out of Bucharest—looked like it had been made of a single piece of aluminum. It stank of bleach, and the toilet tissue had the consistency of cheap wax paper. But the door closed and latched securely, and the noise of the train meant no one would overhear Chapel's communication with Angel.

"What exactly have you been getting up to, sugar?" she asked, as soon as the call went through.

"Don't tell me we made the news sites," Chapel said, his heart sinking.

"No, nothing like that—there's nothing about it anywhere that I can find in the mass media. The Romanian police haven't issued any alerts, either, which means you're off their radar. But the State Department—the U.S. State Department, I mean—got a call today asking to verify your passports. They went through just fine, but we had to turn over your names and your flight itineraries."

That could have gone much worse, Chapel decided. The names on the passports he and Nadia had used were false, and the plane tickets they weren't using would send any pursuers off on the wrong track. It still worried him, though. "A bunch of guys tried to scoop us up in a tea shop on the Strada Lipscani," he told Angel. "We got away. We thought they were looking for this computer tech Nadia likes so much, this Bogdan Vlaicu. He's apparently in trouble with the local mob so I'm assuming it was organized crime. You think they might have requested that passport check?"

"Eastern European gangsters usually don't get a direct line to the State Department," Angel said, mirroring his own thoughts. "Though they might have people in the local government on their payroll. I'll look into this, see who made the request. Most likely it was the local police. If it was, it's strange they wouldn't issue an APB for the two of you, though. Maybe they have a reason to keep this quiet."

"Were you able to see any of what happened?" he asked.

"No. I can only see what wired security cameras see, or what our reconnaissance satellites pick up. There weren't any sats over your horizon at the time. There were some weird traffic reports and a couple posts on Twitter about a shooting in that district, but that was it."

"Two of the gangsters came into the tea shop, and they knew why we were there. We took them down." Chapel was silent for a moment as he thought. "You should have seen Nadia in a fight. She was all over the place, doing high kicks and dodges I didn't think were possible. She looked like Mary Lou Retton at her prime."

"We know she was a gymnast when she was a kid," Angel pointed out.

"This was . . . something else." Something that kept nagging at Chapel. "I've seen moves like that before, somewhere, but I can't remember where. Maybe in a movie." He filed that question away for future consideration and moved on. "As for the men who attacked us, they were pretty well organized. I'd say a dozen men total, in three cars. They were all blond, which didn't strike me as too weird at the time, but now that I say it out loud it makes me wonder. I don't remember seeing a lot of blonds in Bucharest otherwise."

He listened to Angel tap away at her keyboard as she looked something up. "It's not a common hair color there, according to the Internet. Would you believe there's actually maps showing what percentage of the population has what hair color?"

"It's the Internet. There's probably a map of what country has the most nose rings."

Angel giggled. "I'm looking at a map of blonds right now. Eighty percent of Scandinavians are blond, did you know that?"

"These guys weren't Scandinavian," Chapel said. "They had Slavic accents. And judging by their grammar—" He stopped for a second, thinking. "Angel, they were speaking English."

"Really?"

"Yes. Not well, but it was English. It didn't occur to me at the time. But they came straight to me, speaking English."

"So they made you for an American."

"Yeah," Chapel said. "Damn. I thought I was fitting in." He thought about how easily Nadia had changed her appearance, and how she had elicited no stares or questioning looks in the tea shop. How well she'd handled the escape, even knowing exactly when Bogdan's train would show up. "I'm out of my element here. Plunk me down in Afghanistan and nobody would mistake me for a local, but at least I would know how to act and how to not draw too much attention to myself. In Bucharest I might have jeopardized the mission." He shook his head. "Maybe I shouldn't have been the one to—"

"Stop thinking like that right now, sugar," Angel said. "The director approved you for this. There's nobody he trusts more."

"Yeah." Chapel sighed deeply and rubbed his face with his hands. "Okay. Well, let's focus on what we do best. Have you found anything on Bogdan?"

"A lot more than I found on Nadia," Angel said. "Bogdan Vlaicu, alias Aurel21. That's his handle, the hacker nickname he uses on message boards and blog posts. He has a pretty big reputation online as somebody who can break into supposedly secure eCommerce databases. Arrested a couple of times on counts of credit card number running and for being a public nuisance—specifically, for taking over a Romanian political party website and replacing it with hard-core pornography."

"Seriously? This is the guy Nadia thinks is so vital to our mission?"

Angel laughed. "He may be an idiot, but if he is, he's an idiot savant. He's never gone to jail, even when he bragged online about his crimes. The Romanian government cut him a deal each time they arrested him. If he agreed to take down some real cybercriminals—money launderers, online drug dealers—they'd let him off. Hacking the hackers, in other words."

Angel couldn't keep the grudging respect out of her voice. Chapel knew that her own story wasn't that different. Though her real name, her location, and even what she looked like was kept deeply classified, even from him, she'd once told him how she'd ended up working for the Defense Intelligence Agency. Back when she was just a teenager (how long ago that had been was, again, secret), she had thought it would be fun to hack into the Pentagon's servers. Instead of going to jail for the rest of her life, she'd ended up whispering sexily into Chapel's ear. To her, Bogdan might seem like a fellow traveler.

"The guy has chops," Angel said. "He shut down one of the biggest dark net pirated software operations back in 2009 with a simple denial-of-service attack. Basically he flooded the website with fake orders, hundreds of thousands of them coming in every second. That's nothing, that's hacking 101, but it was just a smoke screen. When the criminals shut down their servers to stop the attack, they switched to a backup server for their internal e-mail and even their phones—maybe they thought that the Romanian government couldn't tap into their VoIP connections. Normally they would have been right about that. But Bogdan had secretly hacked the backup server even before he began the denial-of-service attack, so every word they said over the server they thought was still secure got logged and recorded. He took down dozens of cybercriminals in one day, including a guy who was on Interpol's most wanted list."

"That might explain why the local gangsters want him dead," Chapel said, nodding. "And why he always looks like somebody just ran over his childhood dog."

Angel wasn't done, though. "In 2011, he got in trouble again, this time some pretty deep doo-doo. He anonymously posted a document online that claimed the prime minister of Romania had plagiarized his doctoral thesis back in grad school. That doesn't sound like much, but . . . I won't go into the details of Romanian politics, but there was already a feud going between two rival political parties, and it looked like this document might take down the prime minister *and* his party, whether it was true or not. There were riots in the street, and some people got hurt. It didn't help when further charges of corruption kept popping up. The whole mess *still* hasn't been worked out."

"Bogdan doesn't mind stepping on powerful toes, huh?"

"He was arrested for fomenting political unrest. They were ready to throw the book at him. I mean, send him away to prison for life and never let him touch a computer again. But then—damn. Chapel, you're going to sense a theme here."

"You're about to tell me he disappeared."

"Yeah," Angel replied. "Yeah. Just . . . fell off the map. The charges were never dropped, but they were also never prosecuted. There's no record of the case anywhere in the legal databases after a certain date, and nothing whatsoever in Bogdan's file. He just turned into a ghost. You know, the funny thing there is—"

"The funny thing is that was the same year Nadia got her medal," Chapel said, guessing what she was about to say.

"Uh. Yeah," Angel said. "How did you know that?" Sometimes he could still surprise her.

"She said that she'd worked with Bogdan before. Whatever secret thing she was doing that got her that medal, he must have been part of it. She got him out of trouble in exchange for his help."

"There's no evidence for any of that. Nothing you could ever prove. But as a working hypothesis, it makes sense."

Chapel nodded to himself. "Okay. Thanks, Angel. It's good to know who I'm working with, even if that means I'm not allowed to know who they are. Is there anything else you have for me?"

Angel was silent for a while before answering. "There are no new messages on your voice mail, if that's what you mean." No messages from Julia, in other words. "Chapel, if you want to talk about—"

"Not right now," he said.

IN TRANSIT: JULY 15, 20:14

Chapel walked back to the sleeper compartments where Bogdan and Nadia were, passing by a series of windows that showed the countryside rushing past. They were in Bulgaria by now, he estimated, though it was hard to say from what he saw. The sun was an hour away from setting, and it hung like a golden ball over endless fields that stretched away in every direction. In the distance he could just see the Balkan mountains like a pale smudge on the horizon, but they could have been anything. He could have been looking at the American Midwest, or the wheat fields of the Ukraine, or any of a hundred other identical views from a hundred different countries.

It was hard to remember just how far he was from home, though in another way, he couldn't get it off his mind. He was out of his depth here. Nadia knew the local customs and manners, knew how to work a covert operation in this part of the world. But Chapel was just along for the ride. He wasn't even her hired muscle—it was clear she could take care of herself. He really was just here to witness her operation.

He hated feeling like a fifth wheel. Third wheel in this case—Nadia needed Bogdan badly enough to risk getting shot for him.

Chapel took one last look at the fields and sighed and pushed through the automatic door to the sleeper car.

They'd taken two compartments, one for Nadia and one for Bogdan and Chapel to share. He was not surprised to find the two of them in the shared compartment. Bogdan was sitting on the floor, rocking his head back and forth. Maybe to the music in his headphones, but it made him look like he was suffering from some kind of neurological condition. He didn't even look up as Chapel came in. He was tapping the keys of his MP3 player over and over, as if it were a nervous tic.

Nadia was sprawled out on one of the bunks, leafing through a magazine with a lot of splashy color photographs. It looked like a gossip rag, but it was written in a language Chapel didn't recognize, much less read. She looked up at him with a big smile when he came inside.

He took his bag down from the overhead rack and rummaged around inside until he found what he needed. Then he took off his jacket and studied the tear in the left sleeve. It had been ripped during their escape from the construction site and it looked like the damage was too severe to repair with just a simple sewing kit. "I liked this jacket," he said, glancing up to meet Nadia's eye.

"You dress up well," she said, giving him a sympathetic mock frown. "We can get you another one in Istanbul. We have a long layover there."

He nodded and stuck one finger through the hole. "Yeah. I doubt there are any international alerts out for a man with a torn jacket, but you never know." He folded the ruined jacket up and put it on the empty bunk, then started unbuttoning his shirt. "So you're a Siberian, huh?" he asked, mostly just for something to say. To draw attention away from what he was about to do.

She tilted her head to one side. "*Ya Sibiryak, da,*" she confirmed. "And proud of it."

"You said back in the train station that you were Siberian. I'll admit, you're not what I expected a Russian agent to look like."

Nadia laughed. "What, I am not blond and statuesque, with big breasts and sad eyes? I get that a lot. Many people think I'm not Russian. But they forget that only a little bit of Russia is west of the Urals, and European. The vast majority of the Fatherland is in Asia, and many, many Russians look like I do."

"Sorry. I didn't mean to imply anything like—"

She waved away his protest. "I'm not offended. I would imagine that to Americans, Siberia might as well be on the far side of the moon."

Chapel couldn't help but grin. "Growing up, we were always taught Siberia was where they sent you if they wanted to forget you ever existed. We even use it—and I'm sorry if this sounds mean—but we use 'siberia' as a term to refer to, say, the worst table in a restaurant where nobody wants to sit. The table closest to the toilets."

Nadia shook her head in resignation. "A lot of Russians might use it the same way. Many Soviets were exiled there, and many more forced to move there for work. They consider it the end of the world. But others, those born there, love the place. I was born in Yakutia—what they call the Sakha Republic, now."

"You get back there much?"

She sighed and put down her magazine. "Let me guess. Your bosses asked you to find out everything you can about me. So they can make a dossier."

"Just making small talk," he told her.

She laughed. "I take no offense, even if you lie to me. We're in the same line of work; we know the routine. We keep our eyes open and our mouths shut."

Chapel glanced over at Bogdan.

"Don't worry about him; he can't hear us over his music," she said.

Chapel wondered if that was true, but he didn't say anything. He pulled off his shirt and then his undershirt. The barbed wire that had ruined his jacket had cut all the way through three layers of cloth and down into the silicone flesh of his artificial arm.

"You're hurt," Nadia said.

"Not really." He couldn't really see the damage so he reached under the clamp that held the arm on and released it. It went dead as it separated from his body. He used his right hand to lift it away from his shoulder and laid it across his lap.

That made Bogdan's eyes go wide behind their fringe of hair. His repetitive tapping on his MP3 player grew more frenetic, but he said nothing.

Nadia, of course, had seen the arm come off before, back on Donny's party yacht. She jumped down from her bunk and crossed the compartment to run one hand over the silicone prosthetic. The damage was restricted to a thin tear across the bicep. There was no blood, of course, and the wire hadn't cut all the way through the silicone, but the tear was a couple of inches long and it gaped open like a pair of lips. If he left it like that, the damage would only get worse over time, opening a little wider every time he flexed the arm. Luckily he'd brought a repair kit. "Can you help me with this?" he asked. He opened the flat case he'd taken from his luggage and took out a silicone patch. "It's tough to open the packaging with just one hand."

She took the patch—it looked like a large adhesive bandage but was much stronger and more sticky—and peeled away its paper backing. With her small, nimble fingers she laid the patch across the tear and then smoothed it out. It was the same flesh color as the silicone and it was almost invisible once it was on.

"This will hold, until we can send you home?" she asked.

"It'll do. It shouldn't restrict my mobility, and it'll keep the damage from spreading."

She looked up into his eyes, and he was suddenly very aware of how close she was to him. She was beautiful, he realized. *Striking*—the word he'd been using—didn't really do her justice. Her eyes were huge, and very bright and clear, and as they studied him he smelled her perfume, too. Something very subtle and slightly musky.

"I haven't been back to Siberia in over a decade," she said, answering the question he'd asked earlier. "I miss it, yes. If that was your next question."

"Maybe," he told her.

"It's a whole other world, out there," she said, looking out the train window. "Out in the taiga forests. Under the pines . . ." She shook her head. "Nothing like Moscow, or any part of Russia west of the Urals. Not nearly so crowded."

"Some people might say not as developed," Chapel pointed out. He was after something, but he didn't get it, because just then their conversation was interrupted by a curse.

"What the shit?" Bogdan had risen from the floor and come over to the bunk where Chapel's arm lay. He looked at it with wide eyes, holding his hair back maybe so he could see it better. He glanced over at Chapel, then reached out one long, thin finger as if he was going to poke the arm.

"Careful," Chapel said. "When it's off my shoulder, I don't control it. It might grab you if you get too close."

He'd meant it as a joke, but Bogdan turned to look at him with an expression of real fear. He drew his finger back. Then he nodded, once, and went to sit back down. As far away from the arm as he could get. His fingers tapped at the keys of his MP3 player so fast they seemed to blur.

Nadia and Chapel shared a laugh. Then she turned to look at Chapel. "Okay," she said. "Your turn."

"I'm sorry?" he asked.

"I think I will turn in now. Go back to my compartment." She gathered up her magazine and held it against her chest. "But first—you asked me a personal question. So now I get to ask you one."

Chapel gritted his teeth before he answered. He never liked talking about himself. Talking about himself to foreign agents was even lower on his list. But he nodded, eventually. "I guess that's fair."

Nadia scratched herself behind one ear. She twisted her mouth around as if she was trying to think of the best question to ask, as if she would only ever have this one chance. Her eyes narrowed, and she said, "The first day I met you, you were talking about a woman. Someone back in New York."

Every muscle in Chapel's body tensed. Giving away national secrets was one thing, but this—

"You were going to propose."

"Yeah," he said, barely moving his lips.

"Ah. I don't even need to ask. I can see the answer already, on your face. She said no."

"She said no," Chapel confirmed.

Instantly Nadia's face fell. She started to make a sound, the last sound Chapel ever wanted to hear. The sad *ohhh* sound that people made when they felt sorry for you.

"Don't," he growled. Then he shook his head and tried to push away the anger. "I'm sorry. I just—I'd rather not—"

"Of course," she said. She pulled back. "I'm sorry I brought this up."

"It's all right," he forced himself to say.

She nodded and opened the door of the compartment. "You don't want to be comforted, I understand. You still want the pain. Okay. I'll leave you be." She stepped out into the hallway, but she was still looking at him, searching his face. "For now, anyway," she said, and gave him a look he had no idea how to interpret. Then she walked away, toward her own compartment.

He reached over and closed the door. When he turned around, he found Bogdan hovering over his artificial arm, as if daring himself to touch it.

ISTANBUL, TURKEY: JULY 16, 07:32

The train pulled into Sirkeci Terminal an hour or so after sunrise. Bogdan was snoring in his bunk, his headphones slipped over half his face, but Chapel was already up, doing some basic calisthenics in the narrow compartment. Outside the train he saw the city piling up around them, getting denser and smokier with each passing second. He was packed and ready to go long before the wheels stopped rolling.

Nadia came by and helped him pull Bogdan out of his bunk. The hacker looked half dead, even though he'd gotten a full night's sleep. "Is unfair," he moaned. "Is not right. To wake up like this, with no caffeine available."

"We'll get you coffee," Nadia promised him. "Turkey is famous for its coffee!" She gave Chapel a long look. "Come on," she said. "End of the line!"

Chapel gathered up his luggage and kept Bogdan moving, inch by inch, toward the exit from the train. The platform was thronged with people, some trying to get on board even as the passengers debarked. The air was thick with announcements and cries in a number of languages Chapel didn't understand. A child came rushing up with hands outstretched as if he desperately needed help, his face streaked with tears, but one of the train's conductors shouted at him and the boy stopped crying instantly and ran off. "Beggars!" the conductor said to Chapel in English. "Give them a coin, and they will never leave you alone. Be careful of pickpockets!"

Chapel nodded halfhearted thanks to the man and followed Nadia as she headed into the main terminal, a big square room with white and pink walls and arabesque arches and far more people in it than comfort would allow. Nadia steered her way through the crowd so deftly it was all Chapel could do to keep up, with Bogdan in tow. Outside the terminal she led them down a broad road called, of all things, Kennedy Avenue, through a whole new throng of people that made it impossible to see anything. Elbows and shoulders buffeted Chapel constantly and people called out to him over and over, either greeting him or warning him to keep out of their way, he couldn't say. Finally they broke through the press and came to a railing overlooking a broad stretch of water—the Bosphorus, Chapel figured, based on what he knew of the local geography.

Morning fog covered much of the water, still, but Chapel could make out enough to be impressed. The broad ribbon of water cut the city into two halves, each rising up away from the strait on steep hills studded with towers and spires. The water was thick with boats of every imaginable description, from huge tankers and freight ships loaded down with multicolored cargo containers to towering cruise ships to square-nosed ferries to little wooden craft with triangular sails that tacked back and forth across the current.

"Look at the *yalis*," Nadia said, pointing out a line of structures down at the water's edge, crowding both sides of the strait. They were houses of elaborately carved wood that looked as if they floated on the water, giving the impression that the whole city was just one enormous raft bobbing on the current.

It was a beautiful view, Chapel had to admit. The constant roar and blare of traffic behind him, the human press, couldn't spoil that. He found himself almost smiling. He'd always loved the water and watching the way it was in constant motion, constant change.

They found a little place where Bogdan got his coffee, while Nadia and Chapel breakfasted on sweet rolls crusted with nuts and dried fruit. It felt good to be off the train, even in the crowded little restaurant.

"We have hours still, until our plane departs," Nadia said, wiping currant pulp from her fingers with a tiny paper napkin. "How do you wish to spend the time?"

"We should keep moving. I doubt anyone followed us this far," Chapel said, "but we shouldn't take any chances." He looked over at Bogdan. The hacker was going to be a problem, if they needed to keep a low profile. With his very short hair Chapel himself could blend in with the locals, and Nadia's Asian features weren't going to draw much attention in Istanbul. But the tall, lanky Romanian was bound to draw stares. It would be best, Chapel knew, if they could just find some place to lie low, out of sight, but that would mean, say, checking into a hotel. Which would leave a paper trail. The second-best option was to find the biggest crowd possible and disappear inside it.

"Perhaps I may suggest something. Something that has nothing to do with our business," Nadia said. One corner of her mouth curved upward in a sly smile. She put down her napkin and turned to face the windows at the front of the café. "The Hagia Sophia is just a little bit away. It is supposed to be amazing to see."

"You're suggesting we take in the local sights," Chapel said. The idea sounded ridiculous—this wasn't a vacation. But he glanced around at the other people in the café, mostly Turks poring over newspapers or checking their phones before they had to get in to work. There were more than a few tourists, though, recognizable by their casual clothes and the bags they all carried. "That might not be such a bad plan," he said. Among the well-dressed business professionals of Istanbul, Bogdan stood out like a sore thumb. In a crowd of gaudily dressed tourists he might be less conspicuous.

"One must take one's pleasures where one may, yes?" Nadia said. She pushed her chair back and stood up. "This is the last chance we'll have to relax, before things get serious."

They'd already been attacked by Romanian gangsters and had to flee Bucharest ahead of the police. Chapel wondered how serious she expected things to get.

"Before I go anywhere," Bogdan announced, still firmly seated in his chair. "I finish this cup."

The two of them stood and watched while he slurped his coffee.

ISTANBUL, TURKEY: JULY 16, 07:49

They headed down Kennedy Avenue, following the curve of the strait. Soon Chapel could see a big domed structure rising above them, flanked by four needlelike minarets. Helpful signs confirmed this was the Hagia Sophia, one of Istanbul's most important landmarks and a major tourist destination. They joined a mob of people from every country in the world flowing into its forecourt. Signs posted everywhere in a dozen languages told him about the place. "This was built in the year 360?" Chapel said aloud. "Is that . . . is that right?" The signs assured him it was true. They told him the Hagia Sophia had originally been a basilica of the Orthodox Christian

Church, the biggest church in the world for a thousand years. For a while it had been a Roman Catholic cathedral, and then in the Middle Ages it was converted into a mosque. In the twentieth century, it had been converted into a museum.

The building was massive, a sprawling complex of domes topped with golden spikes, with broad stone walls that glowed pink in the morning sun. As they passed through its main entrance into the shadowed interior the temperature seemed to drop ten degrees, and Chapel smelled old stone and wood. When his eyes adjusted, he took in just how big the place was—the walls seemed to stretch upward forever, pierced with rows of arches and massive columns. Round panels displaying Arabic calligraphy hung overhead, so wide each character was taller than Chapel. The walls were lined with golden mosaics or cut from veined marble or rich, colorful stone that gave the place a sense of immense solidity, even as the open space between the walls felt infinite and expansive.

Chapel looked up and saw an enormous dome that stretched so high over his head he felt dwarfed, rendered insignificant. Daylight streamed in through hundreds of arched windows, filling the air under the dome with a bright presence that seemed to shimmer and twist like something trying to take form and existence.

All the noise, all the anger in his head seemed to drain away as he stood there, taking in the sheer immensity of the place. The scale, the power of it. It might well look like a mosque, it might have been packed full of tourists laughing and griping and snapping pictures, but it took Chapel back to a very different place. Strangely enough, it made him remember the little white-paneled church in Florida where, as a boy, he'd gone to services with his mother every Sunday. He had spent those hours fidgeting on the pews that stank of wood polish, bored and wondering what he was missing on TV. But now, in this place, he didn't think about that. He thought of his mother, in her Sunday dress, kneeling with her head bowed in prayer. He thought of the times when the congregation would come together in song, their voices joined over the sound of the church's pipe organ, and how it had felt like there was something there, something bigger than himself. Something special. The people who had built the Hagia Sophia, he knew, had been looking for the same thing. The sacred.

He realized his jaw was hanging open, and he forced himself to look down, at Nadia standing beside him. She looked up at him with a quiet smile.

"Perhaps you think me trivial," she said, "for wanting to see this when there is so much work to be done."

"No," he said, softly. Inside him, something let go, something he'd been holding on to for a long time. He felt strangely at peace. "No, I don't. I'm glad I got to see it myself."

She nodded. "This career we choose, it does not offer us much time to ourselves, to think, to simply be people. We are kept so busy, and our lives could end at any time." She shivered as if she were cold. "I feel I must take advantage, any compensation I can. Being able to see much of the world is one of the best."

She reached over and took his hand. His good, living hand. It was such an innocent and affectionate gesture it didn't occur to him to stop her. Her fingers were warm and soft in his, and after a moment he didn't want to let go.

He closed his eyes, and just for a moment, a short span of time, he was okay. It was like having Julia there with him. Or even more basic than that—just having another human being to share the moment with, to not be alone.

"Happy honeymoon!" someone shouted, and Chapel's eyes opened just as a flash of light dazzled him. His first instinct was to reach for a gun that wasn't there. His second was to pull away from Nadia's hand, as guilt flushed through him and made him want to duck his head.

Then he saw what had happened, and he growled in frustration.

A Turkish man with a camera stood in front of them, grinning from ear to ear.

ISTANBUL, TURKEY: JULY 16, 08:09

"Such a handsome couple. I take your picture," he said. "Then, if you give me your e-mail, your home address, I can send you a copy, all right? You can remember this happy moment forever."

Damn. This was not acceptable. They couldn't leave any trace behind, any sign they'd been here—

not even a picture on some random man's camera. Chapel forced himself to smile. "Can I see the picture? On your camera?"

"Fifty lira for the picture, printed in a lovely frame," the man suggested. "For eighty, I will make smaller prints and send them to all your friends."

"I just need to see the picture first," Chapel said. "I think my eyes were closed."

"If it's no good, okay, I take another," the man tried.

"Just let me see the picture," Chapel said, taking a step closer to him. The man started to turn and move away so Chapel had to reach out and grab his arm. He tore the camera out of the man's hands and let him go.

Instantly the photographer started shouting something in a language that Chapel didn't know. His hand gestures and the look on his face made it very clear what he was trying to communicate.

The last thing Chapel wanted was to have the police come and ask questions. He studied the camera in his hands. The buttons were all labeled with letters and numbers he couldn't figure out, but he managed to bring up the last picture taken. It showed him—his eyes were, in fact, closed—and Nadia, hand in hand. Bogdan was just visible in the background, though he was walking away from them.

Chapel found an icon that looked like a trash can. He deleted the picture and handed the camera back to the photographer.

"This is an outrage!" the man said, in English. "This is not—"

Nadia spoke softly to him in the same language he'd used before. She held up her left hand and pointed at it several times. When that didn't do the trick, she handed him a couple of bank notes.

The photographer made a nasty gesture at Chapel, but he took his camera and left.

"What did you say to him?" Chapel asked.

"I said we were married, but not to each other," she said, with a shrug and a wry smile. "Then I gave him twice what he was asking. I should have led with the money."

Chapel nodded, only half paying attention. He was scanning the crowd, looking for Bogdan. "When was the last time you saw our third?" He raised an eyebrow at Nadia, and her face got very serious, very fast.

"We need to find him," she said, and pushed into the crowd. Chapel went a different direction, looking for anyone tall and thin, looking for headphones.

When he spotted Bogdan, Nadia had already reached him. The hacker had discovered a rank of computerized information kiosks. Each was just a box with a screen and a trackball, designed to give tourist information in several different languages. The screen of each one was displaying pictures of the dome above and the word *Welcome!* in multiple alphabets. The kiosk that Bogdan was using, however, showed a black screen covered in lines of tiny, blurry text.

Even Nadia looked surprised, for once. "How did you . . . ?"

"Is a screen for maintenance," Bogdan explained, moving the trackball across the screen with the deftness of a champion video-game player. "In case system goes down and needs to be fixed. Easy if you know the way in, yes? Hold on." He clicked the ball and the screen lit up with the home page for an Internet browser. "I just go to check my VKontakte page."

Chapel frowned. "What's VKontakte?" he asked.

Nadia looked up at him. "Russian Facebook."

"Oh, no, no, no," Chapel said, grabbing Bogdan's shoulders and pulling him back from the kiosk. "No, we're not going there." He pressed his back up against the screen so Bogdan wouldn't even see it. "Low profile, okay? Coming here wasn't the best idea. We need to stay out of sight. We need to go straight to the airport."

"*Konyechno*," Nadia said, with a weary sigh. "The time to relax is over."

IN TRANSIT: JULY 16, 22:59

Even in his sleep, Bogdan kept tapping away at his MP3 player. He lay twisted up in his seat, his long frame bent to fit into the little legroom he had. His face hung on the seat back as limp and loose as a rubber mask, his mouth open and flecked with drool. The hair that always covered his eyes obscured half his face and made him look barely human.

Another airplane, another night. Economy class this time, just to throw off anyone looking for business-class travelers matching their description. Chapel still couldn't sleep. Nadia sat across the aisle from the two men. Chapel studied her sleeping face and wished he could be next to her, breathing in her perfume, her soft shoulder rubbing up against his. Maybe she would have laid her head against him, used him as a pillow. Maybe he could have put an arm around her for warmth.

Jesus. This had to stop.

He plugged his earbuds into his tablet and booted up his Kazakh language program. Almost as soon as the monotone voice of the vocabulary lesson began it stopped and Angel spoke to him instead.

"How are you doing, baby?" she asked.

The sexy voice speaking to him out of the ether was almost enough to get him to stop thinking about Nadia. He inhaled sharply and put his fingers on the virtual keyboard on the tablet's screen. He wasn't entirely sure how to answer.

"Can you talk, or is this not a good time?" Angel asked, because apparently it had taken him too long to frame his reply.

NO, IT'S FINE, he wrote.

"The director's been pressuring me for an update. I told him you're on your way to Tashkent now. He doesn't like this kind of mission, where he just sends you into the field and you're left to your own devices. I have to say I'm not crazy about it either. I wish we could talk more often, the way we usually do."

ME TOO, Chapel typed. HAS TO BE THIS WAY, THOUGH. WE SPENT DAY IN ISTAN-BUL. VERY NICE PLACE.

"Glad to hear it," Angel said, with a laugh.

ANY NEWS FROM BUCHAREST?

"If you mean, are you still being chased by blond gangsters, I don't think so. The police eventually did put an alert out for two people matching your description, but there were no reports of sightings. And then out of nowhere the alert just . . . went away."

WEIRD.

"Not necessarily. I think they just assumed you left the country when nobody could find you. Most likely they just wanted you to identify the men who tried to scoop you up. I checked, but there's no warrant out for Bogdan Vlaicu, either. I think you got a get out of jail free card, sugar."

GOOD NEWS, I GUESS.

"If anything changes on that front, I'll be watching. So anything else I can do for you tonight?"

He stared at the screen for a while. It only showed the list of language files he was supposedly listening to, but it was the closest he could get to looking at Angel. He'd spent a long time trying to imagine what she looked like, but all he could ever really see in his head was a computer screen. More than once he'd wondered if she was a real human being, or just some kind of very clever artificial intelligence.

She was, he knew, his best friend in the world. The one person he could always rely on. She'd saved his life dozens of times and helped him out in a million ways. He trusted her implicitly—even more than he trusted Director Hollingshead. Maybe more than he'd ever really trusted Julia.

"Sweetie," she said. "I can tell something's on your mind."

Of course she could. He wanted desperately to talk to her, just then. Not just type on a screen. HOLD ON, he tapped out. He got up from his seat and headed back to the lavatories. Inside, sitting on the toilet, he listened to the noise of the engines and the hiss of pressurized air. If he was quiet, it should be all right.

"Angel," he said, barely more than a whisper. "Can you hear me?"

"I can, sugar. You're somewhere secure now?"

"Yeah." He glanced up at the lavatory door. Made sure it was locked. "Listen," he said, "I need to tell you something. Something that's got me worried." He hesitated for a moment longer, but he knew that if he didn't tell her now, he never would. "I've had inappropriate contact with N."

Angel was quiet for so long he thought maybe she'd hung up on him. He should have known better—she never did that.

"Sugar," she said, finally. "Please repeat that. Because I can't believe you said what I think you just said."

Chapel scrubbed at his face with his hands. "I've been . . . fraternizing with her."

"You know that's not okay," Angel told him. "Are you telling me you slept with her? Because that's definitely not okay."

"I know. I know that," Chapel said.

Angel's voice got very soft then, which he knew meant she was being utterly serious. "Have you even considered the possibility that she's a swallow?"

"A what?"

"A . . . you know. The woman who sets up a honey trap."

"You think she's trying to seduce me to learn our secrets?"

"Men will say anything after sex. They have no filters at all." Angel cleared her throat. "At least, that's what I've heard."

"No, no," Chapel said. "It's nothing like that. She would have been way more forward if that was the case. This was—it wasn't much. We just held hands."

"O . . . kay," Angel said.

"I know. I know. I sound like a teenager getting weird about his first crush. But I thought I should tell you. And you should tell the director."

"I could do that," Angel said. "I am required by protocol and professional ethics to do exactly that," she told him. "And you know what would happen then. He would tell you to scrub the mission and come home."

"Yeah. That's why I brought it up. I don't want to give up, but—"

"Or," Angel said, "I could not tell him. We could keep this between us. And you could get your shit together right now."

Angel didn't often swear. She was one of those people who understood that when you save profanity for special occasions, it actually does lend emphasis. Chapel felt like someone had dumped cold water down his back.

"I'm not sure I can," he told her.

Angel almost sounded angry when she replied. "You can and you will. There's a lot depending on this mission, Chapel. Your emotions can't come between you and completing this."

"I know that," he told her. "But—"

"But what? What could be more important than

that? What could come close to measuring up to the fate of the entire world?"

"I'm lonely," he said. "That's all."

Another long silence from her end. He thought he heard some muttering in the background, but with all the noise in the lavatory it was hard to tell.

When she came back, her voice was much softer. "I know you miss Julia," she said. "I know what you're going through."

"Do you?" he asked. "You know what it's like to be dumped by somebody you thought you would spend the rest of your life with?"

"Maybe not . . . exactly, but—"

"I'm human, Angel. I'm just a man. I'm supposed to be this elite soldier, this machine that fights for its country. I'm highly trained and totally professional. But sometimes—sometimes I don't want this anymore. Sometimes I think about getting married and starting a family. This job took that away from me."

"You chose this job."

"I know."

"Do you want to scrub the mission? Do you want to give up?"

"No," Chapel said. "No." Going home now, in disgrace—it wouldn't solve anything. He would still be headed back to an empty apartment. An empty life. "That's why I brought this to you, though. Because maybe I'm not the best judge of my fitness for duty right now."

"I understand," Angel said. "Tell me something. If you put the moves on N right now, I mean, really laid on the charm—you think she would go for it?"

"I can't tell. She's been very friendly. But, well, for one thing—I'm an amputee. A lot of people are nice to me because they think I'm some kind of wounded hero and that I deserve to be treated like a sick kitten or something. Not a lot of people want to . . . to have sex with someone like me. I think maybe she just feels sorry for me."

"There's such a thing as pity sex," Angel pointed out.

Chapel grinned and shook his head. "Not as much as some people might hope. Anyway. No. I don't think I could seduce N without a lot of effort."

"So just don't put in that effort. No more holding hands, right? No more fraternization. Because even if it seems innocent now—she might just be building to something more. You can't know. And you definitely can't trust her."

"Understood," Chapel said. "Angel—thank you. This was weighing on me."

"Always here to help, honey," she told him. "And in fact, I might have something that really does help. I've been doing some more digging on N. Looking for anything that wasn't obvious, something I missed the first time around."

"And you found something," Chapel said, frowning. She wouldn't have brought this up if there was nothing there.

"Yeah, though not something I can prove. N is a pretty slippery fish, and her records are very hard to turn up. But it looks like she might have a criminal record."

IN TRANSIT: JULY 16, 23:14

"I beg your pardon?" Chapel asked.

Angel sounded almost coy as she answered. She got that way sometimes when she'd done a particularly clever thing and wanted to share but didn't want to come off as bragging. "Oh, it's not very serious, really. It's not like she robbed a bank or anything."

"Come on, Angel. Spill."

"A woman matching N's description—and I mean *matching*, height, weight, everything—was picked up by the Moscow police a couple of years ago for subversive political activity. Which probably just means she went to a protest rally and chanted louder than the person next to her. Under Putin, the Russians aren't putting up with much in the way of dissidence."

"What kind of a protest rally?" Chapel asked.

"It was a meeting of a number of student groups, but the focus was on self-determination for ethnic minorities. The protesters were demanding that places like Chechnya, South Ossetia, and some eastern ethnic territories be allowed to split off from the Russian Federation and become their own countries. Their plan was to get a crowd assembled in Red Square and then march across Moscow waving signs and shouting slogans. They didn't get very far. The police moved in and, well, the official record says they 'peacefully dispersed the illegal gathering without incidence of violence.' Which means nobody sued them afterward. I'm guessing they used fire hoses and pepper spray to break things up. A lot of people were arrested, among them somebody who looks and sounds exactly like N. She refused to give her name, which meant she would have been taken into central processing where they could make an ID. Except there's no indication she got there. There's a brief mention of her particulars and her arrest, and then nothing."

"When it comes to N, that's starting to sound familiar," Chapel said.

"Exactly. I figure she waited until she was alone in the police station to tell them she was a government agent, and then they sprang her. It couldn't hurt that she had that medal. I mean, she probably wasn't wearing it at the time, or anything. But the police—and the Putin administration—would have been embarrassed if they had to admit they had arrested a decorated citizen."

"Interesting," Chapel said.

"Yeah. She's not as squeaky clean as she looks, huh?" Angel said. "I kind of like her more now, though. Makes her a little more human."

Chapel thought of the woman he'd left sleeping in her aisle seat. He had no trouble thinking of Nadia as human. But this did change things, a little. Something occurred to him. "Angel—you said the protesters were asking for self-determination for some eastern ethnic territories."

"That's right."

"Which ones?"

Angel tapped at her keyboard for a second. "You want the whole list? There are dozens of them here.

Basically the protesters wanted every ethnic, religious, or language group to have its own autonomous country."

"What about places in Siberia? I mean, specifically, anything close to where Nadia was born, near Yakutsk."

More keys clacking. Then Angel clucked her tongue. "Right on the money. Twelve different areas in Siberia are named on the list, including Yakutia."

"Very interesting," Chapel said.

TASHKENT, UZBEKISTAN: JULY 17, 05:43 (UZT)

The plane set down on a runway near the center of the capital of Uzbekistan just as the sun was coming up. The passengers debarked onto the second floor of a small terminal where the floor was lined with oriental carpets. As Chapel, Nadia, and Bogdan headed down a wide central staircase toward customs and baggage claim a loudspeaker crackled and filled the air with the chanting of a muezzin calling the faithful to dawn prayers. Many of their fellow passengers heeded the call then and there, while less devout travelers streamed around them. It seemed like half the people in the airport were smoking all at the same time, and the air was thick with the stink of tobacco.

Chapel hadn't slept much. He felt like a guitar string tuned too tight, like every breath made his body vibrate uncomfortably. He was going to need a nap, and soon.

There was no trouble with their passports. It took

a while for the bags to come out, but it looked like
no one had gone through them—something Chapel
had worried about. He grabbed his black nylon bag
and followed Nadia out through a pair of glass doors
into the street.

The air of Tashkent shimmered with the last
traces of a morning haze. A breeze swirled down the
sidewalk, already warm, carrying with it the smell
of a desert close by.

The smell made the hair on the back of Chapel's neck stand straight up. He knew that smell,
the ancient dusty spice of it. It smelled just like
Afghanistan—like the place where he'd lost his arm.

Instantly Chapel's muscles reacted, tensing and
pulling his head down. Every day he'd been in Afghanistan, every hour, he'd been in danger. Death
could have come for him at any moment. What had
happened instead was maybe worse. Chapel felt the
old familiar stress headache coming on, like a loop
of wire was wrapped around his skull and it was
constantly tightening.

Get it together, he told himself. This wasn't Afghanistan. That was all over for him, just a memory.

It was so very hard to fight it back.

The physical therapist who had worked with
Chapel after he came home from the war—a fellow
amputee named Top—had once told him that the
percentage of veterans with posttraumatic stress
disorder was one hundred percent. And that the
percentage of wounded veterans with PTSD was
one hundred and fifty percent, because some of
them got it twice. He'd warned Chapel that you
never really left the war behind, that it lived with

you and all you could do was make a place for it in your head, a place you only visited when you had to.

Chapel fought to control his emotions. Part of him wanted to run away. To run back to the plane and beg the pilot to take him away from here. Part of him wanted to curl up in a ball in the corner.

Top would have understood. He'd been to Iraq—and left behind an arm, a leg, and one eye. Maybe he'd gotten PTSD four times over.

Maybe Nadia sensed Chapel stiffen. She put a hand on the small of his back and rubbed the skin there in small circles. It was surprisingly comfortable.

"I'm okay," he told her, and stepped away from her hand.

She didn't reply. She just stepped up the curb and held her arm out, down and away from her body. A car pulled up right away. The driver was smoking, and when he stopped, he rolled down his window and a bluish cloud billowed out, right into Nadia's face. She didn't seem to mind. She leaned in through the window and spoke a few words. Handed over some dollar bills.

"I'll take the front seat," she told Chapel and Bogdan. "The hotel isn't far."

Chapel climbed into the back. Once he was safely inside with the door closed, he shut his eyes.

TASHKENT, UZBEKISTAN: JULY 17, 06:10

Nadia woke him by stroking his cheek with the back of her hand. "Come on," she said. "Time to perform."

Chapel nodded, still groggy, and carefully levered himself out of the back of the car. The new jacket he'd bought in Istanbul reeked of cigarette smoke—the driver of the car must have chain-smoked all the way from the airport. He brushed himself down a little and looked up at the entrance to the hotel. It was a wide portico of giant concrete blocks, broken only by a pair of glass doors and a couple potted ferns that struggled vainly to make the place look less like a Soviet-era dormitory.

A couple of other cars were pulled up out front, their engines left idling as if for a quick getaway. At the end of the drive a bald man in a white button-down shirt was feeding some pigeons from a wax paper sack of breadcrumbs. He looked up when he saw them and started ambling over, shoving his hands in his pockets.

Chapel tried walking past the man, but he changed course so that Chapel would have had to walk right through him to get to the hotel doors.

Interesting.

Trouble, maybe.

"Hello," the man said. "Are you staying here tonight?" His English was accented but fluid, a second language but one he'd been speaking for years.

Nadia stood just behind Chapel and off to one side. As drowsy as he was, he could feel the way she moved, changing her posture the tiniest fraction of a degree, could hear the tiniest gasp of breath she took.

Something was up with this guy.

Chapel narrowed his eyes and gave the man a good once-over, looking to see if he had a weapon on him. He didn't see one, but he saw other things. He saw the waxy skin of the man's bald head, the carefully combed rectitude of his mustache. This was a man who was perfectly groomed at dawn—and not just so he could go feed some pigeons.

Chapel forced himself into character. He'd rehearsed his cover story for hours before leaving the States—now was the time when he needed it. Now that they were in Uzbekistan everything had to be done just so.

"Heard this was the only decent hotel in Tashkent," he said, adding a skeptical look.

The older man nodded agreeably. He didn't smile. Chapel couldn't help but think the man was just as in control of his expression as Chapel was, at that moment. They were both playing parts. Maybe they both knew it. "Oh, all our hotels are excellent. All up to American standards, I think you'll find."

"Uh-huh," Chapel said. "Good plumbing at this one?"

He'd thrown that out as a sort of halfhearted insult, mostly to see if he could get a rise out of the other man. It didn't work. "Oh, yes, yes. You'll be pleased."

Chapel gave the man a curt nod. "Thanks for the tip. You mind?"

The older man feigned a moment of incomprehension, then a slightly longer interval of embarrassment. "Oh, I'm in your way, please, my apologies." He stepped out of Chapel's path and gestured for Nadia to go in first. "Enjoy your time in Uzbekistan, Mr. Chambers."

Chapel turned to face the man, but he was already walking away. As he followed Nadia up the hotel steps, he asked under his breath, "What the hell was that about? And how did he know the name on my passport when we just got here?"

"SNB—the secret police," she whispered back. "They would have called him from the airport so he knew we were coming."

Chapel shook his head and walked in through the glass doors. The message was clear, he supposed. The Uzbek government knew where he was, and they would be watching him. Well, he'd never expected this job to be easy.

At the reception desk Nadia made all the arrangements. Chapel was posing as an executive of an energy conglomerate, looking to invest in natural gas deposits in Uzbekistan's interior. Nadia was supposed to be his personal assistant. Bogdan, who was supposed to be Jeff Chambers's tech guy, wandered around the lobby while Nadia asked about the various services their rooms provided.

Chapel leaned over the counter, interrupting her and staring at the pretty desk clerk. "Nice scarf," he told her.

She reached up and touched it. "Thank you, Mr. Chambers."

"Are our rooms ready? I don't want to hear anything about how they're still being made up. I know it's first thing in the morning. I start work this early, and I expect not to have to sit around waiting for other people to catch up."

The clerk's eyes widened a fraction of an inch, but she didn't flinch. Good for her. Chapel felt like a jerk but that was his cover, and he had to play it perfectly. "As per your request your rooms are available now. Would you like to hear about our spa and exercise rooms, or about our three excellent restaurants?"

"What I want to hear," Chapel told her, "is that I won't be disturbed while I'm here. Think you can handle that?"

"Of course—"

"That means no maid service. No turndown service. It especially means no visitors unless I clear them first. I don't want this to be a problem. I don't want to have to ask about this twice. So when I ask you in a few seconds if my instructions are clear, all I want you to do is say yes. Are my instructions clear?"

"Yes," the clerk said.

"Good girl." Chapel took a hundred-dollar bill from his pocket and laid it on the counter. The clerk just stared at it. "That's for not making me repeat myself."

He grabbed up the keycards the clerk had already laid on the counter and headed for the elevators. "Svetlana," he said, over his shoulder, "I want you ready with my schedule in twenty minutes."

"Of course, sir," Nadia said.

Chapel stepped into the elevator and waited for the doors to close. Only then did he let himself droop and feel tired again.

He'd been in Tashkent for less than an hour and already he could feel how things had changed. Bucharest and Istanbul had just been layovers. This was where the mission really began.

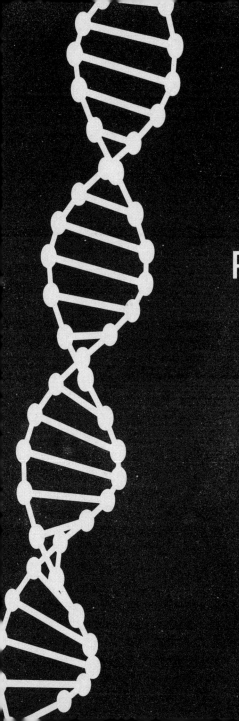

PART III

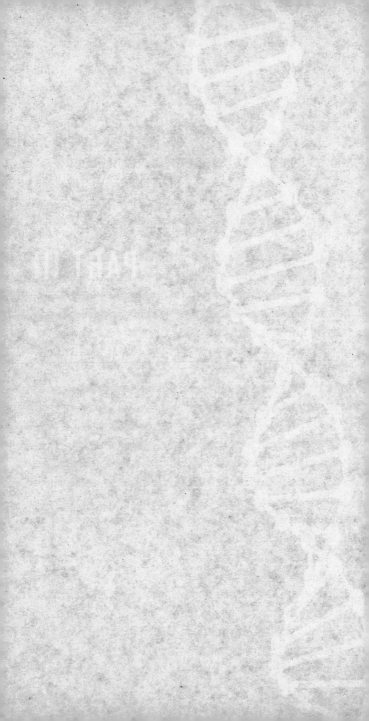

Marshal Konstantin Bulgachenko spent the last night of his life at an exceptionally tasteless party.

There had been many of those, since the fall of the Union. The Soviets had possessed, at least, a sense of decorum—a certain restraint. Oh, the members of the Politburo had had their sprawling dachas on the Black Sea, their Italian mistresses and their fine cars, but in public, in Moscow where the world was watching they had favored cheap suits and proletarian tastes in food, and if they smoked Cuban cigars, they did so behind closed doors.

Nowadays, of course, the world was turned upside down. The power elite of Moscow—the oil executives, the top-end gangsters, the political machinists—lived their lives in the newspapers, on the gossip sites, and their duty was to show their fellow Russians just what wonders and new pleasures capitalism had wrought. Excess had become patriotic, decadence a virtue.

So when one arrived at the door of this particular party in the suburbs of Moscow, one was handed a little spoon carved from bone. Inside the house where camera flashes exploded nonstop, half-naked models walked from room to room with bowls of beluga caviar nestled between their breasts, and they would coo and laugh as fat men dug into their bounty for a taste. In the middle of the house, in its spacious living room, a Japanese sports car had been parked, its tinted windows continuously steamed up from whatever was going on inside. Bulgachenko had not bothered to find out. He had come to the party to speak to one particular person, the American ambassador. Finding the man had taken hours as Bulgachenko was harangued by one notable citizen after another, carried off course by the enforced jollity. He was dragged into rooms where drugs were being ingested openly, where only profuse and eloquent excuses had gotten him free. He was spirited onto a dance floor by an heiress of less than twenty years who did not even know who he was, only that there were medals on his uniform and that he looked like her grandfather. He was ushered with a crooked finger into tense, quiet discussions with small and greasy men who wanted to know just what it would take to corrupt him, men who seemed to want to bribe him simply to prove that he was not above such things.

In the end he had found the ambassador on a back deck, out in the clear night air. The American was a long, thin man with a cloud of white hair on the top of his head. If he'd had a mustache, Bulgachenko thought he might look like the writer Mark Twain. He looked every bit as disgusted as Bulgachenko felt, but as soon as he realized he was not alone on the deck, his manner changed utterly. Like an actor stepping out into a spotlight he came alive, his arms unfolding, his face opening into a wide and benevolent grin.

The expression did not change when Bulgachenko

walked up to him and uttered a few simple words: "It was very warm inside, but out here the air is clear and refreshing." The words were chosen carefully, as banal as they sounded, and the message they conveyed was that while there had been difficulties, they had been taken care of, that Russia still had the highest confidence in the mission. The ambassador responded with a similar pleasantry, this one meaningless in itself: "I like to come out here and look at the lights." Had there been a problem the ambassador would have spoken about the weather.

With that it was done. Bulgachenko made his way back through the party with as much grace as he could muster and headed to his car, an inconspicuous black sedan. He stepped into the back and fastened his seat belt. "I am very tired," he told the driver. "Please take me home."

He must have accidentally inhaled some narcotic smoke, or perhaps simply the perfume of the young heiress had clouded his head—it had certainly been strong enough. It took him some time to realize that the driver of the car was not the usual man, and that he was not driving back toward Moscow, but farther out, into the country.

Even then Bulgachenko did not panic. Though the car was moving in excess of seventy kilometers an hour, still he tried to open his door and jump out. The door was, of course, locked and could not be opened. He had expected no less. He considered reaching over the front seat and strangling the driver, though this would likely end in death for both of them. Even if he did escape, though, he knew that he would simply be picked up at some later time, that he would only be delaying the inevitable. "Will you tell me where we are going, or who it is you work for?" Bulgachenko asked.

The driver did not answer.

They did not go far. Bulgachenko did not recognize the street or even the district of their destination, but that did not matter. The car pulled into a warehouse full of empty shelves and a rolling door was closed behind it. The door unlocked itself, and a man in a black suit reached in to help Bulgachenko out. The man in the black suit did not speak or salute. He simply took Bulgachenko's arm and led him deeper into the warehouse to where a chair sat in the middle of a stretch of open floor. Bulgachenko did not resist as he was forced to sit down, or as his hands and feet were tied to the chair.

No one had bothered to show him a gun, or even a knife. It was implicit that these things were available if they were necessary. There was no line of thugs waiting to catch him if he tried to run. That would have been superfluous—Bulgachenko was an old man, now, and it was clear to everyone involved he would not get far.

This was all very civilized, very formal. It had the stamp of the former KGB all over it. Bulgachenko found that he approved. This made him want to laugh but he resisted the urge.

"You understand," the man in the black suit said, "how this is done. You show no sign of panic. You did not scream for help. You did not attempt to overpower me."

"You sound almost disappointed," Bulgachenko said.

The man in the black suit shrugged. "These

things are easier when the subject is afraid. Fear loosens the tongue."

"So you wish me to talk," Bulgachenko said. "If it will spare me pain, I will tell you what you want to know. I understand how torture is done, yes, and I know it is pointless to resist. But you want me to be afraid? No, I am sorry, I cannot help. I was a child in Stalingrad when the Nazis came. I ate the leather soles of my shoes, even though I knew I would get frostbite and lose some of my toes. Later I lived through the purges of Stalin and the blustering of his heirs and the chaos of the second revolution." Bulgachenko smiled. "I have had a lifetime of fear. I have used up my entire stock of it."

The man in the black suit nodded. "My name is Pavel Kalin."

"That means nothing to me," Bulgachenko said. "Who do you work for?"

"That is not important. Please answer my questions. Where is your agent? Where is Asimova?"

"In Bucharest," Bulgachenko said.

Kalin shook his head. "She left there some time ago. Where is she now? Where is she headed?"

Bulgachenko closed his eyes. If he could have protected poor Nadia, he would have. But there was nothing he could do. This man would get his answer one way or another. Dear, sweet Nadia. "Tashkent," he said.

"Thank you," Kalin told him. "I believe you are telling me the truth."

"Will you release me now? I am the head of FSTEK, as I am sure you know. If I do not return home soon, there will be questions asked."

Kalin gave him a sad smile. "You were replaced in that position at midnight, by governmental decree. Your voluntary retirement papers have already been filed."

"Ah," Bulgachenko said.

Perhaps he had some small supply of fear left in him, after all.

"You understand. You understand how these things work." Kalin sighed deeply. "You do not fight. You comply with my requests, answer my questions. This is a problem in itself. Information come by this easily cannot be trusted. I'm sure you understand this as well." He reached into his jacket pocket and brought something out.

A pair of rusty pliers.

"I apologize, Marshal," the man in the black suit said. "You are a hero of our country. You deserve better than this. But sometimes even heroes lie."

TASHKENT, UZBEKISTAN: JULY 17, 09:42

Chapel woke to the sensation of something poking him in the back, and to a weird unearthly sound, an electronic warbling that rose and fell and occasionally squealed.

He opened his eyes.

He was lying on a bed in a spacious, quite comfortable hotel room. They had taken the largest of the hotel's available suites, one with three bedrooms and a common area as well as a wide balcony that looked out over the center of Tashkent. The rooms were, in fact, quite nice, maybe even better and cleaner than

Chapel's apartment back in Brooklyn. Certainly larger. For a thousand dollars a night it looked like you could find real luxury in Uzbekistan.

Chapel had paid little attention to the rooms once he found a bed. He'd dropped into it without so much as taking his shoes off and fallen asleep instantly.

That explained the pain in his back. He hadn't taken off his artificial arm. The clamps that held it on his shoulder weren't designed to be laid on for very long.

He rolled over on his side and found Nadia standing by the bed. She had changed into a simple sleeveless dress, and she held something about the size of a cigarette lighter with a collapsible antenna mounted on one end. She waved it over the telephone on the bedside table, and it squealed in distress.

She placed one finger across her lips to tell him to stay quiet. She switched off the bug sensor and put it down, then unscrewed the mouthpiece of the telephone. With her fingernails she pried out a tiny circuit board with a microphone mounted on it. She snapped the listening device in half.

"That's the last of them," she said. She jumped onto the bed and sat down next to him, her legs tucked up underneath her. "Good morning, again," she told him. "You played your part very well downstairs."

"I've met enough rich assholes in my life to fake it," he said. He wanted to sit up—felt that would be more appropriate—but he was still tired. "How many bugs did you find?"

"Five. One in each room, including the bathroom, and this one in your phone."

"That seems like a lot," Chapel said, frowning. "You think they doubled up because they knew we were coming?"

"No, I think they just know that anyone staying in these rooms is someone they're going to want to listen to," she told him. She shrugged. "Uzbekistan. It's about as close as you can get these days to how things used to be under the Soviets. There is no conception of civil rights in this country."

Chapel closed his eyes for a second. He tried to force himself to sit up. It didn't quite work. "What will happen when they realize we've deactivated their bugs?" he asked.

"Nothing," she said.

He opened his eyes again to look at her. She had shifted closer to him, until her knees were almost touching him.

She shrugged. "If they said something, that would be admitting there were microphones here in the first place, and they don't want to do that. This is just part of doing business in this part of the world. They try to listen to us. We sweep for their bugs. One reason to have so many is that they hope I will miss one." She smiled. "I didn't. But tomorrow when we are out, they will plant some more, and I'll have to sweep again." She wriggled a little closer, until her knees touched his leg.

Chapel tried to focus. It was hard, with her so close. "How long are we here? How many days, I mean?"

"I will schedule a meeting with my contact here today. This afternoon, most likely, we'll make the arrangements. Then we can head out into the desert, once we have vehicles, equipment, supplies," she said, and put one hand on his arm. His artificial arm. Most people, when they touched it, felt that it was colder than it should be, or they sensed that the skin didn't feel like real human skin. Most people pulled their hand away. They flinched. Not Nadia.

"I should get up," he said. "We have things to do."

"Hmm," she said. Gently she stroked his arm, up and down.

Wrong. So wrong. Not like this, not now—not with Nadia. Not when Julia—

She shifted again, releasing his arm, and he thought he must have misread the signals. Read something into what was happening that wasn't there. She was just curling up on the bed with him—she must be as tired as he was.

She sat up, still very close to him. Looked down into his face. Gave him a tentative little smile. Her mouth a question. He could feel the air prickle between them, feel the hair on his real arm stand on end. He couldn't move, paralyzed by not knowing what was happening here, what was going to happen.

She leaned in close and brushed his lips with hers, just the tiniest suggestion of a kiss. Her lips were so soft, so delicate, barely grazing his own. He could reach up, put an arm around her shoulders, pull her in close . . .

"Wait," he said.

It took all his energy, all his strength to say it, but he managed.

"We can't," he told her.

She slapped the bedcovers beside his head. Then she lowered her forehead to touch his. She was almost on top of him and he felt like if she grabbed his shoulders and pushed him back on the bed, if she straddled him right then and there, he would not be able to resist, he would just have to give in. She was so close. He could just grab her hips, he could—

"*Konyechno*. Of course we can't," she said. She roared in frustration and pulled away. Jumped off the bed and headed for the door to the common room. Her hand hesitated, though, when it touched the knob. "We can't?" she asked, her back to him.

It wasn't too late. One word and she would turn around, come back to the bed, and—

"We can't," he told her.

She opened the door and stepped through. Closed it behind her with a click.

TASHKENT, UZBEKISTAN: JULY 17, 13:17

By lunchtime it was ninety degrees outside. In a shady restaurant at the ground level of the hotel, the three of them ate some *plov*, a local dish of rice and mutton. Chapel didn't have much of an appetite—he mostly just picked at a piece of bread and drank some water. He couldn't meet Nadia's eye throughout the meal. He assumed that the waitstaff would be listening to their conversation, so he kept talking to the bare minimum.

Bogdan ate two plates of rice and asked for more, but Nadia cut him off. "Don't get over full," she told him. "There will be a lot of walking today, in the heat."

The hacker's face fell like a petulant child's. He'd been pouting all morning since he found out there was free Wi-Fi in their suite but he wasn't allowed to use it. "You hire me for computer stuff," he said, "and I cannot so much as check e-mail? Now I cannot eat what I like? Very well, *Mother*."

Nadia laughed and tried to catch Chapel's eye, but he just turned his face away.

When they were done, they headed out into the streets. Their meeting with Nadia's local connection wasn't scheduled for another hour, but she felt they needed the time to shake anyone who might be following them.

"You make anybody?" Chapel asked, as they headed through a strip of parkland. Sprinklers were running nonstop to keep the grass green.

"I don't understand," Nadia said.

Chapel shook his head. Her English was fluent enough that he sometimes forgot she wouldn't know every obscure American idiom. "I mean, did you actually see anyone follow us from the hotel?"

"No," she told him. "Which simply means they're good at it."

"You think we're in danger? I was told the Uzbek government hates Americans."

Nadia sighed and lifted her hands in exasperation. "I think, right now, the secret police are following you—for protection. Yes, they hate Americans, because they're always asking so many uncomfortable questions. About human rights, about the way the government shells its own people out in the countryside. But they love American money. This is a country desperately in need of funds for development. So you—the American plutocrat—they will do anything to keep safe."

"That's good to know," Chapel said.

"Don't allow yourself to get complacent. Let me tell you a story. The president of this country has a nephew, a journalist. About ten years ago he disappeared off the street with no explanation. When your Hillary Clinton came here in 2011, she demanded to see him. He was produced and claimed it was all a misunderstanding, that he had been treated well. But a doctor examined him and saw that he had been starved and kept on psychotropic drugs for years at a time."

"Jesus," Chapel said. "At least we got him released."

That elicited a bitter laugh from Nadia. "A few months after Hillary Clinton left, this journalist called up a friend of his and said he planned on writing a book about his uncle, the president. Even before he finished the phone call, the line went dead and he has not been seen since."

Despite the heat of the day, Chapel felt a chill run down his spine.

"That was the nephew of the president," Nadia pointed out. "A close family member. If your cover is blown while we're here, well . . . imagine what they will do to a foreign spy?"

Chapel gave that some time to sink in. Her story was hard to bring into concordance with what he was seeing with his own eyes. Tashkent as seen from the sidewalks didn't look much like the totalitarian hellhole she made it out to be. The streets were clean and full of cars and trucks and people going about their business. Stores were open and well stocked, full of customers, while the park was crowded with people out enjoying the sun. Every sign in every shop window was printed in two alphabets—Cyrillic and the Latin characters he was used to. "What I see here, though—it looks more like Montreal than Kabul."

"You'd see it if you spent more time here, actually talking to the locals," she told him, keeping her voice low but not whispering—whispering might seem suspicious. "You'd realize that no one here talks about politics. Ever. If you were to ask them about human rights abuses, about the way the government massacres its own people out in the countryside, they would run away from you as if you had started coughing up blood. Politics is never a safe topic in Tashkent, and everything is political. In 2009, the president decided to chop down some historic trees here. Trees the city was famous for. To this day no one knows why he did it. If they asked, they were taken away. This—for trees."

They headed down a crowded shopping street, clearly one of the main thoroughfares of the city. A tourist information kiosk stood on one corner, with a very bored-looking middle-aged women stationed inside. She fanned herself casually, as if she were too bored to even keep cool. On the opposite side of the street was a shop that rented bicycles and mopeds for daily use. Out on the sidewalk were a small number of street vendors. They had hookah pipes and leather-bound books laid out on threadbare blankets, and their eyes moved around constantly. Maybe sizing up potential customers—or maybe keeping an eye out for something else.

"We need to lose our followers," Nadia said. "My contact will not wish to be seen speaking with us."

"It would help if we knew who our followers were," Chapel pointed out. Then he saw something and had an idea. He walked away from Nadia and Bogdan and stooped down over one of the blankets, one selling sticks and cones of incense. The man who ran this impromptu store was wearing a pakol, the traditional soft round hat of an Afghan. Unlike most of the men Chapel had seen in Tashkent, he had a long, thick beard. "*Aya ta pa pashto khabarey kawalai shey?*" he said, asking if the man spoke Pashto.

The man looked up, surprised, and raised his hands in joy. "God is great!" he answered, in that language. "And full of surprises. A white man who speaks my language, and I am sure, has money to buy my wares, yes?"

Chapel got the point. A shared tongue wasn't going to get him anything for free. "You're from Afghanistan?" he asked. Not entirely surprising—Uzbekistan shared a border with Afghanistan, and the Taliban had driven a lot of refugees out of their country with nothing but what they could carry on their backs.

"I have the honor of being born in Waziristan, yes," the vendor replied.

Chapel nodded. Waziristan was where he lost his arm, but he didn't think it would help his case to mention that. "I imagine the local police are no friends of yours," he said, trying hard to remember the correct grammar. "I'm being followed right now."

"Sir, this is Tashkent, and we are foreigners both.

We are all being followed. At night, I think they follow me through my dreams."

Chapel picked up an ornate brass incense burner, the most expensive-looking thing on the blanket, and set it down in front of the man. It would probably fetch five dollars back on Canal Street in New York. He took seven twenty-dollar bills from his wallet, keeping them carefully folded, and used them to tap the incense burner. "Would you be so kind as to point out to me all the . . . special police on this street?" He couldn't remember the word for "secret." He knew the word for "security forces," but that meant something very different in Afghanistan.

A few seconds later, a hundred and forty dollars lighter, and a little bit wiser, Chapel walked back over to Nadia. "Okay," he said. "I've got a plan."

TASHKENT, UZBEKISTAN: JULY 17, 13:38

Nadia and Bogdan headed across the street, into the bicycle rental shop, while Chapel worked his way down the sidewalk, bending low to speak to each of the street vendors. It didn't matter what he said to them, which was good since he didn't share any languages with most of them. Only one spoke English—a teenage boy who looked more Asian than any of the others Chapel met.

"I'm from Russia originally, I mean, my grandparents were Russian," the kid said, shrugging. "Before that, they were Korean. Stalin moved people all over, back in the 1930s, and this is where we ended up."

Chapel nodded. "How did you learn English?" he asked.

The kid shrugged. "Watching your American movies, mostly. And talking to tourists like you. You going to buy something, or were you just so surprised to see a Korean sitting here you needed to ask?"

Chapel looked down at the wares the kid had on offer, a collection of bootleg videos on cheap DVDs. He didn't really register any of the titles—he just pretended to study them while he actually watched what was going on at the far corner of the street. The Afghan merchant he'd paid off was rising from his blanket, speaking to the vendors on either side of him—most likely asking them to watch his stuff. One of them nodded distractedly, and that seemed to be good enough.

The Afghan strolled across the street toward a man who was sitting on a bench there, pretending to read a newspaper. The Afghan had identified this man as one of the three secret policemen working the street. The other two were sitting in a car parked about twenty yards away. Chapel was surprised he hadn't spotted them himself—one of the men in the car was the SNB man with the shaved head who had greeted him when he arrived at the hotel.

Chapel sifted through the bootleg DVDs on the Korean boy's blanket, trying very hard not to show how intently he was watching events unfold. The Afghan sat down on the bench next to the secret policeman and rested one arm on the back of the bench. He spoke a few words, seemingly to himself. Then the secret policeman folded up his newspaper and got up and walked away. After a second the Afghan followed him.

All according to plan. Chapel had paid the Afghan to say he had information on a suspicious American tourist, but he wanted money for it. The two of them headed into the back of the information kiosk, presumably to discuss terms. That would take them a few minutes.

The trickiest part about shaking this tail was going to be convincing the SNB that Chapel, Nadia, and Bogdan were just minding their business, and that they had no intention of evading pursuit. This had to look like it all just happened naturally.

Chapel took a few small bills from his pocket and handed them to the Korean kid. "I've seen all these, but thanks for the conversation," he said. Then he moved down to the next blanket, one that sat just outside of the bicycle rental shop.

Just as he'd hoped, Nadia had come through on her end. She and Bogdan came rolling out of the alley that ran alongside the shop, each of them riding a motor scooter. Bogdan climbed off his and onto the back of Nadia's vehicle, leaving one idling on the sidewalk. Chapel risked a quick glance at the two secret policemen in the car. As expected they were watching him closely. The one he didn't recognize was holding a camera.

Nothing to be done about that—this wasn't like in Istanbul where he could get to that camera and erase his presence. He wondered if that had been part of Nadia's plan all along, to have their presence in Uzbekistan documented by the secret police. Then when they entered Kazakhstan, there would be a trail showing they had not entered through Russia, limiting the Russian government's culpability.

Nothing he could do about that, either. He swung a leg over the idling scooter. The brand name—Vyatka—was emblazoned on its front shield. It was an attractive bottle green color, but that was about all it had going for it. Much of its rear end was held together with patches, and its engine puttered away beneath him with less power than a riding lawn mower. He estimated the thing would have a top speed of about thirty miles an hour, even less than that going uphill.

Still, scooters had their advantages.

"You okay with this?" he asked Nadia.

She strapped a helmet over her black hair and gave him a vampish look from beneath its brim. "Your concern is touching, but I had one of these when I was a teenager." She handed a helmet back to Bogdan, who fussed and fumbled with the straps. She glanced back, and the look of terror on Bogdan's face made her laugh. "Don't worry about me," she said. "Did you ever drive one before?"

"Motorcycles and bicycles, yes. Nothing halfway in between like this. But I'll be fine," Chapel said. Then he hit the throttle and roared out into the street. The engine made a nasty sound as it changed gears, but it didn't die on him as he'd feared it might. He kept accelerating as he drove right past the parked SNB car. Much as he'd expected, as he passed he heard its much more powerful engine kick into life, and in his mirrors he saw it pull away from the curb.

The chase was on.

TASHKENT, UZBEKISTAN: JULY 17, 13:42

They headed down the wide tourist street, Nadia and Bogdan keeping close to Chapel's tail. He pushed his scooter for all the speed he could get, but the SNB car had no trouble keeping up. There was plenty of room for the car to maneuver on the street, even when Chapel used the scooter's small size to wind his way between the other cars. A few drivers shook their fists or shouted at him, but he couldn't understand what they were saying so he ignored them.

The street went on for many blocks. Chapel dropped back a hair until he was riding alongside Nadia. "Left or right up ahead?" he shouted over the mosquito whine of the scooter engines. "We need to get somewhere more crowded."

"Left," she told him, and gunned her scooter forward. She took the turn without slowing down, leaning deep into the curve. Chapel nearly overshot the side street but managed to follow her by jumping up on an empty sidewalk for a second.

Behind them the SNB car made the turn effortlessly. The man with the shaved head was driving and he always stayed a few car lengths back, not so far that Chapel lost sight of him but not so close as to make it blatant that they were being followed.

The side street was almost empty of traffic. There were no stores on this block, just blind doorways that gave no sense of what lay beyond. No pedestrians on the sidewalks, either, which made Chapel uneasy. He had no idea why Nadia had taken this turn—until, without warning, she ducked up a long alleyway to the right. Chapel nearly lost control of his scooter as he spun around to keep up with her, but he kicked off the pavement with one foot and righted himself again.

The alleyway sloped downhill toward a busy street beyond. Clotheslines hung like drab bunting overhead, and windows high on the buildings were propped open to catch any breeze. The alley was just wide enough for the SNB car to follow them, though the driver scraped off half his paint job on a Dumpster at the back of one building. He didn't seem to care—in Chapel's mirrors he could see the man with the shaved head in the driver's seat, and he didn't even look over to see what all the noise was.

This guy was determined, Chapel had to give him that. He wasn't going to let them get away with a little trick driving.

At the end of the alleyway Nadia waved to the right, as if she was going to turn that way. Chapel wondered why she would throw such an obvious signal—then grinned to himself as she shot forward between two cars and into an identical alleyway across the busy street. Her signal had just been a feint. Chapel had to twist around and lean away from an oncoming car as he bounced and rolled across the main street, but he managed to shoot into the second alleyway without crashing. Nadia glanced back over her shoulder at him, smiling. Bogdan looked like he might start screaming at any moment, his eyes rolling under their fringe of hair. He had one arm tight around Nadia's waist, hanging on, while with his other hand he tapped at the keys of his MP3 player. The hacker was crazy, Chapel thought—if he was that scared, why not use both arms to hold on? The key clacking seemed to comfort him, though, like an infant with a security blanket.

Chapel glanced back and saw the SNB car slowly threading its way into traffic in the street behind him. They were gaining significant ground on the car, not least because the downward-sloping alleyways helped their struggling engines.

Up ahead of them the alleyway descended toward a parking garage. Chapel could see flickering sunlight through the open structure. He rushed forward to catch up with Nadia, then pointed at the garage. She nodded back so he took the lead again, using his forward momentum to carry him up a ramp and through the structure, the wind making chopping noises on either side as he flashed past a long rank of parked cars. A second ramp continued up into the higher stories of the garage, but Chapel didn't want to go that way—there would be no way down from up there and he would be trapping himself. Instead he looked for and found an exit from the structure on its far side. A low wall prevented cars from just driving straight through, but there was a gap in that wall for pedestrians who wanted to get to their parking spots. There wasn't a lot of clearance but Chapel threaded the needle and shot through to the other side, just as a car was coming into the garage. The car's horn blared and someone shouted a warning, but Chapel just twisted around and shot past the side of the car, out into a wide street beyond.

Nadia was right on his tail as he blasted through an intersection and slipped between two lanes of traffic. Up ahead he saw that the road opened into a broad plaza with the huge curved wall of a stadium filling up half the sky down there. Traffic swirled around the stadium in a vast gyre, the cars inching forward against gridlock.

Chapel cut some of his speed and let Nadia catch up to him so they could talk again. "Did we lose them?" he asked.

"We must have," she said, as they joined up with the barely moving traffic circle. "There was no way he could get through there."

Chapel nodded and studied the cars around him. The drivers were all staring at them, but that couldn't be helped. An American and a woman who looked like Nadia riding scooters were bound to attract attention in Tashkent.

"So who's this contact we're meeting with?" Chapel asked, as they crept forward, around the circle. They were moving so slowly they had to put their feet down so their scooters didn't fall over. It gave them a chance to talk, though Chapel would have preferred to keep moving—he never liked feeling trapped, even in gridlock.

"She's trustworthy. I know that's what you're asking. At least," Nadia called over to him, over the traffic noise, "we can trust her not to betray us to the SNB."

"That's a big 'at least,'" Chapel said.

Nadia shrugged. "We need certain things for our trip into the desert. Only one person in Tashkent can get us what we need. Therefore, we must trust her. She's a *vory*. You know what that means?"

Chapel grimaced. "Russian mafia."

"The word means 'thief-in-law,' a lawful thief," Nadia told him. "One who follows the thief's code."

"A criminal. Every criminal I ever met followed the same code—do what benefits them, and everyone else can go to hell."

Nadia laughed. "You in the West, you will never understand. The *mafiya*—the gangs—do you know where they came from? The gulags. They were born in Stalin's prison camps. They hate nothing so much as central government. The irony is, they have come to be so powerful, in Moscow and St. Petersburg, they are a kind of government in themselves. The *vory*—"

"Car," Bogdan said.

Chapel stared at the hacker. "Yes, Bogdan, there are lots of cars here," he said.

The Romanian shook his head. "That car," he said, and pointed with one very long finger.

Chapel looked where Bogdan had indicated. "Shit," he said.

It was the car that had been following them, the one carrying the two SNB men, and it had just merged into the traffic circle, about ten cars behind them. Chapel was certain it was the same car because all the paint was scraped off its front quarter panel.

"This guy's persistent," Chapel said.

"Perhaps we should split up," Nadia said. "I can go to the meeting with my *vory*. You can lead these men away, get them off my tail."

Chapel thought of when she'd suggested something similar in Bucharest—when she'd said she could go collect Bogdan on her own. "You asked for a *svidetel*. A witness," he told her. "We go together or not at all."

"All right," Nadia said. She scanned the road ahead. "Up there, do you see? A little street, one where we can—"

She stopped speaking without warning, and Chapel wondered what was going on until, a half second or so later, he heard the sirens.

Coming up the street she'd indicated, their nearest escape route, was a police car with flashing lights.

Chapel had no doubts that it was coming for them.

TASHKENT, UZBEKISTAN: JULY 17, 13:51

"Can they arrest us for shaking our tail?" Chapel asked.

"Not for that, no," Nadia said. "At least—they shouldn't. This is supposed to be a game we play, there are supposed to be informal rules . . . but if they have some other excuse, if we broke traffic laws, even—"

"In other words, if we let that police car pull us over, we're dead," Chapel said. Once they were in an Uzbek police station, it wouldn't take long at all for their cover story to fall apart. And once the authorities knew they were using false identities, it would not be a huge jump to assume they were foreign spies.

Chapel craned his neck around, looking in every direction. The traffic was packed tightly around them. They might thread their way around the cars on their scooters, they might reach another side street with no police car on it, but it would take time, and they needed to move now.

Of course, there was another option. "Nadia," he said. "Follow my lead, okay?"

He didn't wait for confirmation. He twisted his handlebars around and curved around the front of the car on his right, wincing as the driver sounded his horn right in Chapel's ear. He ignored the noise and gunned his throttle, sending his scooter shooting at right angles to the road. There was a nasty bump as he jumped over the curb and up onto the sidewalk beyond. Before him raised the long curved wall of the stadium, set back from the road by a broad plaza where people were lounging on benches and soaking up the sun. The plaza was lined with rough bricks that made his scooter vibrate alarmingly, but Chapel just tightened his grip on his handlebars and opened his throttle as wide as it would go.

Ahead of him pedestrians screamed and jumped out of his way. The scooter had a pathetic little horn that made a weak tooting sound every time he slapped it. He made liberal use of it anyway as he roared across the plaza. In his mirrors he saw Nadia behind him, Bogdan's face pressed down into her neck.

Up ahead, a flight of broad stairs led down toward the main gates of the stadium. Chapel took them at speed, bouncing up and down on his seat, the bones of his skull feeling like they were scraping against each other every time the scooter dropped onto a new step.

The gates ahead were closed, but a walkway led around the curve of the stadium, down at the bottom of the stairs. He leaned to one side and shot by the gates, headed roughly back the way they'd come. There were fewer people down there on the walkway, but there was less room to maneuver, too—Chapel was frankly terrified he was about to run down somebody's decrepit grandmother inching her way along with a walker. Luckily the few people he might have hit were able to scurry out of his way.

On the far side of the stadium was another set of stairs, leading up toward sunlight and another traffic-packed street. Chapel steered up those steps and heard his little engine whine and his wheels squeak as they tried to gain purchase on the upward grade. For a second it looked like the scooter just wouldn't have enough power to get up those steps, but then his front wheel found traction and launched him upward, barely faster than he could have climbed the steps on foot, but it worked.

At the top of the steps was another plaza, not quite as wide as the first one. He zoomed across it, barely aware of the people there, and into the traffic on the far side. More horns, more angry drivers, but in a second he was across the street and headed into an alleyway.

Nadia came up beside him and gestured for him to turn left at the end of the alley. Together they burst out into a street that was nearly empty, a narrow canyon between two blocks of apartment buildings. The fronts of the buildings were painted in rainbow colors, stripes of red and orange and blue that disoriented him for a second. He dropped back and followed Nadia as she headed toward an intersection ahead.

Even before they got there, Chapel heard sirens closing in.

Damn. He'd really thought his little stunt was going to get them free of the pursuit. At least they'd left the SNB car behind.

Maybe there was no other way than to split up. Maybe he should try to lead the police away, let Nadia escape and get to her meeting. Of course, on his own he wouldn't be able to resist the police if they caught him. He could be signing his own death warrant if he split off. Still, the mission was important enough—

Up ahead a traffic light had just turned green and the few cars on the street were surging forward. Nadia, however, pulled up to the intersection and stopped, putting her feet down to stabilize her scooter.

Chapel looked back and saw a police car turn into the block behind them. Its lights flashed across the multicolored apartment blocks, making them shimmer with light.

"What are you doing?" Chapel asked.

Nadia took a deep breath. "Be ready," she said.

Bogdan tapped wildly at his MP3 player, working its controls like they were piano keys.

Behind them the police car was maybe fifty yards behind, and gaining.

"What do you—" Chapel began. He didn't have time to finish his question.

Nadia gunned her throttle and shot forward.

Chapel raced after her. The police car was still accelerating, closing the gap behind them. Then the traffic light changed to red.

It was too soon. The light had just changed to green a few seconds ago. The drivers in the busy cross-street accepted it much faster than Chapel did, however. Even before he'd cleared the intersection, they started nosing forward, filling the space behind him with a wall of metal.

The police car didn't have a chance to stop in time. Chapel heard a terrible crunch of metal smashing into metal. Behind him he heard the police car's siren wail in a much higher pitch for a moment, then fall silent abruptly.

Nadia laughed as she sailed down the nearly empty street beyond the intersection. She turned right into the forecourt of an apartment complex, a little space where the residents stored their bicycles and their trash cans. She stopped, pried Bogdan's arm off her waist, then jumped off her scooter. She was taking off her helmet when Chapel reached her a second later.

"Nice timing," he told her. *A little too nice*, he thought.

"Come," she said. "From here we can go on foot. It's not far to the meeting place."

TASHKENT, UZBEKISTAN: JULY 17, 14:06

The three of them hurried through the streets on foot, stopping now and again to duck into the shadowy vestibule of an apartment building and listen for the sounds of pursuit. They heard no more sirens, saw no more obvious SNB agents. It looked like they'd finally lost their shadows.

The sun was high overhead and it prickled the back of Chapel's neck as they walked out into a broad, open area where the light glared off spotlessly clean concrete. Only a few trees stuck up around the broad plaza to offer any shade. Ahead of them stood a building Chapel immediately assumed was a mosque. It was made of concrete slabs piled up around a massive gothic arch, and at each corner of the building stood a tall, tapering column with a turquoise dome at its top. As he got closer he realized those weren't minarets. The columns looked more like missiles with festively painted warheads.

"Rockets," Nadia explained, when he asked what the columns were. "At least, they are supposed to resemble rockets."

They were far more elaborately decorated than any rocket Chapel had ever seen. But as he got closer he supposed he could see what she meant. The building, it turned out, was just a very ostentatious subway entrance, the main portal into the Kosmonavtlar Station.

They headed down a broad flight of steps into a cool, slightly dim hallway. The pseudo-arabesque exterior gave way to a space-age interior that was no less ornate. The columns that held up the ceiling were a glittering black, while the walls were striped in an elegant blue, more intense near the bottom, fading nearly to white at the top. Set into the walls were round bas-reliefs depicting men in space suits surrounded by swirling stars and planets. Each of them wore the same dead-eyed, resolute expression, except one—Yuri Gagarin, who wore a wide, mischievous grin. Chapel thought back, trying to remember a photo of Gagarin where he wasn't showing that same toothy smile. He couldn't think of one.

Beneath them, under the floor, trains rumbled and sighed and hissed. The station was busy with commuters, people walking quickly in one direction or another, totally ignoring the opulent surroundings.

Chapel couldn't help himself. Despite the danger they were in, despite the nature of the meeting that lay ahead of them, he drank in the bas-reliefs and the wide murals showing the history of space flight, from the earliest astronomers with their clunky telescopes to space stations orbiting the earth.

"You have an interest in cosmonautics?" Nadia asked.

Chapel nodded his head. "When I was a kid, I wanted to be an astronaut when I grew up. I thought about it a lot. Dreamed about it, I guess. What about you?"

Nadia's smile was a trace bittersweet. "I did not want to be a cosmonaut." She tilted her head to one side and reached out to touch Gagarin's sculpted cheek. "I knew I would be one." She looked over at Chapel. "Every day in our classes, we would be reminded. The Union of Soviet Socialist Republics was at the forefront of space science. We were taught that all our futures lay up there, in the cosmos. That we would live on space stations as big as cities and get all our power from the sun. That we would fly to Mars before the millennium was out."

She dropped her hand. "Then the Cold War ended. And somehow, it was no longer our destiny. Oh, we were still the best with our rockets and our space stations. But now it's all about making money, selling space on our rockets to other countries. Funny, is it not? How politics can do that, turn destiny into commerce into . . . nothing."

"I wouldn't exactly call it funny," Chapel said.

Nadia shook her head sadly. Then she turned away and headed down another flight of stairs toward a platform. A train was coming in, but she held back until it had disgorged its passengers and left the station again. When the platform emptied out, she led Chapel and Bogdan to its far end, where the station gave way to a dark tunnel. She looked around for any sign they were being watched, then jumped down to the level of the tracks.

Chapel nodded at a camera mounted on the ceiling.

"No worries," she said. "It's broken."

"How can you tell?"

"Because," she said, "my *vory* friend pays to keep it broken. Come on."

She headed into the almost perfect darkness of the tunnel, hugging the wall away from the electrified rail. Chapel and Bogdan followed, keeping close together.

TASHKENT, UZBEKISTAN: JULY 17, 14:21

The tunnel stretched on ahead of them for miles, perhaps, though it was hard to judge distances in the nearly perfect dark. They trudged along in darkness broken only by too-infrequent lamps, some of which flickered so much their light was worse than nothing. It was all Chapel could do to keep from tripping and breaking his leg.

At one point a train came through. There were shallow alcoves built into the tunnel wall, no more than twelve inches deep. As the air pushed a great belly of wind ahead of it, ruffling their clothing, they had to press themselves back into these narrow holes. The train came so close Chapel thought it would crush him, so fast he was sure its speed alone would tear him out of his hiding place and pull him along with it. He could look in through its windows, see all the people perched on its seats, none of them looking up at him. In a few seconds the train had moved on and he could breathe again.

After another ten minutes of marching through the gloom, they saw a little more light appear ahead. As they drew closer Chapel could see it came from a pair of spotlights mounted on the tunnel ceiling. His eyes had adapted to the darkness, and now they stung when he looked at the harsh bulbs. It was impossible to see anything beyond that glare, and so he was completely surprised when someone shouted out a curt order.

He understood the tone, if not the words. He was being told to halt. Presumably by someone well-enough armed to enforce the command.

He stopped where he was and held his hands out away from his body.

Nadia, on the other hand, gave the unseen voice a

wave. *"Smert' suki!"* she called out, presumably supplying a password.

One of the spotlights swiveled away from them. Chapel blinked away afterimages and saw that up ahead a hole had been blasted in the wall of the tunnel, a ragged portal with edges of broken brick. Beyond was a much softer light, yellow and warm. A man with a rifle—Chapel could only see him in silhouette—stood in that entrance, waving them onward.

The three of them passed through the broken entrance and into a wide, dusty room that looked like the cellar of someone's house. At least, it looked like the cellar of the house of a black marketeer.

The walls were lined with shelves full of cartons of cigarettes and gallon bottles of vodka. At the far end of the room stood a workbench over which hung a row of tools up on pegs. There was a red stain on the workbench that Chapel did not want to investigate. He told himself it was just old paint.

There were two other people in the room, beyond the sentinel who had ushered them in. One was a young man, maybe even younger than Bogdan, in a maroon tracksuit. He held a ridiculously large pistol in each hand. He kept his weapons pointed at the floor.

The other inhabitant of the room was a woman who was maybe ten years older than Chapel. She wore a turtleneck sweater, and despite the years written on her face, her hair was black and silky and formed a great mane around her head and fell nearly to her waist. She wore a necklace with a seagull pendant, and when she saw Nadia, she came running over to kiss her on both cheeks. The two of them spoke for some time in a language that sounded mostly like Russian, though Chapel didn't understand much of the vocabulary. He knew that Russian prison inmates had created their own language, a kind of patois of code words and slang called Fenya—handy for making deals around people who weren't in the loop.

When they were done, they both turned to look at Chapel. "Jim," Nadia said, "meet Varvara. She's an old friend and she's going to help us out."

Chapel held out his hand and the woman shook it.

"Traditionally," Varvara said, her English deeply accented but fluent, "in my country when we welcome someone, we offer them bread and salt. I am afraid unless you wish to smoke or drink, I cannot be so courteous."

Chapel smiled, though he wasn't sure how much he liked this. He wasn't thrilled that Nadia had used his real name, not the Jeff Chambers alias—even if they were all sticking to first names. "Thank you for meeting with us," he said. "Your country, you say— so you're not an Uzbek. You're Russian."

Varvara peered at him through hooded eyes. "An observant man," she said. "People who pay attention can be dangerous."

"Only if they're enemies," Chapel told her. He glanced around at the shelves, then back at the hole in the wall. "This is an ingenious setup you have here."

"Oh?" Varvara asked.

Chapel nodded. "This location—totally hidden, but surprisingly convenient. You pay the train conductors to stop in the middle of the tunnel, just outside your warehouse, probably late at night when the trains are mostly empty. You load your contraband onto the subway trains and they can take your goods anywhere in the city, without the police seeing anything."

Varvara's eyes narrowed. She reached up and touched her seagull pendant. "You are perhaps thinking of informing the police of my operation?"

From the corner of his eye Chapel could see Nadia stiffen, just a little. This wasn't how she had expected this meeting to go.

He ignored her. "Why would I do that? I have no interest in helping such a repressive regime. And I need your friendship if our own plans are going to move forward."

Varvara nodded. "You're just expressing . . . admiration for my resourcefulness, then?"

"Sure. Anyway, even if I wanted to inform on you, I'm sure you could brick this wall back up in an hour, move the goods out of this cellar in even less time. Then you just break through another cellar wall, somewhere else in the city, and resume your operation after only a minor delay."

Varvara went over to the workbench and opened a low cabinet. Chapel was suddenly very aware of the two armed men standing behind him. If Varvara had just decided he was a threat and she wanted to go to work on him with a power drill or a pair of pliers, he wouldn't be able to fight his way out. Maybe he'd pushed a little too hard. He glanced over at Nadia and saw a look of surprise on her face. She hadn't expected him to say anything during this meeting. It looked like she was wondering why he had chosen to antagonize such a dangerous woman.

When Varvara lifted four crystal pony glasses from the cabinet, though, he knew he'd made the right decision. She slammed the glasses down on top of the workbench and reached for a bottle of vodka. Cracking it open, she said, "This one, Nadia dear, this American you should keep." She laughed and poured three generous shots. "You see what he does? He shows he knows my business, that he's two steps ahead of me, just in case I was thinking of betraying him. But he is also clear in that he knows he can't truly hurt me. Very subtle, very sharp." She handed one of the glasses to Chapel. "Are you looking for work, young man? I can always use smart fellows."

"Sorry, I've got my own business to attend to," Chapel told her.

"Then let us discuss it, eh? To mutual trust." She raised her glass high. "You, Jim. You drink first."

Chapel studied the liquor in his glass. He didn't see any sign it had been poisoned or drugged, but then, he wouldn't, would he?

Here goes nothing, he thought, and knocked back the drink. It was harsh, very strong stuff, more like moonshine than the vodka he was used to, but it didn't make his throat close up or his heart stop.

Varvara laughed. "Brave, too. Now. To business. What do you need, Nadia darling, and where do you want it delivered?"

TASHKENT, UZBEKISTAN: JULY 17, 15:11

Three shots of vodka later, Chapel was starting to feel a little off his game, so he refused a fourth. Bogdan sat on the floor, staring morosely at his first shot. He'd been sipping at it for a while, much to the sneering disdain of the two gunmen.

Nadia and Varvara, however, had polished off half of a liter bottle already and were still coming up with things to toast—they were down to local football teams and the glorious memory of some gangster Chapel had never heard of, and they seemed in no hurry to stop. Between drinks they'd hammered out prices for a truck that could cross the desert, a large quantity of purified water, tents, camp stoves, preserved foods, fuel. At one point Varvara had suggested she could get them a very good deal on some camels, which she said would be even better for crossing the desert than the truck. Nadia's eyes lit up at the idea, but Chapel was still sober enough to say no.

"This is how business is done, in this part of the world," Nadia announced, when Chapel suggested that she might slow down on the drinking. Her cheeks were a little red and her eyes a little glazed. "You don't know this because you are—" She stopped herself before announcing to the room that he was an American spy. "You are not used to it," she finished, a little lamely.

Varvara didn't seem impaired at all. She gave Chapel a sly look. "We're almost done. Can I interest you in some Soviet-era maps of the desert? A bit out of date, but they show many things that history has forgotten. Perhaps if I knew what you were looking for, I could help you better."

"What you don't know, the SNB can't beat out of you," Chapel replied. Nadia seemed to find that uproariously funny. She laughed and sputtered and reached for the bottle to pour herself another drink. "Speaking of the local authorities," Chapel said, putting his own glass down on the workbench, "what can you tell us about one who has a shaved head and a bristly mustache?"

"You'll have to be more specific," Varvara said. "That describes half the old men in Uzbekistan."

Nadia laughed at that, too.

"He's definitely ex-military," Chapel said, remembering what he could about the man who'd been following them. "Very disciplined. The first time I met him he was feeding some pigeons."

Varvara nodded her great mane of hair. "*Konyechno*, I figured it was him you meant. Jamshid Mirza. Interesting. You have drawn some very distinguished attention, there. Mirza was a colonel in the old Soviet army, and of course, a KGB man. He's one of the top men in the SNB. You say he's following you personally?"

"Everywhere we go," Chapel confirmed.

Varvara shook her head. "If I hadn't already promised to help you . . . Mirza might scare even me away. If he has taken an interest, he must think you are very important to his country. When you checked in at your hotel, what did you say you were doing in Tashkent?"

Chapel appreciated that she hadn't asked the

direct question—what his cover story was. "I told them I was an American venture capitalist looking into energy development."

Varvara smiled. "This explains it. Mirza is also head of security for Uzbekneftegaz, the state energy concern. Uzbekistan has a number of very productive natural gas fields, up near what is left of the Aral Sea. So far mostly Korean companies have buzzed around these fields, but the government would be very interested in drawing American flies as well. He will be very disappointed when you don't buy up half his country for exploitation."

"In honor of mother earth!" Nadia said, lifting her glass. Varvara lifted her own and they drank. "Source of all Russian wealth, she gives so much and we are so bad to her."

Chapel shook his head. He had no idea what she was on about. "There's one last thing I want to talk about. More equipment."

"Oh?" Varvara asked.

"Guns," Chapel said. "Can you get us some weapons?"

Varvara lifted an eyebrow. "Now I definitely don't want to know what you're doing out in the desert. But yes, yes, of course. All the guns you desire."

"In honor of guns!" Nadia said, and lifted her glass. "If you have enough of them, you don't need politics."

TASHKENT, UZBEKISTAN: JULY 17, 16:04

The negotiations stretched on a while longer. Varvara named an absurdly high price, which Nadia haggled with for a while before getting the total down to a number that was only barely ludicrous. They completed things with one last shot of vodka and a great deal of hugging and cheek-kissing. Varvara even grabbed at Bogdan and kissed him, though he tried to squirm out of her arms the whole time, which she seemed to find endearing rather than insulting.

Varvara made a phone call, and a few minutes later Chapel heard a loud rushing noise and a squeal of brakes as a subway train pulled up at the hole in the wall. The train's doors opened and revealed an empty car. Chapel, Nadia, and Bogdan got on board and took the train back to Kosmonavtlar Station. Once off the train, Nadia almost ran up the stairs. She didn't seem nearly as drunk as she had back in the contraband warehouse, and Chapel wondered how much of that had been for show.

While they were still underground, Chapel leaned in close and asked, "You're certain we can trust Varvara?"

Nadia snorted out a laugh. "Always with you, the trust issues." She smiled and grabbed his arm playfully. "Occupational hazard, yes? If we can trust anyone, it is my friend. She was the wife of a very famous *vory*, a man of impeccable honor. After he died, she took over his operation, something almost unheard of here, but no one can doubt her position now. To be accepted by other thieves she has been ruthless in her time. But she and I get along very well, and she has helped me in the past. It's nice dealing with a woman. All the men, the male *vory*, they just want to fuck me. To prove they can." She gave Chapel a sly look. "I think they watched too many James Bond movies, with the ice queen Russian spies who melt in the arms of the right man."

Chapel ignored the flirtation. "You seem to know a lot of criminals," he said, glancing over at Bogdan, who was lost in his headphones.

"Kleptocracy," Nadia shrugged. "It is how things work here. You want information, you want more than the local government is willing to give, you go underground. In this case, literally."

They headed up the stairs and then had a long walk back to where they'd left the scooters. Nadia turned them in and got her deposit back, and then they returned to the hotel, taking their time, trying to look like innocent tourists.

Chapel was not surprised at all to find a man with a shaved head and an immaculate mustache waiting in the lobby, sitting casually on a leather sofa near the reception desk. Apparently Mirza had come back here after losing them in the city. There was no way to get to the elevators without walking right past him.

"Mister Chambers!" the SNB man called out, as Chapel passed by. "Did you have a good day? See many of our wonderful sights?"

Chapel gave the man a nasty look. "We rented some scooters and took a tour. Can't say I was much impressed."

"It occurs to me we have not been introduced. My name is Jamshid Mirza. Perhaps you'd do me the honor of letting me show you around tomorrow," he said, smiling. "There are some people you should meet."

For a second Chapel was certain he was about to be arrested. He met Mirza's gaze as steadily as he could and tried to think of what to do next. "Sorry," he said. "We have plans. Business."

"Of course. Perhaps you'd like to discuss that business with me? You'll find, I think, that Tashkent can be very friendly to foreign capital. Our policies may seem harsh to you, but we can be very . . . lenient for foreign investors. All manner of things can be forgiven."

"I have no idea what you're talking about, buddy," Chapel said, and headed once more toward the elevators.

He expected Mirza to stop him, or at least make some more cryptic comments, but the SNB man seemed to be done.

Back in the suite Bogdan retired sulkily to his room without a word. Nadia went and got her bug sweeper and went over the usual spots—light fixtures, under the beds and tables, the television set, the phone. She found three new microphones, each of which she destroyed. She dumped the broken circuit boards in a glass ashtray and then rubbed at her forehead with one hand. "I think I need a nap."

"I'm not surprised, the way you were putting away that vodka," Chapel said, smiling at her.

She smiled back. "I know Russians are famous around the world for drinking too much," she said, "and there is some truth to this particular stereotype. I've never had the time to build up a proper Russian liver, though."

"Don't worry," Chapel said. "I'll stand watch while you sleep."

She nodded and turned toward her room. Stepping inside she held the door open for a second. She said nothing, though, and after a few seconds she closed the door behind her.

TASHKENT, UZBEKISTAN: JULY 17, 19:44

Chapel didn't want to risk going down to one of the hotel's restaurants—it was too likely he'd find Mirza there, waiting to ask him more questions. His cover story was ironclad, and if Mirza called up the company that Jeff Chambers supposedly worked for, he would find receptionists and executives to vouch for Chapel's bona fides, but Chapel knew any cover was only as good as one's ability to act. That had never been his forte. If Mirza really started grilling him, Chapel knew he would eventually give himself away. He wouldn't know enough about the geology of natural gas domes or he would forget what town Jeff Chambers was born in, and then Mirza's promised "lenience" would disappear in a hurry.

So he ordered room service, and a few minutes later a smiling bellhop came to the door with three orders of lamb curry and a couple bottles of Baltika 3, the only beer on the menu that Chapel had heard of. Chapel tipped the bellhop to just leave the trays by the door. When the kid was gone, he went over the trays with Nadia's bug finder. It squealed and hissed, but it didn't find anything, so he brought the food inside. Just past the door he found Bogdan waiting, holding a pair of ice tongs over his head.

"Is all I could find," Bogdan said, gesturing at the tongs.

"Okay," Chapel said. "And what exactly did you want them for?"

"In case the boy was an assassin, I would fight him off," the hacker said, putting the tongs down on a table.

Chapel kind of wished the bellhop had been a threat, just so he could have seen what the ensuing battle looked like. Bogdan was so thin he looked like an averagely built bellhop would be able to break him over his knee.

Smiling to himself, Chapel pushed past the hacker, a tray balanced on each hand. The bug finder made a high-pitched shrieking noise, and he nearly dropped the food. Putting the trays down carefully, he picked up the bug finder and waved it over the trays again, thinking maybe he'd missed something. When he got no result, he pointed it at Bogdan and heard it start to screech.

Bogdan stood very still, his eyes wide.

Chapel moved closer, sweeping the bug finder up and down the length of Bogdan's long body. When it passed over the MP3 player, it went crazy.

Chapel looked up into Bogdan's terrified eyes. He switched off the bug finder. "False alarm," he said, and smiled.

Bogdan nodded and tried to smile back. It didn't quite take.

When dinner was set up, Chapel went to Nadia's door and found it was slightly ajar. He pushed it back and looked inside her room and saw her curled up in her bed, one arm flung wide and her small hand dangling over the edge. She was snoring like a steam engine, but her face was open and innocent and he thought—

Well. It didn't matter what he thought.

"Do not wake her," Bogdan whispered. The hacker had come up beside Chapel unnoticed, and Chapel nearly jumped when he spoke. "She may lash out and karate chop you in neck if you touch her now." He pointed at his own ridiculously long neck and shook his head.

"She does look like she could use the sleep," Chapel said. "We'll start without her." He closed her door and went over to the table. "It'll give us a chance to talk. You and I have never had a proper conversation, have we, Bogdan?"

The hacker dropped himself into one of the table's chairs and started picking apart a tray of food. He ignored the beer and drank tap water instead, but he put away an astonishing amount of curry while Chapel sat and watched him. It was clear if they were going to have a conversation, Chapel was going to have to get it rolling.

"So," he said, trying to think of anything the two of them had in common. What he came up with wasn't a great start. "How long have you known Nadia?"

Bogdan peered at him through his fringe of bangs. "Some years."

"Since before 2011?" he asked. The year Nadia got her medal. The year she had worked her biggest mission, as far as Chapel knew.

"No, just then," Bogdan said. "I am not sure this is proper for discussion."

Chapel waved one hand in the air. "I know. It was a secret mission, and you're not supposed to talk about it with people who don't know what you did." He nodded affably and sipped at his beer. "But I'm a secret agent type, too. I know about things."

Bogdan lifted his fork as if he would defend himself with it. Chapel sat back and pretended he wasn't extremely interested in what Nadia had done in 2011. Clearly Bogdan wasn't going to give anything away for free. Luckily, part of Chapel's intelligence training had included a course in cold reading—the art of tricking people into thinking you already knew their secrets, so they could talk about them freely.

"It's okay," he said. "You don't have to tell me anything. I mean, I know most of the details already." He thought of what Nadia's mission might have been. If she'd been working for FSTEK and she'd been in Romania, it had to deal with technology transfer. If she had gotten mixed up with organized crime, that meant she had been tracing something stolen or misappropriated. And Nadia wasn't just a low-level bureaucrat, tracing serial numbers on stolen computers. She would have been working at the very top level of FSTEK's operations. "It was about the missing nukes," Chapel tried, knowing if he had it wrong he would reveal his ignorance. But if he got it right—

Bogdan put his fork down on the table, very carefully. "May I have one of the beers?" he asked, in a very tentative voice.

Chapel popped the cap off the remaining beer and handed it over. Bogdan sucked deeply at the bottle, drinking half of it in one gulp.

Gotcha, Chapel thought.

"I can see why you're so paranoid," he told Bogdan. "No. That's harsh. Let's say—reasonably cautious. You must have pissed off some very powerful people when you took away their radioactive toys. A lot of guys wouldn't have done what you did. They would have been too scared. But you—"

"It was a challenge, yes," Bogdan said. "The bigger the challenge, the harder to resist, sometimes."

Chapel nodded. "And you worked a pretty sweet hack on them."

"The sweetest." Bogdan's eyes were getting brighter, and not just because of the alcohol he'd consumed. People like Bogdan—loners, reclusive intellectual types—had a desperate need to brag when they were in the real world. They worked miracles in the virtual world, in cyberspace, but nobody was there with them to congratulate them on their successes. They told themselves that didn't matter, but it did.

Chapel thought of Angel and the various methods she used to break into encrypted systems. "What did you use? A keystroke logger? Packet sniffer? Or just brute force decryption?" Chapel had no idea what most of those words meant, but he was certain Bogdan would.

"Not even," Bogdan said, looking down at his plate. He was starting to smile, for real this time. "Social engineering," he whispered. "Is always the best way."

"Social engineering?"

Bogdan nodded and put his hands on the table,

fanning his fingers. "Computers, you will see, are very, very good at holding to secrets. They are designed this way. But information is useless if it cannot be accessed by human beings. Someone always knows the passwords. Someone can always get in. You find that someone, you can work them. Hack them, instead of machine. In this case, it was a woman. It was she who made arrangements. You know, meetings between the seller and the buyer. She introduced the parties but had no knowledge of what they sold or how much they paid."

"A cutout," Chapel said. "That's what we call it."

Bogdan nodded. "Did not matter—she was the link, the one at center of deal. Knows everybody, e-mails everybody. Middle-aged woman, single, no babies, yes? Is a common enough problem, in post-feminist world."

"Sure," Chapel said, having no idea what he was getting at.

"She had online dating page. So I seduce her."

Chapel's eyes went wide. The idea of the lanky hacker seducing someone—anyone—was pretty hard to imagine. "What, you bought her flowers, took her for drinks—"

"Online. I created a profile with a fake picture, fake statistics. Same height as me, but that was all. Said I was a banker in Ploiesti—this is a town just north of Bucharest—with a dead wife. Wanted children in a hurry, wanted someone to travel with, grow old with. Best sales pitch possible. She responded and we go to chatting. I looked up love poetry, romantic comedies online, looking for code words. I found the words most often used in successful dating profiles. My e-mails to her are peppered with these words. She never stood a chance."

"Jesus, I feel sorry for her now," Chapel said.

Bogdan shrugged. "To be fair, she was setting up this deal to sell stolen plutonium to a rogue state."

"Yeah, I guess there's that," Chapel replied.

Bogdan had warmed to his topic and didn't want to stop talking. "She responded very quickly, wanted to set up a date. I said my schedule is too hectic, me being a banker, you see? So she gives me her telephone number so we can text, and her private e-mail she checks always."

"And then she started talking about the deal?" Chapel asked.

"No, of course not! If I ask about that, she sees through me in an instant. No. I just want her contact information. As soon as I get it, I delete my profile, and this fabled banker man, he just disappears from the earth. I had her e-mail address, now I need her password. From her VKontakte page I learned the town where she was born—Lugoj; mother's name—Irina Costaforu; favorite movies, everything. I call up the e-mail host service and say I have forgotten my password, can they help? They ask security questions, and I know the answers."

"Her mother's maiden name, the town where she was born—"

"What secondary school she went to, yes, what is her favorite color . . . I am in. They help me change her password, and now I control her e-mail. I download all her contacts and e-mail folders. Then I change this password back to what it was before, so she does not know I have been there."

"You mean she never even suspected what happened?"

"Whole thing, from online profile to download, takes six hours," Bogdan said, really smiling now. "I did it in middle of the night, when she sleeps. I turn this information over to Nadia and my part, it is done."

"Wow," Chapel said. "That's incredible. You stole her e-mail that easily? Remind me never to piss you off!"

Bogdan actually laughed, then, a kind of wheezing, halting noise that made him sound like he was choking. It was the laugh of somebody who hadn't heard a good joke in his entire life and had no practice at laughing. "I am good, yes. The best, maybe."

"I'll say. So this woman you duped, what was her name?"

Instantly Bogdan's face fell. He picked up his fork and speared another piece of lamb. Chapel could tell he'd pushed too hard.

"Sorry," he said. "I forgot myself for a second. You can't talk about this."

"It was a secret mission," Bogdan said. "I take very serious. Nadia would not like if I told you anything, any small detail."

"I understand," Chapel said. "We won't talk about it again."

"Thank you," Bogdan said, and stuffed the lamb in his mouth.

TASHKENT, UZBEKISTAN: JULY 18, 01:34

"These once-a-day phone calls are driving me crazy, sugar," Angel said.

Chapel smiled in the dark of his room. "Me, too. But I have to wait until I'm sure we won't be over-heard." Through the thin walls of the hotel suite he could hear Bogdan snoring in the room next door. The one beer the hacker had drunk with dinner seemed to be enough to put him down for the night. As for Nadia, she'd never woken up for dinner, and the last time he'd checked on her she was still sprawled across her own bed. He needed to get to sleep himself—tomorrow was going to be a big day, the day they illegally crossed the border into Kazakhstan, if everything went right. But first he needed to check in. "We met with a Russian gang-ster today," he told Angel. "She's the one providing our equipment. Her first name was Varvara."

"Let me check the Interpol database," Angel said. He listened to her click away at her keyboard. It was one of the most reassuring sounds he knew—it meant she was looking out for him. "Here we go. Varvara Nikolaevich Lyadova. Wanted in four countries, that's impressive. Arrested on a dozen different charges, ac-tually did jail time on one of them—wow. Murder."

"Yeah?" Chapel asked, suddenly worried.

"Let's look at the case files . . . okay, actually it was conspiracy murder. That's why she only did three years. Looks like her husband killed a rival gangster back in the midnineties and Varvara helped destroy some evidence. A bloody shirt . . . when the police came for her husband, she jammed it in the oven and baked it for thirty minutes at four seventy-five degrees. They pulled it out before it was good and crispy, but at that point it was tainted. They couldn't get any DNA from the blood."

"Huh. So she was loyal to her husband, and kind of smart about it," Chapel said. "The real question is—will she show us that same kind of loyalty? I know she's worked with Nadia before."

"Well, my sources say she's a real Russian gangster, not just a run-of-the-mill criminal. She's what they call a *vory v zakone*, a—"

"'Lawful thief,'" Chapel said, "yeah, I got that from Nadia. Does that really mean anything, though?"

"Probably yes," Angel said. "The Russian gangs are what they call a *Bratva*, a brotherhood. They live by a very strict code. Unless they have a good reason to sell you out—if they think you're a police informant or something—they stick by a deal. Even if they don't care much about moral codes, they have a financial reason to honor their obligations. If they just took your money and never delivered the goods, they would lose their reputation with other *vory*, and that would cost them in the future. From everything I see here, Lyadova is the kind to stick to her word."

Well, that was something, anyway. "Nadia seems to have pretty good contacts in the criminal world. She says that's just how things work over here." Chapel frowned. "Speaking of which—I just had a very informative conversation with your opposite number."

"You mean Bogdan Vlaicu? He's good, but I wouldn't put him in my league," Angel said, sounding a little huffy.

Chapel grinned to himself. "I don't know. I got him to tell me how he hacked into a ring of plutonium smugglers."

"Plutonium?"

"Apparently that was why Nadia got that medal back in 2011. I don't know the details, but I figure the American intelligence community might be interested in knowing that the Russians let some radioactive material walk away back then."

"I think they'd be very interested in knowing about that," Angel said. He could almost hear her sitting up straighter in her chair. "What can you tell me?"

"I can give you a puzzle to work out," he said.

"You always did know the way to a girl's heart, sugar."

Chapel tried to remember exactly what Bogdan had said. "The deal was brokered by a woman whose mother's maiden name was Irina Costaforu. The woman was born in a town in Romania called Lugoj."

"You're going to make this one too easy," Angel said.

Chapel shrugged. "Bogdan seemed to think it was a piece of cake. See what you can figure out. I don't mind telling you—the story of how he got that information was a little chilling. It's way too easy to find out everything about somebody these days."

"If you give all your personal details to a company like Facebook that makes its money by selling personal information to third parties, well . . . maybe you don't really have a lot of right to complain," Angel suggested.

Chapel didn't agree but he let it go. "It got me thinking. If he could break into this woman's e-mail so easily, it shouldn't be too hard to check up on somebody you were worried about. Just to make sure they were okay. You know, without them knowing about it."

"You're right. That would be very easy," Angel said. Any trace of flirtation was gone from her voice, and he knew she had guessed where he was going with this.

"I'm not suggesting that I want to cyberstalk Julia—"

"You just want me to check her e-mail and find out if she's okay," Angel said, completing his sentence. "Think about this one pretty hard, Chapel. Think about if that's what you really want me to do for you."

He sighed and laid the tablet down on the bed beside him. "No," he said.

"No?"

"No, I don't want you to do that."

"Good," she told him. "Because I would have refused. That sort of thing isn't cool. What did she say when she left?"

"She said she would call me. That I should give her some space. That was . . . more than a month ago." He closed his eyes. "Do I sound as pathetic to you as I do to myself, right now?"

"Chapel, I know you miss her. But your relationship status is not a matter of national security. I'm here to help you with your mission, with—"

"I know, Angel," he said. "I know. I just—miss her a lot. I'm only human, you know? I miss her and I wish . . . I wish for a lot of things."

Angel's voice softened. "I get it," she said.

"Okay. Okay. Moving on," Chapel said. "Tomorrow we're going into the desert and—"

He stopped. Focused all his attention on what he'd just heard.

"Angel, I'll call you back."

"Sure, honey."

He pulled off his earphones and hit the power switch on the tablet. Got out of the bed and padded to the door. With his ear up against the thin wood, he held his breath and just listened.

There—he heard it again. The sound of metal scraping against metal. What could it be? He waited until he heard it a third time, then slammed open the door, bursting out into the common room of the suite. If someone had come to plant more bugs—or something worse, he would—

Nadia stood in the middle of the room, wearing nothing but a thin nightgown. She was holding a fork and the lid from one of the room service trays.

"I woke up hungry," she said.

TASHKENT, UZBEKISTAN: JULY 18, 01:49

"I see you couldn't sleep, either," she said, as Chapel stepped out into the common room.

He realized he was staring at her. Moonlight coming in from the balcony doors painted a swath of silver down her arm, the curve of her hip, the long straight muscle in her thigh. He forced himself to look away. "I'm sorry we didn't wake you. Bogdan thought maybe you'd been trained to kill anyone who touched you while you slept."

Nadia grinned around a forkful of cold lamb. "I suppose I needed the rest. The worst part about drinking during the day is that you get the hangover before you go to bed. I seem to have missed most of that, for which I am glad."

Chapel walked over to the table and put his hands on the back of a chair. Her hair was mussed and her eyes were hooded with sleep, still. "Are you going to be able to go back to sleep after you eat that stuff?" he asked.

"Should be no problem."

He nodded. "We've got a lot to do tomorrow, and—"

"Perhaps you should be sleeping yourself," she told him, with a smile. She poured herself a glass of water and drank it down without stopping. "Wouldn't do to be dehydrated before we even reach the desert." She put the glass down and looked over at the balcony doors. "Come get some air with me."

Chapel took a deep breath. *Bad idea*, he thought. *Terrible idea*. "All right," he said.

She stepped out onto the balcony and leaned far out over the concrete railing, way out over a twenty-story drop. Chapel came up behind her, watching the way her shoulders moved under the thin straps of her nightgown.

He reached for her, because he was afraid she might fall. He almost grabbed her arm to pull her back away from the railing. Then he took a breath and dropped his hand.

"I've been waiting so long for this," she said.

"What's that?" he asked.

She smiled at him over her shoulder. Then she leaned forward across the railing, lifting her feet off the balcony floor. A good strong wind at that point might have blown her over the edge. He moved toward her, but she laughed and put her feet back down.

"For years," she said, "I have been working toward this moment. Toward shutting down Perimeter. Now it's finally happening. It feels . . ."

Chapel almost sighed in relief, but stopped himself. "Unreal?" he asked.

"No," she said. "No. This is very real. More real than anything in a long time. The world we live in, people like you and me—that is what never feels real to me. I think you must understand what I mean. We are sent out into the field, never really knowing what we're after. We gather intelligence, we neutralize threats." She shrugged. "Then it is home again, or what we call home, and 'thank you for your service.' No one explains why we did what we did. No one acknowledges we were ever there. Even our names are secrets. We are never allowed to mean anything, in case we are lost. But tomorrow— tomorrow I'm going to do something important. Something meaningful. And at least one person in the world will know I was there, that *I* did it."

She turned to look at him. She reached for his hand, and he took it without a thought. Her small fingers stroked the hair on his artificial knuckles. "You will know, Jim. You'll be my *svidetel*. You won't forget me, as soon as I disappear."

She lifted his hand to her lips, kissed it.

"Nadia," he said, breathing out her name in a soft warning.

She shook her head. Kissed his hand again. He tried to pull it away, but she clutched at his fingers.

She brought the hand up to her face and made it

cup her cheek. "Do you feel this?" she asked, rubbing her cheek against his silicone skin.

"Yes," he told her. "Not as much as with the other one." He could feel basic textures with the artificial hand, some temperature differences. He could definitely feel how soft her skin was.

"And this?" she asked, moving his hand. Pressing it against her breast. Through the thin fabric of her nightgown he could feel her nipple hardening.

"Nadia—"

"Shh. Just a moment," she said. Her eyes were closed. She lifted his hand away from her body but didn't let go of it.

It wasn't his real hand. It wasn't him that had touched her like that, it was a machine. It wasn't him. That was an utter lie, but lies can be useful things. If this ended now, if she stopped, he could forgive himself, he could—

She brought the hand down past her waist. Turned a little so she could maneuver it inside her panties, press it against her soft and yielding flesh. One finger slipped inside her effortlessly and he felt her warmth, felt how wet she was.

He tried to pull back, pull away, but his fingers brushed her clitoris and she trembled, her body as tight and as tense as a violin string. He stroked her there and her shoulders jumped. Her eyes were closed and her mouth slightly open, her breath deeper and stronger than before.

This isn't me, he tried to tell himself. *It's the fake arm, it's not me.*

He started to take his hand away, but she brought both of hers down, covering his hand, pressing it back into place. He felt like this was inevitable, that it couldn't be stopped now, not when it had already gone too far. He made a small circle with his fingertip and she sagged, as if her knees were getting weak. He touched her again and felt the heat of her body between them, filling the thin sliver of air between her and his real body, his own flesh. He could put his other arm around her, draw her closer, but, no, he didn't dare, this was wrong; he couldn't keep doing this, he thought, even as his fingers found her clitoris again. His thumb and index finger held it from either side in the softest grasp, moving up and down the tiniest distance. He released her and she gasped; touched her again and she made a sound like a bird inside a cage that's just been unlocked.

"Yes," she whispered, as he moved his hand, such tiny, precise movements, "Please," she said, and he increased the speed, the pressure, but just by the smallest amount. "Don't stop," she said. "Jim, please, don't . . . don't stop . . . don't . . ."

She was hunched over his arm, her head down, only an inch from crashing into his chest. If any part of her touched him, he knew he would have to stop, but she was agile enough to balance herself there as if she knew, as if she knew that was the only way this could keep happening. He could feel her gasping breath on his skin, but even as her hair slid down across her face it didn't touch him. Only his hand was in contact with her body at all, only his fingertips.

He felt her start to shake, felt her body squeeze under his hand. And then with one convulsive noise like a sob she was there, the cage was open, the bird was free, its wings thrashing and taking flight . . .

She lifted her hands toward his shoulders as she came, reached for his actual flesh, his body, and he knew if she touched him once, he would not be able to resist, that he would scoop her up in his arms and carry her back to his bed and he would make love to her—no, at this point, the way he was feeling, he would *fuck* her. If she touched him. If she touched him at all.

He drew his artificial hand back, out of her panties, away from her. She stopped reaching for him. She let him go.

At the door leading back into the suite, he turned and looked at her there, in the moonlight. Her head was bowed and her hands gripped the railing and she was still trembling. "It's all right," she said. "You did nothing wrong. Try to get some sleep."

He hurried back to his room and locked the door behind him. Sat down on his bed and reached up and unlatched the artificial arm, felt the clamps release and the arm fall away from him. He caught it with his good hand and wondered what to do with it. He wanted to throw it across the room. Smash it into pieces.

It hadn't been long enough. For all he knew, Julia was trying to call him right then, trying to get back in touch and tell him she'd made a mistake.

No, he told himself. *No, she hasn't called. She's not going to call. And Nadia is right here. Just waiting for me to get over myself.*

Of course—there was the other reason this couldn't happen. The fact that she was a foreign agent and that she might have orders to seduce him, to pump him for information.

He shook his head. He couldn't resolve this. Couldn't figure it out at all.

He cleaned and plugged the arm into a wall socket so it could recharge. Then he went back and sat on the bed and scrubbed at his face with his good hand, covered his eyes as if to keep anyone else from seeing what was happening there, behind them.

He did not sleep at all that night.

IN TRANSIT: JULY 18, 05:43

Nadia ordered down for breakfast the next morning, so they wouldn't have to go down to the lobby and maybe run into Mirza. A huge platter of fruit and nuts and coffee and rolls came up to the room. Bogdan ate heartily, but Chapel and Nadia both just picked at the meal. Chapel drank a cup of coffee and announced he was ready to go.

Nadia looked at him and he looked away, as simple as that. Neither of them said anything, neither of them did anything to indicate that something had changed. "We'll head down the back stairwell," Nadia said. "There's a service entrance at the back of the hotel. It will be monitored by cameras, but I doubt there will be anyone waiting for us there."

Chapel nodded and hefted his bag. He led the way out into the hall, checking both ways to make sure it was clear before gesturing for the others to follow him. They weren't expecting any trouble, but they wanted very much to get out of Tashkent without being followed.

It was a long walk down the stairs and then a short bustle through the kitchens of the hotel. A chef looked up and scowled at them, but he was too busy to say anything or chase them out of his stainless steel domain. The service entrance was unlocked and unguarded, and soon they were out into the alleyway behind the hotel, the early morning air already thick with exhaust fumes and the tape-recorded chant of a muezzin calling the faithful to prayer.

It wasn't far to the metro station, just a few blocks, but it took far longer because they had to stay in the alleyways and back courts the whole way, sticking to where the night's shadows still hadn't been eroded by the rising sun. They never crossed a street or turned a corner without checking for watchers, for any sign of a tail.

They made it to the metro without incident. Boarded the first train to come along. Changed at the next station, took the next train, changed again. They got a few looks from early commuters, but the people of Tashkent were used to minding their own business and no one spoke to them.

Finally they took one last metro line to Tashkent Central Station in Mirabad, where Nadia bought three tickets with cash. She bought the tickets for the 8:30 train to Bukhara, though they had no intention of going that far. "It's a shame. Bukhara's lovely," she said. "It's one of the stops on the old Silk Road, and a UNESCO World Heritage site for its historic central—"

"Please," Chapel said, shaking his overcaffeinated, sleep-deprived head. "Don't play tour guide today."

She laughed and tried to meet his eye, but he looked away. That simple.

The train was right on time. There were SNB

people on the platform. Anyone could have made them out for secret police the way they scanned everyone's face and asked random passengers for their tickets and papers. They didn't seem to be looking for anyone in particular. Chapel gave them a wide berth and herded Bogdan and Nadia into the first car on the train. It set off on time, and within fifteen minutes they watched Tashkent fade away from the car's windows, its dense streets thinning out to residential neighborhoods, to wide, open green spaces full of trees, and finally to cultivated fields.

No one came bustling into the car demanding papers. No men with shaved heads and mustaches appeared on the local platforms they stopped at. Nobody even called Jeff Chambers on his cell phone to ask when he was coming down from his room.

Eventually, Chapel let himself relax. A little. He exhaled deeply and plopped back in his seat and let the waves of exhaustion crash through him, driving all thoughts from his head.

Nadia smiled from the seat across from his. Tried to catch his eye.

He turned his head to the side to watch the dusty-looking crops stream by, the sun glinting on irrigation ditches and the occasional stream.

It was that simple. He just had to never meet her eye again, and he would be fine.

IN TRANSIT: JULY 18: 10:14

The train passed through the city of Samarkand, Uzbekistan's second biggest. Chapel was sure it was important historically, and the name conjured up visions of a glittering past, of caravans of camels and spice merchants and dancing girls in veils, but the train didn't stop long enough for him to even get a decent look at it.

Nor was he awake enough to pay much attention. He kept slipping into a doze, a sort of half-sleeping state where he was only minimally aware of his surroundings. He slipped in and out of dreams of swirling cigarette smoke—the car was full of it, even with the windows open—of brown landscape rushing by him, of the constant swaying of the train, of Nadia's perfume, of Bogdan's incessant clicking.

He blinked his eyes to try to clear them, but he was having trouble focusing. He could hear Bogdan's fingers moving, make out a fluttering motion when he looked over at the hacker sitting next to him, but that was all. He fought through it, fought for consciousness, and saw Bogdan clicking away at his MP3 player, like he always did.

This time, though, something about it bothered him.

Bogdan was facing away from him, looking up the aisle between the rows of seats. He had his big headphones on, as always. His fingers were moving over the keys on the MP3 player the way a clarinetist might work the keys of his instrument. It looked like there were more keys on the MP3 player than Chapel would have expected—more than enough to pause or stop the music, fast-forward or reverse. The main body of the player was wrapped in duct tape, and it looked like Bogdan had modified a commercial unit to his own specifications.

Something else bothered Chapel about the setup, as well. Though he had rarely seen Bogdan without the headphones on, he'd never heard any music coming from them. They might just be very well insulated, but Chapel had never seen a pair of headphones that didn't leak at least a little sound.

Chapel turned away, wanting to shake his head and just let it go. So the kid was obsessed with his music, so what? Plenty of people his age spent their whole lives with headphones on. Bogdan was exactly the sort of person who would want to block out the real world as much as possible. The constant clicking at the keys was just a nervous tic. Chapel had no idea if he was constantly zooming back and forward within a given track, or just adjusting the volume up and down, up and down.

He should just go back to sleep, he thought. He should just—

Inside his head something came together, a pair of jigsaw puzzle pieces fitting perfectly to each other and showing a glimpse of a bigger picture.

He forced himself to sit up, to stretch for a moment. Blood rushed back into his head and his extremities and he breathed deeply, pushing oxygen into his tired tissues. He stood up and reached for his small travel bag, pulling it down from the overhead bin. Across from him Nadia stirred and opened one eye—it looked like she'd been fully asleep.

"Just going to freshen up," he told her.

She turned her head to the side and fell asleep again, instantly.

He pushed his way through the men in the aisle who were smoking and laughing at jokes in languages he couldn't understand. In the tiny lavatory of the train car he opened his travel bag and took out his tablet and his own earphones. As soon as they were in place Angel greeted him.

"We weren't supposed to talk again until tonight, sweetie," she said. "Everything okay?"

"Fine, probably. I just thought of something I wanted to talk to you about. It concerns our young Romanian friend."

"Vlaicu? What's he up to now?"

"I'm not sure." Chapel tried to figure out how to express his intuition. "We've been keeping him away from computers this whole time, anything with a screen and a keyboard."

"Probably wise," Angel said, "though if he's anything like me, that's got to smart. It would be like being hopelessly nearsighted and the people around you won't let you have your glasses."

"I'm sure he'll survive a few days without the Internet. The thing is, I'm not sure he has to—I mean, I think he might have found a way to get online anyway."

Angel suddenly sounded very excited. "You think he's hiding something on his person? Well, maybe. A smartphone, or a tablet—"

"Nothing like that." He described the MP3 player to her. "Last night when I was sweeping our rooms for bugs, the player made the bug finder go through the roof. I don't know. It seems unlikely. There's no screen, and maybe about ten keys total. Could you even make a computer like that? I know it sounds impossible—"

"Not at all, actually. The original computers

didn't have screens or keyboards—they used punch cards."

"Yeah, but I'm talking about something a little more sophisticated," Chapel said.

"Well," Angel said, "Maybe. There was a famous case of a bunch of computer science guys from the University of California, back in the eighties. They built computers into their shoes, using their toes to work the controls."

"Shoe computers? Did they do anything useful?"

Angel laughed. "They took Las Vegas for a bundle, actually. They worked out a way to predict where a roulette ball was going to land and rigged the game."

"Jesus. I think Bogdan might have been hacking this whole time. When we were trying to lose our tail in Tashkent yesterday, I think he changed a traffic light, or at least made it change faster. And he—and Nadia—always seem to know when subway trains are about to arrive."

"That's pretty easy stuff. Let me think about this," Angel said. She sounded almost breathless. "I mean, you could reduce your inputs down to a small number of keystrokes if you used modal shifts, you know, like holding down a shift or control key to change the character you type on a normal keyboard. Say you have two mode keys, and eight input keys; that gives you twenty-four basic key combinations, which is almost enough for a complete alphabetic input, and that doesn't even include multimode inputs, conditional mode inputs—"

"You're saying it could be done," Chapel said. "But how would he remember all those combinations?"

"Just by practice," Angel replied. "You do anything long enough and it becomes second nature. Do you remember exactly where, on a standard keyboard, the H key is? But I imagine you could type the word 'hello' without having to think about it."

"And let me guess, he doesn't need a screen, because—"

"The headphones!" Angel actually laughed in excitement. "This guy's brilliant! He probably just used a normal text-to-speech module, the kind that blind people use. They can't see a screen, so the computer just reads everything on the screen aloud for them. Those headphones tell him where he is on the net, and he uses the keys to move from page to page, to enter form data, to—"

"This is all guesswork," Chapel said.

"True," Angel said, disappointed. "Except . . . maybe we can find out for sure."

"You have some way to scan for computers?" Chapel asked, incredulous. "By satellite?"

"No. But the tablet you're using now does. It has a Wi-Fi transponder built into it. It can scan for wireless networks. That's just standard equipment on any wireless device. I can use it to triangulate a specific network. Let me ping it . . . there. There are a couple of dozen wireless networks in your local area right now."

"Really? In the middle of rural Uzbekistan?"

Angel laughed. "Don't start expecting to freeload off somebody else's wireless so you can download a bunch of YouTube videos. The signals I'm getting are way too weak for you to access—they might be miles away—but I can still detect them. They get stronger the closer you get to them. Go back to your seat now but leave your tablet turned on. When you're sitting next to Vlaicu, touch the screen so I know you're close. If one of the signals ramps up superhigh at that moment, I'll know it's his."

"And you'll be able to tell me what he's looking at on the Internet?"

Angel sounded apologetic when she answered. "Well . . . no. The signal will still be locked and encrypted, and even I can't beat 256-bit encryption. But at least you'll know your hunch was right. What will you do then? Confront him? Confront Nadia?"

He thought about that. "Telling her I know about Bogdan's computer won't get me very far. Even if she admits she's had him hacking away this whole time, so what? I've had you doing the same thing. It's not like she'll give me Bogdan's password and we all get to share information, especially since I'm not letting her know about you. If you had enough time, do you think there's any way you could break through his encryption? Maybe figure out his password?"

"Not directly. Not with a brute force hack. But maybe I can do something. I don't know. Let me think about it. For now, let's just find out if you're right. If he even has a working computer."

"Okay. Talk to you soon."

Chapel slipped the tablet into his pocket, his earphones still in place, and stepped out of the lavatory. When he got back to his seat, he climbed over Bogdan's long legs and sat back down, not even looking at the hacker, just watching the world blur past the windows. He settled himself in, then reached into his pocket and tapped the screen of the tablet.

For a second nothing happened. But then, in a very quiet voice, Angel whispered in his ear: "Gotcha."

VOBKENT, UZBEKISTAN: JULY 18, 16:32

The train only stopped for a minute in the town of Vobkent, as if it were in a hurry to finish the last leg of its voyage to Bukhara. They had to rush to get their bags down and struggle through all the people standing in the aisle, but they managed to get down to the platform before the train chugged away again, leaving them behind.

On the map Vobkent had looked like little more than a flyspeck, but from the ground it was a vibrant, if sleepy little place, full of shops selling chicken feed and textiles. There was even a bit of tourist business—they saw a couple of European backpackers headed toward a minaret in the center of town. Its main attraction for Nadia, however, was that it was far enough away from Tashkent that it didn't merit a significant SNB presence.

"Varvara said the truck and the supplies would be waiting on the north edge of town, in an abandoned battery farm," she told Chapel.

Chapel nodded and folded up the map he'd been staring at, trying to get some sense of where they were headed. He scanned the street for taxis but found none. "I guess we're walking," he said.

"It's only about a mile," Nadia said, and started off at a brisk pace, her bag swinging from her arm.

It had been a hot day, and the late afternoon was

showing no signs of cooling off. Before long Chapel had to wipe his brow. The streets of Vobkent were wide and open to the sun, and the smell of the desert was everywhere—everywhere, at least, that didn't smell of chickens. They passed through the center of the town, through a zone of little shops selling phone cards and soft drinks, and then into a more residential neighborhood where old women sat in the shade of their doorways, fanning themselves with beautiful little pieces of cloth. Chapel tried to smile a lot and look at the architecture so he would seem like a lost tourist, though he supposed he wasn't dressed for the part. He'd taken off his suit jacket and rolled up his sleeves, but he still looked like American energy executive Jeff Chambers. He'd brought clothes more appropriate for the desert, but he hadn't had a chance to change since they left Tashkent that morning.

As they headed up a dusty avenue where the only shade came from the occasional tree, Nadia dropped back to walk alongside him. He didn't move away from her, but he didn't glance her way, either.

"We will not speak of what happened last night, apparently," she said, her voice low. She didn't look at him when she spoke, as if they were trading vital secrets. "I understand that you need some time to think."

"Yeah," Chapel said. He considered adding something, then decided against it. If he didn't talk about what had happened, he didn't need to think about it either. Instead he could focus on wondering what Bogdan was doing with his makeshift computer. The hacker was walking ahead of them, his long legs barely shuffling along but still managing to eat up the distance. As he walked he tapped at his MP3 player, as he always did.

"You will not even look at me now, it seems," Nadia said.

Chapel shrugged. He adjusted his bag on his shoulder and made a point of turning to face her, still walking the whole time. He forced himself to look at her eyes.

What he saw there made him turn away again.

She didn't look angry. She wasn't winking or throwing suggestive looks his way either. She just looked sad. Like she understood, perfectly, how complex things were for him but she just wished they were ... different. Simpler.

He imagined he probably looked much the same way.

"I'm not sure," she said, when they were safely looking in different directions again, "what you thought was going to happen between us. We're not the kind of people whose lives move toward oaths and ceremonies in little white churches. I wasn't looking for a golden ring."

Chapel had to squeeze his eyes shut for a second when he thought of the little jewelry box that was probably still sitting on the hall table back in Brooklyn.

"Our lives are not our own," Nadia said. "We don't get to make long-term plans."

Chapel grunted in frustration. "I know that better than anyone," he told her. "And I thought we weren't going to talk about this."

"Forgive me," Nadia said. "But I really need to. She left you, Jim. She set you free."

"It doesn't work that way."

"Of course it does." Nadia moved toward him, as if she would grab his arm. He took a step in the opposite direction, and from the corner of his eye he saw her drop her hands in frustration. "You have no obligation to a woman who—"

"Nadia!" he said, loud enough to make Bogdan turn around and look. Much louder than he'd intended to. "Look," he said, lowering his voice. "I think in some weird way you're actually trying to help. That you think I need to hear this. But everything you say is just making it worse."

He was pretty sure she stared at him then, stared at him with wide eyes. He wouldn't know because he refused to look in her direction. He turned his face away until he couldn't even see her shadow.

Eventually she gave up on him and hurried forward to catch up with Bogdan. The two of them carried on some light conversation in what sounded to Chapel like Romanian. He couldn't have followed it if he wanted to.

The road they were on petered out after another half mile or so. The shops and houses gave way to larger structures—warehouses, factory farms, and light industrial workshops. No one was on the street out there, and judging by the boarded-up doors and the broken windows it looked like the district had seen better days. It wasn't much farther to their destination, a nondescript shed of a building maybe a hundred yards long but only one story high. Like many of the buildings they'd passed it was surrounded by a high chain-link fence, but the gate of this one was ajar.

Nadia dropped back to point it out to Chapel. "Come on," she said. "We still have a job to do, and we must do it together. Whether you like it or not."

"Fine," Chapel said. "We can be professionals, at least."

Nadia shook her head and sighed. Then she strode forward, toward the open gate. Chapel and Bogdan followed close on her heels.

VOBKENT, UZBEKISTAN: JULY 18, 17:03

It was clear right away that the shed had not been used in a long time. Its walls were made of corrugated tin that had turned white in the sun and rotted away in some places, big holes in the structure that showed only darkness and swirling dust. The ground around the shed was strewn with old litter—plastic shopping bags that skittered across the concrete like insects, old tractor tires full of stagnant water, broken wooden pallets. Climbing over all the debris took some work, since Chapel didn't want to accidentally step on a rusty nail and give himself tetanus. Nadia scampered over it like a mountain goat, of course, while Bogdan carefully and painstakingly navigated around the trash, moving each foot carefully before setting it down as if he would be contaminated just by touching anything.

The front of the shed ended in a tall doorway wide enough to drive a car through. It was locked up tight, with a massive rusted padlock hanging from a chain with links as thick as Nadia's wrists. She rattled the chain for a second then let it drop back with a bang. "There must be a side entrance," she said.

Chapel scanned the street behind them. This wasn't the kind of place tourists should be investigating. Anyone who saw them now might remember the strange foreigners wandering around the abandoned battery farm—and if they remembered them, they could tell the SNB what they'd seen. Luckily the street was deserted.

Nadia made her way around the shed, climbing over a pile of blown-out old tires so high she could have climbed up onto the roof from its top. When she came down on the other side she was out of view, so Chapel hurried to follow as best he could. He heard her call out, and when he finally caught up with her, he saw she'd found a doorway that wasn't locked.

He followed her inside, into the low, dim interior of the place. The far end of the shed was wide open and let in enough sunlight to dazzle him. He could only make out the rough outlines of what he saw. The walls were lined on both sides with hundreds of chicken coops, tiny cages made of thin wire. Narrow conveyor belts ran along beneath the coops, perhaps to catch the eggs the chickens had once laid. There didn't seem to be anything alive inside the shed now except some ants that crawled over his hand when he touched the door frame. He shook them off and walked farther inside.

At the far end, near the open doors, he could make out the silhouette of the truck. It was bigger than he'd expected, a high square-cabined thing with a shovel-shaped nose that made it look more like a troop carrier than a commercial vehicle. It sat on eight massive fat tires, each with its own elaborate suspension. He supposed it needed all those tires to gain purchase on sand, but he could imagine less conspicuous vehicles to use on a covert mission.

"Hello?" Nadia called out, her voice echoing off the steel rafters of the shed.

There was no answer.

Chapel came up beside her, wondering why this felt wrong.

"Someone was supposed to be here to show us how the truck works," Nadia said. "Varvara told me that someone would be here."

Chapel nodded and walked ahead of her, toward the truck. He tried to keep his ears open to any sound, but his shoes crunched on the old dust and debris that covered the shed's floor.

His eyes were slowly adjusting to the weird light in the shed. He thought he saw something inside the cab of the truck—maybe their contact had fallen asleep in there and hadn't woken when Nadia called. Chapel hurried over to the driver's-side door. It was five feet up off the ground, reached by a short folding ladder. He climbed up, holding on to the door's handle, and tried to peer inside through the smudged glass of the window.

That was when he saw the bullet hole.

The glass of the truck's windshield had been punctured by a small-caliber round—he guessed a rifle shot—leaving the familiar cobweb-shaped cracks in the glass. Their contact was inside but he wasn't moving. Chapel pulled open the door and reached inside, barely catching the man as he slumped out of the cab and started falling toward the floor of the shed.

Chapel let the body fall the rest of the way, then jumped down to examine it.

"Someone beat us here," he whispered, and gestured for Nadia to get down. If the shooter was still somewhere nearby, if the rifle was trained on anyone who approached the truck—

But the gunshot Chapel expected never came.

He ducked low and studied the body. The man had been about Bogdan's age, just a kid. He had dark hair and a sad little excuse for a goatee, and the expression on his face was one of surprise. The shot had gone in through his left eye, probably killing him instantly. "Jesus," Chapel breathed.

Nadia came up behind him, ducking low to use one of the truck's tires for cover.

"Who did this?" Chapel asked her, keeping his voice down.

"How would I know that?"

"Those gangsters who were chasing Bogdan? Would they come this far? Or maybe Varvara has some enemies? Think, Nadia."

She shook her head, but even in the half-light he could tell from her face that she knew something. He started to demand more answers, but he was interrupted as Bogdan shouted for them.

"I'll get him," Nadia said.

Chapel nodded. "There should be guns in the truck—I'll look for them." He climbed back up the side of the truck, feeling very exposed. If the sniper was still out there somewhere . . . but he got inside the cab without being shot. There were four seats inside, big bucket seats that looked like they belonged in an airplane instead of a land vehicle. The driver's seat was covered in sticky blood that hadn't had a chance to dry, even in the stuffy cab. Their contact must have been killed recently.

There was a hatch set into the back of the cab, between the rear two seats, which led to the cargo compartment at the rear of the truck. Keeping his head down Chapel moved back there and opened the narrow hatch, then slipped back into darkness. Light streaming in from the cab showed him there was a lamp set into the ceiling of the cargo compartment, but he couldn't see how to switch it on—and wouldn't have if he could, since that would have given any hypothetical sniper a great target to work with.

Slowly Chapel's eyes adjusted to the darkness. The cargo compartment was packed full of supplies. Most of the room was taken up by fuel and water tanks and huge spare tires. There were some crates toward the back, next to the rear doors. The guns had to be there. He climbed in over the spare tires and started making his way over to the crates, then stopped in place when he heard a sound.

A series of sounds—a repetitive banging noise, like someone hitting metal with a hammer. The sound a sledgehammer might make as it pounded on a rusty padlock.

Someone was trying to get into the shed.

VOBKENT, UZBEKISTAN: JULY 18, 17:22

Chapel moved to the back doors of the truck and felt around until he found the latch that opened them. He eased one of the doors open just a crack so he could see outside.

The locked doors of the shed rattled and banged, and he could see dust sifting down across them. They hadn't been opened in a long time, and they screeched as the lock broke and they sagged open. He heard someone shout, and then the doors flew open all at once and four men came rushing through, each of them carrying a pistol. Three of them were blond, and one wore glasses.

It was the same man he'd fought back in Bucharest, one of the gangsters who'd come for them when they were picking up Bogdan.

Had the Romanian gangsters followed them all this way? It seemed unlikely but Chapel definitely recognized the man's face. Glasses even had a bandage on his left wrist—where Chapel had stomped on it.

The four men moved quickly into the shed, spreading out, their pistols covering the decrepit chicken coops, the rafters overhead, the dead body of Varvara's driver. They weren't trying to be subtle, this time—they looked like they expected a fight.

Well, Chapel aimed to give them one.

With the back door of the truck cracked open, a little light spilled into the cargo compartment. Just enough for Chapel to make out the various boxes and crates stowed there. One looked very familiar to him, a long, narrow wooden crate. He reached for its lid and found that it wasn't—thank God—nailed shut. Inside he found a bunch of torn-up newspapers that stank of gun oil. He reached in and felt around to see what kind of weapons Varvara had provided.

She hadn't stinted on the firepower. He felt a couple of pistols in there and the long wooden stock of an AK-47 assault rifle. There were clips for each of the firearms, already loaded with bullets.

Outside of the truck the four men moved step by step through the shed, their guns up and ready. Chapel had no idea where Nadia or Bogdan might be. He had to assume he was on his own for this. He pulled out the AK-47 and one of its curved clips.

Now came the tricky part. He slotted the clip and drove it home, as gently as he could. It made a sharp click as it locked into place, a sound the whole world was probably familiar with from hearing it in so many movies.

Outside the truck someone spoke, but he couldn't catch the words. They must have heard the click.

He couldn't give them a chance to figure out where it came from. He slid the firing selector on the rifle all the way down, to semiauto, and kicked open the truck doors, then jumped backward out of the truck and down onto the floor of the shed.

The four gunmen must have split up, two on either side of the truck. On the left side, one had climbed up the ladder to look inside the cab. Another had bent to look under the truck in case anyone was hiding there.

Chapel didn't waste time looking for the other two. He brought the rifle up and squeezed the trigger, releasing a burst of three rounds into the body of the one hanging on the side of the cab. The man fell away from the truck instantly, and Chapel swiveled around even as the one looking under the truck started to stand back up.

The man had time to look over at Chapel, time for his features to take on an expression of surprise. Chapel's second burst caught him in the chest and knocked him sprawling backward, onto the floor.

The noise of his firing echoed loud enough in the shed to drive any thoughts out of Chapel's head. He moved on instinct, dodging left around the side of the truck, keeping his body behind one of the huge tires. He heard movement on the other side of the vehicle—the two men who had gone to the right, moving to react to the sudden attack.

They were smart enough, or disciplined enough, not to just come running around the side of the truck and straight into Chapel's line of fire. He heard them shout back and forth, and though he couldn't understand their words, he was sure they were making a plan to flank him. One would come around the front of the truck, the other around the back. He wouldn't be able to fend them both off at once.

He had to move. He looked toward the open end of the shed, the same direction the truck was pointed. There might still be a sniper back there, the one who had killed Varvara's driver. He glanced to the other side, toward the doors the gunmen had come through. There could be more of them out there, waiting for anyone foolish enough to come running out of the shed. The noise of the rifle fire would have alerted them, and they would be ready if Chapel showed his face.

The truck was too high to climb. He considered ducking underneath it, but if either of the remaining gunmen even glanced down there, he would be a sitting duck.

It was while he was thinking about what to do that he heard gunshots outside the shed, out front—pistol fire, and then someone screaming. He glanced out and saw a blur of movement, something fast bouncing around the piles of decayed wooden pallets. It took him a moment to realize it was a human being. He saw it drop to the ground and roll on its shoulder, then spring back up to its feet.

It was Nadia, he realized. She had found another gunman hiding in a pile of tires. The killer brought up his pistol to shoot her, but she was already striking, her hands clenched together for a blow that knocked the pistol right out of the gunman's grip. He tried to recover, but she was just too fast for him, her knee coming up to catch him in the groin. As he bent forward she struck the back of his neck and put him down.

Behind her, another gunman was climbing up on a rusted water heater, lifting his pistol to aim at her head. She would never see him in time.

VOBKENT, UZBEKISTAN: JULY 18, 17:26

Chapel didn't think about what he did next. He didn't have time. Roaring like a bull to draw attention, he dashed toward the open front doors of the shed, not even bothering to keep his head down. The gunman who had aimed at Nadia turned a few degrees to the side.

Chapel lifted his rifle and fired a burst into the gunman's midsection, making him twist and fall backward off the water heater. His pistol spun up into the air.

Nadia darted across the open space in front of the doors and dove for the pistol, sliding across the trash on her side. She didn't quite catch the gun before it hit the ground, but Chapel could have sworn it was still spinning when she snatched it up.

He started to ask if she was all right, but then she lifted the pistol and pointed it right at him. He ducked to the side, and she fired twice, one shot, a beat, a second shot, neat as that.

Behind him he heard someone gasp in pain. Of course—he'd left two gunmen back there, Glasses and the dark-haired one. Chapel ducked down and turned to look. The dark-haired one was on the ground, clutching a wound on his neck. Blood streamed down his shirt inside his suit jacket.

"There's another one in there," Chapel told Nadia.

"I know," she said. She fired again, but she must not have hit Glasses because she shook her head. "I told you, I am a crap shot."

Chapel wanted to laugh. He figured the dark-haired gunman would disagree. He grabbed her arm and pulled her into the cover of a pile of rotten tires.

"Any more of them out here?" he asked.

She shrugged. "I saw three. All accounted for."

"You saw three, or there were three?"

Nadia scowled. "There are no guarantees in this life."

Chapel checked his weapon. There was still half a clip left in the AK-47. "Where's Bogdan?" he asked.

"I don't know. I came out to look for him and that is when I saw these men. Jim—he is almost certainly dead, or captured. The latter case is very bad, because—"

Chapel shook his head. "Not now. I can't think about the future. There's still at least one guy in that shed with a pistol, not to mention the sniper who took out Varvara's driver—"

He jumped when he heard a gun go off inside the shed. There was a bloodcurdling scream and then another gunshot, and then nothing. The second shot had stopped the screaming, presumably for good.

"What the . . . was that the sniper?" Chapel asked, even though it was clear Nadia couldn't answer.

Instead, someone else did. "The marksman is dead," someone called from inside the shed. "Though he did not die easily. He told me many things first, Mr. Chambers."

Chapel knew that voice, though it took him a second to be sure of it.

"Mirza?" he shouted, when he'd put it together.

"The very same. I am going to come out now. Please hold your fire. We have matters to discuss."

Chapel pointed his rifle at the doors of the shed. Nadia lifted her pistol.

The SNB man walked out into the light. He wore a thin Windbreaker over his button-down shirt. His mustache was as neatly combed as ever, and his head shone like a cue ball in the sunlight. He was smiling. He also held a boxy machine pistol in his hands, the barrel of it pointed at them.

Chapel could have taken him out then and there, but there was no guarantee Mirza wouldn't shoot back at the same time. The machine pistol was more than capable of killing both Chapel and Nadia before Mirza died. It looked like a stalemate.

"I have taken care of a problem for you, Mister Chambers," Mirza said. "The fellow back there with the spectacles will not bother you again."

"These guys weren't working for you?" Chapel asked.

"Indeed, no," Mirza said. "May I approach you, do you think?"

"You're fine right there." Chapel wanted to look over at Nadia, see if she could make any sense out of this. He had no idea what his next move should be. "I will say thanks. These assholes were following us for a while."

"Yes," Mirza confirmed. "They arrived in Tashkent last night. When I learned they were looking for you, I followed them all the way here. Just one of the many ways I have sought to be useful to you, Mr. Chambers. I think perhaps it is time you reciprocated. Perhaps by putting down your weapon."

"Sure," Chapel said. "Just let me make sure of a couple of things first. These guys were Romanian gangsters, looking for my computer geek. You seen him around here anywhere?"

Mirza laughed. "Do you know the most difficult part of my job, Mister Chambers? People give me false information all the time. The difficult part is knowing when people are simply ignorant, or mistaken, or when they are intentionally lying. These men were not Romanian."

"They weren't?" Chapel asked.

"Ah, that sounds like a man who has been misinformed. No. They were Russians. And they were not looking for your computer specialist. They were looking for Nadia Asimova."

"They . . . what?" Chapel asked.

"Oh, did you think her name was actually Svetlana Shulkina? You see how difficult it becomes when people lie to us? I really think it is time for us to talk man-to-man. So put down your weapons, please."

"And what happens then?" Chapel asked, though mostly just to stall for time to think. Mirza had blown Nadia's cover but far worse than that—the gunmen were Russians, and they were chasing Nadia, which meant . . .

"You and I will return to Tashkent. You will explain to me how you came to be involved with a Russian criminal. Not that I particularly care— however, it will be useful information when I negotiate with your company. I will schedule meetings with the top men in the Interior Ministry. You and I will find a way for your company to work with Uzbekistan."

"You're going to blackmail me into making a bad deal, huh?" Apparently Mirza still thought he was Jeff Chambers, energy executive. So part of the cover story remained intact.

"You'll still make money here, Chambers," Mirza said. "But perhaps you will not rob my country as mercilessly as you'd hoped."

Chapel shook his head. "What about my assistant?"

"Asimova? Well." He shrugged, though not so much that his aim wavered. "I will kill her, of course. She is wanted alive or dead, and she has already shown she is a fighter. She will be much easier to ship home in a crate."

VOBKENT, UZBEKISTAN: JULY 18, 17:39

Chapel didn't even need to think about the deal. "It's not going to happen, Mirza. Put down *your* gun, and we'll talk about what happens next."

Mirza didn't flinch. "That would seem foolish. There would be no reason for Asimova not to shoot me, then."

Chapel sighed in frustration. "We all need to calm down and think. We need to find a way to make sure nobody gets shot."

"Are you sleeping with her, Mr. Chambers? Has she seduced you? I think you are not realizing that this is a rescue mission. I am here to protect you from her, first and foremost. I have also protected you from the Russian spies who were sent to retrieve her. I assure you, they had orders to kill you as well. Their plan was to have their sniper pick the two of you off. When that did not happen—thanks to me, alone—they stormed into this place to finish the job. I admire your ability to survive that attack, but you could not have done so without my help. I am your only friend here, Mr. Chambers, whether you believe it or not."

Chapel frowned in thought. "If she puts down her weapon—"

"This is not a matter for discussion," Mirza said.

"Goddamnit, it is! This is your only chance of getting out of here alive, Mirza," Chapel said.

Nadia did not turn away from the SNB man as she spoke. She was too smart to drop her guard even for an instant. "Jeff," she said, because apparently she'd figured out as well that his cover wasn't compromised, "this man is a *butcher*. He works for a government that routinely slaughters its own people, just to maintain political control—"

"I'm not going to kill a man in cold blood," Chapel told her. "I don't care if he deserves it or not. Put down your gun."

She stared at him with questioning eyes. She was trying to decide, he thought, if he was speaking truthfully—or if he only intended to disarm Mirza so that he could be killed safely.

It was the kind of business they were in, where that kind of moral calculus was acceptable. Chapel had no doubt that if Rupert Hollingshead were there just then, the old man would advise him that killing Mirza was the only way forward.

But Hollingshead wasn't there. And despite what people consistently seemed to believe, Jim Chapel was no murderer. He killed only in self-defense.

Eventually, Nadia dropped her pistol and raised her hands above her head. She was trusting him to do the right thing here.

Even if her definition of the right thing and his were different.

"Now. Mirza. You saved my life, and maybe what you're saying about Svetlana is true," Chapel said. "If you want to save anything out of this mess, you'll put your gun down, as well."

The SNB man inhaled sharply. Then he dropped the machine pistol.

"All right," Chapel said, and he nodded slowly. "Now I'm going to tell you how this ends. She and I are going to get into that truck, and we're going to drive away. You won't follow us." He couldn't read Mirza's face. He knew he couldn't trust the man. But he had to move forward. "You're not going to report any of this to your superiors. We're going to drive to Afghanistan, we're going to leave your country as quickly as possible, and we're never coming back. Do you understand?"

Mirza smiled. It was not a warm smile. "I understand that you believe this will happen," he said.

"He'll hound us," Nadia protested. "He'll send an army after us—Jeff—"

"I'm giving you a chance, Mirza," Chapel said. "A chance to—"

He stopped in midsentence because he'd heard something. Someone was moving around back in the shed, back near the truck. But there wasn't supposed to be anyone still alive back there—all four of the Russians were dead, there was no one—

Time slowed, then, as things happened very fast.

Mirza started turning, his eyes still locked on Chapel and his AK-47. His hands lifted, as if he were reaching for another weapon, or as if he wanted to surrender. Chapel would never know which.

Because suddenly Bogdan was standing in the doors of the shed, an assault rifle gripped in both of his skinny hands. His hair had blown back and his eyes were very wide, as was his mouth, showing bared teeth. The depressive hacker was gone, replaced by some vicious Romanian monster out of legend as he squeezed his trigger and fired thirty rounds on full automatic, the bullets tearing Mirza's chest to ribbons.

The SNB man didn't even have time to look surprised.

VOBKENT, UZBEKISTAN: JULY 18, 17:45

"Oh crap," Chapel said, staring at what remained of Jamshid Mirza.

Nadia, without a word, bent down and picked up her pistol again.

"What?" Bogdan asked.

The hacker's face had relaxed again, now that his enemy was dead. His bangs fell back down over his eyes, and other than the fact he was still holding an assault rifle, he looked exactly as he always had.

"Something is wrong?" he said.

"Where were you?" Nadia asked. "I went looking for you."

"I hear people come, so I hide," Bogdan said. He lifted his shoulders and let them sag again. "In the chicken coops, yes? Then I see men coming, with weapons, I think I am dead. The American killed those men, and later, the Uzbek killed another one. But he is our enemy, so I went in truck and found guns and kill him."

"That . . . makes sense," Nadia said.

"Was right thing to do, yes? He is our enemy?"

"He . . . was," Nadia agreed. "Jim?"

Chapel wanted very much to sit down. He wanted time to figure out what had happened and where everything went wrong.

Sometimes in life you don't get what you want.

"Okay," he said. "We need to . . . we have to . . ."

There was a course forward, a series of steps he could take that would get them out of there and to a place of safety. He was getting stuck, though, on the first step. He couldn't think straight, couldn't—

"We need to hide these bodies," he said. Because that had to be the first thing they did.

His moment of doubt passed. One of the most useful things the army had ever taught him was that motion and activity were a passable substitute for a rational plan. "It may already be too late. Maybe someone in one of the buildings nearby heard something. Maybe they'll come to look. Maybe they'll find Mirza and report his death, and his friends in the SNB will know he was assigned to watch us. I'm sure he told them where he was headed, he would be a fool not to leave word with somebody that he was coming here, and Mirza didn't seem like a fool."

"He fell for your cover story," Nadia pointed out.

"The cover was solid. Yours, on the other hand—"

That was a whole other kettle of fish. He hadn't even begun to process what Mirza had said about Nadia. That she was wanted by the Russian government. That the blond thugs had not, in fact, been Romanian gangsters looking for Bogdan but Russian security men sent to kill *her*.

If he started down that path, he was going to have to question all kinds of things that so far he had comfortably taken for granted.

Later, he told himself.

"Never mind. Help me with these bodies. Bogdan, see if you can find a tarp or something. A sheet, a cloth, plastic—it doesn't matter. We need to hide this mess as best we can and be out of here as soon as damned possible."

He realized he was babbling, that he was talking more than he was thinking, but he didn't care. He started hauling bodies around, then, and talking through the process helped him not think too much about what he was doing, about what he'd already done to the dead men. With Nadia's help he got them inside the shed, where at least they wouldn't be seen from the street. Bogdan found some old stained blankets in the pile of trash that filled the lot, and Chapel covered the bodies because that seemed more respectful than just letting them lie there on the dirty shed floor.

When it was done, he got the three of them in the truck. The driver's seat was still wet with blood, the blood of Varvara's man. There was still a bullet hole in the windshield. He ignored these things. He got the truck in gear and drove out of the shed. There was just room to drive the big truck around to the gates at the front of the lot, though it took a lot of maneuvering. Nadia jumped out and pushed the gates open wide enough so that Chapel could drive through them. Then she jumped back in the truck, and Chapel put it back in gear.

"Head north," she told him. "If we can get out into the open desert, away from the main roads, we have a chance to—"

"No," he told her.

"No?"

"No. We head southeast. To Afghanistan. Like I said."

Nadia shook her head. "That doesn't make any sense. It is exactly the wrong direction!"

"No," Chapel said. "Afghanistan."

"But why?"

"Because," he told her, "we're aborting the mission."

IN TRANSIT: JULY 18, 18:22

Nadia was right about one thing—they needed to get into the desert before anyone came looking for them. Chapel took the truck to the edge of town and then rolled off the road, into a scrubby field of weeds. Ahead of them lay irrigation ditches and a few cultivated cotton fields and then nothing but sand as far as the eye could see. Though the truck was hardly inconspicuous, it was clearly meant for crossing rough terrain. The big tires always found something to grip, and the wide wheel base kept them from pitching about too much even when the ground rose and fell beneath them.

The seats weren't exactly comfortable, just a thin layer of padding over flat steel, and he imagined he would get pretty sore if he tried driving the truck all day. But the Afghan border was only a hundred miles away or so, and once they were across they could simply find the nearest American troops and then they would be safe. Hollingshead would get them space on a transport plane headed back to the States and they would be home free.

All they had to do was cross that hundred miles of desert before the SNB realized that Mirza was missing and started looking for them.

Bogdan sat in the back and clicked away at his MP3 player/computer. Chapel didn't know what he was doing with his improvised keyboard and didn't much care at that point.

Nadia, of course, didn't like his plan. She pleaded with him constantly to turn back, to head north again.

"I'm the lead agent on this mission," she said, staring at him from the passenger seat. "I'm ordering you to go back."

He didn't even turn his head to look at her.

"Jim, please," Nadia said. "Just listen to me for one moment. I've spent years of my life planning this operation. If we just stop now, I'll never get another chance."

"You have no chance now," Chapel told her. "If we headed for Kazakhstan, how far do you think we would get? Even if we made it across the border, the SNB would just call up their friends over there and tell them that three dangerous fugitives were headed into their territory in a vehicle that any reconnaissance plane could pick up in a second. And that's even assuming they don't tell the Russians about us."

She looked away, out through her window over the endless rippling landscape of sand.

"You know, the Russians? The people who are trying to kill you?" he asked. He was angry, and he didn't care if he was shouting. "The people you said you worked for?"

"Jim—"

"You came to us claiming to represent the Russian government. You said this mission was sanctioned by the Kremlin. You lied to us, Nadia. You lied to me."

"It's not how you think," she insisted. "It's . . . I admit that things have become complicated. But—"

"Who do you really work for?" he demanded.

"FSTEK. My superior is Marshal Bulgachenko." She reached over and for a second he thought she was going to grab the wheel. Instead she reached for his arm. He shrugged her off. "I didn't lie. I just omitted some of the truth."

"Jesus," he said. He smacked the steering wheel with his artificial hand. "You put me in danger, Nadia."

"I know."

"You tricked the government of the United States into supporting this mission."

"*Konyechno*, but—"

"You saw the Russian hit squad in Bucharest and you let me think they were just local gangsters and we could run away from them."

"This is true."

"Stop saying that! I'm not sure you even know what the word 'true' means."

She reached for him again and he shoved her away, harder than he'd meant to. She curled up in the far end of her seat, staring at him.

"Bogdan," she said, in a soft voice.

Chapel started to ask a question, at least to vent his confusion. It took him a second to realize she wasn't talking to him.

Bogdan tapped some keys on his MP3 player, and suddenly the truck's engine died. It wheezed to a stop, the truck halfway up a sand dune, its nose pointed at the sky. For a second it just hung there as if it had hit a brick wall. Then it slipped backward a few yards as it lost its grip on the loose sand.

Chapel stared at the dashboard. All the controls were labeled in Cyrillic characters, but the needles on all the gauges had dropped to zero—even the fuel gauge. All power had been cut to the engine and to the displays.

"Clever," Chapel said. "Let me guess. Antitheft controls."

Nadia's voice was much easier to hear without the engine noise drowning it out. "This vehicle is of Russian military manufacture. We had a problem, a few years back, with our soldiers stealing our equipment. They weren't getting paid, you see—they were owed a great deal of back pay—and many of them figured they were then justified to simply drive their vehicles off their bases and sell them on the black market. So we installed a chip in every vehicle to make sure this could not be done. Bogdan has simply activated that chip. He can deactivate it, if I feel he should."

"If I agree to continue with this crazy mission, you mean."

"*Konyechno*. Exactly. I still need you, Jim. I need my *svidetel*."

Chapel glared at her for a while. He said nothing.

Eventually, when she didn't relent just because he looked at her funny, he gave up. He popped open the door of the truck and jumped out, landing in the soft sand. It took a second to get used to the yielding ground, but he managed. Step by halting step, he started marching, to the southeast.

Behind him Nadia leaned out of the cab door. She called after him, shouting his name over and over, as he went on, placing his feet carefully on the shifting sand.

He didn't get very far.

"Jim," she called, when he had taken maybe a dozen steps. "Jim, I think it is time to call your boss."

"He's not going to like you any more than I do right now," he called back.

"Even so." Her face was set, her normally jovial features very, very serious suddenly. "Jim, I think you should get Angel on the line."

That was enough to stop him.

"I beg your pardon?" he demanded.

SOUTHEAST OF VOBKENT, UZBEKISTAN: JULY 18, 18:56

Nadia jumped down onto the sand and walked toward him. "You need to contact Angel and set up an immediate call with Director Hollingshead," she said.

"Listen," Chapel told her, "I don't know what you think you know—"

"Did you think I never wondered why you spent so much time in bathrooms with your tablet?" she asked. "Did you think I would not listen in?"

Her face had changed in the last few seconds. The softness, the friendliness, was gone. Now she looked like a soldier. Resolute, unapologetic, and unflinching.

"You spied on me?" he asked, though it sounded lame even to his own ears.

"Of course I did. That is what we do," she said. "And please, do not take this moral tone with me. I know you did the same—just yesterday, when you attempted to question Bogdan about my previous mission. You made some very educated guesses, didn't you? You asked him about a plutonium theft, convinced him you knew everything so there was no harm in talking. I admire your skills, Jim."

Chapel shook his head. "So we're putting all our cards on the table," he said. "Okay. Tell me what's really going on. Tell me about the Russians hunting you."

"I will tell Director Hollingshead. You may listen while I do."

Chapel stared at her, unable to process the way she'd changed. Unable to reconcile the Nadia he'd seen before with this woman.

When he was done trying—and failing—he went over to the truck and climbed the ladder to the cab. He went to his bag and took out his tablet. Before climbing back out of the truck he looked over at Bogdan.

The hacker was curled up in one of the backseats, clicking away at his MP3 player. Looking bored, mostly. He didn't look at all like a man who had slaughtered an Uzbek security agent with an assault rifle. He didn't look like the kind of guy who could screw up a mission in the time it took to empty a clip of bullets.

It seemed like today was the day he learned who everybody really was. He reached over and grabbed the headphones off Bogdan's head. The Romanian flinched and made a noise that might have been a halfhearted protest, but Chapel ignored it. He pulled the headphone jack out of the MP3 player and shoved the headphones into his own bag. For good measure he grabbed the MP3 player—Bogdan's connection to the outside world—and shoved that in his pocket.

"What is the meaning?" Bogdan asked, his voice high, almost squeaky. Maybe that was how he expressed outrage.

"You get this stuff back when I'm sure you won't get me killed with it," Chapel told him. Bogdan had more to say, but Chapel didn't listen. He climbed out of the cab and staggered across the sand. Nadia was waiting for him under a tree a few dozen yards away, the only shade available from the evening sun.

He stared at her for a second, gritting his teeth. Then he switched on his tablet.

"Angel," he said.

She answered immediately. "Sugar? Are you alone? I'm showing you don't have your headphones plugged into this tablet. Is it safe to talk?"

"No," Chapel said, "but we need to anyway. Nadia knows all about you, apparently. Though watch what you say anyway. She's tricky."

"I . . . see. Agent Asimova? Can you hear me?"

"Yes, miss," Nadia said. "It is a pleasure to make your acquaintance at long last."

Angel sounded pretty wary when she replied. "Likewise, I'm sure," she said. "Um, I'm not really sure this is kosher. Sugar, you know what the director said about—"

"We both know what he said. Let's not go into it now. Angel, I need you to call the director, actually.

We need to discuss whether or not we're going to scrub the mission. Things have gotten . . . complicated."

Angel's only reply to that was to switch the tablet over to its telephone screen. Digits appeared one by one there as if Chapel had typed them in: 01 00 000 000-000-0000. Chapel had seen numbers like that before—it meant Angel wasn't taking any chances, not even letting Nadia see what American area code she was calling. The 01 at the beginning was just a country code, indicating the call was headed to the United States.

Chapel set the tablet in between two low branches on the tree, so that it faced both him and Nadia at eye level. Hollingshead answered almost immediately. It would be midmorning in Washington, and he most likely would have had a line open with Angel anyway, just to monitor the mission in Uzbekistan. His face appeared on the screen, with just a plain neutral background behind him that didn't give away anything about where he was. He looked out of the screen with genial eyes that opened a lot wider when he saw Nadia peering back at him.

"Son?" he said. "This is a little unexpected."

"I understand, sir, and if circumstances were different, I wouldn't be contacting you like this. But things have gotten bad over here. Very bad." He explained as quickly as he could how Mirza had followed them to the truck's location, and how Bogdan had killed him. He repeated what Mirza had told him—that Nadia had a price on her head, that the Russians wanted her dead or alive. Nadia glanced away when he said that, as if she were ashamed.

Well, good, he thought. She should be. "She lied to us, sir. She misrepresented her support."

"Young lady," Hollingshead said, blinking behind his thick glasses, "this is quite serious. You understand that? You involved the United States in this mission with the understanding that your country was fully in line."

"I know this, sir," she said. "You have my apology."

"I'm going to want a bit more than that."

She nodded. "Yes, it is true, there are Russians who . . . disagree with what I am doing. My country is very large, and it has many, many security agencies. I think you will understand when I say they do not always cooperate, yes?"

Hollingshead sighed. "All too well." Chapel knew why that thought exasperated the old man. The secret directorate in the Pentagon had fought brush wars with American civilian intelligence groups in the past—one of which involved a CIA assassin sent to take Chapel's life.

"There are men, mostly ex-KGB," Nadia explained, "who think Perimeter should be kept intact. That it is a vital part of the Fatherland's defenses. These men have power in the Kremlin, power enough to call for my execution—or worse. Men who would very much like to torture me for the information I possess. I have avoided their clutches this far, but I knew they would come eventually."

"And you chose not to tell us this, when you came to us for help."

Nadia shrugged. "You would have said no, I thought."

Hollingshead's frown deepened. "You're quite

right about that." He turned to look at Chapel. "Son—what's your plan now?"

"I'm thinking we should abort," he told the director. "Exfiltrate immediately and return home while we still have the chance. As for Asimova—"

"No," she said. "No, I do not agree. There is no reason to stop now. We have no reason to believe that the SNB knows of our plans, or that they are even tracing us right now. They cannot know our destination. If we move quickly, if we drive all night, we can be in Kazakhstan before dawn. This is not the time to turn back."

"I see," Hollingshead said. "Well, now, this is a dilemma. You're supposed to be lead on this mission. But I gave you that courtesy because I thought I knew who you were. I have to say, I'm inclined to Jim's way of thinking."

Chapel nodded. "Very good, sir, I'll—"

"No!" Nadia said again. "No, I will not accept this! Do you have any idea how long I have worked toward this goal? What I sacrificed to get this far?"

Hollingshead frowned. "Agent Asimova, who do you even work for?" he asked.

"FSTEK, as I have always said," she told him. "Call Marshal Bulgachenko. He will vouch for me, as he already has."

Hollingshead took off his glasses, presumably to polish them offscreen. "I'm afraid I have some bad news for you. Marshal Bulgachenko turned in his resignation a few days ago. And then . . . well, there's no pleasant way to say this. His body was found the next morning, floating in the Neva River."

"He is . . . dead? Konstantin? Dead?" Nadia

asked. She put her hands over her face and turned away from the screen. "No, please, it cannot be so. It cannot! He was . . . he was a father to me, do you understand?"

"I'm sorry you had to hear it like this," Hollingshead told her. "But certainly you can see how that changes things."

She didn't respond. She was too busy weeping.

Chapel fought down an urge to reach for her, to comfort her. He needed to stop thinking those kind of thoughts, and he needed to stop right now.

"Sir," he said, "whatever we plan on doing, we need to do it fast. Every minute we wait the SNB gets closer to finding Mirza's body—and when they do, they'll put every resource they have into finding us."

"Understood, son. Agent Asimova, how did you get into this mess?"

"I will tell you," she said, through her hands. "I will tell you everything."

SOUTHEAST OF VOBKENT, UZBEKISTAN: JULY 18, 19:12

Nadia fell down on her knees in the sand. When she pulled her hands away from her face, Chapel saw that her tears, at least, had been real.

"It was Konstantin Bulgachenko who recruited me, out of college," she said.

She looked up at Chapel, then at the tablet. She cleared her throat noisily and wiped at her cheeks. "Forgive me. This is a long story."

"Make it shorter," Chapel growled. "We need to move."

Nadia lifted her shoulders, then let them drop. "I will try."

Then she started talking.

"I studied nuclear engineering, in the college. I thought I would return home, to Yakutia, and work there for a mining company, digging uranium out of the ground to help build nuclear power plants. Instead the marshal came to see me. He took me to lunch. He was not a charming man, but . . . endearing in his way. He wore his uniform and his flat cap and he never smiled. He looked like something from a history book, from the Soviet days, and I was young enough then to find such a thing romantic. He said he had seen my records and he was very impressed. He said he had a job for me, one that would make a real difference in the world. I was young—a student still. That idea appealed to me. I thought I had a choice, that I could accept or decline his offer, but of course there was no choice at all. I had already been recruited. Otherwise he would never have been able to talk to me like he did that day.

"He told me that after the fall of the Soviet Union, a large amount of military hardware had gone missing—stolen by the soldiers who once guarded it, sold on the black market. This was hardly news. I was young and thought I knew everything and I laughed . . . until he told me that some of that hardware, approximately one hundred and fifty kilograms of it, was plutonium. Enough to build perhaps twenty-fire hydrogen bombs. And he had no idea where it might be. I did not laugh then.

"His organization, FSTEK, had been given the task of quietly finding that material and returning it to Russian control. He said they had already recovered some ten kilograms. He said he needed people like me, people who understood nuclear materials, to find the rest.

"I did not know it during that lunch, but already I had become a state secret. I did not go home to my dormitory after that. I have never been back since. The marshal spirited me away immediately and cut me off from the world I knew. I was not allowed to speak with my friends or even my family. My things were taken to a new apartment in Moscow, a place that I did not leave for another six months without an escort.

"Perhaps I should have been terrified. Instead, I was exhilarated. I had work to do, vital work—work that could save countless lives. Work to be proud of. Before he had used police techniques to find the nuclear material. The process was slow—it required too much human intelligence. With Geiger counters and satellites, I made the work much more efficient. In my first six months, I managed to locate another fifty kilograms of the missing plutonium—often, only a few grams at a time. In Kiev, we found some in an abandoned factory. More in a garbage pit near Krasnoyarsk. The worst was when we found sixty canisters, nearly three full kilograms, in a railroad siding outside of Moscow, hidden in among general stores and supplies for the maintenance of trains. The men who worked there, the railroad men, they had seen the canisters every day, had walked past them and never even wondered what was inside. One of the canisters was not properly shielded, and it . . . leaked. Most of the men I spoke to are . . . dead now."

She shook her head. "This was our worst discovery. It was not, however, the most dangerous. We found two kilograms were sitting in a warehouse in Bucharest. We tracked the men who had moved the plutonium to that warehouse. We found they were gangsters, the worst kind of criminal. And that they had a buyer—a man known to have affiliations with North Korea. The material had to be recovered, at any cost.

"We could not simply go there and take it away from them. We had no authority outside the borders of Russia. We needed someone who could infiltrate the gang and steal the material. This is when I became a true operative. I begged Marshal Bulgachenko to allow me to go, personally, to recover the material. He did not wish to agree. He thought of me as a child still, a little girl, incapable of such a thing. I did my best to persuade him I was the right one for the job. In the end I believe he relented only because I already knew all the details. Choosing another agent would mean briefing them, telling them secrets that were vital to state security.

"I received intensive training before the mission began. I took a crash course in the Romanian language. I learned how to fire a gun, though I was never very good at that—no marksman, certainly. I was given combat training, hand-to-hand fighting techniques and the like, by a man who had been a trainer for the Spetsnaz, our special forces. That was the hardest part: day after day of exercises, of sparring and then fighting with blunted knives. Every night I would come home to my bed bruised and sore in new places, desperately tired, but I would have to stay up to read more intelligence reports, more daily updates on the Romanian gang.

"Jim, you have heard some of the actual mission. I went to Romania, where the transfer was to take place. There I found Bogdan. He was in desperate trouble, about to be arrested for sedition. The sentence would be death. In exchange for his life—I do not know how it was arranged, someone made a deal—in exchange for immunity, he agreed to hack into the files of the gang, and of the buyers.

"When Bogdan told me where the exchange was to be made, in a parking structure in Bucharest, I went there with twenty men, all of them highly trained soldiers. Things . . . went wrong. The gangsters were ready for us somehow; they were armed with machine guns. The buyers came with their own security. There was a firefight that lasted for nearly ten minutes, and at the end only I and two of my soldiers remained standing. All of us were wounded.

"There was no time . . . the local police were closing in. The gangsters had reinforcements coming. I did not have time to think things through. I made . . . I made a very bad mistake. The plutonium was in a bag, a kind of duffel bag with lead shielding. I picked it up and carried it from that place. I had to make my way most carefully out of Romania, often by hitchhiking or stowing away on trains. I could not allow myself to be caught by police, you see—not with what I was carrying. For six weeks I never let that bag out of my sight, not until I was back in Russia. I took it to an FSTEK facility and there, finally, I turned it over to technicians who could dispose of it properly.

"They opened the bag and took out the plutonium and I thought I was done, that my mission was over and a success. It was only then one of the technicians—he was dressed in a full hazard suit, and he would only touch the bag with lead-lined gloves. He looked at me with eyes that were . . . very sad. He opened the bag and showed me the lead lining, the shielding that had protected me from the radioactivity over those six weeks.

"He showed me there was a hole in it. During the firefight, a bullet had pierced the bag. Cut almost clear through the lining.

"For six weeks I had been carrying a bag full of the most toxic substance the world has ever seen. For six weeks, it had been poisoning me. And I never knew."

SOUTHEAST OF VOBKENT, UZBEKISTAN: JULY 18, 19:33

"You were—irradiated?" Chapel asked, barely able to believe her story.

"The lining was not pierced entirely. If it had been, I would have died within hours of picking up that bag. As it was I only received a moderate dose of radiation."

"How much?" Chapel asked.

She shrugged. "Perhaps twenty, maybe thirty millisieverts per day."

Chapel was unsure what that meant.

Nadia looked him straight in the eye. "It was the equivalent, say, of having my whole body x-rayed once per day. For more than forty days in a row. It is a . . . significant exposure."

She stood up and went over to the tablet hanging in the tree. She spoke directly to Hollingshead as she went on. "I was examined by many doctors. They told me there was one immediate effect: I was now sterile. The radiation had destroyed all my eggs. I will never have children, now. But this seemed less important to them than the other effect, that I had increased my possibility of dying from cancer at an early age. I asked them for specifics, but they said with cancer there was no such thing, that one could never predict what would happen. I asked for an estimate, a guess. I said, what is the percentage chance that I will die of a cancer before I am forty?

"They said, ninety-nine percent."

"Nadia," Chapel said, though he had no idea what he would say next. How do you comfort someone who's gotten news like that?

She ignored his sympathy. "I went to Marshal Bulgachenko and told him all this and he wept. He had a bottle of vodka in his desk, still sealed. He said it had been given to him by Andropov. He opened it that night and we talked for a very long time, talked and drank. I could not seem to get drunk, or perhaps not drunk enough. The marshal said I should retire from FSTEK, retire and move somewhere pretty and end my days looking at water. The sea, the ocean . . . I said no. I said instead I wished to use what time remained to me to do something vital. Something useful.

"The marshal told me he had something in mind. It was very, very secret but we had finished off his special bottle by then and I think he would have told me anything. He spoke of Perimeter that night, and it was the first time I ever heard of it. He told me what it had been designed to do. He told me of the great shame around it, that so much of it was forgotten, untouchable. He said it had long been his dream to dismantle Perimeter.

"At first I thought nothing of it, that this was some Cold War fable, that it did not matter to us today. But when I sobered up, when I went back to work, I did some research. I found little, but enough to intrigue me. I dug deeper, and at every turn it seemed the system was more crazy, more dangerous. In the end I became obsessed. I discovered that the greatest secret, Perimeter's forgotten location, had been kept in a certain document, a list of secret facilities known only to the KGB. This list was destroyed, no copies remained . . . but one. One in a KGB library no one had visited since the fall of the Union. I tracked it down. I held it in my hand, the map reference, and committed it to my memory. This would be the last thing I would do, the thing that would justify my sacrifice. I would destroy Perimeter.

"I went back to the marshal and told him what I'd found. I said I was ready, that I would do this thing in the time I had. I was exultant. Only then did he tell me it was impossible. Already I had met some resistance. There were people in the FSB— this is the successor to the KGB—who felt that any change, any diminishment in the nuclear arsenal was a sign of weakness and therefore unacceptable. There were others whose reputations, whose careers, would be damaged if it were revealed how they had let Perimeter get away from them." Nadia shrugged. "I had been threatened. I thought nothing of it. I was going to die young; why worry about some menacing fools? But the marshal knew better. He understood interdepartmental politics better than I. FSTEK is an autonomous body, on paper. In reality it is subordinate to FSB. Despite all I had done, all I had achieved, he could not get approval for this mission."

"I notice, young lady, that it didn't stop you," Hollingshead said.

"At first, I obeyed. I was no rebel, to go against the entire intelligence community for one personal crusade. But then something changed . . . I was receiving monthly physicals. Monthly CT scans, to check my bones, my pancreas, my liver, for any sign of cancer. Six months ago one of these scans came back positive. It is in me, now. It is deep inside my organs, where it is impossible to cut out. The doctors called me in, spoke with me at great length. Before they could barely look at me. Now they found me fascinating. I would be a wonderful test subject—physically fit, perfectly healthy except for this one thing. I had a good chance of surviving some new experimental treatments. Chemotherapies untried before. New advances in, of all things, radiation therapy. Hope blossomed inside me—how could it not? I thought perhaps the last few years had all been a terrible dream. That my impending death might be averted.

"That was when they explained. No, they could not save me. They could extend my life by a few years, perhaps, years I would spend in a bed, in constant nausea and agony, years of suffering instead of a relatively quick death.

"I could only stare at them. They were ghouls—I could see in their eyes they were already mentally carving up my corpse to see how well their treatments had worked. I . . . assaulted one. Struck him down right there in the hospital. He was more surprised than hurt. Did I not wish to give myself to the glory of medicine, to the advancement of the healing arts? Did I not wish for my tragedy to have some meaning, some purpose?

"I went to the marshal again, this time with a plan in my hands. A document describing how I would defeat Perimeter, what I still required—the one-time pad—how I would acquire it. I had written the plan in such a way that two or three people could make it happen, and no one need to know it was being done until it was accomplished. The same plan I presented to you, Director. The plan we have followed so far.

"The marshal tried to stop me, but I was done with men telling me what could be accomplished. What was *possible*. What was *politically viable*. Enough, I told him. I go to Washington with or without your blessing. Maybe the Americans would laugh at me, maybe they would arrest me. But still I would go.

"The marshal was the man who made me what I am. He understood me like no one else. He could see in my eyes that I would do this thing. Still he did not say yes—but he did not stop me from going to America. From contacting you. I had no idea if he would back me the way I hoped, even when I met with you the first time. I did not know what would happen. When you said yes, well . . ."

She shook her head. "Here we are. You know the

truth, now. You know what I have done, and why. I will go on to Kazakhstan with or without Jim. I will finish what I started. They tell me I have only months left, months of good health and then a quick decline. They tell me the end will be painful if I do not seek medical treatment, but that it will be over in a week or so." She looked back over her shoulder at Chapel. "I will not get a second chance at this."

Chapel just stood there, uncertain what he should do or say.

But that was Hollingshead's job, after all.

"Young lady," the director said, "that's quite a story. But it doesn't change a damned thing."

SOUTHEAST OF VOBKENT, UZBEKISTAN: JULY 18, 19:49

Nadia stared at the tablet, her face a mask of disbelief.

Hollingshead had the decency to look away as he explained himself. "This has already gone too far. You've implicated the United States in what could turn into an international incident. You tricked us into conspiring with you when you had no national credentials. That's simply unconscionable. Your actions have led to the death of an Uzbek government official—"

"A butcher of his people," Nadia pointed out.

Hollingshead shook his head. "I'll lose no sleep over Mirza's demise. But the government of Uzbekistan will not just forget about him. They'll want to know why he died, and if they turn to me for answers, I will have none."

"Then I will go on alone, as I say—"

"Not without my authorization," Hollingshead told her. "Damnation, girl, don't you see? They saw Chapel in Tashkent. They photographed him. If you're caught in Kazakhstan, if the Russians catch up with you, they will get Chapel's name from you one way or another. They will trace him back to us. So I cannot allow you to proceed alone. If necessary, I will order Chapel to detain you, by force."

"Sir," Chapel said, though he wasn't sure if he was trying to protest or acknowledging that he was ready to follow orders.

"But what then? Will you turn me over to the FSB who hunt me, with an apology? Will you tell the whole world how you were duped by a rogue agent?" Nadia demanded, her eyes flashing.

"If that were necessary, yes, I would do exactly that. I would hand you to them on a silver platter if I thought it would smooth things over."

"Knowing, as you must, what they would do? How they would torture me, until they were satisfied they knew everything? How then they would put a bullet in my brain, and bury me in an unmarked grave?" Nadia said.

"Yes," Hollingshead said, almost growling. "In a heartbeat."

Sometimes Chapel forgot that the director's bow ties and his thick glasses and his genial manner were a carefully studied act, meant to disarm the people he spoke with, to get them to trust him. Sometimes he forgot that before Hollingshead had become a spymaster, he'd been an admiral in the United States Navy. And that you didn't get to that rank in the armed forces without having solid titanium vertebrae. Chapel found himself standing at attention, unconsciously adopting the posture of a soldier in the midst of an old-fashioned full-on ass-chewing.

"Fortunately—for you at least, young lady," Hollingshead went on, his voice softening by the narrowest degree, "it needn't come to that. Chapel can escort you back to the United States. Once you're here we will protect you from the FSB. We will strive to make the remainder of your life comfortable. Of course, you'll have to sing for your supper. You'll be questioned, and while I do not torture those who fall under my microscope, I can assure you that we will be thorough. You will tell us everything you know, every tiny detail, every name, place, and date before we're done with you. But you won't be hunted down like a dog. That, Agent Asimova, is the very best you can hope for right now."

"You're assuming Chapel can subdue me," Nadia said, baring her teeth.

"Are you really going to make me find out?" Hollingshead asked her.

Nadia had a pistol tucked into her belt.

Chapel had one, too.

If it happened—if he was given the order to detain her—it wasn't going to be a fistfight. It would be over very quickly, and one of them was going to get shot. Maybe killed.

He didn't know if he could do that.

Hollingshead and Nadia stared each other down, through the screen of the tablet. Maybe, Chapel thought, maybe if he moved fast enough, and quietly enough, he could anticipate the order. Maybe he could get his arm around her neck, put pressure on her carotid artery, knock her out before she could react . . .

Maybe it would work. But maybe not.

Spetsnaz. She said she'd been trained by the Spetsnaz, the Russian special forces, and he knew it was true. Those acrobatic moves she'd used in Bucharest and again at the shed in Vobkent, the high kicks, the twisting evasions—he knew he'd seen them before. Back in Ranger school, his trainer Bigelow had showed him videos of those moves and told him just how dangerous they were. If he tried to choke her out, she would have a dozen different ways to reverse his attack, to put him at the disadvantage—

"Wait," he said.

Nadia turned to face him. On the tablet's screen he saw Director Hollingshead nod, just to indicate Chapel had his attention.

"Maybe," he said, "maybe there's a way to still pull this off."

SOUTHEAST OF VOBKENT, UZBEKISTAN: JULY 18, 20:01

Chapel scrubbed at his face. It had been a hot day and he felt grimy and very tired, but he forced himself to focus.

"Son," Hollingshead said through the tablet, "I think we all want to—"

"Sir, just . . . please. Just hear me out. When Mirza tracked us down, he blew Nadia's cover—the Russians told him who she was. But he never figured out that I wasn't who I said I was. He still thought I was Jeff Chambers, that I was a venture capitalist looking to invest in Uzbek energy concerns. He thought he could blackmail me, holding over my head the fact that I'd somehow gotten involved with a Russian criminal. We can use that. We can make it look like Nadia kidnapped Chambers and is on the run, but still in Uzbekistan."

He glanced over at the truck, a few yards away. "I don't think the SNB knows about the truck. Neither do the Russians. The three of us can drive to Kazakhstan right now and get out of the country. Meanwhile Angel can plant some false information—phone in anonymous tips, saying that we've been sighted, getting on a train in Bukhara, say, or trying to cross into Afghanistan. You know Angel can make it sound good, make it sound like credible intelligence. Maybe . . . maybe she can pose as someone from Chambers's company back in the States and demand to know where he is. The SNB will put all their resources to tracking us down in their own country. They'll have no reason to alert the Kazakhs, and no reason to go looking for a giant desert-crossing truck. Perimeter is only a few days from the border, it won't take us very long to get there. By the time they figure out we're gone, we can already have completed the mission."

"And then what? How do you get out of there? Once you leave Uzbekistan, coming back won't be an option," Hollingshead pointed out. That had been the original plan, to retrace their steps, but Chapel had to agree it was no longer possible. "And you can't very well exfiltrate through Russia."

Chapel nodded, thinking hard. "We go out through the Caspian Sea. You can send a submarine to pick us up from the Kazakhstan shore, take us to . . ." He went over the map of Asia in his head. "Azerbaijan." It was the closest thing to a NATO country in the region, the nearest place where they could expect a warm welcome. "From there we can just take a commercial flight back to the States."

"That . . . could work," the director said, though he still sounded skeptical.

"Angel can arrange the whole thing. Sir—we can do this."

Hollingshead frowned. "Son," he said, very softly, "weren't, ah, you the one calling to scrub the mission in the first place?"

"Yes. But only because I didn't know the whole story."

"Don't let emotion cloud your judgment," the director told him.

Chapel shook his head. "Sir, I get it. I just—" He tried to think of some way to explain why he'd changed his mind. Nothing he thought of would sway the director. But he thought he knew one argument that might. "Sir. When you first brought me into your directorate, when you gave me this job, you told me what you wanted to do. What your directorate was designed to do."

"I remember, son."

Chapel nodded. "You said you wanted to shake all the skeletons out of the closets of the Cold War. You wanted to find every dangerous thing left over from seventy years of fighting communism, all the obsolete secret stuff just waiting to come back and bite us when we least expected it. Well. It seems to me that Perimeter ought to be job one."

Hollingshead watched him closely through the tablet. Chapel had the sense the director doubted that he was thinking logically. But the argument was sound. Nadia's last operation—her life's work—was aligned perfectly with Hollingshead's mission statement. Turning back now, aborting the operation, thwarted both of them.

Maybe it would be enough.

"The risks you'd be taking on are, well, astronomical," Hollingshead pointed out.

"I've never shied away from risk before, sir," Chapel pointed out.

The director nodded. "True enough. That's my job." He shook his head. "This mission already required violating the sovereignty of Kazakhstan. Now you're talking about running counter to the security interests of Russia. We can't afford to antagonize the bear, son. If the Russians discover that we ran a mission behind their backs, conspired with someone they've declared an outlaw . . . the diplomatic blowback could be horrendous. Ordinarily I couldn't even consider doing such a thing without a direct order from the president."

"We don't have time to run this through channels," Chapel pointed out.

"No, we don't. But if I were to authorize something like this and it blew up, you know who would take the blame, don't you? You understand what this would do to me and my directorate?"

"I understand that if we fail, I'll most likely be dead. Or left to rot in a Russian prison for the rest of my life," Chapel pointed out. "Sir, this is a once-in-a-lifetime chance. We can take down one of the biggest nuclear threats mankind was ever stupid enough to build, but we have to do it now. If we wait, the Russians will just put a fence around the thing and we'll never be able to touch it."

Hollingshead stared at him through the thick lenses of his glasses. If it were anyone else, any other intelligence director, Chapel knew how this would end. Any spymaster but Hollingshead would simply shut the mission down. Call for further study, or declare the whole operation untenable. Anyone else would cover his or her ass.

Hollingshead, though—the man had principles. He still had things he believed in. And more than once that had led to him doing something real, something good, for his country. It was why he still had his job, because the president needed somebody with the backbone to actually get things done.

"Jim, you're asking for a lot. Make it worth my while," Hollingshead said. "Agent Asimova," he called.

Nadia looked up at the screen. She'd been silent since finishing her story, as if it had taken all the wind out of her sails to relive all that. "Yes, sir?" she asked.

Hollingshead cleared his throat. "You are absolutely certain you can dismantle Perimeter? If you can get to it, you can shut it down for good?"

"*Konyechno*," she said.

"Don't just say 'of course' as if this were something easy. You convince me this is worth putting so much at jeopardy."

"Sir, it will be done. It is all I have left in my life to do," she told him.

Hollingshead was silent for a long while. On the screen Chapel could see the wheels turning behind his eyes, the calculations being worked through, the numbers crunched. It was the kind of decision he was glad he didn't have to make himself.

"All right," the director said, finally. "Get moving, don't stop for anything—and let me make this very clear: *do not get caught*. No matter what."

"Understood," Chapel said, and grabbed the tablet off the tree before the screen even went dark.

IN TRANSIT: JULY 18: 21:24

Night fell before they'd gotten very far. At the wheel of the big truck Chapel felt a little relief once they were out of the sun—he was an intelligence operative and the shadows were always more comfortable for him—but even so he was keyed up enough to hunch forward in his seat, every nerve strained as he wondered where the next threat would come from.

Angel kept a very close ear on the police band chatter in Uzbekistan, listening for any sign that they were being pursued. No one had reported Mirza's death, yet, nor was there any sign that the SNB was worried. That gave them a little breathing room.

The quickest route to Kazakhstan would have been to drive straight north, through the desert, but that way lay danger. To curb drug trafficking, the Kazakhs had built a high fence with barbed wire and floodlights along the border. Patrols swept the area every night, focusing on the main roads from Tashkent to Astana, the Kazakh capital. To the west, however, where there were no roads and only a few farms, the border was much more porous.

So they took the truck northwest, past Vobkent, using the best roads they could find. As long as they weren't being actively pursued, they wanted to make the best time they could, and that meant sticking to graded surfaces. The truck was designed to cross sand and slickrock, but it was still a lot faster on a highway.

Chapel worried at first that the truck was going to give them away, that it was just too conspicuous with its eight wheels and its high cab. It turned out that wasn't a problem. North of Vobkent the roads were almost deserted, and what little traffic they did see was all construction vehicles and big segmented trucks hauling goods back toward Tashkent. The desert-crossing truck didn't stand out at all—if they'd been driving a late-model sedan, *that* would have drawn more attention.

"The northern half of Uzbekistan is all desert," Nadia explained. "The Kyzyl Kum, three hundred thousand square kilometers of nothing but sand. Almost no one lives there, other than a few herders. The people who come there come for work, to dig for gold, uranium, natural gas, live back in the cities. They are all headed home now for their dinners, tired and uninterested in us."

"Fine," Chapel said. "I won't feel comfortable until we're out of anyone's sight, though." He still wasn't sure he'd made the right decision. How much had Nadia's story affected him? He thought of himself as a logical person, a smart guy who at least tried not to make dumb mistakes. But her revelation, the fact that she was dying—he wasn't heartless, after all. Had he allowed himself to be swayed?

He supposed it didn't matter now. In for a penny, in for a pound.

He glanced at the tablet sitting between them, wedged under the emergency brake. Angel would be sending their pursuers in the wrong direction, he knew. She was too busy to talk, and now was hardly the right time, with Nadia sitting next to him, but he desperately wanted to know what she thought.

In the backseat Bogdan was busy, too. Chapel had returned his makeshift computer, and the hacker was raiding the SNB's archives, looking for anything they thought they knew about Jeff Chambers and his mysterious assistant Svetlana. So far Bogdan had turned up nothing to worry them, but if Mirza had left some case notes behind, or even a voice mail to his superiors telling them where he was headed before he disappeared—

"Jim," Nadia said. "I want to thank you."

He glanced over at her. "For changing my mind?"

"For allowing me to finish my mission," she said. "It means . . . a great deal that you trust me. That you believe in me."

"I believe in what we're doing," he told her, and left it at that.

This woman had lied to him. She could do it again. Maybe there was more to her story she wasn't sharing, maybe—

"Sugar," Angel said, "you're going to see the town of Zarafshan coming up in a few miles. You might want to detour around it."

"Understood," he told the tablet.

Diverting around the population center took enough of his attention to keep his doubts and fears in the back of his mind for a while. The town wasn't very big, but there weren't a lot of roads around it, either, so he had to go off-road for a while. He had to admit he was impressed when the big tires grabbed at the sandy soil and they barely lost any speed. Varvara had done right by them.

Beyond Zarafshan the road turned into little more than a gravelly track that stretched on for many more miles, slowly but steadily turning into nothing more than a ribbon of slightly paler dirt in the midst of the desert. At one point they saw the lights of a village up ahead and had to go off-road for a few miles to stay clear. Eventually the road disappeared altogether, and they entered the Kyzyl Kum proper. To either side there was nothing to see but sand dunes, no oases or rivers or even many trees to break up the horizon.

There was no turning back. Chapel might have his doubts, but it was time to put them aside.

IN TRANSIT: JULY 19, 03:37

They took turns, one of them driving through the night while the other rested. Both of them were too alert to really sleep, though, and driving through the desert was never going to be a restful experience.

The truck was an old military vehicle designed by the Soviet Union for prospecting work in the open desert, and it had been built extraordinarily well. It had special filters in its air intakes to keep out blown sand. It had a doubly redundant coolant system to cope with the heat of the desert sun, and special heating filaments wrapped around the fuel lines to handle the bitterly cold night. Even the groove pattern on its massive tires had been designed to offer the best possible grip on the sand.

After driving for nearly four hours, Chapel cursed the designers anyway, cursed them for not considering what a thinly padded seat could do to a human tailbone.

Nadia shrugged when he told her how sore his ass was. "The Soviets, they were brilliant in their way. They understood machines, basic engineering, so much better than anyone else," she told him, "because they had to. They had such a large country to conquer. But they never built a car seat that a human being would want to sit on, and their chocolate is terrible."

"Got to have your priorities, I guess," Chapel said, shifting on what felt like a bare metal bench. The rivets in the steel dug into him no matter how he held himself.

It didn't help that the damned landscape wouldn't just lie flat. The desert was a great rumpled sheet of long crescent-shaped barchan dunes, giant mounds of sand that moved grain by grain as the wind carried them along. There was no way to drive around the dunes, so the truck had to constantly climb the face of each one, powering its way up the face, then scramble down the far side with the engine almost idling. It was like riding the world's most boring roller coaster, and at the bottom of every dune the truck came down with a jolt no matter how carefully Chapel steered into the impact, launching him into the air. He thought Bogdan had the right idea. After moaning for nearly an hour about the rough ride, the Romanian had wedged himself down into the leg well between the front and back seats. Maybe the carpeting on the floorboards was thicker than the seat upholstery.

Chapel peered out through the windshield, anticipating the next dune. They had gotten lucky in that the moon was new, and only starlight lit up the landscape. With the truck's banks of lights turned off, that would make them hard to spot, even by satellites. It gave them a fighting chance. "You really hate the Soviets, don't you?" he asked. "Ever since we started this mission, all you've done is tell me how awful they were."

Nadia shrugged. "It is a national pastime. We all live in their shadow now. We live with their mistakes every day." She clutched her arms around herself. Even in the heated cab it was cold—outside the night winds would be truly bitter, despite the warmth of the day.

"And the Russians, now? The Russian Federation? How do you feel about them? They're trying to kill you, after all."

Nadia looked over at him with guarded eyes. He'd touched something, but he wasn't sure what. "You doubt my patriotism? Tell me, do you support everything your government does? Every member of your Congress, every elected official?"

Chapel frowned as he peered ahead into the endless waves of sand. "My government tried to kill me, once," he said. "Well, one of its organizations did, anyway. Governments, even good ones, aren't ever really of one mind. As for Congress, well, I guess hating Congress is *our* national pastime. Sometimes I think we elect our politicians just so we'll have something to be angry about. Yeah, there are things about America I don't like. It doesn't stop me loving my country. Fighting for it. I guess I'm asking how you feel about your country, not its leaders."

"My country," she said, a little bitterness in her voice. "This is the problem with Russia, calling it one country." She shivered a little. "Strange that I feel so cold now, when in Siberia this might be a pleasant day in spring. I've been away so long. Siberia is my country. I hope to see it again before . . . well. Before I die."

"Nadia, I didn't mean to—" he began.

She shook her head to stop him. "I do not want your pity. Moscow, where I have lived for many years . . . it is very nice, in its own way; you can buy nice clothes any time of the day or night. You can see all the foreign movies there. But the people throw their trash into the street. The river stinks. My people would never let that happen. My grandfather was an Evenki shaman. Do you know what that is?"

"Not even a clue."

Nadia never turned to look at him. Whatever she saw through the windshield, he was pretty sure it wasn't the desert. "He went from village to village in the forest, healing the sick, fighting with ghosts. He rode around on a reindeer. When I was an infant, he would hold me on his lap, on the back of his reindeer. I can almost remember that. I can definitely remember how it smelled."

She smiled at the thought. Closed her eyes and lay back in her seat.

"That is my country, the back of that reindeer. The trees of the taiga. The people of the forest. I will fight and die for them, to keep them safe. Whether Moscow approves or not."

"I believe you," Chapel said.

She opened her eyes. Turned and looked at him.

"That was what got you arrested, wasn't it?"

"I beg your pardon?"

Chapel thought back to what Angel had told him. "You were arrested a few years ago at a protest rally in Moscow. One that was calling for Siberian independence, among other things. You didn't give your name, and you were released right away. But you were there, weren't you?"

"Angel is very, very good at what she does," Nadia said. She shifted away from him in her seat, as if she might throw open her door and jump out of the truck.

He'd definitely hit a nerve. "Yeah," he said. "She is."

"If you have a question to ask, then ask it," Nadia told him.

Chapel was careful not to push too hard. What he was getting at was a tricky thing to talk about, even now. "You say that Siberia is your country, not Moscow. That makes me wonder something. Why is Siberia still part of Russia?"

"Now you're asking me riddles."

He shook his head. "No. Listen, I'm curious about this. When the Soviet Union fell, just about everybody jumped ship. Everybody from Belarus to Tajikistan decided they wanted nothing to do with Russia anymore. But not Siberia."

"It's true," Nadia said.

"Why is that?"

"When the Union fell, every ethnic group in the Union was given a choice to declare for self-determination. But Moscow wished to hold as much territory as possible. Some groups were . . . urged more strongly than others to stay. The truth is, Russia could not afford to lose Siberia. All the country's wealth is there."

"Oil, you mean," Chapel said.

"Yes, definitely there is oil in Siberia. Not to mention gold, and diamonds, and rare metals. And of course there is Vladivostok, which is the only way Russia has to reach Asian markets, and one of its very few port cities that does not freeze over every winter. No, Yeltsin was very much interested in holding on to Siberian territory, and Putin agrees. At the time of the breakup, perhaps, something could have been done. There was political momentum, then. But now—Putin has made it very clear that Moscow will not give up any more territory. Look at what he has done to Chechnya."

"But you think it would be a good thing, if Siberia split with Moscow?"

Nadia sighed and wrapped her arms around herself as if she were cold. "The Soviets plundered Siberia for its resources, without much compunction. Putin has been, if anything, worse. The land is being strip-mined, the trees cleared in great swaths. No one seems to care if the forest is poisoned, as long as they get what lies beneath. Do I think the people who actually live there would make better stewards of the land? Yes. *Konyechno*."

"You feel strongly enough to get arrested for saying so," Chapel pointed out.

"What is this?" Nadia demanded. "What are you asking?"

He turned and gave her a hard look. "You lied to me once. When you said that you had the blessing of Moscow for this operation. I want all the cards on the table. You don't work for FSTEK anymore. You've shown political leanings in the past. Who are you working for now?"

"You'll never really trust me again. I see that," Nadia told him. "But you already know the answer to that question. I work for Marshal Bulgachenko."

"Who's dead," Chapel pointed out.

"Yes. I work for his memory. And I work to make the world safer for everyone. Jim, I have very little time left. I have dedicated all of it to bringing down Perimeter. Is that so hard to believe?"

Chapel started to answer, but he stopped when his tablet chimed and the screen lit up with a map.

Talk about timing, he thought.

"You're almost there," Angel told him. "The border's just a few miles up ahead. Time to get careful."

IN TRANSIT: JULY 19, 04:02

"I'm getting the live feed from a weather satellite that's about to break your horizon," Angel told him. Chapel nodded, even though he knew she couldn't see him. "You're still clear of the border, though if you get too much closer, you'll definitely draw some attention."

Ahead of the truck was nothing but sand— endless dunes of it, a slightly paler black than the night sky. There were no posted warnings, no signs telling him where the border was. He only had Angel's word for where the dividing line fell. She was being very careful with that—she didn't trust Google maps, which could be off by whole miles in places, so she had downloaded some very, very detailed maps from the CIA's databases. Using the GPS in the tablet, she was able to tell where the truck was within a few yards.

"Okay, satellite's up. I see . . . I see a couple of things, actually," she said. He heard her clacking away at a keyboard. "Stand by."

Chapel dropped the truck into neutral. They were down in the shadow between two dunes, and he could see nothing at all.

The border between Uzbekistan and Kazakhstan was long and much of it ran through trackless desert. Until recently no one had ever bothered to patrol the dividing line at all. But one of the main drug pipelines that brought opium poppies and refined heroin into Russia ran across this border, in almost a straight shot from Afghanistan. The fence and the border checkpoints north of Tashkent had been built to stop that flow, but of course the drug runners had simply diverted around the obstruction and now they moved most of their product through the Kyzyl Kum. In recent years the Russians had started paying the Kazakhs to keep an eye on their desert frontier to stem that tide. There had been problems—a few farmers who had never even known which country they lived in had been shot while herding their sheep. And plenty of drugs still got through—coverage was still spotty. It was a lot of ground to cover for Kazakhstan's small military.

But if even one drug interdiction helicopter spotted Chapel's team, if they fell afoul of even a single man working border patrol, their whole mission would fall apart.

"Okay," Angel said. "Still working. But you can creep forward a little. The nearest helicopter is twenty miles away from you and heading west."

Chapel goosed the engine, trying and failing to keep it from roaring as the wheels bit into the dune ahead and started pulling the truck up the long, sweeping face. They were in the most danger at the crests of the dunes, where starlight might glitter on their windows. Chapel hit the top of the dune and raced back down to its bottom.

"Head east for a minute," Angel said. "Okay, stop. Wait there."

In the dark Chapel gritted his teeth and waited. He couldn't see what Angel saw. He couldn't see anything. He was already exhausted from driving all night, and this anxious game of hide-and-seek made him feel like the bones of his skull were grinding against each other. He glanced over at Nadia and saw her staring out her window, as if she could help by keeping an eye out. The problem was, if they so much as saw the lights of a border patrol unit or heard the chopping noise of a helicopter, they were already dead.

"North. Go now," Angel said. "Now! Okay, slow down, slower. Head northwest . . . stop. Stop, stop, stop!"

Chapel drove down into the shelter between two dunes and cut his engine.

"Hang tight," Angel whispered. "There's a helicopter about three kilometers to your north. That's just inside their range of vision. Just . . . don't move. Try not to make any noise, in case they have long-range microphones."

Chapel all but held his breath. With the engine off, the cab of the truck started to get very cold, very quickly. He looked over and saw Nadia shivering, her lips pressed tightly together.

She was trying to keep her teeth from chattering.

Chapel took his hands off the wheel, as if he might accidentally switch the engine back on and give them away. He held his hands up in the air, almost afraid to put them down in case they made a noise when they hit the upholstery.

He could hear the engine ticking, pinging as it cooled. He could hear a drift of sand come tumbling down the dune in front of him, stirred by the wind. He could hear his own heart beating.

No. No, that tiny sound, softer even than the noise the sand made, that wasn't his heartbeat. As fast as his pulse was racing, it wasn't going fast enough to make that sound. It had to be something else. It had to be the sound of the helicopter. Was it getting closer? Was it getting louder, or was he just imagining that?

In the shadow of the dune, the truck's roof was nearly invisible, but if anyone thought to look at it, it would seem wrong. It was too square, in this country of curving dunes. Someone could see them, someone with night-vision goggles could have spotted them, called for the helicopter to investigate . . . as the helo got closer, its FLIR sensors would pick up their body heat inside the cab, so much warmer than the surrounding sand. Maybe, just maybe there was a chance the helo crew would think they were animals, camels or wild pigs or whatever else lived out here, maybe they would shrug off the heat signature, but more likely they would come closer still, get a better look, and then . . .

"Okay," Angel said, her voice startlingly loud in the enclosed cab. Even Bogdan jumped, lifting his long neck in the backseat and staring at Chapel and Nadia.

"Okay, give it another minute. Then head due north, and keep going," Angel told them. "I think you're clear."

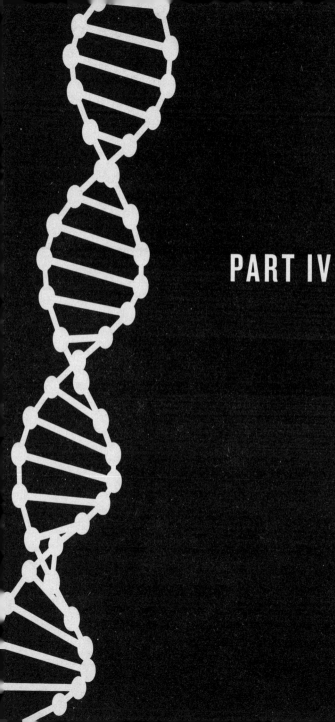

PART IV

Abdulla Zokirov had been born in the countryside of Uzbekistan shortly before the fall of the Soviet Union. He had never known a time when orders from Moscow shaped every aspect of his life, had never lived under the yoke of atheists far to the north who wished for nothing more than to trample his religion and his ethnic heritage. He had joined the Uzbek armed forces when he was a teenager and then the SNB when he finished his tour of duty and had spent most of his life studying police reports in Tashkent, under the tutelage of the legendary Jamshid Mirza. He had never traveled farther than Bukhara in his life, had never been outside his national borders.

Still, there was inside him an abiding hatred for all ethnic Russians. It was simply part of his DNA.

So when a pale-faced man in a black suit appeared in the dawn light at the entrance to the abandoned poultry shed in the outskirts of Vobkent, Zokirov's hackles went up right away. Here was some mindless functionary from the frozen north come putting his nose in where it did not belong.

Zokirov removed his latex gloves—he had been examining one of the dead bodies that lay rotting in the cool darkness of the shed—and strode over to tell the Russian he was not welcome, that this was a crime scene and an internal Uzbek matter and he should just go home.

Then he saw the man's eyes, and he forgot every word he'd meant to say.

Jamshid Mirza—who was now one of those corpses in the dark—had often spoken of the KGB in tones of reverence mixed with utter loathing. He had once been an agent of that now-defunct organization, and he had talked of how they all cultivated a particular look, a stare, a piercing expression they called the Eye of the Dead Fish. It was a look that conveyed a particular message to anyone it fell upon. *You are not a human being,* the stare implied. *You do not have any rights. You will do what I say or I will shoot you without a moment's hesitation. Even if you do exactly as I say, I may shoot you anyway, and if you beg for your life, you will only disgust me.*

It was a lot for one look to say. Abdulla Zokirov had always thought Mirza was being dramatic, when he spoke of the Eye of the Dead Fish. No man could say so much with a single glance.

But this Russian, this man who had intruded on Zokirov's work, had the Eye. And it spoke volumes.

"These men belonged to me," the Russian said, kicking the hand of one of corpses. Most of the dead men in the shed were, in fact, Russians. None of them had any identification on their bodies, and Zokirov had been wondering who had sent them here to die. He did not nod or express satisfaction at learning this new fact. "I am Senior Lieutenant Pavel Kalin, of Counter Intelligence," the Russian said. "I will take over here now."

It took a moment for Zokirov to realize that

Kalin was speaking not in Uzbek but in Russian. Of course Zokirov knew the language—it was a second unofficial tongue of his country, legacy of an age of tyranny. He was a bit ashamed that when he answered, he spoke in Russian, too.

"This one," Zokirov said, pointing to Mirza, "is ours. It's clear that he killed some of your men. Most likely because they had no jurisdiction here, and no permits for their weapons."

Kalin glanced around the shed. There was not much for him to see, Zokirov knew. The bodies, of course, but beyond that only a little stain of oil on the floor. It was still wet, which meant there had been a vehicle there recently, but now it was gone.

"There were three others. A Russian woman, an American, and a Romanian," Kalin said. He did not seem to have taken the hint about jurisdiction.

"Yes, Svetlana Shulkina, Jeff—"

Kalin clucked his tongue. "Those names mean nothing. They had a vehicle—a large truck, I think." He bent down and touched the oil stain with two fingers. "I do not know who killed whom here, and I do not care in the least. The ones I want are the ones who fled." He looked over at one of the corpses, the one that wore spectacles. "Next time I will not send policemen to do the work of soldiers. I will take the bodies of my men. You will not put their deaths in your report. You may do with your dead man as you please, but you will not make any mention that there were Russians here. Am I understood?"

Zokirov was an agent of the SNB. He was accustomed to a certain level of respect from his peers, and from a great measure of fear and obedience from common folk. He straightened his spine and tried to think of what Mirza might have said. "This is an internal matter of the Republic of Uzbekistan. Interfering with a police investigation is an offense, and—"

Kalin stood up very suddenly and slapped Zokirov across the face.

A cold fear washed through Zokirov, a certainty that if Kalin were to kill him in the next moment, there would be no consequences, no repercussions. Zokirov had worked in state security long enough to know that some men were above the law, even international law. Such men did not need papers or clearances to get their way.

He closed his mouth.

Then he opened it again. "Forgive me," he said. "I am happy to cooperate with your investigation. Let me tell you our theory. Our man, Mirza, confronted your agents here and killed them. The three you are looking for then killed Mirza. They departed in a large desert-going truck, and we believe they are headed for—"

"I know exactly where they are going," Kalin said.

Zokirov did not ask him to share this information.

KYZYLORDA PROVINCE, KAZAKHSTAN: JULY 19, 04:22 (OMSST)

It was cold out there. Even in the middle of the desert, even after a long day of the sun baking the sands without relief. It was cold—nearly freezing.

It was empty, empty in an enormous way. The desert was not lifeless, not by any means. Through the windshield Chapel could see a landscape painted silver by the moon and dotted sparsely with scrub grass and tiny bushes all the way to the horizon. Once or twice the truck startled a lizard or a small mammal out of its burrow and sent it scampering for cover in the cold sand. But these exceptions only served to highlight just how little there was out there, just how much of nothing the truck rumbled through. No roads. No sign of human life at all. No trees, anywhere. No clouds overhead. No mountains, no hills, and definitely no water.

Only the dunes. The endless barchan dunes, rises where the wind had sculpted the sand into gentle soft shapes that could run for miles in either direction. Dunes furrowed by moving air, with a constant spray feathering from their tops. Dunes that looked like moving waves in the dark, like swells in an endless sea.

Chapel found himself glancing over at Nadia time and again, at her sleeping face lit a quiet green by the dashboard lights. Just to see something human, something on a scale he felt comfortable with. He was glad she was there.

In the backseat, behind Chapel, Bogdan snored and whimpered in his sleep, like a beaten dog. After a while Chapel was even glad for that noise, that human noise.

Chapel braked to a gentle stop in the dark lee between two dunes. He let the truck settle, let it slide around a little on the loose sand. Listened to its engine idling away. He rubbed at his face with his hands. Drank a little water.

He touched Nadia's shoulder and she opened one

eye. In the dark cab of the truck, she stared at him as if she didn't recognize him, as if she had no idea where she was.

"Your turn," he whispered.

She sat up, one side of her face obscured by the shadow of her hair. "*Chto?*" she asked. Then she shook her head and sat up much straighter, looking forward through the windshield. She took a deep breath and nodded. "Sorry. My turn." She tried to stifle a yawn, but failed. She squeezed her eyes shut, hard, then opened them again.

"Never mind," he said. "Go back to sleep. I can keep driving for a while."

She turned to face him. "No. It is my duty. I don't shirk."

He started to protest but he could see in her face she fully intended to take her shift. They switched places, which involved a certain amount of awkward crawling over each other. She said nothing and didn't act embarrassed or uncomfortable. Chapel kept his own feelings to himself.

She put the truck in gear and got them moving again. Chapel knew he ought to try to get some sleep, but he was still too dazed, too hypnotized by the desert outside the windows to close his eyes. He drank some more water and watched the dunes go by.

KYZYLORDA PROVINCE, KAZAKHSTAN: JULY 19, 06:12

Traveling during the day was just too dangerous. Besides, they were all exhausted and desperately needed some sleep. Nadia parked the truck in the lee of a tall dune that would give them shade for most of the day. Chapel jumped out with a shovel and spread some sand across the dark roof of the truck. It wouldn't pass a close inspection, but any satellites or helicopters overhead would be less likely to see them. Working with Nadia, he hung tarps across the windows of the cab and then they crawled back inside. The interior of the cab was dim, lit up only by some orange light, those few sunbeams already strong enough to pierce the thick canvas. The night's chill lingered in the air, in the metal surfaces all around Chapel. He sank down onto the seat that had been tormenting him all night and suddenly it felt very, very comfortable.

"There's a tent, back in the supplies," Nadia told him. "I think I am too tired to put it up, though."

"I'm too tired to keep talking about this," he replied.

She made a noise that was something like a laugh, but required less energy.

Bogdan was already asleep in the back, curled up in one of the seats. "He might at least have helped with the tarps," Nadia said.

Chapel shook his head. "He's the talent, right? The mission specialist. We're the grunts. When he wakes up, he'll probably expect breakfast to be ready."

"There is dried fruit and some canned meat back there," Nadia said.

He waved a hand at her to make her stop talking.

Whether she did or didn't made no difference. He was out like a light.

He dreamed of standing on the deck of a seagoing boat that rose and fell and rocked with the waves as a storm lashed its sails. A long night of going up and down and over sand dunes had left his brain still swaying, perhaps.

When he woke, it was to find himself coated in sweat. His left, artificial arm was resting on the metal door handle and when he brought it up to his face he got a good whiff of scorched silicone. The inside of the cab was oppressive with heat, like it had been stuffed full of hot packing peanuts while he slept. The air was so dry it parched his throat.

He wiped the sweat away from his face—pinpricks of moisture broke out on his forehead and his nose the second he dried them off. He looked over and saw Nadia sleeping in the passenger seat, her brow wrinkled, her shirt glued to her shoulder and back with sweat.

He couldn't take it. He grabbed the tablet and cracked open his door. The tarp that hung over the windows pushed back against him, but he struggled through it and down the ladder, onto the sand below.

Fresh air whistled into his lungs, but even through closed eyelids the sun burned his retinas. He pushed one hand against his eyes as if to wring the sunlight out and stumbled around even as the heat cooked his back.

It had been hot in Tashkent, but nothing like this. "Angel," he called out. "Angel, are you there?"

"I'm here, sugar," she said.

He had no idea what the time difference was between Kazakhstan and . . . wherever she was. She sounded well rested, though.

"What's the temperature here?" he asked.

"You sure you want to know?" she asked him. When he didn't reply, she said, "It's about a hundred and twenty."

He couldn't believe it. "Fahrenheit?"

Angel laughed. "A hundred and twenty Celsius would kill you."

Chapel had heard stories about heat like that from guys he knew who fought in Iraq. Afghanistan had never been that hot—in fact, up in the mountains it had been downright chilly. He couldn't remember if he'd ever felt heat like this. He could just crack his eyelids if he forced himself. The sunlight was still blinding, but it looked like there might be a patch of shade off to his left. He hurried toward it, staggering through the loose sand—and tripped over something and went sprawling.

In the shade he could see a little better. Still not very well—and if he turned his head even slightly and looked out at the sand where the sun beat down, stabbing pain would burn through his head. He peered into the shadows and saw Bogdan sitting there, leaning back against a pile of sand. The Romanian had his knees up near his ears, having folded himself like an insect into the small patch of shade.

"Sorry," Chapel said, because he realized that what he'd tripped over was Bogdan's feet.

"Is okay, yes." Bogdan lifted a heavy canteen and waggled it. "Drink. Drink or you will dehydrate and die."

Chapel took the canteen and sucked up a thick mouthful of warm water. He forced himself to swallow it slowly, to make it last.

"Is hot enough for you, yes?" Bogdan asked.

Chapel nearly spat out all the water in his mouth. He held it in with his hand—in a land like this water wasn't something you could waste on a spit-take.

In point of fact, now that he was in the shade, the heat felt almost bearable. He remembered that was the secret of dry heat—moist air conveyed heat much better than dry air, so people who lived in places like Arizona could stay relatively comfortable as long as they were under a roof. The tiny patch of shade under the dune in Kazakhstan was its own miniature oasis as far as he was concerned.

He sipped at the water. Bogdan, after his initial foray into conversation, seemed uninterested in talking further, and that was fine with Chapel. A few minutes after he'd arrived in the shade he saw the canvas covering the truck shimmer and shake and then Nadia came running over toward them with a whoop. She pushed Bogdan to one side to find her own patch of shelter from the sun.

"We should move the truck," Chapel said. "It's just soaking up heat right now. That can't be good for our supplies or our electronics."

"Give me one moment, please," Nadia said. She pressed the palms of her hands against her eyes. Shook out her hair, sending drops of sweat flying. "You could have woken me, when you stepped out," she said, staring daggers at him.

Chapel laughed. "All I could think about at that moment was getting away from the heat. Sorry." He handed her the canteen. "I'll move the truck. There has to be some more shade around here somewhere."

IN TRANSIT: JULY 19, 20:30

While Nadia drove, coaxing the engine of the truck to move while it was still overheated from sitting in the desert all day, Chapel studied a map of Kazakhstan. "I had no idea this place was so huge." He unfolded another section of map and sighed. Judging by the scale, you could fit all of western Europe into the borders of Kazakhstan and still have some room left over. "And all of this," he said, moving his hand in a circle over the southern central part, more than half of the country, "is desert? I can see why, if you wanted to hide something, this would make a good spot. I'm not as clear on how we're going to find it."

"I have the map coordinates, and our GPS will take us there. Angel will help, will she not, if we get lost? Don't worry." Nadia turned and looked at him. She had been cool with him ever since he'd questioned her politics, just before they crossed the border. But the prospect of reaching Perimeter soon seemed to melt some of that ice. "We're so very close, now. This night, and then just a bit tomorrow."

Chapel nodded. "And then we hit Perimeter and then . . . it's over," he said. "We exfiltrate and go our separate ways. What will you do with . . . damn. There's no good way to circle around this. What will you do with the time you have left?"

"I have some ideas. No point in getting ahead of myself, but I've thought of it. I have at least six months, I think, before the pain will get too bad. I will see my home again."

"Back to Russia? Where they want you dead?"

"I know how to stay under their radar, so to speak," she told him. A wan smile crossed her face. "They taught me very well how to not be seen. Anyway, if they catch me, what of it? They kill me?" She watched the dunes for a while, keeping both hands on the wheel as the truck tried to slew to one side on the downward face of a dune. "What about you?"

"Me?"

"Yes, you. I'm sure you cannot tell me what your next mission is. I'm sure all your movements are classified. But do you have to go back to the States right away?"

Chapel hadn't even considered it. He'd always figured he would go back and try to find Julia and talk to her, find out why she had broken things off. Find out if maybe there was a way forward. But that was seeming increasingly unlikely. Every day that passed, and she still hadn't called, made him feel more like that chapter of his life was over. Like he should move on, as much as he didn't want to.

Thinking that through, actually saying it to himself if only in his head, felt like tearing a bandage off a fresh wound. It hurt.

"Jim?" Nadia said.

"Sorry. Just thinking."

Nadia was quiet for a while, her eyes staying focused on the ground ahead. "I wondered," she said, finally, "if maybe . . . if you had some time before you had to go back . . ."

"Nadia—"

"Just. Just listen, for now. Don't answer. If you

had some time, maybe you could come with me. Come see my Siberia."

"You don't want to be with your family?" he asked.

She shook her head. "My father died many years ago. My mother moved away, to Vietnam. My childhood friends . . . they will not remember me now. I don't want to be alone when I go back. That's all."

"Nadia—you don't even know me. Not really."

"I don't have time for long acquaintance now," she said, with a bittersweet smile. "I know you're a good man. I feel it when I stand next to you. Just think on it." She turned her face away from him as if she was watching an intersection for oncoming traffic. Not that there was likely to be another vehicle for a hundred miles in any direction. Chapel understood that she just didn't want him to see her eyes, just then.

They drove in silence for a long time. Maybe an hour. Nadia checked the tablet occasionally, to make sure they were still on course.

They never saw another human being, not even a light on the horizon. At one point they had to cross a major road—the local equivalent of a superhighway. Angel said it was clear in both directions, so Nadia eased the truck onto the road surface. "This is an important road. Over there," she said, pointing through the passenger's-side window. "About thirty kilometers, is Baikonur. The cosmodrome."

"Where they launch the rockets," Chapel said.

"The—the Soyuz. Soyuzes. Whatever, the rockets that go to the International Space Station."

"We won't see a launch on this trip, I'm afraid," she told him. Her smile was back, her enthusiasm.

"That's too bad. I'd have liked to see something like that," Chapel told her.

She laughed. "I'll make a tourist of you yet. Maybe you'll come to Siberia just for the sights."

Within a few minutes they had left the road behind, so that Chapel couldn't even see it in their mirrors.

KYZYLORDA PROVINCE, KAZAKHSTAN: JULY 20, 04:38

"So far, sugar, your plan is working."

Nadia was setting up the tent in the lee of a massive boulder. Bogdan had wandered off to urinate, so Chapel had figured it was an excellent time to check in. "Did the SNB find Mirza's body?" he asked.

"They did," Angel told him. "And they went nuts over it. They figured out very quickly that the other dead people were all Russians, but they seem to have assumed they were gangsters, not Russian agents. There's a manhunt going on right now in Uzbekistan, every cop in the country looking for you and Nadia. They're assuming you've already gotten away, but they aren't taking chances."

"Did you spread those false sightings I asked for?" he said.

Angel laughed. "We got lucky and I didn't have to. Somebody blew through a border crossing into Tajikistan, just six hours after Mirza stopped reporting in. Most likely it was just smugglers, but they assumed it had to be Nadia at the wheel. They've got an all-points-bulletin out for you in Tajikistan, but they aren't very hopeful. Apparently there's no love lost between the two countries, and they don't expect much cooperation."

"That's good news. What about the Russians? Have you heard any chatter from them, about Nadia?"

"Those communications are a lot better guarded than the internal stuff in Uzbekistan, I'm afraid. I'm not having a lot of luck intercepting their reports. But I do know they sent a new group of agents to Uzbekistan yesterday. They aren't just going to give up—they'll follow her wherever she tries to run."

Chapel sighed. "I figured as much. Hopefully we can keep one step ahead of them until this is done. It won't be long now—tomorrow, in fact."

"I'll run as much interference for you as I can," Angel promised.

"You're the best, Angel."

"Darn right. Chapel—listen. I just want to go on the record here and say I don't like this."

"You don't like what?"

Angel sounded more frustrated than he'd ever heard her before. "This . . . openness. This perestroika you've reached with Nadia. I don't like the fact that she knows who I am."

"Nobody knows who you are, Angel."

"She shouldn't even know I exist. How did she find out? You said she overheard you talking to me. But I know you, Chapel. You aren't that careless. Unless you're getting sloppy over there."

Chapel was glad she couldn't see him blush. "It was my own fault. If I'd kept typing instead of talking to you out loud . . . well. Frankly, I prefer it this way. I hated having to always run to the bathroom every time I needed to talk to you."

"If you say so," Angel told him. "I just wonder. She got a lot of information out of something she just happened to overhear."

"She's a spy," Chapel pointed out. "We tend to be perceptive people."

"Okay. The director seems semiokay with how things are, though he's asking for constant updates. He wants to know everything that goes on over there, and most of what I can tell him is just what I can see from the satellites. Everything's okay? You haven't seen any sign of more Russian assassins?"

"No, nothing," Chapel told her.

"And what about . . . the other thing. Fraternization. Anything to report there?"

Now Chapel was really glad she couldn't see him. "I've rejected a few advances," he said, which was technically true. That night on the balcony of the hotel, their last night in Tashkent . . . he had, in fact, stopped himself. But not before things had already gone too far. "I'm behaving myself," he told Angel.

"Good. Good. I'm really glad to hear that. Because . . . there's something I've been struggling with. Something I wasn't sure I should tell you about, because I know you're not going to like it. It's about Julia."

Chapel felt his heart lurch in his chest. He swallowed, painfully, as a sort of electric jolt ran through his body. "Did she call?" he managed to ask.

"She called me," Angel said, very softly. "She . . . she was looking for you. Wanted to know if I could get a message to you. She knows she's not supposed to call me unless it's an emergency, but she said she couldn't get hold of you any other way."

"Was it an emergency?"

Angel seemed to have to force the words out. "No. No, it wasn't. She called because . . . because she wanted to know if she could move back into the apartment, the one you shared in Brooklyn. She wanted to know if you had moved your stuff out yet. It's been more than a month, after all."

Chapel wanted to bang his head on the dashboard. He resisted the urge. "What are you saying, Angel? She's evicting me?" The lease was in Julia's name, after all. Secret agents weren't supposed to sign legal documents if they could help it.

"It sounded like she assumed you would move out on your own," Angel told him. "I told her you couldn't be reached right now, and that you wouldn't be able to move your things. She said there was no rush, but that she'd really like to move back in. Sweetie—I'm so sorry. I know how this must make you feel—"

Anger started welling up in Chapel like his blood vessels would burst with it. "You don't, actually. You have no idea," he said, far more curtly than he'd meant to. "You . . . you don't."

"I'm on your side," Angel pointed out.

Chapel felt blood surge through his head, felt like he was going to explode. He reached over and grabbed the dashboard with both hands. Clung to it until he felt like the sharp metal would cut into his fingers. He felt like he might stop breathing. He felt like he might die right then and there.

He brought one leg up and kicked, hard, at the dashboard, not caring if he smashed the gauges and instruments there. Maybe wanting to do just that.

But the Soviets had built the truck to take the occasional blow, and he didn't even leave a dent. He lifted his leg to kick again, but then he stopped himself.

Tried to breathe.

"Yeah. Yeah, I know. Well. I guess." He had no idea what to say. No idea what to do next. As he had so many times before, he forced himself to fall back on his training. When you got frantic on the battlefield, he knew, when shells were bursting around you and fear and confusion threatened to take over your brain, you started making mistakes. You stopped doing all the little things that kept you alive.

Focus on the little things, he told himself. He could take care of the logistical details. It might mean nothing, it might not change how he felt at all, but it was at least something he could accomplish. "Angel, can you arrange for someone to go and collect my things? There's not much, just some clothes and a few boxes of papers. It should all fit in a cheap storage locker." His whole life back in the States and it would probably fill two suitcases. He thought back to what Nadia had said, about what this job did to you, how it made you a nonperson, and he wanted to laugh. *We leave no trace, no mark we were ever there.* Maybe he should tell Angel to burn all his things in a trash can. Just throw everything away—how appealing was that idea? Just chuck it all. Maybe not just his things. Maybe throw everything away. Fly off to Siberia with Nadia and find out how far he could run before he had to start thinking again.

No. That wasn't . . . it wasn't possible. He knew that. Even if he was having trouble remembering why.

"Just . . . just move the stuff. And send me the bill."

"I'll do that," Angel said.

"Yeah."

He ended the connection on the tablet before he could say anything else. Popped the door of the truck and jumped down into the sand. Nadia had the tent set up and she stood next to it, watching his face. She was smiling when she first saw him, but maybe the look on his face scared her. It made her stop smiling, at any rate.

The sun was almost up. Chapel said nothing to anyone, he just crawled in the tent and made room for himself. Took off his artificial arm and laid it down next to him like he planned on using it as a pillow.

Nadia and Bogdan came inside after a while and settled down themselves. Bogdan and Chapel on the sides, Nadia in the middle. There was no pretense of privacy or personal space—the tent wasn't big enough for that.

An hour later, maybe, Chapel still hadn't fallen asleep and he was just listening to Bogdan snore, listening to any noise that would drive thoughts out of his head. The sound the sand made as it rolled down the face of the boulder behind the tent. The flutter and snap of the canvas tent in the night breeze.

Nadia breathing behind him. He could just feel her warm breath on the back of his neck. It felt good—it was cold inside the tent—but then each time it went away he shivered, chilled again until her breath washed over his skin again.

He turned over on his other side, careful not to make too much noise or shake the tent. Rolled over until he was facing her. He wanted to see her sleeping face. The tent was almost perfectly dark, the rising sun blocked by the boulder behind the tent. But there was just enough light to glint on her open eyes.

She wasn't sleeping either.

He was too angry, too hurt, too confused to worry about social niceties. He reached over and brushed her cheek with the back of his fingers. His real fingers. She blinked—he could only tell from the way the light in her eyes vanished for a moment—but she didn't move, not away from him, not toward him.

He leaned in and kissed her. Gently, just a touch.

It felt good. It felt natural. There was comfort there. But it was like putting a Band-Aid on a gaping wound. It wasn't going to be enough.

He couldn't trust her. No matter how much he wanted to.

She reached for his hand, but he pulled it away. He rolled over on his side again, facing away from her.

Scooted over so he didn't feel her breath on his skin anymore.

KYZYLORDA PROVINCE, KAZAKHSTAN: JULY 20, 20:22

Chapel woke to find the tent shaking, its poles rattling against each other. His first thought was that he'd woken up to an earthquake.

He turned over and looked around and saw that instead it was Bogdan, wrestling with a sheet, trying to get up and onto his feet. The hacker turned and stared at Chapel. "Must pee. Now."

"I'm not stopping you," Chapel said.

Bogdan managed to get untangled from the sheet and stumbled forward into the flap of the tent, his long fingers running up and down the seam looking for the zipper. He eventually found it and he yanked it downward, spilling light and heat into the tent. It was enough to wake Nadia, who covered her eyes with her hands as she sat up. Bogdan stepped outside of the tent, making no attempt to close it again behind him.

"Is it time to get up, now?" Nadia asked, looking like she would much rather go back to sleep. "Is it time to—"

She didn't finish her thought. Bogdan came racing back into the tent, as quickly as he'd left.

His eyes were wide and staring under their fringe of hair. He'd gone as white as a ghost.

"Get gun, shoot them! Do it now!" he said, his voice an octave higher than usual.

Chapel glanced at Nadia. She was wide awake now. She put one hand behind herself, reaching for a pistol. Chapel picked up his arm and clamped it onto his shoulder. "What did you see?" he asked Bogdan.

"No time! Just shoot!" the hacker exclaimed.

Chapel pushed him out of the way and peered out through the tent flap, expecting to see half the Russian army out there. What he saw instead made him jump back nearly as fast as Bogdan had.

"Giant lizards," he said. He forced himself to look out of the tent again.

Surrounding the tent were maybe a dozen big reptiles, some of them seven feet long. Their lean bodies and long tails were striped and spotted in desert colors, for camouflage maybe, but Chapel had no trouble seeing them. Their tapered snouts were open, showing rows of vicious triangular fangs and pink, wet mouths, and they hissed angrily when Chapel poked his head out through the flap.

"Desert monitors," Nadia said, coming up beside him to take a look for herself. "Not uncommon in the Kyzyl Kum. This rock we have been using for shelter must be their den."

"They're as big as I am. Their jaws are big enough to swallow my head," Chapel said. Maybe that was an exaggeration, but not much of one. "What do they eat? Tourists?"

"Wild sheep, mostly." Nadia put her weapon down.

"So they're carnivorous," Chapel said.

"*Konyechno*. You have seen so many plants in this desert for them to eat?"

"Great." Chapel reached for his assault rifle, but she grabbed his arm.

"No! You can't shoot them," she said.

"We're surrounded by giant carnivorous lizards. This is about as close as I'm ever going to get to being attacked by dinosaurs," Chapel said, as if explaining himself to a child. "I am not in the mood. You want to worry about animal rights, you can—"

Nadia shook her head. "If you fire a weapon, even in the air, the entire group will attack us at once and tear their way in through the tent to get at us."

"Uh-huh," Chapel said.

"Also, they are venomous," she pointed out.

"Jesus." Chapel put his rifle down. "So what *do* we do?"

"I will strike the tent. Bogdan," she said, "you gather up our things. Then the three of us will walk very slowly to the truck and drive away. I do not think they will attack if we are calm and do not overly antagonize them."

It was probably the worst plan Chapel had ever heard. The problem was, he couldn't think of another one. He slung his rifle over his shoulder and grabbed a pistol from the floor of the tent. They'd taken the precaution of bringing plenty of weapons with them, in case they were attacked while they were sleeping. He knew Nadia was right, that if he started shooting they would be quickly overrun, but he wasn't about to go out there unarmed.

Behind him the tent started to collapse as Nadia unscrewed the poles that held it up. Bogdan pressed up close behind Chapel as if he was afraid of being hit by fallen canvas. *Now or never*, Chapel thought.

He stepped out of the tent, the pistol held loose and low in his hand. The monitors all watched him with their yellow eyes as he took a step farther into their midst. The truck was about seven yards away— directly behind the pack of lizards. He could run for it, but the way the reptiles all crouched, their legs bent taut, made him think that was a bad idea.

The nearest one—and the biggest, bigger than Chapel—closed its jaw and lifted its snout in the air, turning it one way, then the other. Its huge eye stayed locked on him. As he watched, it flicked a nictitating membrane across its pupil. Chapel knew more than he wanted to about nictitating membranes. He knew, for instance, that the monitor could see him just fine through the cloudy third eyelid.

Bogdan and Nadia were close behind him. He lifted his free hand a few inches, to tell them to stay back. Then he took another step forward.

The big monitor opened its mouth and made a noise that wasn't so much a hiss as the sound of a steam boiler about to burst apart at the seams. Other monitors started moving, spreading out, flanking them. For solitary animals they understood just fine how to work as a pack.

"Stay calm," Nadia said. "Do not make sudden moves."

"Jesus," Chapel said. "What's that smell?" The odor wafting off the monitors was like rotten eggs, or maybe dead flesh. A deep, earthy, animal smell that made the hairs inside Chapel's nose prickle.

"Musk," Nadia told him. "That explains why there are so many here in one place. This must be the mating season. Animals can be so direct about these things."

"Ha ha," Chapel said. "Not the time for that. Okay, I'm going to start moving toward the truck. Just stay behind me, all right? If we split up, they'll probably try to isolate the weakest of us or something. So, Bogdan, you stay very close."

"I can tell when I am insulted," the hacker said with a sniff.

Chapel stopped talking, then. He edged sideways a little, which the big monitor seemed to find acceptable, then took another step forward, barely inching his way ahead. The monitor started opening his mouth again.

"I heard you," Chapel told it. "I heard you the first time. I'm just going to head this way, all right?"

He took a step to the side, and the monitor closed its mouth. Jesus, he thought. This was the world's worst game of Simon Says.

"Jim," Nadia said.

"Hold on." He took another step to the side. That brought him closer to another big monitor, this one maybe five feet long. It was crouching low, its jaw nearly scraping the sand. Chapel wished he knew what that meant—whether it was about to attack, or if it was showing submission. He kind of doubted it was that second thing. "Just—"

"Jim," she said once more.

He glanced behind him. The look on her face was very serious. She was pointing upward. He followed her finger and saw the top of the boulder. There were about six more monitors up there, perched ten feet up over his head, and they were all peering down at him, flexing their back legs like they were about to jump.

"Damn," he said. "These guys are good. We're going to have to run for it. Bogdan, you first—"

"Jim, no," Nadia suggested.

"—then Nadia, be ready to fight, I'll bring up the rear—Now!"

Bogdan at least knew the score. He burst past Chapel, running as fast as his long legs would carry him. One small monitor tried to snap at him, but he vaulted over it, moving far more gracefully than Chapel would have expected.

With a sigh Nadia dropped the bundled tent and sprinted after the hacker, a pistol in either of her hands. She tracked them around to aim at the monitors as she ran, but she didn't fire. Chapel was already moving by then, coming up close behind her, keeping an eye on the biggest of the reptiles, the one that was clearly the alpha male.

The alpha was moving, too. Coming right for him. Chapel threw an arm across his face, but the monitor slapped his legs out from under him with one big claw, its talons shredding his pant leg. It twisted its head around, and he saw its eye staring into his face as its jaws came down to disembowel him with one bite. He barely managed to get his arm down across his abdomen before the darting attack connected.

"Jim!" Nadia screamed. "Jim, the venom!"

Down on the ground Chapel stared up into the face of the thing that had his arm in a vise lock. Like an alligator—he'd seen plenty of those back in Florida—it started twisting its head back and forth, trying to tear off a piece of him. The venom, brown and thick, spread through the flesh of his arm.

Or rather, the silicone simulated flesh of his artificial arm.

He tried desperately to get up, to get at least one foot under him. It was tough to do with a hundred and fifty pounds of lizard thrashing around on top of him. His prosthetic had saved him for the moment, but he knew his time was limited—any second now the other monitors would move in for the attack, swarming him from every side. Some of them were bound to get their poisonous jaws into his living flesh.

"Come on, you son of a bitch," Chapel shouted, yanking his arm back, trying to free it from the monitor's grip. Those teeth wouldn't let go, but at least he managed to get up on his feet again. He looked around and saw half a dozen of the bigger lizards coming toward him, taking their time, their tails lashing the sand into deep furrows.

He'd lost his pistol when he was knocked down. The rifle was still slung across his back, but there was no way to reach it with one hand. His only hope was to get back, closer to the truck. He shouted for Bogdan and Nadia to get in, then dug his feet into the shifting sand and danced backward, pulling the monitor along with him. The monster didn't even try to dig its claws into the sand—it let itself be pulled along, saving all its energy to use to hold on to the arm. The other reptiles scampered after Chapel, but at least for the moment they didn't attack.

If Nadia had been a better shot, maybe she could have driven some of them back. As it was, especially in the fading light, he was glad she didn't try. Inch by inch, step by agonizing step he moved toward the truck, the alpha just digging his teeth deeper and deeper into the artificial arm. Chapel considered releasing the arm, just loosing the clamps that held it to his body and leaving it behind, but he couldn't bear the thought. He staggered backward, through the stink and the hissing, and suddenly his back rammed into the side of the truck.

The monitors came after him, moving faster now. The pack knew it was in danger of letting its prey escape and they would do anything they could to stop that. Chapel reached up with his free arm, trying to find the handle of the truck door without looking.

Then Nadia reached down and grabbed him

with both hands and pulled. "Drive!" she shouted to Bogdan. "The pedal on the right!"

With his free hand Chapel found the ladder on the side of the cab. He wrapped his good arm through and around one of the rungs and just held on as the truck roared to life and started moving away from the rock and the pack of lizards. The monitors tried to chase after it, but in seconds it was moving too fast for them and they fell behind.

All of them except the alpha, who hadn't so much as loosened its death grip on Chapel's arm. It was dragged along, its feet paddling wildly on the sand but unable to gain purchase.

On the outside of the cab Chapel clung on for dear life as Bogdan took them straight up the side of a dune and then over the top. Chapel's legs swung free—as did the alpha, whose big eyes showed no terror at all as its body flopped through the air.

Nadia leaned out of the window of the truck, a pistol in her hand. She pointed it at the monitor's eye, but the lizard flopped around so much she couldn't seem to line up a shot. "I can't risk shooting you!" she shouted over the noise of the engine.

"Hit it between the eyes!" Chapel shouted back.

Nadia twisted around until she was sitting on the windowsill. She held the pistol by its barrel and brought its grip down hard on top of the monitor's head.

It was enough to make the monitor blink its nictitating membranes, but nothing more. Its grip didn't loosen at all.

Chapel cursed and shouted at the monitor, but that didn't help either. The truck crested another dune at speed and nearly threw him, his legs flying out wide from the body of the cab. One foot got tangled with the monitor's front leg.

Maybe, he thought—just maybe—

Chapel lifted his feet and planted his boots on the monitor's shoulders. The reptile thrashed but there was nowhere for it to go to get away from him. Chapel braced himself as best he could and then pushed down with his feet, shoving the monitor's body away from him, using every bit of strength he had.

The alpha responded by tightening its grip still further. Its teeth tore deep into the silicone flesh of Chapel's artificial arm and then, with a sickening slowness, tore right through it. The flesh came away in one big chunk, no longer attached to the arm at all.

For a moment the monitor seemed to float in midair, its jaw already chewing at the chunk of prosthetic arm, but then it disappeared as it fell away from the truck, rolling over and over along the sand. Chapel just had time to see it spit out a mouthful of silicone before it fell away behind them.

He looked down at his artificial arm. The silicone sleeve was just a ragged mess, still brown at the edges with venom. He tried flexing the arm and it worked—apparently the reptile hadn't damaged any of the actuators under the skin.

Using both hands, he climbed up and through the window of the truck, landing in Nadia's lap.

"Are they after us still?" Bogdan asked. He was hunched over the steering wheel, his eyes wide and staring.

"Just drive," Chapel told him.

KARAGANDY PROVINCE, KAZAKHSTAN: JULY 20, 21:07

In the backseat, Chapel poured water over the torn flesh of his arm to try to wash away the last of the venom.

"One of those little sticky bandages you carry isn't going to be enough," Nadia said, prodding the torn skin with a pen. The motors and pistons underneath whined a little as his arm moved, even though he was trying to hold it still. "This saved your life, did it not?"

"Wouldn't be the first time." Chapel reached one-handed for the truck's bulky medical kit and flipped its catch. Supplies spilled out onto the seat beside him—suture kits, antihistamine tablets, a thin plastic splint. He picked up a roll of gauze and brought it toward his mouth to unspool it.

"Let me," Nadia said. She spun out a long length of fabric and started wrapping it tightly around Chapel's arm. The damage was all confined to the forearm and the wrist and it didn't take long for her to wrap it all up.

He looked into the kit and found a small pair of scissors secured to the lid of the case with a nylon loop. He handed them over and she cut the gauze, then tucked the end neatly inside the wrapping and used white tape to keep it in place. She looked up at him with questioning eyes. "In America, do mothers kiss their children's scrapes to make them better?"

"Better not," he told her. "There might still be some venom on there."

She shook her head and laughed. "You are infuriating, Mr. Chapel. But I will let you run hot and cold a while longer before I simply attack you out of unbearable desire. Otherwise you might think me too aggressive. I am told this is unattractive to American men."

He knew she was fishing for a compliment, so he said nothing. There was a perverse kind of pleasure to torturing her like that, as if he could get back at Julia for all the pain she'd caused him by being cruel to Nadia. Even as he realized that he felt like a jerk, but not enough to give in to her charms.

She shrugged dramatically and then climbed back into the front passenger seat. He didn't seem to have broken the buoyant mood that had come over her in the last few hours. Nothing could—they were getting close to Perimeter, and she could barely sit still. Ignoring him, she chattered amiably with Bogdan in Romanian. Chapel couldn't follow the language so he didn't bother to try.

Instead he lay back in the seat, trying to ignore the way Bogdan's inexpert driving tossed him up and down every time they passed over a dune. Even as the night darkened, he could see the landscape beyond the windows was changing, getting rougher. Instead of an unbroken sea of sand, now when he looked outside what he often saw was rocks, big rocks—more than boulders. Small hills, then the start of big ones.

He realized with some surprise they were coming to the edge of the desert.

How long had it been since they'd left Uzbekistan? It felt like no time at all—or forever, he couldn't decide. Maybe it was more like they'd left Earth altogether, that they'd been driving across the face of the moon. What he'd seen of Kazakhstan had been just as desolate, as uninhabited. The Kyzyl Kum seemed to belong more to the desert monitors than to people.

For Chapel, who had grown up in the suburban sprawl of Florida where he'd never been more than a mile from the nearest town, it was unimaginable that you could have all this land, this huge expanse, and not fill it up with strip malls and housing developments. Sure, it was a desert, ridiculously hot during the day and freezing cold at night—but that hadn't stopped western expansion back in the States. Then again, the Soviet Union had been a lot bigger than America—a whole empire, with room enough for tracts of land that just went unused, like this place, like Nadia's Siberia.

In the distance, ahead of them, part of the night sky was obscured. Above it spread a wealth of stars, a glittering abundance of the kind you never saw in America, a night sky paved with light. Below the dividing line was only darkness. It took Chapel a while to realize those were mountains ahead of them, blocking out the sky.

Nadia glanced back over her seat to look at him. "There," she said, pointing at the shadow. "That is where we are going. That is where we find Perimeter."

Even in the dark cab of the truck, her eyes shone.

KARAGANDY PROVINCE, KAZAKHSTAN: JULY 20, 23:41

"It will not be much longer," she said. "The northern shore of the Aral Sea is over there," she said, pointing west. "The coordinates I have for Perimeter suggest it is some fifty kilometers inland from there."

Chapel moved to look between the seats and out the windshield. Bogdan's driving was erratic, and he couldn't seem to keep a steady speed, but it wasn't like he was going to crash into anything—even as the landscape grew rockier and less sandy, there was still plenty of room to maneuver. The mountains ahead looked just as far away as they ever had, still off in some impossible distance.

"How will we know when we arrive?" he asked. "I doubt there's going to be a big neon sign announcing the location."

"Hardly," Nadia said. "I do not actually know if we will see anything. The installation will be all underground, dug out of bedrock deep enough that it can survive a direct hit from an atomic weapon. There will be some way to enter, a cover as if for a manhole or the like, perhaps. Even that will be camouflaged, though. Perimeter was designed never to be found by the wrong people."

Chapel nodded. "And how accurate are your map references? Are we going to have to hunt for this entrance when we get there?"

"They are accurate to one-tenth of one second of a degree," Nadia claimed. "Do not worry. I did not come so far just to miss it now."

As they got closer, the low hills gave way to looming pinnacles of rock, towers of limestone carved into incredible shapes by ancient oceans. They rose up ahead and blocked out the stars, and Chapel couldn't help but see them as silent guardians, soldiers standing watch to make sure no one ever discovered the secret buried here.

The dark mass on the horizon, the mountains Chapel had been watching for hours, started to gain a little definition. Dead ahead stood a long massif of rock that lifted above the sand dunes like the curtain wall of a castle. As they drew closer still, Chapel could see the rocky barrier was broken in some places, cracked open by ravines and even winding box canyons. One of those canyons seemed darker than the others.

"Perimeter will be there," Nadia said, consulting the GPS on the tablet. "Those shadows—I hope it is not overgrown with brush that we will have to clear away."

A few seconds later Chapel said, "I don't think that will be a problem." The shadows were too regular, too blocky in shape. That wasn't brush. It was a collection of structures definitely built by human hands. Nature didn't build that straight or that repetitively.

Bogdan stepped on the brake, and the truck rocked to a stop a few hundred meters from the entrance to the canyon. From there it was quite easy to see that the defile was full of buildings. It looked like there was a whole town sheltered between the walls of the canyon.

For a while the three of them stared at the canyon

in hushed silence, trying to make out features in the shadowy place. Moonlight lit up the sand and rocks on either side of them, but the canyon hid its secrets well, casting a pall of darkness over the sleeping buildings.

"You weren't expecting this," Chapel said.

"No," Nadia said. She unlatched her door and jumped down into the sand.

"Wait," Chapel called, and jumped down after her. No lights showed in the town, but that didn't mean it was uninhabited—or for that matter, that it wasn't surrounded by a minefield. He hurried after Nadia as she staggered forward, across the desert floor, toward the dark interior of the canyon. Toward the town there. As Chapel raced after her he saw a sign hung in front of the closest building. He struggled to make out the words, then to transliterate the Cyrillic characters. "Aralsk-30," he whispered.

Nadia turned and faced him. Her hair blew across her eyes in the breeze that came down the canyon. She hugged herself, perhaps against the night's chill, perhaps to contain some of her excitement. "A secret city," she said. "Of course!"

ARALSK-30, KAZAKHSTAN: JULY 21, 00:02

Chapel knew something about the secret cities.

They had been built by Stalin, mostly back before the Space Race. Back before reconnaissance satellites, when the Soviets still believed they could keep big secrets hidden inside their borders. People had lived and worked in the secret cities, just like normal cities, but they were also secret installations—weapons laboratories, factories constructing biological weapons or atomic bombs, even farms where experimental livestock could be raised. They were constructed by slave labor, dissidents and criminals and sometimes just people who belonged to ethnic groups the politburo didn't like. When the building was complete, the slaves would be shipped off to the next project and the city's actual residents would move in—scientists and workers who could be trusted to tell no one, not even their families, where they lived. The cities were built far from civilization, in places where people weren't likely to stumble on them, and they were never, ever mentioned in official documents. They didn't appear on any maps, and they didn't even get their own names—they just took the name of the nearest town and a number to describe how far away they were, so they had names like Arzamas-16 or Chelyabinsk-65—or Aralsk-30.

The most advanced science that the Soviets did happened in the secret cities. So did some of their worst atrocities. The NSA had compiled a list of all the cities and what was known about them, but it was believed it was incomplete—some of them had been hidden so carefully that they still hadn't been found, decades after spy satellites had mapped every inch of the former Soviet Union. Some of the secret cities hid in deep forests or on the tops of mountains. Some were believed to be housed in enormous underground bunkers, though that might just be an urban legend.

Whatever reason the Soviets had had for building Aralsk-30, they'd hidden it very well. The walls of the box canyon would shield it from view from all but one side, the direction from which they'd approached it, and the shadows of the canyon walls might hide it even from eyes in the sky.

"Have you ever heard of this place?" Chapel asked.

Nadia shook her head. She seemed too overwhelmed to speak. Years of her life to find this place and it had still surprised her. Without a glance backward she raced down the main street of the town, deep into the canyon.

"Wait!" Chapel called after her, but she was already gone.

In the dark of night she was likely to get lost, or trip over something and break a leg. Chapel called back to Bogdan, telling him to turn on the truck's lights. The sudden blast of illumination blinded Chapel for a second, so he had to put one hand over his eyes and look away. He hadn't realized just how dark it was out here and how much his eyes had adapted.

He jogged back to the truck and climbed up the ladder on the driver's side, so he could look in the window and tell Bogdan to start moving forward, slowly, into the town.

Jesus, Chapel thought. Secret cities tended to be guarded with fences and watchtowers and sentry patrols. What if Nadia ran in there and stumbled right into an ambush?

The truck rumbled forward, off the sand and onto the first paved road it had touched since they passed Baikonur. The lights swept across a row of squat, square buildings with broken windows and boarded-up doors. There was a searchlight on the roof of the cab. Chapel scrambled up on top of the truck so he could move its beam around manually. He shone it through empty, open windows and saw nothing but broken furniture and old dust.

The noise and the light seemed perverse in that dead place. It made him jumpy and anxious. He felt like at any second people should come pouring out of these old buildings, maybe the descendants of the old inhabitants, devolved into savagery after being left behind for so long. Or maybe they had all left because the place was contaminated, maybe some old experiment had gone wrong and flooded this place with radioactivity or plague germs—

He shook his head. He was letting his imagination spin out of control. This was just an old ghost town, nothing to be afraid of. He shone his light down into a guard post at the corner of two intersecting streets. Nobody there. The booth was empty.

"Nadia!" he called out. There was no answer.

Aralsk-30 wasn't very large. There were only the two main streets, which met at the center of the town. The squat buildings near the canyon entrance must be dormitories, he decided, living quarters for the people who had worked here. Past the intersection lay big buildings that must be factories, judging by the forest of smokestacks that stuck up from their rooftops. Maybe there had been other things here once, shops and bars and places for the workers to blow off steam, but now it all just looked like decaying concrete and broken glass. Sand was everywhere, in a thin film over the streets, in great drifts up against the lee sides of the buildings. It had blown in through any open doorway and clogged some of the buildings until it poured out through second-story windows. Falling rocks from the canyon walls had crushed in some of the smaller structures. At least there was no sign of barbed wire or mass graves, and if there were mines, the truck hadn't rolled over any of them so far.

Bogdan drove up to the intersection and stopped. "Which way?" he called out, over the noise of the truck's engine.

"Just park it here," Chapel shouted back. He tilted the searchlight back to illuminate the intersection. It was just wide enough for two vehicles to pass each other, but a little space in its exact center had been cleared for a bronze statue that stood twenty feet high. The light washed over the face of Vladimir Lenin, then down his chest to show that he held an oversize hammer in one hand and a sickle in the other.

There had been statues like that in every town in the Soviet Union, once, dozens of them in some places. Chapel had read recently that while the Russian Federation officials did their best to tear them all down, there had been so many they still hadn't managed to get them all, not even twenty years after the end of communism. Well, here was one more to add to the list.

He climbed down the side of the cab, then ducked in through the passenger-side window. In the big glove compartment he found what he was looking for—a flashlight, a big model with a rubberized grip and a body that could hold an old dry cell battery. He climbed back out of the truck and shone his light around the buildings that surrounded the intersection. "Nadia!" he called out again.

There was no answer, but when he pointed his light at the ground he saw the footprints she'd left in the blown sand. They were clear enough that he could read them like a map of how she'd moved through the town, stopping to look in a window here, ducking through a sand-clogged doorway there. They ended at a side door of one of the big factory buildings. Its door had been sealed with rotten boards, but it looked like Nadia had just pulled them free with her bare hands so she could get inside. The wood was silvered and smooth with age on the outside, but where she'd broken it he could still see the yellowish grain inside, bright in his flashlight beam.

He trotted after her, though before he went inside he took one last look around. If people were hiding in the shadows, squatting in the abandoned buildings, they'd done a good job of staying hidden. He had to assume this place was deserted.

As he passed into the darkness of the factory he felt cold air wash over his face. It was frigid inside, colder even than the desert night outside. He could smell rusting metal and rotting plaster, and something else, something sharp and organic. Maybe some birds or wild sheep had gotten inside and died there.

He heard a noise ahead of him and swung his beam around. He nearly jumped when it lit up a human form, but then he saw it was just Nadia. The electric light washed out her features and turned her eyes to glass, making her look spooky and unreal.

She blinked in irritation—the light must have hurt her dark-adapted eyes—so he swung it away again, pointing it up at the rafters of the building. The factory floor seemed to be one vast open space, the ceiling held up by a spiderweb of thin steel beams, punched with regular round holes to keep them light. He brought the light down the wall, illuminating old posters showing happy workers being safe and productive. Blotchy white mold had eaten into the ancient paper.

"This is the perfect place," Nadia said, her voice strange and disembodied in a place that must have known silence for so many years. "If you want to hide something of crucial importance, where do you put it? Underneath something that is already hidden. Even I never guessed they would put a city on top of Perimeter."

Chapel kept his light moving. Sitting on the factory floor were dozens of big machines, what looked like hydraulic presses festooned with handles and wheels and pull-chains. He had no idea what they were for, what kind of work had been done here. Maybe the workers of Aralsk-30 had built components for the rockets that were launched at Baikonur. Maybe they'd been working on nuclear weapons.

"Is this place safe?" he asked.

Nadia laughed. "It's the unfeeling black heart of the Russian nuclear arsenal. You're worried there might be asbestos in the walls?"

He brought the light around to shine on her again. She didn't blink so painfully this time.

"We must find the entrance to Perimeter," she said. "It could be in any of these buildings."

"Let's get started," he said.

ARALSK-30, KAZAKHSTAN: JULY 21, 04:47

They'd looked everywhere. Twice.

The entrance to the computer facility wasn't in any of the dormitories. Well, they'd expected that, but still they'd gone over every wall looking for concealed doors, sliding panels, hollow places in walls that should have been solid. Where the sand had piled up, they'd dug it away. Chapel had found some tools, including a sledgehammer, and he smashed a hundred or so holes in all the floors and walls, finding only solid concrete beneath.

They had no better luck in the guard posts or the empty buildings whose purposes were not immediately evident. The factories took a long time to search but were in fact easier than the smaller buildings since they had fewer walls. They learned a little about Aralsk-30 in their search, for all the good it did them. From what little evidence remained it seemed that the secret city had been devoted to making white phosphorous bullets. There had been a time when those had been controversial, forbidden by international treaties, so it made sense that they would be manufactured in a secret place. They weren't important enough, however, that enemies of Russia would bother raiding the canyon city. "They were smart when they hid Perimeter here," Chapel said, with a sort of grudging respect. "Even if you knew this place was secret, you wouldn't bother with it."

Nadia wiped sweat from her forehead. It was freezing inside the buildings, but the two of them had been working hard. "I wonder if the people who lived here knew what they protected. Not the workers in the factories, of course. But there would have been a commanding officer in charge here. Someone perhaps who was given this post as a punishment. I wonder if even he knew what he was hiding."

In the beam of the flashlight Chapel could see her face. The concern there, the worry. Maybe even doubt. "We'll find it," he told her, his voice soft.

"Of course we will," she said, but there was a sigh underneath the words.

He thought of how long she'd looked for this place. How much of her dwindling life she'd sacrificed for it. Had she really done all this work just because she wanted to leave the world better than she'd found it? Maybe a grand obsession was the only thing that could keep her from really thinking about the ugly death that was coming for her.

He reached over and put a hand on her shoulder. Gave it a friendly squeeze that turned into something more, his fingers trailing across her back.

For once, though, she didn't respond. For the first time since he'd met her, it seemed she had better things to do than flirt with him.

"It will be dawn soon," she told him. "I had hoped to find it and dismantle it tonight. We will be stuck here all day, now—it is still too dangerous to move when the sun is up. It might be dangerous to stay, as well."

"No one has any idea we're here," Chapel told her. "Look at this place—it's been lost for decades. Even if they were looking for us, how would they find us? This place isn't on any map. Nobody knows about it."

She shrugged. "If I could find it . . . no, never mind. I was thinking we might check the canyon walls. Something could be hidden in the rocks, camouflaged to look like natural stone."

"Good idea," Chapel told her. He threw his sledgehammer into a corner of the room. Walking past her he stepped out into the night. The sky was turning a weird electric blue—the sun was coming up, as she'd said—but it was still dark enough out that he could barely see the truck sitting in the intersection. They'd turned off all its lights for security and to save battery power.

Bogdan was fast asleep in the driver's seat. Chapel climbed up the side of the cab and looked in the window. "Wake up, buddy," he said. "Come on. We need your help."

The hacker opened one bleary eye, which rotated in Chapel's direction. He did not look happy. Chapel laughed and patted him on the arm. "Come on. Time to earn your pay, right?"

"What do you want?" Bogdan asked.

"Nadia wants to check the canyon walls, but we can't see a thing out here. I need you to move the truck to the end of this street and get all its lights on the rocks over there. Think you can handle that?"

"Yes, yes, is possible," Bogdan said. "I am driver now. Tell me where to go, boss, and there I go. Good boy Bogdan, the driver man."

"Best-paid driver man in Eurasia," Chapel told him. He waved one finger in a circle. "Let's get moving."

He jumped down from the cab as Bogdan woke the engine. Nadia had come outside to stand in the road, clutching herself for warmth. Chapel started heading over to her, intending to put his arm around her. Behind him the truck started to move, its big tires moaning as they dug into the sand.

"We'll spend all day looking, if we have to," Chapel told Nadia, raising his voice over the noise of the truck engine. "And tomorrow, too. If that's what it—"

"Bogdan!" Nadia cried out. "You're in the wrong gear! Reverse! Reverse!"

Chapel whirled around to see the truck rolling steadily forward. He heard Romanian words coming from the cab that sounded pretty nasty. His eyes went wide as he saw the truck slam into the big statue of Lenin in the middle of the intersection.

The statue rang like a bell—and then made a horrible crumpling noise as the impact smashed in one side of its base. Lenin started to lean forward as if he were giving a benediction.

"Jesus, if that thing falls on the truck we'll be stranded out here," Chapel said. He rushed forward and grabbed for the ladder on the side of the cab, intending to shove Bogdan aside and take the wheel himself. Lenin shifted another few degrees forward as Bogdan stripped the gears, trying to move the truck. Just as Chapel reached the truck's ladder, the bronze statue made a horrible groaning noise and then something snapped, a horrible, popping noise like a whole piece of the statue had just broken off under tension and shot off into the dark.

Somehow Bogdan managed to get the truck into reverse and move it away from the statue, back toward the canyon entrance. It turned out not to be necessary, because the statue never did fall over.

Chapel was less concerned about Lenin's fate, though, then what had broken off the statue base. Moving around behind it, keeping a close eye on the shifting metal mass above him, he came around to the back and saw there was a large hole in the base, now. The outline of the hole was strangely regular, not what he expected at all.

It was rectangular in shape, about six feet high and three feet wide. The corners of the hole were neatly rounded.

It looked like nothing so much in Chapel's experience as the shape of the hatches on the *Kurchatov*. It looked like a doorway.

"Nadia," he called out. "Nadia! Bring the flashlight over here!"

ARALSK-30, KAZAKHSTAN: JULY 21, 05:02

The base, and the statue above it, were both hollow, but they weren't empty. Inside the base was a little room, just big enough for three people to cram inside. Set into one wall was a Cyrillic keyboard and a bank of lights. All of them were dark.

Inside the statue was a pipe rising straight up into the air. A wire ran from the base of the pipe, down along the wall, and into the floor. "*Konyechno*," Nadia said. "I wondered why a town of this size needed such a large monument."

"Not just to remind Russians far from home what they were working for?" Chapel asked, though he'd guessed what she was going to say.

"It's a shortwave antenna," she told him. "Perimeter must listen, always, for data from its monitoring stations and for the buzz tone from Moscow. Remember? It does not activate until that buzz tone goes silent." She played her light along the pipe, up toward the inside of Lenin's head. "A shortwave antenna out here might be noticed, but not some grandiose statue. Clever, clever."

"This is the lock, yes?" Bogdan said, reaching toward the keyboard.

Nadia slapped his hand away. "Yes, it is. Do not touch it, whatever you do." She ushered them all back out into the predawn light. "We must take our time, now. Though I want to very much to get started."

Chapel nodded, thinking of all the prep work they should do. He ran down the job assignments in his head. "Honestly, we're all tired. It's been a long night, and we should get some sleep. But I know that isn't going to happen—none of us wants to wait any longer; we want to do this. First I should tell Angel what we found," Chapel said. "She can get our escape route ready for us." The timing would be crucial—the submarine had to appear on the coast of the Caspian Sea just when they arrived. If it was spotted in Kazakh waters, it would be fired on without warning. Angel needed as much advance warning as she could get. "We need to move the truck, too, just in case the statue falls over. We need to check all our equipment, everything we'll need once we're inside. That's Bogdan's department. As for you—"

"Yes?" she asked, looking at him. Before he answered her, though, her eyes strayed back to the door in the base of the statue. She couldn't not look at it.

"Why don't you just take a second and pat yourself on the back?"

When she looked at him with uncomprehending eyes, he couldn't help but laugh out loud.

"You did it, Nadia," he told her. "You made it happen."

"Don't shout hop-la before you jump," she told him.

It was his turn to look confused.

Bogdan sneered in disgust. "Is Russian proverb. Means, not to be counting chickens before they are born."

Chapel laughed again. He knew it was true— nothing was finished, not yet. But he couldn't help but be excited. The mission was nearly complete. He ran all the way back to the truck.

ARALSK-30, KAZAKHSTAN: JULY 21, 05:23

"Jim, do you have the one-time pad?"

Chapel took it from his pocket and turned it over in his hands. When he'd went diving for the pad in the wreck of the *Kurchatov*, he'd had no idea it would lead him here. The little black book still smelled of an ocean on the other side of the world. He handed it to her as if it was dangerous in itself, as if it might explode.

"A code word must be enciphered, then entered very carefully into this keyboard," she told them. "Only this will open the way."

"So let's get started," Chapel told her. "You know how to work the pad?" He'd studied the matrices of numbers and Cyrillic characters in the one-time pad and never been able to make hide nor hair of it. "You know the code word?"

"I do," she said, but raised both hands for patience. "It must be done precisely, though. One mistake and—pfft—it is over. The panel and the door will lock themselves down, and the system will know we are intruders."

"What will it do then?" Chapel asked, looking around at the metallic walls of the statue. "Electrify this thing?"

"Worse," Nadia replied. "It will switch Perimeter into active mode. Arm the system. Then only a special signal from Moscow will turn it off again."

"You're saying if you press the wrong button, we will have made this damned thing worse than it was before? More dangerous?"

"Indeed."

Chapel shook his head. "Better let Bogdan do it, then."

Nadia looked almost hurt.

"He has the nimblest fingers I've ever seen," he told her. "You brought him along for a reason, right?"

"Yes." She closed her eyes for a moment and

pressed the one-time pad to her chest. "All right." She opened the book to the last page, the one dated 25 December 1991. Christmas Day, the last day of the Soviet Union.

Bogdan went over to the panel. He cracked his knuckles a few times, then let his fingers hover over the keyboard. "Am ready," he said.

Nadia inhaled deeply. She looked at the pad, matching each letter of the code word with the matching entry on the grid. Then she spoke each enciphered letter out loud, one at a time, very slowly.

"Kah. Ehr. Ah. Ehs. Ehn. Ee kratkoyeh. Ee kratkoyeh. Ehl. Oo. Cheh."

As she spoke each letter, Bogdan dutifully typed it on the keyboard. When he was finished, he drew his hands away quickly so as not to accidentally type an additional letter.

On the row of lightbulbs above the keyboard, a single lamp lit up with a dull yellow glow.

Nothing else happened.

"Did it—was—" Chapel had no idea what to say.

Nadia looked at the two men, a growing horror writ on her face. Had they got it wrong? Had they just armed Perimeter and left the world in constant danger of nuclear annihilation?

"Does it—maybe this is just the code entry panel, the actual door is somewhere else," Chapel said, which sounded stupid to his own ears. "Maybe—"

He stopped then because he'd heard something, very soft and far away. It came from below his feet, the sound of a machine moving on a rusty track.

Then the floor of the statue lurched and dropped half an inch. Chapel and Bogdan staggered back away from the walls, toward the door. Nadia dropped into a crouch, one hand on the floor. She looked like a cat.

The floor dropped another few inches without warning. There was a horrible grinding noise, and the rattle of a massive chain. Something broke with a snap, and then the floor started lowering, smoothly and slowly, sliding down into the earth with all three of them still on it.

It was an elevator. It was an elevator and it was going to take them to Perimeter. The code had worked.

BELOW ARALSK-30, KAZAKHSTAN: JULY 21, 05:33

The elevator descended through a concrete tube, its walls stained with white sediment. There was no light inside the tube except the flashlight that Chapel held. He shone it at the wall and saw some markings there—numbers, telling them how far they had descended.

-5, he read. He imagined that meant they'd already dropped five meters below the canyon floor.

He realized he was holding his breath. He let it out noisily.

As if they'd been waiting for his example, Nadia and Bogdan exhaled, too.

-10. Something was written on the wall in Cyrillic. He could just make out the word *sekretno* before it passed out of the light again. Probably some kind of dire warning about unauthorized access, and what would happen to any traitor who dared enter this place.

-15. Bogdan sat down on the floor. Maybe he thought the elevator was taking too long.

-20.

-25.

-30. A few more meters and the elevator stopped. One side of the tube was open, with just a metal folding gate blocking the way. Chapel reached out and grabbed the handle. The gate was rusted and didn't want to open. He put a little elbow grease into it and it screeched in its track, opening wide enough to let them out.

Nadia jumped, her shoulders rising toward her ears.

"What's wrong?" Chapel asked. His voice echoed weirdly in the underground chamber.

"Nothing. Nothing," she said, shaking her head so her hair swung around. "We just need to be careful. Perimeter is designed to resist what we plan. The keyboard panel above was not its only safeguard. If it decides we do not belong here, it will activate itself."

"Moving a gate might do that?" Chapel asked.

"No. No, almost certainly not."

Chapel made a mental note not to touch anything else.

The three of them stepped out of the elevator onto a shiny concrete floor, painted battleship gray. A thunking noise sounded above their heads and lights came on, revealing a short corridor ahead of them. The walls were a dismal green, and as shiny as the floor. There was surprisingly little dust.

An archway led off to their left, into a little room

with some tool cabinets and a single cot. The sheets on the cot stank of mildew—which Chapel found reassuring. It meant this place hadn't been used in a long time. The tools were placed neatly in their racks, and they were as shiny as when they'd been made. Maybe they had never been used. "What's all this for?" Chapel asked. "I thought this system was completely automated."

"Every system needs maintenance, sometimes."

Chapel shrugged and looked down the hall. There were more thunking noises, and lights came on down there, too, illuminating a spiral staircase leading downward. The steps were made of steel that had been perforated to keep them light. They didn't look as rusted as the gate had been.

Nadia led the way down the stairs. Lights kept coming on as they advanced, anticipating what they might want to be able to see. At one point they heard the sound of a tape being rewound—Chapel might have been the only one of them old enough to remember what that sounded like—and then music started playing from speakers mounted on the ceiling. *Classical*, he thought.

"Tchaikovsky," Nadia told him, as if she'd read his mind.

"Why?" he asked.

"Why does it play music for us? Do you know about Chernobyl, about the Excluded Zone?"

"Sure," Chapel said. "All the land around the nuclear plant there is irradiated, so nobody's allowed inside. There's a whole city in there that's fenced off and abandoned."

"Pripyat," Nadia said. "It is called Pripyat. In the

early days, just after the disaster, when someone did have to go there—scientists, mostly—they would get very frightened. Not because of the radiation but because it was too silent. There were no other people for miles. No birds sang—the birds all died. So they had loudspeakers mounted throughout the zone, loudspeakers that played music all the time, all day. I've seen video and it is very haunting, that music. But perhaps better than nothing at all."

"So Perimeter is playing us music so we don't get creeped out down here?" Chapel asked. "I have to say, it's not working."

The spiral staircase took them down into a cave, a mostly spherical space hollowed out of the bedrock. Like a vast bubble in the stone. At the end of the staircase was a narrow catwalk that led to a circular platform that seemed to hover in empty air. Chapel shone his flashlight down and saw that the platform was mounted on huge springs, each coil as thick as one of his legs.

"Shock absorbers," Nadia told him. "If there is an earthquake, or a nuclear strike shakes the earth, those will absorb all vibration."

Sitting on the platform were a number of upright rectangular boxes, each about the size of a bookcase. Together they looked to Chapel like some kind of space age Stonehenge. A simple desk stood in the middle of the boxes, and sitting on the desk was a television screen and a keyboard.

The cave had not been designed for comfort or human convenience. Big klieg lights shone down from above, illuminating the platform in a harsh light that made for long, stark shadows. Heavy cables snaked across the platform and disappeared into the darkness below the springs. If you tripped over one of those, you might fall off the platform and drop twenty feet before you hit the jagged rocks below. Chapel wondered if now he knew the purpose of the cot in the tool room. Even if you didn't plan on spending the night down here, the tool room was a human space, a place that was actually designed to be used by people. The platform certainly wasn't.

"That's it, isn't it?" Chapel asked. "Those boxes—"

"Yes," Nadia whispered. "Those are the data banks. And the terminal, there on the desk, it is the only access point. This place, this cave . . . is Perimeter. You know, I never really believed I would see this."

"You weren't supposed to. Nobody was." The three of them moved forward, onto the platform. The light streamed down all around them. On the faces of the data banks huge spools of magnetic tape turned slowly, while polling lights flashed on and off as bits of data moved through the system like red blood corpuscles drifting through arteries and veins. Chapel felt something like awe, or reverence. Like what he had felt in the Hagia Sofia, when, for the first time, Nadia had taken his hand. There was something here larger than them, bigger than human scale—

The spell broke instantly when Bogdan started laughing.

Chapel spun around to look at the Romanian. Bogdan was bent over, studying one of the data banks. There was a big, goofy smile on his face, and his eyes were sparkling. Chapel had never seen the hacker so animated, not even when he'd killed Mirza.

"What's so funny?" he demanded.

"Is like old man's computer!" Bogdan exclaimed. He slapped one of his long thighs. "Is what everybody so afraid of? Is end of world, here? I see more advanced calculators, in my time."

PERIMETER: JULY 21, 05:38

"He's got a point," Nadia said. "This system was installed in the early 1980s and never upgraded. You could probably fit all its data in one little corner of a smartphone and carry it around with you."

"That would make it the world's most dangerous smartphone," Chapel pointed out, "since then you would have the launch codes for every nuclear missile in Russia." He looked around at the data banks, standing in a circle around the desk. Each had two big reels of magnetic tape on its front, behind a plastic dust cover. "Jesus. I haven't seen a reel-to-reel system like this since I was a kid, and that was just for recording music. What happens if one of these tapes breaks? They used to do that all the time."

"One of them has," Nadia said, pointing at one of the data banks. A dull red light flashed on its control panel. "That's why there are eight of them. Each one must contain the entire program and database, so that even if seven of them broke at once, the last one could still function. Remember up top, where we saw one lamp lit above the keyboard? I believe that indicated that one of the reels was reporting an error."

"So we can just grab these tapes and go?" Chapel asked. "That would cripple this thing, right?"

"I wouldn't recommend it. That is one of those safeguards I told you about. If you lift the covers and remove one of the tapes, Perimeter activates itself automatically, and—"

"—and it can't be shut down again until Moscow sends the right signal," Chapel finished.

"For the same reason we cannot blow this place up with C4 or smash the data banks with a lead pipe, even."

He nodded. "So we can't touch this thing without activating it, and we don't want that. So what do we do here?"

"You and I do nothing. This is why we brought Bogdan," Nadia said.

Both of them turned to look at the Romanian. Bogdan wove his fingers together and cracked his knuckles with a sickening pop. He took off his MP3 player and his headphones and set them down on top of one of the data banks, then went to the desk and sat down before the terminal.

"Is my turn," he said. "Bogdan for the win, yes?"

Chapel went to stand behind the hacker and look over his shoulder. "How are you going to break in to the system?" he asked, suddenly nervous. If Bogdan did this wrong, would it activate Perimeter? Maybe it would launch the missiles out of pure paranoia. Chapel tried to remember some of the things Angel had done to computers on his behalf. "Are you going to try a brute force approach? Run a logging script?

Or do you think there's a backdoor you can exploit to get you past the firewall?"

The Romanian looked up at him with a sneer. Then he reached over and switched on the monitor. It took a second to warm up, but when it did Chapel saw nothing on the screen but a greenish-white rectangle in the top left corner of the screen.

Bogdan tapped one key on the keyboard—the Cyrillic equivalent of a D.

Instantly the screen filled up with green text, line after line of Cyrillic characters Chapel couldn't begin to read.

"So I am in," Bogdan said.

Nadia smiled. "Jim, you forget. This computer isn't connected to any others. It predates even the earliest forms of the Internet. It doesn't even have password protection—or rather, it did, but we've already broken that, when we turned on the elevator."

Chapel nodded. "If you're in here, if you're sitting in that chair, it assumes you're an authorized user," he said. "Okay. So shut this thing down and we can go."

"It's not *quite* that simple," Nadia told him. "We don't just need to shut it down. As you know now, there are people in Russia who want Perimeter to remain functional. The same ones who tried to kill us."

The ones who had put a price on Nadia's head, Chapel thought—they'd only tried to kill him because he was standing next to her at the time. But he didn't say as much.

Nadia shook her head. "If we just shut this down, they'll figure out what we've done, eventually.

They'll come here and they'll start it back up. No, we must be more subtle. Bogdan is going to cripple Perimeter—but he will leave it so it looks functional. So that *it* thinks it is functional, and it will tell so to anyone who comes down here to ask."

"Yes, yes," Bogdan said. He tapped some keys and new lines of text appeared on the screen. "This I do. And this I do much easier if he does not lean over my head this whole time."

It took Chapel a second to realize Bogdan was asking for some space.

Maybe it was time to give the Romanian his due. This was his area of expertise. If you wanted something blown up or shot at, if you wanted to sneak in to a secure area without being seen, Chapel was your man. But now it was Bogdan's time to shine.

"Sorry," he said, and took a step back.

Bogdan cleared his throat. Apparently that wasn't enough space.

"Come, Jim," Nadia said, grabbing his hand. "We'll let him get to it. I have something else for us to do, just now."

PERIMETER: JULY 21, 05:49

From the way Nadia kept laughing, Chapel knew exactly where she was taking him. He didn't resist.

He wanted this. He hadn't wanted anything so much in a long time.

As she led him out of the cave, up the spiral staircase, the music from the overhead loudspeakers changed. "Rimsky-Korsakov," she said, and laughed. He didn't know why. He didn't care about the music. She kept turning back and trailing her fingers across his chest. The second time she did it, he grabbed her by the hips and pulled her to him and kissed her. He wanted to pick her up and carry her. By the time they reached the little cot in the tool room, his shirt was off. He started to take off his artificial arm but she stopped him, kissing down from his shoulder to his fingertips. He pulled her shirt away from her neck and kissed the hollow of her throat, the top of her breasts.

She wasn't laughing by that point.

He pulled her shirt over her head and bent down to put his face between her breasts, to drink in the smell of her, the smoothness of her skin, her warmth. With his right hand he cupped her breast, his thumb stroking the nipple until she shivered and curled against him. She looked up at him with wide eyes and he kissed her deeply, even as he slipped his hand down across her flat stomach and inside the waistband of her shorts. He felt lace and pushed his fingers under it, felt the sparse hair between her legs. She swiveled around, rubbing against him with her whole body until she was facing away from him. She pulled his left arm around her until he was holding her tight, then she grabbed his right hand and pushed it farther down until his fingers sank inside of her. She was already wet and he met no resistance as he slid his fingers back and forth, back and forth, slowly, rhythmically.

Her back pulsed against his chest, her body jerking every time his thumb made contact with her clitoris. At the same time her ass rubbed against his crotch, which felt maddening and amazing at the same time. She let out a trapped breath with a little moan and just when he thought he couldn't wait any longer, that he was going to have to throw her down on the cot, her whole body shuddered and went limp and she fell away from him, tumbling gracefully around until she was sitting on the cot in front of him. She lifted his hand to her face and looked deeply into his eyes, then licked her own wetness from his fingers.

He started grabbing for her shoulders, intent on pushing her down onto the cot, but she batted his hands away with a laugh. She unzipped his shorts and pulled everything down until he stood naked before her.

She took him into her mouth and he was certain that just that would make him come, but she held him back, her tongue playing along the tip of his penis but never quite letting him thrust away.

Then she stopped. With her hand on him, she drew her head back and looked up at him. "Is it okay that we're doing this?" she asked. "Is this—"

"Don't ask me that yet," he warned her. Already they'd gone too far for him to stop, even if he'd wanted to. If she was willing, and he wanted her this badly, what could be the harm? Julia had thrown him away, pushed him out of her life. He had no obligation to her now. Hollingshead and Angel never had to know about this.

She lay back on the cot, pulling down her shorts and her black lace panties. She twisted on the cot, reaching for him.

He climbed on top of her, and it was no effort at

all to slip inside her. Their bodies just meshed and it was happening, he was thrusting against her hips and he knew it wouldn't take long. Once he'd passed this border, he knew he would never look back. He would never hesitate again.

She wrapped her arms around his neck, pulling him toward her. She pressed her face into the crook of his shoulder and made a little whimpering sound that he knew wasn't a cry of pain. He pushed into her, desperate with need, with lust, with anguish that had to be expressed somehow. She rose off the bed to meet him, her hips smashing against his as he pushed harder and harder into her and her whimper became a plaintive wail. And then it happened, the dam broke, and all his pain, all his frustration came rushing out of him as his muscles locked, as his face writhed in a grimace of release.

He fell on top of her, panting and spent. He would never be able to put into words what had just happened, what he'd let go, but he felt empty and light and clean for the first time in weeks. He felt like he was floating in limitless space, and he didn't dare open his eyes.

He opened his eyes. She was stroking his hair, shushing him as he started to struggle up onto his hands. She pulled him close. "You must savor this," she told him. "Truly feel it. Let nothing else intrude. This is what I've learned."

He closed his eyes again and just lay there, letting the blood pound in his ears, letting his chest heave for air. The floating sensation came back, though not as strong as before. It slipped away from him, little by little.

He rolled off her onto his side, grabbed her with both his arms and pulled her close to him. Her lips found his and they just kissed for a while, their tongues finding each other slowly, searchingly. The emptiness he'd felt began to fill up with her, her presence, her smell, her body heat. His hands roamed across her back, grasped at her buttocks. She moved across him sinuously, with all the grace of the gymnast she'd once been, and then she was on top of him, lying across his chest, her breasts against his skin.

His hand just seemed to find her on its own, his fingers twining inside her. He felt her shake and knew she wanted more. He didn't need to do the work this time—she moved against his hand, pressing herself against it then sliding away, pressing again, sliding away until she'd built up a rhythm that made her breath come fast. Her mouth was against his ear and he felt her wet exhalations on his skin, felt the muscles of her face and neck tense as she rubbed herself to a climax against his fingers, his palm, his wrist. As she rode it out he was surprised to find that he was hard again—he hadn't recovered that quickly since high school.

She hooked one leg over him and twisted around until she was upright, her hands on his chest holding her above him. She reached down and guided him inside her in one quick motion, then she bent to kiss him and rose again to ride on top of him, moving up and down steadily. A thin sheen of sweat covered her face and the top of her chest and her eyes were squinted shut and he realized she was still in the throes of her orgasm, that she hadn't stopped coming.

She surprised him again, this time by rocking up onto one leg and swinging the other one across him, then turning around so she was facing away from him but still engulfing him. She reached down and grabbed his ankles as she moved against him, rising and falling, her muscular ass grinding back and forth against him. He pushed himself up with his arms and then reached forward to hold her, his hands grabbing her hips and pulling her down hard against his body, hard enough she let out an explosive cry. "I can feel all of you," she told him. "I can feel you inside me." She grabbed his hands and lifted them to her breasts. Sitting on his lap like that she lifted and fell with just the muscles of her thighs and slowly, slowly drew him onward, closer and closer. He pulled his good hand away from her breast and reached down to find her clitoris, making tiny circles on it with his forefinger and she burst, her body heaving as he came inside her, as they came together, as they rocked back and forth and both cried out.

The third time was a lot slower, but no less intense. Both of them had a lot of tension to burn off.

PERIMETER, JULY 21, 08:45

Chapel must have dozed off, because he woke to the smell of their sex, to Nadia wrapped around him, a rumpled sheet hanging from her shoulder—

—and Bogdan standing over them, looking down at them through his bangs.

Chapel licked his lips—they were very dry—and

grunted out something like a question. He'd meant to ask what Bogdan thought he was doing there, but it mostly came out as a growl of surprise.

"Is finished," Bogdan said.

"What?" Nadia asked, twisting around until she was sitting up, the sheet wrapped around her breasts. "What did you say, Bogdan?"

"The reprogramming work, is done, yes? Yes," Bogdan said. "I have finished."

"That's . . . great," Chapel managed to say. He grabbed for his shorts and found that he'd picked up Nadia's by mistake. They were tiny in his hand. Sheepishly, he handed them to her. "Great stuff, Bogdan. Thanks for, uh, letting us know. Why don't we meet you down in the cave and you can . . . show us what you did."

Bogdan didn't move. He wasn't leering at Nadia's near nakedness—nor Chapel's—but he didn't seem ready to go.

"Is time, I guess," the Romanian said. Then he let out a very long, very put-upon sigh.

"Time for what?" Nadia asked him.

"Is time, my usefulness it is complete. So now is time when you shoot me, yes? So I am no witness. Yes, I know how this works."

Nadia laughed. "Bogdan! Nobody's going to do that."

"Yeah," Chapel said. "We're the good guys."

Bogdan just shrugged.

"If you could . . . just . . ." Chapel shook his head. "Bogdan, we need to get dressed. We'd prefer to do that without you watching us."

The hacker nodded. For a second longer he just

stood there. "You are sure you do not wish to shoot me? Only, I would prefer, if so, that is done quickly. I do not wish to draw things out, as they say."

It was Chapel's turn to laugh. He jumped up off the cot and clapped the hacker on his shoulder. "Nobody wants to kill you. In fact, if you're interested in a job in America, I think maybe we could work something out." Chapel already had Angel as his in-house hacker, but he imagined Hollingshead could find some use for the Romanian. Anybody who understood Russian computers as well as Bogdan did would find plenty of work. "You'd be safe, there, and—"

"He does not know?" Bogdan asked. He was looking at Nadia.

"Go wait in the cave," she told him, harsher than before.

When he was gone, Nadia got off the cot and wrapped her arms around Chapel, kissing his chest and then leaning her cheek against his skin.

He pulled away. "What is it I'm supposed to know?" he asked.

She looked confused for a second. Maybe even hurt. "After all this," she said, gesturing at the cot—which was leaning on one buckled leg and would never be the same again—"still you question me like some enemy agent?"

"When I asked why you were spying on my conversations with Angel, you said it was just part of the job. Nothing personal." He put one hand against her cheek, and after a second she rubbed her face against his palm. "What am I supposed to know?" he demanded.

She hissed in frustration and started grabbing her clothes. "I'll tell you. In a minute. Just let us see first what Bogdan has done."

They dressed without another word and then hurried down the spiral staircase. Bogdan was standing next to the terminal desk. Chapel couldn't tell if he looked bored or proud or sad that his work was done—all those expressions looked pretty much the same on Bogdan's face.

"Show us," Nadia said.

"Is nothing to see." Bogdan tapped a key on Perimeter's keyboard and the screen filled with Cyrillic text. It looked exactly the same as it had the first time Chapel had seen it. He still couldn't understand any of it. "No change shows, as you asked. No one will know I was here. But! The system does not work now."

Chapel frowned. "How's that?"

Bogdan nodded. He tapped some more keys and more, but different, text appeared on the screen. Just as meaningless to Chapel. "I have put small subroutine in this program. Nothing that looks out of place. In normal times, if Perimeter activates, its first step is to query its atmospheric sensors, yes? It looks for heat, for light, for change in the barometer. If a signature is found, a specific signature for nuclear blast, then, and only then, Perimeter launches all missiles."

"Sure," Chapel said. "That's what we don't want it to do."

Bogdan nodded. "So now, is extra step. If Perimeter checks sensors and finds such a signature, it goes to a new line in program that tells to check whether

Perimeter has been activated. If is activated, it checks sensors. If sensors show signature, it checks for activation. If activated, check sensors . . . goes on forever, like this, but never gets to launch codes."

"An infinite loop," Chapel said, finally getting it. "It can never finish the program."

Nadia clapped her hands in delight. "That's perfect! And you hid your work?"

"Yes, yes. No one will find it unless they know exactly where to look. No sign of tampering, no obvious code insertions. No one will know system is broken, unless they make Perimeter launch, and nothing happens."

"That's . . . kind of brilliant. Bogdan, you're a genius," Chapel said. He fought back an urge to grab the Romanian and give him a hug. He turned to Nadia. He knew there was a big goofy grin on his face, but he didn't care. "This is what you had planned all along, isn't it? I thought you were going to blow Perimeter up, or just take a fire axe to those data banks. But you knew that wouldn't work. You did it, Nadia. You did it!"

"I could not have come this far without you, my *svidetel*," Nadia said, smiling at him. "My dear witness. You will tell the Americans it is done? That Perimeter is no longer a threat?"

"Absolutely. And then—who knows. This thing has been holding back any kind of nuclear disarmament talks for years. Maybe, someday we can live in a world without all these nukes. Maybe the world can finally stop worrying about the apocalypse and start getting things turned around . . . there's just one last thing we need to consider."

Nadia shook her head, but she was close to laughing with joy. "There is? What is it?"

"What did Bogdan think I was supposed to know?"

Her face fell instantly. She frowned and started to turn away, but then she stopped and looked him right in the eye. "Bogdan will not be going with you to America," she said, "because he's coming with me."

"Where?" Chapel asked.

"That's the big question." She inhaled sharply. "There is something I have wanted to tell you. Something about my mission—something you are not cleared for, but I think, at this point, such niceties are unnecessary."

Chapel could feel the muscles tensing up in his neck. She had lied to him once already about the mission—when she claimed she had unequivocal support from the Russian government. If there was more, if she had misled him further—

"You know I am an agent of FSTEK. At least, I was. If Marshal Bulgachenko is dead, then the bureau for which I worked is . . . no more. He *was* that office. I am an agent now with no agency."

Chapel shook his head. "It's not like that matters anyway. You can't go back to Moscow. They'd shoot you the second you stepped off the plane."

She nodded. "*Konyechno.* But my plan was never to return to Moscow, not even at the start. You see, the marshal and I, we had something in common. Something we believed in. It was why he chose me, why he allowed me to take on this mission, even after he knew I was dying. We thought we could make a grand play, a great leap that would carry our common dream forward, to—"

She stopped in midsentence, as if she'd been frozen in place.

Chapel frowned but just watched as she tilted her head to the side. "Bogdan," she whispered. "What does that mean?" She pointed at the terminal desk.

Bogdan and Chapel both turned to look at the screen there. A line of Cyrillic characters had appeared in bright green. They flashed alarmingly as if demanding attention.

"Oh," Bogdan said. "This is shit."

"What kind of shit?" Nadia asked.

"Is saying, someone is here. Up top," Bogdan said. He looked almost ashamed, as if it were his fault.

"It can tell that? That there's something out of place up in Aralsk-30? Tell me it's just picking up our truck," Chapel demanded.

"If it makes you happy, yes, yes, I will tell you this. But is lie."

ARALSK-30, KAZAKHSTAN: JULY 21, 08:59

Bogdan grabbed his MP3 player off the top of the data bank where he'd left it. Chapel checked the assault rifle he had carried down into the cave. None of them said anything. There was nothing to say, until they knew what they faced.

They came up the elevator into punishing sunlight—after the cool darkness of Perimeter's cave, the heat and brightness of the desert above hit Chapel like a wall and it took him a second to adjust.

Even with his eyes clamped shut, though, he could hear the helicopter just fine.

Shielding his eyes with his hands, he cursed when he saw it not a mile away, floating over the desert floor as if it were pinned to the air. It looked like a standard Russian military chopper—a Kamov Ka-60. Something occurred to him about it, though. "Nadia—that helicopter's a newer Russian model. Does Kazakhstan have any of those?"

An agent of FSTEK, he knew, would have that information memorized. "No, none—they use Mil Mi-24s, only."

Chapel nodded. "Then that's not some random Kazakh patrol." The idea had been unlikely, anyway. What reason would the Kazakh military have to be out here, in the middle of an uninhabited desert? There was no sign anyone had visited Aralsk-30 in years. Why would they do so now?

No, this helicopter was Russian, and the pilot didn't care if he was seen violating Kazakh sovereignty. There was only one explanation. The assassins had come back for Nadia, and this time they weren't foolish enough to just send a couple of thugs with pistols. This time they intended to finish the job.

"How did they find us?" Nadia asked. "We were so careful to hide our movements. They couldn't have been following us all this time."

Chapel shook his head. "Maybe they didn't need to."

The helicopter looked like it wasn't moving at all, just slowly getting bigger, which meant it was headed directly for them. Chapel estimated they had a minute at most before it arrived.

He turned to Nadia. "Who knew you were

coming to dismantle Perimeter? Besides you and the marshal, did anyone—"

"No! I can only think they tracked us by satellite, or—oh, no. They killed Marshal Bulgachenko. But they must have . . . questioned him first."

Chapel wished he had time to comfort her, but there was no time left for anything but tactics. "It doesn't matter right now. Come on—we need to get into that building over there." He pointed at one of the buildings that had partially filled with sand. "Maybe they won't see us. Maybe we can just wait them out."

"You think this likely?" Bogdan asked.

"No," Chapel said, and jogged across the intersection, away from the statue.

ARALSK-30, KAZAKHSTAN: JULY 21, 09:01

They crouched low under the sill of a broken window inside the shade of the building. Chapel risked a quick glance over the edge and saw the helicopter circling Aralsk-30, high enough up to avoid the walls of the canyon. He held his breath and closed his eyes and listened to the sound of its rotor chopping up the air, silently praying for that sound to diminish, to lessen, to indicate that the helicopter was moving away. That the pilot had given up his search, having found nothing.

Instead the noise got louder. The Ka-60 was coming closer, lower. He heard its noise echo off the dead faces of the buildings and knew it was coming in to land.

Beside him Nadia looked terrified. One of her hands reached for his and he took it. He would give her what comfort he could, as pointless as it might seem.

Bogdan had curled up, his knees up in front of his chin. He looked like he might be asleep, though Chapel doubted even the Romanian could relax at a moment like this.

He waited until he couldn't stand it anymore, then took another quick peek over the windowsill.

The helicopter had landed near the mouth of the canyon, its rotor kicking up great clouds of dust that obscured much of what was going on. But dark shapes moved through that dust and Chapel knew that the chopper had off-loaded its passengers. He couldn't get a good head count on them through the dust, but he thought there might be half a dozen. Six armed assassins, then. And no way out. The only way to escape the canyon was through its mouth, right past those men.

He whispered to Nadia, telling her what he'd seen.

"Even if we could get past them all, even if we could get the truck out of here—the helicopter could just follow us. There's no way we could outrun it, not over the desert, and there's no cover for us to make for. And that's even if we *could* get to the truck. I have my rifle, you have a pistol. Not much firepower, considering what we're facing."

Nadia set her jaw, accepting the inevitable, perhaps.

"They'll try to take you alive, for questioning," he told her.

"I'm more worried about Bogdan," she said.

Chapel grunted in surprise. It might have been a laugh, under different circumstances.

"If they take Bogdan, if they question him—he can tell them what he did to Perimeter. Tell them how to change the program back. All our work would be for nothing, then."

Chapel hadn't thought of that.

A different kind of man, the kind of agent that Hollingshead should have sent on this mission, would have been able to think about the situation without passion, without qualm. Such a man might have come to one inescapable conclusion.

The course forward was to shoot Bogdan, to make sure his information couldn't be retrieved. And then probably shoot Nadia, and himself, for good measure. If none of them could be questioned—call it what it was, Chapel thought, *tortured*—then their secrets would remain safe.

If Hollingshead had picked some twenty-five-year-old Navy SEAL for this mission, or some MARSOC jarhead, some kid with no ties, no family, no obligations to anything but his country—such a man wouldn't have hesitated.

But Chapel wasn't one of those men. He thought of what his old trainer, Bigelow, had said about him.

You're a smart guy, Chapel. But for some reason when you're beat, you get dumb. You get too dumb to just give up.

So shooting each other in a horrific game of round robin was just out of the question. They were going to have to live through this, or at least try. Chapel racked his brain trying to think of a plan. Anything at all.

What he came up with sounded absurd even as he outlined it to Nadia. She didn't laugh, though. Maybe she was willing to clutch at straws just as much as he was.

"You're going to have to take out those assassins, as best you can. You're going to move from building to building, cover to cover, and get to the truck. There are better weapons for you there—assault rifles, anyway, and the two of you can use those to shoot your way out of the canyon."

"And what about the helicopter?" she asked.

"That's my job," he told her.

ARALSK-30, KAZAKHSTAN: JULY 21, 09:07

Chapel headed up to the roof of the building, up where he could get a better view. The building had a flat top lined with tar paper that burned in the sun. A two-foot-high lip ran all the way around it, providing enough cover for Chapel to lie down on the scorching roof and be invisible from the street level. He could poke his head over the lip just enough to see what was going on without exposing himself unduly to enemy fire.

It would have been a great position to set up a sniper nest, if he had a sniper rifle. The AK-47 he carried just didn't count. He could theoretically give Nadia some covering fire from up there. If he'd had enough bullets.

He didn't, though. He had one magazine of thirty rounds, and he was going to need all of them. So as the assassins spread out through the streets, covering doorways and starting their search, Chapel could only watch and hope.

A little voice in the back of his head kept nagging at him. *She's a terrible shot*, it said. *She's outgunned, and she doesn't have any body armor. Bogdan will slow her down.*

He tried to ignore that voice. He'd seen her fight before, and he knew she was dangerous. The Spetsnaz training she'd received would have to see her through.

Once they were clear of the helicopter's rotor wash, Chapel could see that the assassins were a different breed than they'd faced before. These wore heavy kit, ballistic vests and helmets with neck protection. They carried short-barreled carbines, probably the AKS-74U variant of the rifle Chapel held. Those stumpy little weapons sacrificed a lot of range, but they made up for it by being easier to use in urban warfare scenarios—just like this one. At least one of the assassins had grenades hanging from his harness, and another one was carrying some kind of tactical shotgun.

They broke into teams of two so they could cover more ground. One group approached the statue—and the truck that was parked next to it. If they thought to shoot out the truck's tires, or its engine block, Chapel's plan would be ruined. Luckily the thought didn't seem to occur to them. One of them climbed inside the truck and looked around while the other covered him. After a few seconds, the assassin climbed back out of the cab and gave a hand signal that had to mean the truck was all clear. The two of them moved on.

The second group of two headed for the dormitory buildings near the mouth of the canyon. They disappeared through a doorway and Chapel lost sight of them.

The third group headed for the factories at the end of the canyon, their weapons tracking the broken windows. They moved fast, but they didn't leave themselves exposed—wherever they went they kept a wall at their back, or one of them twisted around to cover their rear. These guys were professionals, and they weren't going to take any chances.

At the entrance to one of the factories, one of them readied a grenade—probably a CS tear gas grenade, by the look of it—while the other covered the intersection with his rifle. They gestured back and forth, not making a single sound, then stepped inside the factory together.

The second they were through the empty doorway, into the darkness of the factory building, Nadia appeared in the door of an administration building across the street. She glanced up at Chapel where he hid on the rooftop.

He looked around for the other groups. Both of them were inside buildings, out of sight. Chapel risked a quick wave at Nadia to let her know it was momentarily clear.

Nadia ducked low and ran across the street, to press herself up against the outside wall of the factory.

For a long, tense minute nothing happened. Chapel had an idea of what Nadia had planned, and he also knew that if either of the other two groups emerged from their buildings in that time, they would see her in a second. Nadia stood perfectly exposed to anyone watching from the street.

Then the group in the factory came back out into the light. It would take them a second for their eyes to adjust to the light, Chapel knew.

Nadia didn't give them the chance. She swung around in one fluid motion, raising her pistol and holding it in front of her in both hands.

She was a terrible shot. The assassins were wearing body armor.

It didn't matter.

She knew they would kill her if she didn't kill them, so she went for the best possible shot. Her pistol was only inches from the lead assassin's face when she fired. Even from the other side of the intersection Chapel could see the man's eye explode in a cloud of blood.

He dropped his grenade and brought his hands up to his face, but he was already collapsing, already dying. The grenade hit the ground and bounced away from the door, and for a second Chapel thought Nadia was diving to catch it. But she had something else in mind. The dead assassin's carbine was on a strap around his neck. It would have taken too long for her to get it loose so she just slid in under his falling body and used him as a shield, grabbing the carbine and twisting it upward to fire into the body of his partner. At that range she couldn't miss, and the carbine was powerful enough to tear through his body armor.

It also made one hell of a racket, clearly audible all over town, even with the noise of the helicopter. Chapel saw movement in one of the dormitory buildings, a flash of dark fabric in one of the second-floor windows. The other assassins had heard Nadia's shots, and it wouldn't be long before they ran over to investigate.

Meanwhile the tear gas grenade went off in the street, a huge white cloud jumping out of it instantaneously. Nadia freed the carbine from its strap and cradled it to her chest as she rolled inside the factory building, away from the cloud.

Two assassins came out of an administration building that fronted on the intersection, just as the wind carried the cloud of tear gas straight at them. They wore gas masks and it didn't affect them, but it did cut down on their visibility. They jogged toward the factory building, clearly intent on investigating what had just happened.

Surely Nadia would have expected that. Surely she would have moved on already, slipping out the back of the factory. The only way to win a fight like this was to move constantly, to maintain the element of surprise. Chapel was sure Nadia knew that—she'd been trained for this kind of fighting, just as he had.

He wanted to keep watching the factory, to see what happened next, to make sure she was okay. But he didn't get the chance to see her next move.

Up at the mouth of the canyon, the helicopter was already lifting into the air. It was going to provide air support to the assassins on the ground. If it spotted Nadia, even for an instant, the jig was up.

Chapel had to make sure that didn't happen.

ARALSK-30, KAZAKHSTAN: JULY 21, 09:12

The helicopter drifted slowly toward the center of town, toward the Lenin statue, staying low but not so low it risked colliding with any of the buildings. It moved through the air like a starving predator, hunting desperately for any sign of prey. Chapel kept his head down so the pilot wouldn't see him, waiting for his chance.

Down in the intersection, the tear gas cloud was already beginning to disperse, shredded by the downward wash of air from the chopper's rotor. One of the assassin teams moved through the thinning cloud toward the factory, their carbines swiveling back and forth in case Nadia showed herself.

Chapel couldn't see the other team, the one that had gone into the dormitories. They must be holding back, as a reserve, or simply as spotters. The Russians weren't taking any chances.

Time to give them something new to worry about. As the helicopter neared Chapel's position, he readied himself, then jumped up and started firing. His rifle's bullets tore through the thin metal skin of the helicopter, leaving bright holes in the dark paint of its fuselage. He didn't hit anything vital— this was a military helicopter, and all its important equipment would be protected by armor plate—but he definitely got its attention.

Its beak-shaped nose started to swing around in slow motion, and he got a good look into the canopy. He cursed when he saw there were two people in there, a pilot and a copilot. The Ka-60 had a big rectangular front viewport, much like the windshield of a car. In Ranger school they'd taught Chapel just how difficult it was to snipe someone through a windshield—the curved glass distorted your view, and it also tended to refract the trajectory of any bullet that passed through it. He tried for a shot at the pilot anyway. That was one vital piece of equipment he could conceivably hit.

His bullets starred the viewport, sending a gentle rain of glittering glass cubes falling toward the street below. The helicopter jerked sideways and raised its nose, looking very much like a startled dragonfly. Chapel had time to see that he hadn't hit either of the pilots, though the copilot had shed his safety webbing and was running back toward the main body of the aircraft.

Then the nose came up farther and he could only see the belly of the helicopter as it reared back and fell away from him, pulling out of range. Chapel let it go and looked down into the streets. Both members of the assassin team he could see were looking up at him, though their carbines were still aimed at street level. He desperately wanted to fire a burst into them, to make them jump, but he didn't dare waste bullets. He'd already fired twelve rounds of his thirty into the helicopter and there was a long fight coming.

Nor, it turned out, did he need to shoot at them. Even as he watched them watching him, Nadia was sneaking up behind them, crouched so low she was nearly walking on her knees. She fired a quick salvo into their backs and then darted away, into the shadowy interior of an administration building.

Chapel wanted to cheer as he saw them dance and jump. One of them was bleeding from a wound at his hip as they ran for cover. Chapel ignored them and studied the dormitory buildings, looking for any sign of the third team. He was so intent on his search he almost missed what the helicopter was doing.

The Ka-60 had turned broadside to him, hovering over the statue fifty yards away. It bobbed slightly as it hung in the air there, then stabilized itself until it was motionless, seeming almost glued to the air.

Its side hatch slid open—the movement was enough to make Chapel look—and the copilot peered out for a moment, then ducked back inside. A second later the long narrow shape of a heavy machine gun rolled forward, four barrels sticking out through the side hatch to glint in the sunlight.

Chapel recognized the gun—a Yak-B Gatling gun that could pump out four thousand rounds every minute. Standard equipment on most Russian attack helicopters, though the Ka-60 normally didn't carry one. The helicopter must have been modified to carry it at the expense of crew seats. It opened fire almost instantly with a grinding noise that made every muscle in Chapel's body twitch.

He dove backward, under the short wall that screened the rooftop. His face hit the searing tar paper as bullets lanced over him, chewing up the roof only a few feet from where he lay. If the pilot ascended even a few dozen feet, the gunner would have a perfect view of Chapel, wherever he was on the roof.

It was definitely time to move.

He waited until he heard the Gatling gun start to spin down, then pushed himself up on his hands and dashed for the stairway that led down inside the building. The helicopter started firing again before he reached the stairs, but he managed to get down into cover behind thick walls, even as dust and shards of broken concrete rained down on him. Something hurt, but he didn't have time to think about it. He hurried into the center of the building where he would be safe from the Gatling gun and pressed himself up against a wall, gaining just a little space to breathe.

Something really started to hurt by then. It didn't matter—he could walk. And he had to find some way to deal with the helicopter. As long as it was airborne, there was no way to get away in the truck, no hope for him or for Nadia or Bogdan.

He checked his rifle, even though the pain was getting pretty intense. His clip was still half full, and everything looked in order . . .

Goddamnit, that hurt.

He realized he was being foolish. If he was really injured, he could bleed out in minutes. He just hadn't wanted to acknowledge that he was wounded. He looked down, then, and saw a huge oblong gash in his leg. It was bleeding profusely, but he didn't think any arteries were pierced, and none of the bones were broken.

Still, it had to be taken care of. He tore off his shirt and ripped it into strips. He could barely manage a quick field dressing, but at least that would slow the blood loss. While he was tying off the bandage, he heard something, and he stopped rigid in place.

He'd heard someone whisper.

He grabbed his rifle and almost fired a burst into the shadows—

—before he realized it was Nadia, and she was calling his name.

ARALSK-30, KAZAKHSTAN: JULY 21, 09:19

He realized that he'd lost track of her, and that she must have run into his building as she moved around the intersection. She would have known he was still there, of course—she only had to look for the building currently being demolished by the helicopter. It was a terrible risk, though, for them to be in the same building at the same time. If the assassins had a bomb or even just more tear gas grenades—

"Jim," she breathed. "Oh, thank God you are still alive!"

She came out of the shadows and rushed over to put an arm around him. He thought she was trying to embrace him and wanted to tell her there was no time for that, but then he realized he had been falling over and she was coming to support him.

"You're hurt," she said.

"I'll be fine. What's the situation?"

"We are about to be killed," she said.

Chapel grunted in frustration and pushed his back up against the wall. "That's not what I meant. There were six of them on the ground. You got two over by the factories, then wounded another one when they spotted me. I'm pretty sure two of them are still holed up in the dormitories; they're probably watching the entrance to the canyon, ready to gun us down if we try to run into the desert, and—"

"Eight," she said.

He shut up and just stared at her.

"What?" he asked, when she didn't elaborate.

"There were eight of them on the ground, by my count."

Chapel wanted to close his eyes and sit down and just stop thinking then. He wanted to pretend like none of this was happening.

He couldn't do that, of course.

"I counted six," he told her. "I was planning on six." But it had been hard to get an accurate count when they jumped out of the helicopter. The rotor had been kicking up so much dust, and he'd been far enough away he could have counted wrong. "Okay, there were eight. Now there are six and one is wounded. Then there's this helicopter. The second we step out of this building, it's going to mow us down." He thought of something, then. Something that should have always been there, in the middle of his plans. "Where's Bogdan?" he asked.

"In the truck," she said. "Hiding under some crates. I got him in there while the killers were still distracted."

Chapel forced a grin, despite the pain in his leg. Damn, but Nadia was good at this. The truck was probably the safest place for the hacker to be. The assassins had already checked the vehicle and cleared it. They would have no reason to check it again, at least not until they were sure they'd secured the area.

"It might be possible," Nadia said. "Not likely, mind you. But possible that we could draw enough attention away from the truck that he could drive out of here alone. Of course, we would have to sacrifice both our lives to get him clear."

"If we don't take care of the helicopter, he won't get very far. And do you think it would even occur to him to take that kind of initiative?"

Nadia's shoulders swiveled around in a complicated shrug as she wrestled with her thoughts. "No," she said, finally.

Chapel nodded. "Okay. So, slightly different plan. I go up on the roof and shoot down this helicopter—if I can, which is a big hypothetical. In the chaos you run for the truck and drive the hell out of here. Assuming these assholes don't shoot out your tires or get a lucky shot and kill you at the wheel, you can get to the Caspian Sea and meet the submarine there; it can take you to—"

"That is the most foolish plan I have ever heard," Nadia told him.

"You have a better one?"

"Yes," she told him. "I go to the roof. You drive the truck."

Chapel could guess her logic. He knew perfectly well what she was thinking. She had only a few months to live, even if she did escape from Aralsk-30. Sacrificing herself here and now wouldn't do much to shorten her life expectancy.

He knew he couldn't let her do it, though. He couldn't let this woman, this incredible person, just throw her life away, no matter how short it might be. He didn't understand his feelings for her. He didn't know that he ever would. But they were real.

He would do everything in his power to make sure she lived, for as long as she could. To make sure she escaped.

He also knew that she would try to argue him

around if he said anything like that. She would tell him he was being an idiot, an emotional idiot, and maybe she would be right. So he needed another reason why it couldn't be her.

"You're a lousy shot," he said.

Her eyes flared with something similar to—but not quite the same as—anger. He could tell she knew he was right. She pressed her lips together very hard, until they turned white. She twisted her face away from his. Then she brought it back very fast and kissed him, deeply, passionately. For what they both knew was the last time.

She broke away from him and ran toward the front of the building. He headed back toward the stairs.

ARALSK-30, KAZAKHSTAN: JULY 21, 09:25

Even before he could reach the roof, the helicopter came for him, strafing the broken windows on the upper floor of the building. Concrete dust puffed from each of the windows in turn, and the window-sills crumbled away, rotten after years of exposure to the desert sun. Debris crunched under his feet as he ran for cover between two windows, then ducked down to keep out of sight.

The Gatling gun spun down and he took his chance, leaning out the window to fire off a quick burst at the gunner in the side hatch. He didn't hit anything important, but the helicopter bobbed away a little—clearly the pilot didn't want to risk a stray shot hitting a fuel line or an ammo box.

The likelihood of that was minimal, though. Chapel needed to kill the pilot if he was to have any chance of bringing the helicopter down. That was going to take a miracle. He wished he had his tablet with him, that he could talk to Angel—not just because she could give him an idea of what the battle looked like at ground level. He wanted to tell her good-bye as well.

He wasn't going to get his miracle by hiding in cover. He ducked low under a windowsill and dashed over to another window, several yards down. If he could keep the gunner guessing where he was going to shoot from next, that might buy him a little time.

He heard shots from below, carbine rounds. That could be Nadia or it could be one of the assassins. Clearly they planned on storming this building, finishing him off if the helicopter couldn't. He could only hope Nadia was ready for that kind of assault.

He poked his rifle barrel out of the window, then risked a quick look. The nose of the helicopter was ten yards away from him. He could see right through the viewport, could see the pilot hunched over his controls.

He was never going to get a better chance than this. He lifted his weapon, lined up the sights—

And saw the pilot glance up and see him, the Russian's face instantly going white with fear. Chapel took his shot, firing a tight burst right into the viewport.

Glass splintered and flew, but the pilot was already moving. The third shot of Chapel's burst didn't even hit the viewport, instead digging into the fuselage between the canopy and the side hatch. Worthless.

Except—Chapel wasn't sure it was even possible, but yes, he could definitely see a tinge of red on the broken glass of the viewport. The helicopter didn't just fall out of the sky, but he knew he had struck the pilot, wounded him at least.

Not that it mattered. The helicopter was already pulling away, drawing back to a range where Chapel would be unlikely to hit the aircraft at all. He howled in frustration—then cut himself off in midgrowl as he saw the Gatling gun's barrels moving, tracking around. In an instant it would fire again; he needed to move—

—Except the Gatling gun wasn't turning toward him. The gunner had lowered his elevation, tilting the barrels down so they could fire into the street.

No. No, no, no, Chapel thought, the words hammering in his brain like fists on steel. Nadia was down there, moving already, dashing for safety as the Gatling gun homed in on her position. It didn't need to be accurate. It didn't need to conserve ammunition. It could just hose her down with bullets, chop her to pieces.

Roaring with anguish, Chapel leaned far out of the window and pointed his rifle at the gunner, barely visible behind the mass of his weapon. Chapel held down his trigger and sprayed bullets as best he could into the man, so far away, so far out of reach. His rifle clicked dry and he wanted to throw the damned thing at the gunner, as useless a gesture as it might be.

Down in the street Nadia zigged and zagged, trying to keep the gunner from drawing a bead on her. She was fast, so very fast, but in a second it wouldn't matter, the gunner would just start painting the ground with lead—

And that was when Chapel got his miracle.

Or was it even a miracle? Maybe Nadia had planned for it to happen. Maybe she'd been that smart. Maybe Chapel had hit the helicopter pilot harder than he thought, maybe the pilot was losing blood and getting dizzy, not paying attention like he should.

Chapel would never know why it happened. But it did happen, so fast Chapel couldn't even process the details.

The helicopter had to move back to give the gunner a good angle of fire on Nadia. It had to move back to get away from Chapel and his AK-47. It had already been flying very low, only a few dozen feet off the ground, below the level of the surrounding buildings. The pilot must have assumed he had plenty of clearance, though, because he was in the middle of the wide intersection.

He didn't have enough clearance. The very tip of one of his rotor blades brushed, ever so gently, the bronze face of Vladimir Lenin.

The blade was made of a tough composite material, but it was thin and the statue was thick, hard bronze. The blade twisted and bent faster than any human eye could follow and knocked backward into another blade in the space of an eyeblink. Suddenly there was nothing holding the helicopter up in the air and it fell, its rotor like the crooked wings of a squashed bug. It hit the ground hard, its nose smashing into the base of the statue, its tail twisting around and around until it snapped off and flew across the intersection to collide with a building on the far side.

It brought up an incredible cloud of dust and debris, a vast wave of murk that hid everything from Chapel's view. He saw flashes of light inside the cloud—gunfire—and knew that Nadia was making her move, running for the truck.

Something buried deep in Chapel's brain, some survival instinct, started shouting at him then. If he could reach the truck himself, if he could run over there in the dust, when the assassins couldn't see him, if he could get away with Nadia and Bogdan—

He didn't let it turn into a full-fledged thought, much less a concrete plan. He just started running and hoped for the best. Down the stairs, two at a time. He missed one riser when his wounded leg went out from under him, but he was so full of adrenaline at that point he caught himself on the handrail and just kept running. Down to the ground floor, the door just in front of him. A shape appeared in the doorway, a human form in silhouette. Chapel didn't waste time trying to make out any details. He brought his shoulder down and smashed into the shape like a linebacker, bowling over one of the assassins. He didn't even slow down as he plunged into the debris cloud, even as things whizzed and rocketed past his head. Maybe they were bullets, maybe they were parts of the helicopter that flew off in the crash. He didn't care. If one of them struck him, he would go down, he knew that much, but there was nothing he could do about that, no way to prevent it.

The truck was ahead of him, a big square shape

slightly darker than the dust and sand blowing up around him. It was still so far away, and he heard shouting, and knew he was being chased, but if he kept running, if he kept moving—his leg hurt, bad, but—but—

He came out of the cloud gasping for breath, moving as fast as his wounded leg would carry him. The truck was no more than sixty yards away. Its taillights were lit, and he knew Nadia was in the driver seat, waiting for him, Bogdan sitting next to her; if he could just make it over there, they could be gone, laughing as they rocketed through the desert, just like before, before they'd found Perimeter—

"Ostanovis!" someone shouted. *"Ya pristelu tebya!"*

Another shape appeared in front of Chapel, a human shape again. He tried to swat it away, but the shape just took a step backward. Then it lifted a tactical shotgun and pointed the barrel right at Chapel's chest.

He stared at the man, suddenly very focused, very clear. He could grab the barrel of the shotgun, push it away from him. He knew a couple different techniques to twist it out of the assassin's hands, to get it away from him. Then it would be his shotgun.

Now that he was thinking clearly, though, he knew how stupid that idea was. In his head he could hear Bigelow's voice, as clear as if his ranger instructor was standing next to him. "There's no way you're going to win this. The lesson I'm supposed to teach you today is that up against a man with a gun, you can't win if you're unarmed. You have to put your hands up and surrender."

Chapel glanced over at the truck. Nadia hadn't

moved. She was waiting—waiting for him. She must have seen him running toward her. She must be watching right now in her mirrors.

If she hesitated even a few seconds more, the assassins would regroup and go after her and it would be over. They would shoot out her tires, leave her stranded, surround the truck and just fill it full of bullets or pump it full of tear gas and take her alive. Chapel didn't know which would be worse.

She was waiting for him.

He looked at the assassin facing him. Looked into the man's eyes. Then he grabbed for the barrel of the shotgun.

It went off before he even touched it. Something thudded into his chest, and he felt like he'd been hit by a hammer. It didn't knock him over, though. He glanced down and was surprised by what he saw—a little yellow plastic box was sticking out of his ribs, anchored by two tiny barbs that had pierced his skin.

It wasn't lead shot or a slug the assassin had fired. It was a Taser round, a self-contained electric incapacitation device. It went off in the same moment he realized what it must be.

Every muscle in Chapel's body triggered at once. He curled in on himself, screaming in pain, as he dropped to the ground. He twitched and shook and drooled and there was nothing he could do—he stayed conscious through the whole thing; his eyes were open, but he could do nothing but look over at the truck and beg Nadia, silently, to drive away.

Just go, he told her. *Just go.* If she could get Bogdan to the submarine—if she could get away—

He saw the truck sit motionless for way too long. He could feel her hesitating.

Go, he urged her.

He saw the taillights flare as the engine was thrown into gear. And then the steel toe of a combat boot hit him in the head, and he didn't see any more.

BENEATH THE CASPIAN SEA: JULY 22, 00:14 (IST)

Captain Ronald Mahen walked on rubber-soled shoes from the engine compartment of his submarine, the USS *Cincinnatus*, up to the bridge. He placed each foot carefully, to make as little sound as possible.

The seamen he passed saluted smartly but made a point of not coming to attention—that would mean moving their feet, and their shoes might squeak on the deck plating. When he reached the bridge, he climbed up to the conning tower and saw his SEAL team exactly where he'd left them, crammed into a space too small for them, much too small when you included the mass of the inflatable boat they would use if he sent the order for them to go ashore.

He nodded at them, and they nodded back. No words were exchanged.

For nearly thirty-six hours now the *Cincinnatus* had been keeping station off the coast of Kazakhstan, just outside national waters. Twice in that time a vessel had passed overhead, well within passive sonar range. It was impossible to know who owned those craft—they could be fishing boats, or they could be naval ships of one country or another, equipped with hydrophones. For nearly thirty-six hours, not a word had been spoken aboard the submarine. Most of the crew remained in their quarters, passing the time as best they could without making a sound.

Captain Mahen climbed back down to the bridge and looked around at his officers. They looked to him for any sign that the wait might be over, but he had nothing to give them. They were in danger of losing their edge through sheer inactivity and loss of sleep, but he couldn't even sigh and shake his head.

He went aft to his cabin and switched on his laptop. Even the gentle hum of its fans was a risk, but he needed to know. He waited for the machine to make contact and then typed a quick message, careful not to let his fingers click too loudly on the keys.

STANDING BY. REQUEST NEW INFORMATION.

The response came almost instantly. He had no idea who spoke to him through this particular link, but he had to admit they were diligent—he had never had to wait for more than a few seconds to get a return message.

NO NEW INFORMATION. MISSION PARAMETERS UNCHANGED.

This time the temptation to sigh was almost unbearable. The *Cincinnatus* had vital work to do south of here, off the coast of Iran. For the last six weeks, she and her crew had been monitoring training exercises by the Iranian navy's newest Hendijan class missile craft, learning all they could about the boats' capabilities, range, and armament. They had been dragged away for this secret mission on very little notice, and already it had cost them dearly.

Still, his orders came from very high up. He was to approach a certain point on the Kazakhstan coast and take aboard three individuals. They had been expected to arrive almost a full day ago, and still there was no sign of them.

Captain Mahen's orders had come from very high up, indeed—straight from the Pentagon. But aboard his submarine the captain was one rank below God. The decision to stay and wait longer was entirely at his discretion—his duty to keep his crew safe had to come first.

The time had come.

ABORTING MISSION AS OF 00:30 LOCAL TIME, he typed.

For once the reply took longer than expected. Was the person on the other end of this connection hesitating? Was he or she waiting for instructions from a superior? An icon on the screen flashed to indicate that a new message was incoming, but for long minutes Captain Mahen could only listen to his laptop drone away and wonder if anyone up on the surface could hear it. Hydrophones were very sophisticated these days, very sensitive, and the slightest sound could betray the presence of the *Cincinnatus* . . .

REQUEST ONE MORE DAY.

Captain Mahen stared at the screen in amazement. Another twenty-four hours? His crew would be useless if he kept them at alert that long. Unthinkable. He had no idea who these people were he was supposed to pick up, but he was certain of one thing—they weren't coming. They had to be covert operatives, if he was smuggling them out of Kazakhstan like this. People like that knew better than to be late for an exfiltration.

His hands hovered over the keyboard. He made up his mind.

ABORTING MISSION.

The reply came almost before he'd finished.

PLEASE, it said.

This time he couldn't resist an actual grunt of frustration, though he clapped his hand over his mouth as the noise escaped him. No naval officer would ever send a message like that. Had he been talking to a civilian the whole time?

He didn't take orders from civilians.

ABORTING MISSION. I WISH YOUR PEOPLE LUCK, BUT THAT'S ALL I CAN OFFER. COMMUNICATION ENDS.

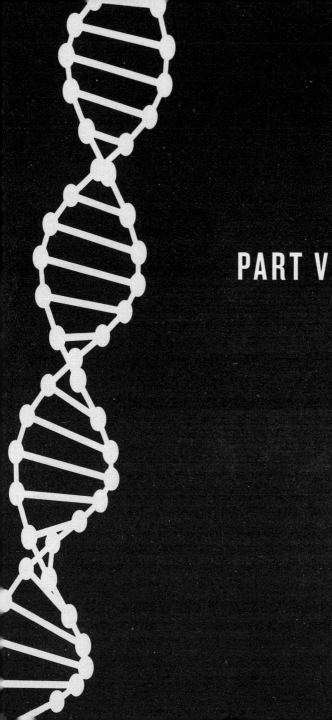

PART V

Everything hurt.

Chapel had experienced enough physical pain in his life to know the difference between sore muscles and actual tissue damage. He knew what it felt like to wake up after having been beaten while one was unconscious. He knew what gunshot wounds felt like, and how to tell if he had broken bones.

He'd also had enough training to know that internal damage was tricky. You might feel a little achy for a day or two and then drop dead because of bruising on your liver. You might feel horrible agony, racking, excruciating pain, and be just fine after a few days resting in a soft bed.

He tried to assess how badly he'd been injured and realized he just couldn't be sure. He might be dying, or he might just have been hit by a freight train. He knew that the idea of sitting up was laughable. The way his torso felt he would be lucky to open his eyes and see that he was still in one piece.

He opened his eyes.

Eye, anyway. He opened one of them. The other was too swollen to budge. His good eye gave him a very blurry image of a lot of sunlight and a sky so blue it looked like you could just step into it and fall forever, fall upward until you hit outer space.

Opening the eye had been a bad idea. The light

buzzed around in his head, chasing any rational thoughts around. There were multicolored halos around every object he looked at—not that he could focus enough to make out what those objects were. He knew what that meant: a concussion. And a bad one, definitely.

Which meant that, as much as he wanted to close his eye again and go back to sleep, he absolutely shouldn't. You could go to sleep with a concussion and never wake up. He forced himself to keep the eye open. Fought back each wave of exhaustion as it came for him, pushed back until it was gone and he could brace for the next one.

Damn, everything really hurt.

He tried to concentrate on piecing together what had happened to him. There had been a helicopter—no—two helicopters, there had been—there had—

He felt the desperate need to throw up, and a certainty that he shouldn't, that throwing up was another bad idea, just like falling asleep. He was lying on his back, he thought. He could drown in his own vomit if he threw up now.

Concentrate, he told himself. *What happened? How many helicopters?*

One, at first. He had not quite shot it down, but it crashed. Nadia and Bogdan had—had they gotten away or not? Had they—

That thought brought on a new wave, one of panic. A desperate need to move, to run, to *do something*. Yet another bad idea. If his neck was broken, or if—

Concentrate.

The helicopter had crashed. He'd been Tased, then kicked. He had blacked out for a while. Most likely he'd been beaten while he was unconscious, because he couldn't remember hurting this much when he blacked out.

When he came to, another helicopter was on its way. Descending, getting bigger as it came down from the sky. It looked like it was going to land on top of him. He had seen a flag painted on its side and for a second he'd been excited, thrilled, because he saw red, white, and blue.

Wrong flag, though. The colors had been horizontal stripes, white, blue, and red.

Shit, he thought. That was the Russian flag. The Russians had him.

Now he was here under this incredibly blue sky. There were people around him, people who weren't paying any attention to him. He couldn't make out their faces. He heard them talking, heard at least one word he understood. *Glas.* That was the Russian word for eye, or for sight. They had noticed that his eye was open.

He didn't think that was a good thing.

The people around him started moving faster. He couldn't see what they were doing. One of them was above him, another beneath, and then he felt himself moving, being moved. He tried to warn them, tried to tell them his neck might be broken, but either they weren't listening or they couldn't hear him. He wasn't sure his throat was working right. Wasn't sure he was making a sound.

They moved him for a long time. Occasionally someone else would loom over him, another human shape. A few words would be spoken and then he would start moving again.

They took him into a dark place. That was a little better—the light had really been hurting his eye. But the darkness was going to make it hard to stay awake. The dark place stank, enough to make him gag. It smelled of something foul and . . . rusted metal? Maybe. Maybe that was the smell of blood.

His eye adjusted to the darkness, though it took a very long time.

A shape appeared above him, in the dark. A human face. He could see it more clearly this time, without all the sunlight blasting his vision. He could tell this new person had a long, thin face, and that he wore a black suit with a white shirt and a black tie. The high contrast helped. The person in the black suit studied him for a very long time.

"Who are you?" Chapel asked. He could hear the noise he'd made, at least. He was certain he'd said something, though whether or not he'd actually formed words was debatable.

He must have made himself understood on some level, because the person in the black suit answered him. In English. "I am Senior Lieutenant Pavel Kalin. I'm going to be doing your interview. I'll get you something for the pain in a moment, but first I need you to answer some basic questions."

Name, rank, and serial number, Chapel thought— the three things you were supposed to provide to your captors when you were taken prisoner. Except he couldn't even provide that much. Announcing that he *had* a serial number would be the same as saying he was an American serviceman and therefore a spy. "I can't . . . can't . . ."

"Are you allergic to codeine or any other pain-killing medications? What about penicillin, erythromycin, sulfa drugs? I'm sorry, I can't understand what you're saying."

"Where . . . where am I?"

"The sooner you provide us with your medical information, the quicker we can get moving," Kalin told him. "No? You don't wish to cooperate with your treatment personnel?" Kalin took something from his pocket. A little notebook. He jotted down a quick entry and then put the notebook away. He waved someone over, someone in a white coat who put a hypodermic needle in Chapel's neck. He was too beat up to fight them off.

"Can't . . . sleep," he managed to rasp out. "Concussion . . ."

"Don't worry," Kalin told him. "If your heart stops, we'll resuscitate you. As many times as necessary."

IN TRANSIT: JULY 22, 15:33

When Chapel woke next, he was moving. The room he was in was moving. He could feel it swaying back and forth, bouncing up and down. He had no idea what was going on.

He was naked. His left arm was gone—just missing, nowhere to be found. He was lying on a pile of blankets that hadn't been washed in a while, or maybe it was him that stank. It was unbearably hot in the room, and sweat crawled across his skin like prickling ants.

He wasn't dead. He was groggy and weak, but he wasn't dead. He could move, crawl even, if he was careful. His body still ached everywhere, and standing up was impossible in the moving room, but he could just about get around. There was a tiny bit of light coming in from one side of the room. He moved over there as best he could and found that the source of the light was a crack in the wall. He pressed his eye up against it and for a second saw nothing but dazzling light. Even though it hurt his eye, it felt good after the near total darkness of the moving room.

When his eye had adjusted to the light, he saw a dashed white line streaming away from him. A road, then—a highway. The "room" he was in must be a shipping container mounted on a flatbed truck. He was being taken somewhere. They had simply stuffed him in the back of a cargo container and then shipped him off. He had no idea where he was going or what would happen there, no idea if they were going to—

Best to focus on what he *could* know.

The light was coming in through a crack between two doors at the back of the container. He pushed against the doors, tried lifting them with his hand, but they wouldn't budge. They were locked from the outside, and he was too weak to do much but strain against them.

Crawling around the inside of the container, he defined his world very quickly. There were only two things in the container beyond himself: a pile of blankets he'd been using as a bed, and a bucket in one corner. The bucket was the source of the terrible smell in the container. It had been used before Chapel arrived, and no one had bothered to clean it out.

He sat down and watched the bucket for a while. It rattled and bounced and constantly threatened to fall over and spill its contents all over the floor. Somehow it never did.

He might have slept again. Without anything to do but watch the bucket, it was hard to tell.

Time passed.

A lot of time.

Eventually the container stopped moving. He heard the squeal of the truck's brakes. He heard someone talking outside, but he couldn't understand the words.

The doors at the back of the container opened and he was blinded again. Men in uniforms came inside and grabbed him, hauling him to his feet. They pulled a thin gown over his head and then he was dragged out of the container and along the side of a building. They came around a corner and Senior Lieutenant Kalin was there, waiting for them.

Kalin took a quick look at Chapel and nodded. The soldiers carrying him started moving again.

They marched him through an alleyway between two brick buildings, neither of which had windows, just blank walls. He let his head fall back and looked up and saw a sky grimy with smog, streaked with trails of smoke.

Up ahead, the alleyway ended in a broad courtyard. At its far side was a big building with curved walls, so that it looked like a drum. It was made of concrete stained black in places. It had a lot of windows, but all of them were covered with bars. An ambulance stood out in front of the building, with Cyrillic lettering on its sides.

"Where am I?" he asked.

Surprisingly, Kalin answered. "Magnitogorsk," he said. "A municipal asylum for the mentally ill."

Chapel stared up at the round building. He was marched toward its front doors, wide glass doors that looked like the entrance to a hospital emergency room. Inside a team of doctors and nurses waited, staring out at him. Ready for him to rant and rave or grow violent or just start screaming. Ready for anything he might try.

So this is where I'm going to spend the rest of my life.

He could only hope it wasn't going to be a long one.

MAGNITOGORSK, RUSSIA: JULY 22, 22:14 (YEKT)

They threw him in a little empty room—a cell, no point in giving it a prettier name—and locked the door behind him. They left him there in the dark, and no matter how many times he pounded on the door and shouted, nobody came.

They left him to think about what had happened.

He'd been taken captive by the Russians, by the FSB—the security service. The KGB, for all intents and purposes, just with a brand-new name. There was no chance of escape, now. They would see to that. There was definitely no chance of a rescue. If Pavel Kalin had personally flown to Washington and asked Rupert Hollingshead if he wanted Chapel back, Hollingshead would have no choice but to say he'd never heard of a Jim Chapel. He would disavow the mission. What else could the director do? Admit he'd sent an American agent to sabotage a Russian military installation?

Chapel had known that going in. He'd known it when he'd joined the Rangers, and when he'd started working for military intelligence. It was how the game was played. Once he was in the field he was on his own, responsible for his own fate.

Well. He'd screwed that up pretty well.

Back in Ranger school, his instructor Bigelow had told him about what might happen if he was captured by the enemy. "Don't expect humane treatment. Don't expect them to treat you like a normal POW," he'd warned. "Spies don't go to country club prisons. They'll want to know all your secrets, and they won't ask politely. Now, if they start asking you for classified information, what do you give them?"

"Name, rank, and serial number, right?" Chapel had asked. "I just keep my mouth shut. If they put a gun to my head and threaten to kill me if I don't talk, well, I guess I let them shoot me."

Bigelow had sighed and shook his head. "They're not going to make it that easy. They'll torture you. You're a tough guy. You can take a lot of punishment, I've seen to that. But they'll have all the time in the world, and it doesn't take much more than a pair of pliers to make even a tough guy talk. Believe me, you won't be able to hold out forever. They'll get what they want, sooner or later. One way or another."

"So what do I do? Just spill the beans at the first possible opportunity? Save myself from being tortured?"

"Absolutely not. You hold out as long as you can. Every day you resist, every hour, you give your handlers back home more time to minimize the damage your information can do. You give us time to change our codes, or move our troops to a new location, or set up new covers for your fellow agents. Any little crumb of time you can give us is useful. So you hold out. You bear the pain the best you can, and you hold out as long as you possibly can. When you finally do break, well, that's natural, that's human. But you think of your country and your duty, and you make the enemy work for it."

Alone in the dark cell Chapel nodded to himself, promising himself he would fight. That he wouldn't go down easy.

He had to admit, though, if only to himself—he was scared.

MAGNITOGORSK, RUSSIA: JULY 23, 09:14

"Are you ready? Let us begin." Kalin took out his notebook and a silver pen.

He sat on a chair that was the only piece of furniture in the room. The place they'd stuck Chapel was not quite a padded cell—its walls were actually lined with ceramic tile—but it was designed so that an inmate would find nothing inside with which to hurt himself. There was no way to commit suicide there. The windows were covered in thick, impact-resistant plastic. The room's sole lighting fixture was recessed into the ceiling, well out of reach. There was no knob on the inside of the door. Kalin had to bring the chair in with him, and presumably he would take it with him when he left.

Chapel supposed you could bash your head

against the wall until one of the tiles cracked. Use that to cut your own throat. You would need a lot of determination, though. You would need more strength than Chapel had.

"Where's my arm?" Chapel asked. "When I was detained, I had a prosthetic left arm. What did you do with it?"

"We had to make sure it wasn't a weapon," Kalin said. He shrugged. "I'm afraid that in the process of analyzing it, the arm was destroyed. You won't see it again."

Chapel inhaled sharply. Then he nodded. He'd gotten by in the past with one arm. He knew how to live like that; he could do it again. There were other, more pressing concerns. "Are you going to feed me?"

"Subject has requested food," Kalin announced, and made a note of it. "Do you have any dietary requirements? Perhaps religious in nature?"

Chapel stared at Kalin. Did he think Chapel was a Muslim? Or maybe an agent of Mossad? "I haven't been given any food for more than twenty-four hours. That's a violation of the Geneva Convention."

"Which applies only to soldiers taken as prisoners of war. Are you a soldier?"

Chapel said nothing. He wanted to sit down but that meant sitting on the floor, and he wouldn't give Kalin the psychological advantage.

"At the moment, we don't even know your name. Are you willing to tell us your name? Once we have that, we can begin to process you correctly," Kalin told him. "We'll know how to move forward."

Chapel turned his face away. If he admitted to

being a soldier, then his presence at Aralsk-30 might be construed as an act of war. He could, instead, fall back on his cover and claim to be Jeff Chambers. But even if the cover held up, that would make him a criminal, a trespasser, and that would give Kalin the right to charge him and put him into the Russian court system. He did not have any faith that would improve his situation.

"All right," Kalin said. "You aren't interested in answering questions, I can see that." He put his notebook away and stood up. "I'm in no rush. We're really just filling in a few blanks here. Once I have a statement from you, I can file a report, but honestly, it doesn't matter. Asimova and Vlaicu are dead, and you're in custody, so there's no need for alacrity."

Dead?

Nadia and Bogdan were dead?

That got Chapel's attention. He whirled around to study Kalin's face, looking for any sign the man was lying.

If he was, it was impossible to tell. Kalin might have been carved from a block of marble. "You didn't know, did you? Perhaps you thought they got away. Of course we couldn't let that happen. We picked up the truck less than an hour after it left Aralsk-30. They were unwilling to surrender, and we had already sustained some casualties, so the order was given to fire rockets on the vehicle. There wasn't much left of them, just enough to identify the bodies."

Chapel dropped his head. Nadia was dead. After all he'd done to try to get her and Bogdan safely away, after everything—

"So you see, this is just a formality. But I do like to be thorough. We'll see how you feel tomorrow, after you've spent the night with us."

MAGNITOGORSK, RUSSIA: JULY 24, 03:22

"Just let me sleep!" Chapel howled, as they held him down and poured energy shots down his throat. The orderlies laughed and shouted in his face—the words were in Russian, but it didn't matter that he couldn't understand; the meaning was clear. Loud music blared from speakers in the ceiling and the light kept getting brighter—then they were throwing ice water on him, dousing him in it until he shivered and cried out, and still they were laughing, laughing—

MAGNITOGORSK, RUSSIA: JULY 24, 07:49

Sleep deprivation.

It was a kind of torture. Chapel's head was reeling, and his eyes wouldn't focus properly. He felt like hell, felt like he wanted to throw up but that wasn't it, it wasn't his stomach; his brain wanted to purge, to—to just stop, to—to—

Kalin came in, dragging his chair. The way its legs squeaked on the tiles made Chapel want to cringe in the corner and wrap his arm around his head. He forced himself to stand still, up against one wall, with an expression of stoic indifference on his face.

"Good morning," Kalin said. "How are you feeling?"

"Fine," Chapel insisted.

Kalin didn't laugh. He sat down in his chair and took out his notebook.

"Are you ready to tell me your name?" he asked.

Chapel bit back a profanity.

"Perhaps you'd like to tell me how you met the terrorist Asimova?"

Chapel scowled. "She was no—"

Kalin waited, pen poised over his notebook. "Yes?" he said.

Chapel screwed his eyes shut. Bit his tongue to keep it from moving. He'd come very close to giving himself away, there. Far too close. Sleep deprivation took away your filters, made you say things without thinking about them first.

He had to be very, very careful now. He took the time, let the pounding in his head recede. Waited until he was totally in control again before speaking.

"I have no idea who you're talking about," he said. A small, pointless act of defiance. But it helped him straighten out his back and stand taller.

"That's interesting. Especially given what we found when we tested your clothing. Forgive me if this is a bit . . . tasteless, but it's germane to our conversation. We found traces of semen in your underwear. We also found her DNA—hairs, skin cells. Do you understand what that suggests?"

"That you're some kind of underwear pervert?" Chapel asked. Childish, he knew. He could have done better if he could just think. Just think straight.

Kalin pursed his lips. "You do understand that you're under investigation? Anything you say will be subject to verification."

Chapel looked out the window. Or rather, he looked at the thick plastic that covered the window, and the bars beyond. He could see very little through those barriers. Just a sky the color of rotten tin.

Kalin waited patiently for a while before proceeding. "Subject does not acknowledge that he is under investigation," he noted, eventually. "Exhibits signs of mental disorganization. Does not appear to follow logical questions."

"That sounds like a psychological profile," Chapel said. "I guess I am in an asylum, so it makes sense. What was that last night, a therapy session?"

"A method of persuasion," Kalin said. "We have several at our disposal."

"Sure. The KGB were always the experts in torture and interrogation," Chapel said.

"I'm not KGB. The KGB doesn't exist anymore."

"You're FSB, then," Chapel pointed out. An organization that had been created, instituted, and staffed almost exclusively by former KGB agents.

"There *is* a difference, you know. The FSB is committed to human rights. We don't hook up anyone to car batteries or pull out their fingernails with pliers. We won't stick you in a cage full of rats." Kalin laughed as if such things were quaint, old-fashioned practices, like writing with quill pens or traveling in horse-drawn buggies. "We won't take you out in the courtyard and just shoot you."

"Too messy," Chapel said. "So how will you do it?"

"Do what?"

Chapel forced himself to grin. "Maybe you'll inject me with polonium. That's one of your techniques, right? Or maybe you'll just let me starve."

Kalin started writing in his notebook again. "Subject indulges paranoid fantasies. Believes he is to be killed. Believes he is important enough to be executed in violation of the rule of law."

Chapel wanted to rip the notebook out of the bastard's hand. "We both know how this ends," he shouted.

"Do we? If I were to kill you, that would make it impossible for me to get the information I need. It would mean I couldn't finish my report. No, no. I'm going to keep you healthy for as long as it takes."

A little voice started screaming inside Chapel's head, then. A voice of panic. It threatened to overwhelm him.

He fought it back.

"Let's try to get back on course, all right?" Kalin asked. "Tell me your name."

"You haven't figured that out, yet? In your investigation?"

Kalin favored him with a cold smile. "I know that a man named Jack Carlson is wanted in Romania for destruction of property and discharging a firearm in public. I know that a man named Jeff Chambers is wanted for questioning in Uzbekistan. Since both of those men fit your description, and both were seen in the company of the terrorist Asimova, I think we can safely assume neither of those men really exist. I would like your real name. The one you use in America."

Chapel turned away from Kalin. He started

pacing back and forth, trying to get his blood moving so he could think more clearly. He hadn't told Kalin he was an American. It wasn't exactly hard to figure that one out, but if Kalin knew that much, then he must have already figured out that Chapel was a spy, that—

"Tell me your name. That's all. Then I'll let you sleep."

"My name," Chapel said. Oh, God. If Kalin knew so much already, what would it hurt? And to sleep—even if it was just a nap, just a catnap, a little sleep—

"Yes," Kalin said. He held his pen over his notebook.

"My name is Napoleon Bonaparte. Put that in your psych profile."

MAGNITOGORSK, RUSSIA: JULY 24, 21:22

That night they took him out to the courtyard and made him walk in circles. Every time he flagged, every time he tried to stop in place and close his eyes, even for a second, an orderly would hit him with a baton. Not hard. Just enough to get him moving again. They had a knack for finding the bruises he already had and prodding those. They seemed to think it was funny when he jumped away from them. They started brandishing their batons at him even when he was moving, just to see him flinch.

In Ranger school, his trainer Bigelow had told him that a soldier needed to be able to sleep anywhere, anytime, under any conditions. "Sometimes you'll be in the field for days on end. Behind enemy lines, or just in the middle of a battle that goes on and on. Your inclination will be to keep going, to just not sleep. Don't do it. Even one night without sleep has the same effect as drinking three shots of tequila. It's like being too drunk to drive. Your reaction time slows way down. You stop thinking about what you're doing and you go on autopilot. You know what happens to a soldier who stops thinking on the battlefield?"

"He gets killed, sir," Chapel had replied.

Bigelow had nodded. "That's right. So you're going to learn to sleep in a foxhole with artillery going off right next to you. You're going to learn to sleep in a puddle of mud—to sleep standing up, if need be. You'll learn to sleep for twenty minutes and feel as fresh as a daisy. You'll—"

His reverie was interrupted by a quick blow to the bullet wound on his leg. Chapel shouted in pain and hopped forward on his other foot, while an orderly in a white coat laughed in his face. The man's breath stank of meat.

For hours they kept him moving. He couldn't keep up the pace, so the blows came more and more often. Eventually even the pain and the jeers couldn't keep him from just shuffling his feet, stumbling along as they pulled his arm and dragged him. He fell down on his knees, and they dragged him back up to his feet. His chin dropped to his chest, and someone grabbed his hair and pulled it back.

He kept moving, as best he could. It got to the point where he wanted it, wanted to keep walking, because the alternative was so hellish. It got to the point where he wanted to please the orderlies, make them happy—if he could just walk, if he could walk a few more steps, maybe they would stop laughing—

He must have blacked out. He must have just collapsed. Because suddenly his face hurt like he'd scraped it on the pavement, and when he opened his eyes, he saw feet all around him, shoes—and then Kalin, who was squatting down next to him. Squatting and holding an empty hypodermic needle.

Chapel reared up like a startled bull, whooping for breath. His eyes snapped wide open, and he could feel his heart jumping around in his chest like it was trying to break free of his rib cage. Every muscle in his body twitched and shook, and he had a desperate need to urinate.

"What—did—you—give—me?" he demanded, through chattering teeth.

Kalin flicked the end of his needle. "Adrenaline," he said. "Not quite enough to give you a heart attack, but enough to keep you awake. Now. Back on your feet."

MAGNITOGORSK, RUSSIA: JULY 25, 13:42

"Are you ready to tell me your name?" Kalin asked, pen poised.

Chapel couldn't stop blinking. His eyes hurt, a deep, dull ache. He moved his head to try to get away from it. It didn't work. His eyes hurt. He—he had already—he'd already—his eyes hurt.

He was pretty sure there had been more in the last needle than just adrenaline.

"Drugging me. You're . . . you're drugging me, that's—that's illegal, it's—you're giving me medical treatment without my consent. You can't—it's illegal."

"What is your name?" Kalin asked.

"I know my rights!" Chapel shouted. He tried to grab for the notebook, but Kalin was too fast for him, yanking it out of the way. Chapel turned around and went to the wall and pressed his face against it. He scratched at his scalp. "You have to let me shower. You have to feed me. You have to let me sleep. You can't drug me like this. I have rights!"

"Human beings have rights," Kalin pointed out.

"Exactly. Yes. Human beings have rights," Chapel said. He knew how he sounded. He knew how he was acting. He couldn't help it. He needed to sleep. But he couldn't sleep, not with the drugs they'd given him. He couldn't sleep. He couldn't sit down, couldn't stand still.

His eyes hurt. A deep, profound ache. His eyes wanted to sleep. They wanted to close, but they couldn't. He could only blink, over and over and over again.

"You don't seem to have a name."

"I have a name! You can't have it," Chapel insisted.

"If you don't have a name," Kalin said, as if Chapel hadn't spoken, "that makes you a nonperson. Nonpersons don't have any rights."

Chapel turned and stared at him. Staring was easy. His eyes wouldn't close. *I'm a person*, he thought. *I am a person. I am a person.*

"If you tell me your name, you can sleep. You can eat. We'll even hose you down," Kalin said, with a smile.

"I—I have a name," Chapel insisted.

"I know. Just tell me what it is. Really, what's the worst that can happen?"

Chapel tried to remember. He tried to remember why he couldn't give this man his name. He was sure there was a good reason. He just had it. He just had the reason, he just had to remember. Remember why—

Kalin clicked his pen. Got ready to write something down.

"In your own time," he said.

Chapel stared and stared and stared. He opened his mouth. He felt like something was going to come out. Words. Two words. A name.

"Indira Gandhi," he said.

The look on Kalin's face made him laugh. And laugh and laugh.

"David Cameron," he tried, which was even funnier. Then he thought of the funniest name of all.

"My name is Senior Lieutenant Pavel Kalin, and I'll be conducting your interview," he said. And that was just hysterical.

He was still laughing when Kalin got up and picked up his chair. The notebook was nowhere to be seen.

"I apologize," Kalin said.

Chapel stopped laughing instantly.

"I underestimated you," Kalin told him. "It's clear you've been trained to counter this kind of persuasion. Sleep deprivation isn't going to work on you."

"It's—not?"

"We find it highly effective with most people. But there are limits to what can be done this way.

Sleep deprivation can even be fatal if it's taken too far. The first queen Elizabeth of England died of insomnia, did you know that?"

"That's my name," Chapel tried. "Queen Elizabeth."

Kalin shook his head. "I could keep you awake longer, but then you would die. And that wouldn't help me finish my report. So go ahead and sleep." He shrugged and headed for the door. "The drugs will wear off in a few hours, and then I imagine you'll sleep very well indeed. That's good. I'll want you clear-headed tomorrow."

"Tomorrow? What happens then?"

"That's when we take things to the next level."

MAGNITOGORSK, RUSSIA: JULY 26, 08:01

Chapel woke up on the tiled floor of his room, his eyes slowly opening. He stretched out his arm, his legs, luxuriating in how rested he felt. He was sore from lying all night on the hard tiles, but he didn't care. He felt a million times better than he had the day before.

He was considering his options—most of which involved rolling over and taking a nap—when there was a knock at the door. It opened before he could even realize he should say something, and an orderly came in, bearing a tray of food. Dry toast and some water. Chapel didn't protest how plain it was. His stomach had shrunk from going without for so long, and he probably couldn't have handled anything more complex. The orderly left again without a word, before Chapel could ask for more.

A little while later a different orderly came in and took the tray away. Then Kalin came in, carrying two chairs. He set them down facing each other and gestured for Chapel to sit in one of them.

"You look well," Kalin told him, with a smile that showed some actual warmth. "I'm glad. You know I don't want to cause you pain, don't you? I hope you understand that. That I don't take any pleasure in what we've done to you."

Chapel considered sneering, but he didn't want to give Kalin the satisfaction.

"You don't want to give me your name, we've established that," Kalin told him. He made a dismissive gesture, as if he were shooing away a pesky insect. "Okay. *Konyechno*, as we say in Russia."

Chapel forced himself not to flinch, hearing Nadia's favorite word out of this man's mouth.

"You know the term? It means more than just 'okay' or 'of course.' There's no exact translation into English. Perhaps you have heard of our famous Slavic fatalism. The way we simply accept that the world is not made for our pleasure, to our desires. We say '*konyechno*' to mean this. Perhaps the best English equivalent would be, 'What are you going to do?'"

"So you've given up? You're going to release me with an official apology?"

Kalin smiled again. "American optimism. Perhaps that's what won the Cold War. Okay. All right. *Konyechno*. I give up . . . at least, I will stop asking for your name. There are other questions that I'd like answers to. I'd like to know how you met the terrorist Asimova." He took his pen and his notebook out. "I'd like to know what you were doing at Aralsk-30. I'd like to know what her plan was. She was in charge, yes? She was giving the orders? We've established that much, but I'd like confirmation."

"For your report."

"Yes. Exactly. For my report. Where should we start?"

"Sorry," Chapel said. "I don't have the answers you want."

"You mean you won't give them to me," Kalin suggested.

"Believe what you want," Chapel said. He draped his arm over the back of his chair. It was immensely comforting to have furniture at his disposal again. "So where I'm from—"

"Which is?" Kalin asked, his pen coming up.

"—the police have this tactic they use during interrogations," Chapel went on, "called Good Cop Bad Cop. Two police officers enter the interrogation room and the first one threatens the suspect with jail. He shouts and demands answers and slams the wall and gets right up in the suspect's face. The suspect, naturally, refuses to answer anything. He's afraid of the bad cop, you see."

"Understandably."

Chapel nodded. "Eventually, the bad cop gets so frustrated he says he has to leave the room. That he's going to hurt the suspect if he has to look at him for one more second. The other cop, the good cop, closes the door behind him and tells the suspect how sorry he is, that the bad cop is a hothead and dangerous and he wishes he didn't have to work with him. He tells the suspect that things aren't actually so bad, that he understands why the suspect did what he did. He promises him all kinds of favors. He gets the suspect coffee or food. He makes friends with the suspect. Of course, it's all an act. Both cops know it. But it's surprisingly effective. Given the chance to talk to a friendly face, many suspects will just give themselves away."

"Interesting," Kalin said. "But I don't see the point. There's only one of me."

"Exactly," Chapel said. "That's why this isn't going to work. I'll never think of you as a friend, Kalin. And I'll never answer your questions."

The senior lieutenant nodded in understanding and tapped his pen on the edge of his notebook. "You *have* been trained to resist interrogation, haven't you? Very impressive. Very good. But you're wrong about one thing—I'm not trying to fool you here. I harbor no illusions that you're going to start to like me. I am not trying to instill Stockholm syndrome in you, no, nothing like that."

"Okay," Chapel said.

"No, no. You see, I wasn't trained by American policemen. I was trained by the KGB. You understand, of course, that the old men I learned from were experts at this sort of thing. Masters of getting at secrets. They had their own technique. One of them, one of the most simple, one of the most effective was based on the idea of operant conditioning. Do you know the term? No? Let me tell you how it works. I begin with something bad, something unpleasant. Say, I keep a man awake for days until he begins to break down psychologically. Then— out of nowhere—I stop. I let him sleep. I give him food. I let him feel good again, safe again. I let him remember what it was like to be warm and comfortable. I let him remember how much he has lost. Because—and this is the effective part—it makes what comes next so very, very much worse."

Chapel froze in his chair. He forced himself not to give anything away.

Kalin rose from his chair. "Come," he said. "Let's take a walk. I want you to see the next step."

MAGNITOGORSK, RUSSIA: JULY 26, 08:20

Kalin led him out into a wide hallway that curved gently as it followed the round shape of the hospital. They passed by a number of doors, some of which were ajar, though Chapel could see nothing in the rooms beyond. He wondered for the first time if he were the only inmate here.

One door opened, and a pair of big orderlies stepped out. They nodded respectfully to Kalin and then fell in behind him and Chapel. They said nothing, and they didn't meet Chapel's eye.

"Torture," Kalin told Chapel as they walked, "has a rather long history. As soon as there were kings and priests, I imagine, there was a need for torturers. As long as there were heretics and dissidents. Think of all the ways it used to be done—the rack, the iron maiden, the thumbscrews. An enormous amount of human ingenuity has gone into finding ways to make people talk. But in ancient times it was always looked on as a craft. Perhaps an art form. It took the KGB to bring torture into the modern era.

To bring science to the problem of persuasion. To make a technology out of it."

They reached a junction in the corridor, and Kalin gestured for them to walk deeper into the building, away from the windows.

"For seventy years they worked at it, testing out new techniques, new drugs, new methods of causing pain. They studied how their subjects responded to each tactic. They made charts and graphs of how long human beings could withstand, say, having hot irons placed against the soles of their feet, or how long they could go without food before they would begin raving. They tested all the famous truth serums—scopolamine, sodium pentathol, amobarbital—measuring each dosage so carefully, compiling lists of control questions and polygraph results. For decades they honed and refined their methods, always looking for the new way, the *best* way to reach the truth."

They came to a bank of elevators. Kalin summoned one with the press of a button and they all stepped inside, the orderlies flanking Chapel on either side. Maybe they thought he was going to attack Kalin. Try to kill him.

He'd thought about it. But he knew that no matter how much satisfaction he might get from strangling his interrogator, it would make no difference. Moscow would just send another one straightaway.

As the elevator descended, Kalin continued his lecture. "After seventy years of this, most of what they had learned was what *didn't* work. How useless most torture really was. Cause enough pain and a man will tell you anything—but you can never know if what he tells you is true or simply what he thinks you want to hear. Testimony given under the influence of drugs is as likely to be fabricated—pure fantasy—as it is to reflect reality. But they did learn one basic principle about torture. One thing they could be sure of: every subject is different."

The elevator doors opened, and they stepped out. Chapel thought they might be in the basement of the hospital. The air was much cooler down there, and a little clammy. The walls were all tiled, and drains were set at periodic intervals in the floor, as if this level needed to be hosed down frequently. Even the lighting was different—harsher, more direct. Instead of the recessed bulbs on the higher floors, here the light came from hanging lamps, each of them inside its own steel cage.

It was not a good place. Combined with the subject of Kalin's speech, it was enough to make Chapel's skin crawl.

"Some men resist pain better than others. Some can go longer without food. The same dosage of a truth drug might open one man up and kill another." Kalin shrugged. "All very frustrating. But some agent of the KGB, some man who will be forever nameless, took this problem and saw that it was actually an opportunity in disguise. If every subject responded to torture differently, then it was clear to him that the torture must be changed to suit the subject. That effective torture meant finding the one thing, the one breaking point, that would work for a given subject. If a man is afraid of spiders, for instance—if he has a phobia of them, then you will get more out of him by sticking his hand in a box full of the things than you would from weeks of a drug regimen. If a man loves his wife, you threaten *her*, not him. The trick, of course, is finding out just what the breaking point, the weak spot, is. Especially with a subject who won't even tell you his name."

They came to a section of corridor lined with long rectangular windows. Beyond the glass was only darkness. Kalin went over to one and flipped a switch, turning on lights in the room beyond.

Chapel wanted to run away. He didn't want to know what was in that room, what Kalin thought was going to make him crack. He started to turn—it was involuntary—but the orderlies just grabbed him then. Held him in place.

"Take a look," Kalin said.

Chapel forced himself to look through the window. His imagination, he knew, was running away from him; it couldn't possibly be as bad as what his own mind could come up with. He looked and saw—

Nothing much. On the other side of the glass was what looked like a standard operating room. There was a slablike operating table and a couple of cabinets. A tank of anesthetic gas. Lights that could be shone directly on the table. That was it.

No box full of spiders. No Julia with a gun to her head.

Just an operating room.

"I've been watching you for some time now. When you first came to me, I had your prosthetic arm taken away. I thought that would leave you vulnerable, that you would have difficulty doing the most basic tasks. But I was wrong—you operate just fine with one arm. You have learned over time how to get by with only half the usual number of hands. That's very commendable. I wonder if you could learn the same lesson all over again?"

Chapel's eyes went wide. "No," he said. "No. You can't. You wouldn't."

"I can. I will. You are a nonperson. I can do anything to you I desire," Kalin said. "You don't even have a name. Tomorrow, if you do not answer all of my questions, I will bring you back here and we will cut off your right arm. And then you will have no arms at all. It will be interesting to see just how well you can adapt to *that*."

MAGNITOGORSK, RUSSIA: JULY 26, 14:33

They left him alone all day. An orderly came by with food a couple of times, but he didn't respond to Chapel's halting questions, even when he tried to ask them in Russian. It was clear that Kalin had given the order that Chapel be left to his own thoughts.

Which was a kind of torture all in itself.

"You hold out as long as you can," Bigelow had told him. Every day he kept silent was another day for Hollingshead to distance himself and the DIA from Chapel's activities. Another day for Angel to scrub his existence off the official records. Another day to make it look like the United States had never sent an agent to sabotage Perimeter.

But Bigelow had also told him there would come a time when he wouldn't be able to hold out any longer. When the pressure was just too much.

He'd already given one arm for his country. Was he supposed to give the other one, too? Objectively he knew the answer to that question. If he was willing to give his life for America, why not an arm? He'd already proven once that he could survive that kind of loss. That he could learn to have a meaningful life as an amputee. He thought back to when he'd come home from Afghanistan, and he'd worked with a physical trainer named Top, learning how to live with one arm. Top had been a sergeant in Iraq who had lost an arm, a leg, and an eye to a roadside bomb. The man had given more than anyone could reasonably ask, but he'd never complained—and he'd never let it slow him down. With Top's help, Chapel had learned to adjust.

Of course, part of that adjustment was getting a magic prosthetic that worked almost as well as what he'd lost. The artificial arm had made a huge difference in his life, made so many things possible for him. But that arm was gone. Kalin wouldn't give him another one, and he certainly wouldn't give him two. He would spend the rest of his life in this hospital—maybe years—struggling to learn to use his feet to feed himself, to clean himself.

And even that wouldn't be the end of it. Once Kalin had taken his right arm—what would be the next step? If somehow Chapel managed to stay silent even through another amputation, Kalin wouldn't just give up. He would find some other way to get the information he wanted.

There came a point where your country could ask no more of you, Chapel thought. There came a point where no matter how many oaths and promises you'd made, no matter how sincerely you had sworn to defend the honor of your country, you had to let go. You had to give in.

Maybe he had reached that point.

MAGNITOGORSK, RUSSIA: JULY 27, 07:00

He was asleep when they came for him. Two big orderlies in white tunics picked him up and carried him out of his cell. Kalin waited for him by the elevator that led down to the surgical theaters.

Kalin had his notebook in one hand, and his pen in the other.

He was tapping the pen against the edge of the notebook. Impatient.

Somehow that was the thing that made Chapel snap. That made him try to fight.

One orderly held his arm, the other had his neck. He didn't know if they were really hospital employees or FSB agents—but he could tell by how thoroughly, how efficiently they held him, that they'd had some training in how to restrain a violent person.

They'd never tried to hold on to an Army Ranger before, though.

Chapel's legs were free. He stopped walking and forced them to drag him until his legs were dangling behind him, his bare feet squeaking on the slick floor. He brought one leg up and hooked it around the knee of the orderly holding his arm. The man wasn't ready for that and he stumbled. The other orderly tried to compensate, but Chapel threw his weight to the side and all three of them went down in a heap.

The orderly who held his arm saw the floor coming toward his face and let go, using his hands to catch himself. That was all Chapel needed. He brought his arm back and delivered a nasty punch right to the kidney of the orderly holding his neck. The man's breath exploded out of his mouth, and his grip slackened.

Chapel wrestled his way clear and scrambled to his feet. He could see Kalin reaching into his jacket pocket, maybe going for a weapon. If he went for Kalin, Chapel knew that would give the orderlies a chance to come at him from behind, so he ignored Kalin and dashed down the hall in the other direction.

He heard shouting behind him, but he ignored it. He came to the junction in the corridor, the place where it met the hallway that followed the curve of the building. Where would the stairs be? He'd seen them when he was brought here for the first time, but now he couldn't remember—did he go left or right?

He had to pick one. He went right.

They'd made a mistake in letting him eat and sleep. He'd recovered some of his strength, and he had always been a fast runner. He dashed past a series of doorways, some of them open to show empty rooms. He remembered the bars on the windows, the impact-resistant plastic that covered them on the inside. No point entering any of those rooms. He needed to find an exit, a way out of the hospital altogether, if he had any chance of getting away.

Up ahead the curved hallway opened into a sort

of lobby. There were restrooms up there, and—yes—a bank of elevators. He had no time to wait for one of those, but he knew that generally where you found elevators you found emergency stairs as well.

He got lucky. If the door to the stairs had been labeled in Russian, he would have just passed it by—he couldn't read the Cyrillic characters. But the doorway also showed a pictogram of someone running down steps ahead of a cartoon flame. Fire stairs—perfect. He hit the door with his shoulder and found, as he'd expected, that it was locked. Fire safety was less important than not letting your inmates escape, he supposed. He hit the door again, and again.

Behind him he heard rubber shoes chirping on the linoleum floor.

He hit the door again and the lock snapped. Cheap manufacture, not meant for this kind of abuse. Chapel burst through the door and down a flight of concrete steps. It was dark in the stairwell but as he descended, taking the steps two and three at a time, automatic lights flickered on overhead.

He had no idea even what floor he was on, or how many flights down the street was, but he didn't care. He heard people yelling at each other above him and just kept hurtling down the steps, fast enough that if he missed a riser he would probably fall and break his neck.

He didn't fall. One flight down, dash across the landing, two flights, another landing, three flights—

He heard someone moving below him, footsteps hurrying up the stairs toward him. He heard the squawk of a portable radio and knew the hospital's security guards had been alerted about an escape attempt. Well, he would just have to improvise.

Four flights down, five, and then he ran around a landing and saw a man below him, a man in a dark green uniform carrying a radio in one hand and a heavy wooden baton in the other. No gun.

Chapel launched himself off the landing, into the air. He came crashing down hard on top of the security guard, whose body broke his fall. The man cried, something in Russian Chapel didn't understand. Chapel grabbed the baton out of the man's hand and hit him a couple of times with it, hit him until he stopped protesting.

Then he was off again. Down another flight. Another. Up ahead the stairs ended at a short corridor. At the end of that corridor was a sign covered in warnings and writing he couldn't read. The door had a push bar and it looked like an alarm would sound if it was opened. It had to be an emergency exit to the street.

If he could get through that door, if Chapel could get out into the world, he could count on his training for what to do next. Find some clothes, get some money, find some way to contact Varvara and her *vory* friends, find a way out of Russia—

He hit the push bar at full speed, expecting the door to crash open, expecting to spill out into sunlight and chill morning air and freedom, and—

The door didn't open.

The push bar moved under his weight. He could feel a latch inside the door retract, could feel the door shift in its jamb. But it wouldn't open.

It must have been sealed off somehow. Maybe the

security detail had a way to lock it remotely, and they'd sealed off every exit from the hospital as soon as they heard an inmate was loose. Maybe the door was just rusted into place.

Chapel hit the door with his shoulder, hit it again and again until he felt like he was going to break the bones in his one good arm. Still it wouldn't open. He could hear people coming up behind him, hear them getting closer, and there was nowhere to go except back, right into their path. He hit the door with his left shoulder, probably damaging the sensitive electrodes implanted in his stump, but who cared, what did it matter, anything could be fixed—

A needle sank deep into his neck. He whirled around, as ferocious as a tiger, to find Kalin right next to him. He thought he would kill the man then and there, bite his throat out if need be, gouge him in the eyes, smash his trachea . . .

. . . but he suddenly . . . felt very . . . woozy. Very . . . weak.

"Only a sedative," Kalin said.

Chapel sank down to the floor. He just wanted to sit down for a second. Then he would start fighting again.

"Not too much," Kalin said. The FSB man squatted next to him, to look in his eyes. "Half a dose, really. I need you conscious for what comes next."

MAGNITOGORSK, RUSSIA: JULY 27, 07:13

Four orderlies, this time. Even though Chapel would have found it hard to stand under his own power. His head felt light, and even his teeth felt numb. Well. He'd won a small victory, then. A tiny, barely meaningful one.

When they cut off his arm, it wasn't going to hurt as much. The sedative would help kill a little of the pain.

His eyes rolled around to look at Kalin, and he realized that he was being asked a question. He had floated away for a little while there. Kalin smiled and repeated his query, very slowly.

"What is your name?"

Chapel smiled back.

"You do understand, don't you? If you have a name, that makes you a human being. That gives you certain rights. I won't be able to amputate your arm if you have rights. But only if you have a name. What is your name?"

"Marie Antoinette," Chapel told him.

The drug didn't take away the fear. It didn't keep his fight-or-flight reflex from kicking in. Inside his head Chapel was screaming, begging to be released. But he could use the drug, use how sluggish it made his muscles. He could at least pretend to be composed.

He promised himself he would hold out right until the last minute. That he wouldn't give in until they strapped him down on the operating table. Who knew? Maybe this was all a bluff. Maybe Kalin wouldn't go through with it.

Yeah, right, he thought. He knew better. That wasn't the way the world worked. Not his world, anyway.

"How did you meet the terrorist Asimova?" Kalin asked.

"She wasn't a terrorist," Chapel said. "She was a patriot. More of a patriot to Russia than you are, asshole."

Kalin beamed. "So you admit you knew her. This is getting us somewhere."

Damn, Chapel thought. He'd slipped up. Maybe the sedative had hit him harder than he'd thought.

"How did you make contact with her? Who was her handler? Tell me this much and I will put off your surgery for a day. Come, come, my friend. What does it matter? She's dead—there is no need to protect her now. How did you meet her?"

"Go fuck yourself."

Kalin sighed in frustration.

Well, now. There was another little victory. Chapel was really racking them up. He'd managed to annoy the senior lieutenant.

Maybe he could force the man to raise his voice before they cut off his legs, too.

The elevator doors opened on the basement level. Tiled walls and bad lighting. Not much longer now.

"You can still save yourself. Your arm. How traumatic it must have been, when the first one came off. How you must have raged against God and your country, that they would take so much from you. Do you really want to go through this again? Answer one question and this ends, right now," Kalin told him.

Chapel fixed him with a steely gaze. He was just about out of those. Out of defiance. He knew that when he saw the bone saw, when he heard it whine, he would lose. He would give in.

But . . . not just yet.

Every second he held out was worth it. Angel

could erase a lot of data in a second. She could take his name out of a lot of databases.

"We shall go back to the beginning," Kalin said. "Just give me your name. Your real name."

The stress, the panic, was burning through the drug in his bloodstream. Chapel lifted his head—it felt a little easier now. "No," he said.

They passed by a dark window. Another one. The next window was already lit up. That was their destination.

"Tell me your name," Kalin asked, and he gave a friendly little laugh. "Just a name. Tell me your name, and I will send you back to your cell."

Through the lit window, Chapel could see the operating table. It was draped with a sterile white cloth now. There was a tray next to it, a tray holding instruments. And there was a man standing next to the table wearing surgical scrubs. Had they brought in a real surgeon for this? What doctor would actually perform an unnecessary amputation? What about the Hippocratic oath? What about First Do No Harm?

Chapel knew perfectly well there were doctors in the world who would cut his arm off with no hesitation. He knew Kalin would have such a doctor on his payroll.

"Your name," Kalin said.

Chapel closed his eyes.

Kalin grabbed his face and squeezed until his eyes opened again.

"Your name. Tell me your name."

Chapel heard a bell ring. Then he heard a bunch of people walking quickly over the linoleum floor. Getting closer.

Kalin glanced backward, toward the elevator. What he saw there didn't seem to please him. "Only one thing can help you," he told Chapel.

Inside the surgical theater someone turned on a bone saw. Chapel would have recognized that sound anywhere.

This was it—the moment he'd promised himself he was allowed to surrender.

"What is your name?" Kalin asked, shouting in his face.

Chapel opened his mouth. He didn't know what was going to come out—he wasn't in control of his tongue anymore. He started making sounds, and he couldn't fight it, couldn't help himself.

"His name," someone else said, someone behind him, "is James Chapel. Captain James Chapel. He's an American agent, working under direct orders from the Washington Pentagon."

Chapel and Kalin both turned to look.

The man who had spoken wore the long greatcoat and cap of a Russian army officer. Judging by the epaulets and all the medals on his chest he was of high rank. He did not smile as he approached them.

"He is also," the officer said, "now under my authority." He spoke some more, in Russian, far too fast for Chapel to make out any words. Kalin replied with surprise and anger, but then the officer held up a piece of paper and let Kalin read it.

Whatever was written there made Kalin turn white as the snow in Siberia.

He glanced over at Chapel, still being held up by the orderlies. Then he nodded, just once. The officer said something else, but Kalin didn't respond.

He put his notebook and his pen back in his pocket, and then he started walking toward the elevator.

In the surgical theater, the doctor turned off his bone saw.

MAGNITOGORSK, RUSSIA: JULY 27, 08:20

It was . . . hard to believe.

It was hard to accept that this wasn't a trick. Some subtle ruse on Kalin's part, a way to make Chapel talk. Somehow the Russians had learned who he was. Now that his name wasn't so important, they were going to fool him into believing that it was over, that he wasn't going to be tortured anymore. Then he would start talking because, why not? Surely this was some kind of trick.

"I am Colonel Mikhail Valits, of the RVSN," the soldier told him.

"The Strategic Rocket Forces," Chapel said. That was the branch of the Russian military that controlled all the land-based nuclear missiles. "You must know why I'm here, then, so you don't need to ask."

Valits looked slightly confused. His English wasn't as good as Kalin's—Chapel could clearly see him sound out each word before he spoke it. Maybe he didn't understand. "If you will please come with me, we have much to discuss."

"I'm a prisoner here. You don't have to say please," Chapel told him.

Valits looked over at the orderlies and barked a question at them. They responded in Russian Chapel couldn't follow, but one of them mimicked plunging a hypodermic needle into his own neck. They were telling Valits that Chapel had been drugged.

"*Konyechno.*" Valits sighed, making it sound like the weariest word in the Russian language. He took Chapel's arm and helped him walk. He led Chapel back to the elevator. They had to wait for it to return, since Kalin had already used it to leave the basement.

Valits said nothing as they rode up to the ground floor of the hospital. He took Chapel down a short corridor and into a large room with lots of windows. It looked like some kind of lounge, maybe for the patients or perhaps the doctors who had once worked there. A boxy television set hung from a bracket in the ceiling, and there were a number of tables and stuffed armchairs scattered around the room. Everything looked dusty, and Chapel remembered wondering if he was the only inmate in the entire place.

A woman was waiting for them when they entered. She was sitting at one of the tables, hunched over an expensive-looking tablet, maybe checking her e-mail. She wore a smart business suit, and her hair was piled up on top of her head. When she looked up, Chapel saw she wore tortoise-shell-rimmed glasses and had eyes the color of used dishwater. She was maybe thirty years old, but probably younger.

And she was an American.

He could tell, instantly. Something about how white her teeth were, how her hair was cut. Maybe just the corn-fed good looks or the fact that, unlike every Russian Chapel had met except Nadia, this woman didn't look like she expected to be arrested at any second. Funny. He'd been away from his home country so long that other Americans had started to look strange to him.

She didn't smile as she stood up, and she held her tablet in one hand as she held out the other to shake his. She glanced at his stump and visibly shuddered. "One big horror show after another," she said, and laughed, as if she had made a funny joke.

Chapel didn't mind. He was used to people being polite about his missing arm—too polite. They pretended like it didn't bother them, or they tried to suppress their disgust. This woman didn't seem to care if he knew how she felt.

That was almost enough to make him like her on the spot. Of course, the fact that she was an American—and that her presence here almost proved that this wasn't an elaborate ruse concocted by Kalin to make him talk—made him want to hug her and weep.

"What's your name?" he asked her. He wanted to laugh out loud. "Sorry—you don't have to answer if you don't want to."

The woman's lips pursed in confusion. She looked over at Valits, but clearly she didn't find any help there. She rolled her eyes and sighed theatrically. Her sigh sounded very different from Valits's—it was the sigh of someone for whom boredom is the greatest pain imaginable.

She sat back down and tapped at the screen of her tablet. "I'm Natalie Hobbes. I'm an attaché with the office of the United States Ambassador to the Russian Federation." She glanced up at him. "Are you going to sit down, or what?"

Chapel had been a prisoner for only a few days, but it had been long enough to make him think he needed to be asked first. He sat down, gratefully— the drug in his system still made him feel weak— and rested his hand on the table.

"I'm supposed to check you out and give you something, and then Colonel Valits is going to show you a video. Shouldn't take long. I hope not—I'm supposed to be at a poetry reading tonight back in Moscow." She rolled her eyes again. "Arts outreach. I hate poetry, but you have to show a pretty face every once in a while to keep everybody happy." She looked up at Valits. "Is there any coffee?"

The colonel reared back as if she'd spit in his face. He was not the kind of man that fetched coffee for other people. "I'll see what I can do," he told her, and walked away.

"God, I hate this part of Russia. The smog is thicker here than in L.A., I swear," Hobbes said. She looked up at Chapel for a moment. "You don't look so hot. Were you mistreated while you were detained here?"

Chapel couldn't help it anymore. He laughed—a full-body belly laugh, enough to make him double over and make tears run from his eyes.

MAGNITOGORSK, RUSSIA: JULY 27, 08:47

Natalie Hobbes stood up from the table. "I really don't need this," she said. "I think I'll be going, now."

Chapel started to reach for her, to grab her and

make her sit down again. She flinched away from him, though, and he held up his hand to show he meant no harm. "Please," he said, "I apologize. I didn't mean to—"

"To freak me out?" she asked, looking very angry.

"Right. Look, I can't tell you how grateful I am that you've come for me. I thought I was going to . . . well, I thought I was going to be here for a very long time." It was clear she had no idea what kind of hell he'd been through in the hospital. No point freaking her out more. "I know what I must look like. But, please, I'm ready to go. Right now. The sooner the better."

She squinted at him, her nose wrinkling upward, as if she had forgotten her glasses and was having trouble seeing him clearly. He realized it must be how she expressed confusion. "They didn't brief you, did they? I'm not here to take you home. You're still under arrest. You're not going anywhere unless Colonel Valits says so."

Chapel glanced over to the door of the room, where the colonel had reappeared holding two steaming coffee cups.

"I was given two tasks here," Hobbes told him. "One was to verify you were still alive and in no immediate danger. That's done. The other thing was—this." She reached into her purse and took out a small manila envelope. She threw it down on the table. "It came over this morning in the diplomatic pouch, addressed to you. Even in this stupid country, prisoners are allowed to get mail."

Chapel could only stare at her. This wasn't a

rescue? He was still under arrest? He couldn't bear the thought of going back to his cell, to wait for Kalin to come for him.

He picked up the envelope and turned it around in his hands, almost afraid to open it. Kalin had nearly broken him. If this was just a message from Hollingshead, telling him he was on his own . . . But the envelope was too heavy to just be a letter. It bulged from trying to hold its contents.

Only one way to find out what it meant. He tore open the envelope and spilled it out onto the table. A cheap disposable cell phone and a hands-free unit.

It might have been gold and rubies. Chapel put the hands-free unit in his ear and powered up the phone.

"Angel?" he said.

She answered him a second later. "Chapel? Is that . . . of course it's you. Oh, sugar, I am so glad to hear your voice, you can't even know."

"I bet I can," Chapel told her. He closed his eyes and tried not to weep. The sexy voice of his operator in his ear was something he had thought he would never hear again. "Angel," he said. He couldn't think of more words. "Angel."

"Sweetie, there's a lot to talk about. But you're alive—that's the main thing. Oh, thank God. You're still alive."

MAGNITOGORSK, RUSSIA: JULY 27, 08:59

"First things first," Angel said. "This signal is encrypted, and the hands-free set has noise-canceling technology. But if they have a powerful enough microphone—and I bet they do—they can still hear what I'm saying in your ear. And of course they'll hear everything you say to me. There's not a lot we can do about that, but we're going to try to be discreet, right?"

"Of course," Chapel said.

Across the table Hobbes took her coffee from Valits without a word and sipped at it. She made a face.

"You're probably looking at Natalie Hobbes," Angel said. "She's the real deal. A junior staffer from the American embassy. Rich parents, went to Harvard, pretty much fell into this job—we've vetted her from this end and we don't see any reason to think the Russians might have turned her. She's on our side, in other words. As long as she's in the room you're safe."

"She's already talking about leaving," Chapel said.

"Just make sure she sticks around until you talk to Colonel Valits. As for him—he's not an FSB agent, I'm about eighty percent sure on that. He might shoot you, but . . . look, I don't know what you've been going through there in Magnitogorsk. I think maybe I don't want to know the details. But, sweetie, whatever he is, he's better than the people you've been dealing with. He's your best bet, so keep him happy."

"Got it," Chapel said.

"You're not free. You're still under arrest, and you're a prisoner of the Russian legal system."

"What am I charged with?" Chapel asked.

"They claim they picked you up just inside the Russian border, raving and disoriented. They've arrested you for a couple penny-ante crimes—being a public nuisance, defacing public property, whatever. That's enough for them to hold you. They claim you're a danger to yourself and others, and they're working on having you committed as a mental patient. If they do, that's the last anyone will hear of you. Ever."

"Jesus," Chapel said.

"It's bad. I wish I could tell you otherwise, but . . . it's bad. And you know there's not much we can do to help you. Until Colonel Valits came into the picture, we were following the standard protocol for agents captured in the field."

Which meant that the United States government had disavowed Chapel, just as he'd thought. They'd denied all knowledge of him, or any responsibility for his actions. He nodded. He understood that. "What I don't get is why that changed."

"I'll let Colonel Valits give you the details," Angel said, "but . . . he's got a problem. A very serious problem. I convinced him you were the only person in the world who could fix it. Whatever you do, make sure you don't convince him otherwise."

Chapel looked over at the colonel. The man was staring at Hobbes with open hatred. He clearly couldn't wait for her to leave.

"There are no guarantees here, sugar," Angel said. "No promises that you're going to get to come home. But if you play your cards right, you might have a chance to do some good, still. To fix things."

"Fix things?"

Angel was silent for a moment. "You know I'm on your side," she said, softly. "You know I care about you."

"I do," he told her.

"But even I have to say . . . look, Chapel, you really fucked up. *We* really fucked up here. Trusting Nadia . . . I think about it now and I wonder how any of us were fooled, even for a second."

Chapel wanted to ask what she meant, but Colonel Valits had turned to stare at him. The Russian cleared his throat noisily. Clearly he was ready to begin.

MAGNITOGORSK, RUSSIA: JULY 27, 09:14

Once Natalie Hobbes had left—Chapel tried to get her to stay, but she refused—Colonel Valits went over to the television hanging from the ceiling and attached a portable DVD player. He glanced over at an orderly who was standing near the door and barked a quick command. The orderly couldn't get out of the room fast enough.

"You are a fool," Valits told Chapel.

Chapel had no idea what he was talking about, so he didn't protest.

"You are an utter fool. Your country was taken in by a con artist. A terrorist who fed you a pack of lies. And you ate them up." He waited with his jaw set, as if he expected Chapel to throw a punch or something. When that didn't happen, he nodded and went on. "This is what your superior told me, and it is the only explanation that is acceptable. Because if I learn you knew who you were working with, then you, also, are a terrorist, and I will kill you myself."

Chapel wished someone would tell him what was going on.

The colonel pushed a button on the DVD player and the screen lit up with a grainy black-and-white image. Chapel had trouble telling what he was looking at. It seemed to be security-camera footage showing the inside of a warehouse. A long, cylindrical shape filled most of the view. It looked like a rocket lying on its side.

Or a missile. As Chapel took in more details he realized it was, in fact, an ICBM. An intercontinental ballistic missile. A nuke.

This one was missing its warhead. The complicated electronics package was revealed, a tangle of wires and motherboards that handled the targeting and steering for the missile once it was in flight. Chapel was no expert on missiles, but he thought it looked like this one had been partially dismantled for repair or maintenance.

"You know what this is?" Valits asked.

Chapel tried to remember everything he knew about Russian nuclear weapons. In the month before he'd left for Bucharest, while he'd been researching Perimeter as best he could, he'd memorized quite a lot. "It's an RT 2PM Topol," he said. A kind of missile that could be loaded on a motorized crawler and launched from anywhere. The Topol system was largely obsolete, but Chapel knew the Russians still had a hundred and fifty or so of them still in service.

The colonel nodded. "So you are a fool, but an educated fool. That makes things a little easier. This film was taken in the city of Izhevsk, a little more than twenty-four hours ago. It could have happened in many places. Ever since we realized what Asimova stole, we have been attempting to remove the remote launch units from all our arsenal. At least, we were attempting to do so, until this happened."

On the screen a couple of workers in coveralls were busy at the front of the missile, carefully untangling the exposed wires in the electronics package. There was no sound, but clearly something had happened in the warehouse, because suddenly one of the workers jumped away from the missile and ran offscreen. The other worker turned around to watch him go.

He should have run with his friend. One whole side of the screen went white, solid featureless white. At first Chapel thought it must be a glitch, that the camera was malfunctioning, but then he realized what he was seeing.

The missile's thrusters were firing. On its side, in a warehouse, with half its guts exposed, the Topol was trying to launch.

The whole screen went white, with clouds of sparks filling up the view for a moment before the view cut to nothing but static.

"The missile attempted to carry out its programming," Valits said. He switched off the television and removed the DVD player. He took the disc out and snapped it in half, then pocketed the pieces—clearly no one else was allowed to see this. "It was given a launch command, and it fired its engines. It even attempted to right itself, to begin a steering burn that would take it toward its intended target."

"What was the target?" Chapel asked.

"Sacramento, California," Valits told him, without a shred of apology in his voice. "Of course, it was impossible for the missile to reach that place. And it had no warhead—that was removed before the workers began to dismantle the electronics. Still. It carried enough fuel to level the warehouse and every building in the surrounding block. It had mostly disintegrated by that point, but still it had enough thrust to carry it one kilometer across the sky of Izhevsk and destroy an office building on the far side of the town. It happened in the middle of the night and casualties were limited. Both men you saw in this video are dead, however, and there are many injuries in Izhevsk."

Chapel forced his jaw not to drop.

"The launch command came from the Perimeter system," he guessed. "Via a shortwave signal, from Aralsk-30."

Valits raised one eyebrow. "I am glad you do not feign ignorance. Or innocence. Yes, it was a Perimeter protocol command that told the missile to launch. However, you are wrong. The command did not come from Kazakhstan. In fact, we do not believe it was even carried over the shortwave band, though it mimicked such a signal perfectly. No, Perimeter did not launch this Topol. Perimeter does not have the capacity to launch a single missile at a time. It must launch them all, or none. The event in Izhevsk was an isolated launch. Thank God, it was the only missile that launched that night."

"So," Chapel said, "what you're telling me is that someone . . . stole all the launch codes from the Perimeter data banks. And now they can fire any missile at your arsenal, whenever they want to."

"Yes," Valits said. "*She* can."

She?

A lot of thoughts raced through Chapel's brain at that moment. Many of them didn't make sense, while others were just emotions—panic, confusion, anger, fear.

One rose to the surface right away, however.

Nadia is still alive.

MAGNITOGORSK, RUSSIA: JULY 27, 09:19

Valits folded his hands together and watched Chapel with hooded eyes. "There was a message. It came in at the same time the missile launched in Izhevsk. It gave us some instructions. Some demands. We are not to attempt to dismantle any more of our weapons. And we are to raise a plebiscite concerning greater autonomy for the republics of the Far Eastern Federal District."

"I'm afraid I don't understand," Chapel said. "When you say Far Eastern—"

"It means Siberia," Valits said. "The eastern half, anyway. The Sakha Republic, as well as the maritime oblasts such as Amur, Primorskiy, Sakhalin Island . . . it is all worded very politically, very carefully, but it amounts to a call for secession. Now, do you know anyone who has an interest in Siberian self-determination who might also have access to the Perimeter codes?"

Chapel shook his head. "Kalin told me she was killed," he insisted.

"Kalin is a security man, and therefore a liar by profession," Valits told him. "Most likely he wished to convince you there would be no harm in sharing Asimova's secrets if she was dead. She escaped, along with the Romanian, at the same time that you were captured. No sign of her was found after that, but now we know what she has been doing. What you helped her achieve."

Chapel took a deep breath. "We didn't steal any codes. I was there the whole time, there was no way that . . ."

But of course, Chapel hadn't watched Bogdan the entire time the hacker had access to Perimeter's terminal. Bogdan could have told Perimeter to read out all the codes, and then recorded them somehow.

He remembered, then, something that he had barely noticed at the time. When Bogdan went to the terminal he had placed his MP3 player on top of one of the data banks. Was it possible?

"Excuse me one moment," Chapel said. He turned his head to the side and said, "Angel, are you still there?"

"Always, honey."

"I need to know if something is possible. Could you build a device, a . . . a data logger of some kind, say something the size of an MP3 player. Could you make one that would copy information from a reel-to-reel data tape at a distance?" It sounded impossible, but he was consistently surprised at what they could do with computers these days.

"No problem," Angel told him. "When the read/write head of a tape player moves across a tape it releases tiny bursts of electromagnetic radiation, and if you have a way to record those bursts and then interpret them as data, sure. You would need the tape to actually be running at the time, though you could fast-forward through it and still record all the information."

Bogdan had made only a small change to Perimeter's programming. He would have had plenty of time to run the whole tape. "And the data we're talking about, all the launch codes—you could fit that on the memory of an MP3 player?"

"Absolutely. Those codes are just strings of numbers and characters, probably sixteen digits long each. There's more data in one MP3 file than in ten thousand launch codes."

Chapel closed his eyes. He could feel a very bad headache coming on. "So Bogdan was in on it the whole time. Everybody was in on it but me."

He was moving toward one inescapable conclusion. He really didn't want to get there. He had one protest left.

"When Nadia—Asimova—came to us, in Washington, we vetted her," he told Valits. "We made sure, as much as we could, that she was real. An agent of FSTEK. She was vouched for personally by Marshal Bulgachenko."

"Konstantin Bulgachenko was born in Vladivostok in 1951," Valits told him. "Do you know enough geography to know where that is? It is in Siberia."

"So you're saying—"

"Bulgachenko and Asimova were a cabal of Siberian separatists. We do not know if they infiltrated FSTEK with the express intent of forwarding their political aims, or if they only realized their shared cause after she was recruited. It is immaterial. Bulgachenko is dead Asimova has become a terrorist."

He couldn't resist it anymore. The conclusion was right there in front of him, and he couldn't even look away.

Nadia had betrayed him.

She had used him, tricked him into joining her crusade. Unwittingly he had helped her steal the entire Russian nuclear arsenal for the cause of Siberian independence—and by so doing implicated the United States in an international incident worse than anything he'd ever heard of before.

She had betrayed him.

Nadia. The woman he had . . . the woman he had begun to . . . the woman he'd started to feel . . .

Nadia had played him like a fish on a line.

MAGNITOGORSK, RUSSIA: JULY 27, 09:30

No. It couldn't be. Nadia wasn't a terrorist—not Nadia—not the warm, funny woman he'd fallen for. Not the cheerful, doomed woman who just wanted to make the world a little safer before she died. Not the Nadia who had sacrificed so much to track down missing plutonium, not her.

No, she'd been a patriot! They'd given her a medal, the Russians had given her a medal for her service, they had . . .

She had been a patriot, hadn't she? *Just not to the country*, he thought.

How many times had she told him about the abuses and crimes of the Russian government? She'd framed it as criticism of the Soviets, not the current Russian government, but plenty of times she'd spoken of how unfair it was that Siberia was tied to Moscow—*ya Sibiryak*, she'd said. I am a Siberian.

The whole time. She had been lying the whole time. When they found out that the FSB was chasing her, that they wanted her dead—he should have aborted the mission then. He should have, but he'd persuaded Hollingshead into letting them continue. Because he had believed. He had believed in Nadia. Believed that she wanted the same thing he did, an end to the madness of Perimeter, of nuclear proliferation.

And the whole time all she wanted was to control the missiles herself.

She had come to Washington with the means to dismantle Perimeter and it had sounded so good, so possible. So worthwhile. She had convinced Hollingshead to send him after the one-time pad in the wreck of the *Kurchatov*. She had convinced Chapel to help her fight her way to Aralsk-30. The whole time she'd known they would never have gone along with it if they knew her true aim.

Where was she now? Was she laughing at him? Laughing at how easy it was to seduce the cripple? There had been so many signs; how had he missed them all? She had spied on him when he spoke to Angel; she'd even admitted as much. She had consorted with organized criminals. She had killed Russian agents and violated the sovereignty of three different countries.

And he'd been by her side the whole time.

He couldn't take it. He couldn't take the betrayal. In a rage, he jumped up and grabbed the nearest chair and threw it across the room. He kicked another chair and sent it clattering across the floor. He roared in anger, the veins in his temples throbbing until he thought they might burst.

"I had no idea," he told Valits. "The whole time—I had no idea."

The colonel hadn't moved, hadn't flinched, throughout Chapel's rampage. He nodded just once now. "Surprisingly," he said, "I believe you."

Chapel dropped his head. He was breathing hard, and every muscle in his body was tense, but the anger was already draining from him. He was already starting to move on to self-loathing.

Valits rose and straightened his uniform tunic. "Unfortunately, Moscow has no choice. We must see your actions as an act of espionage, if not of war."

"We have more to lose than you do," Chapel pointed out. "If she launches those missiles, they'll head straight for my country. For New York. For Chicago. For Washington."

Valits shrugged. *Konyechno,* he was saying. "It would seem, then, that we have a mutual problem."

"Yeah," Chapel told him. "And one solution. We get Asimova before she can press the button. But how exactly do we do that?"

"This," Valits said, "is why I am talking to you now, instead of leaving you to the devices of Senior Lieutenant Kalin. Because I have been led to believe that you are the only man in the world who can find her."

MAGNITOGORSK, RUSSIA: JULY 27, 09:39

"Of course," Valits explained, "we have attempted to track her location. We find that the signal she is using, however—the one that sent the launch signal to Izhevsk, and the one that carried her demands—is untraceable. It was not a shortwave signal, though it had similar characteristics. We were able to determine it was bounced off a satellite. That means she could be anywhere in the world right now. If she is smart, she will be very far from any Russian holdings. She might be in your country, even.

"It is possible she was not that smart. We have teams of soldiers out looking for her everywhere from St. Petersburg to the farthest eastern islands. We do not have enough manpower to cover the entire Russian Federation, but we have been concentrating on major cities—places where she could have access to high-end signal equipment."

"I'm guessing you haven't turned up anything yet," Chapel said.

"Nothing. There is no trace of her anywhere. We sent envoys to speak with the top leaders of the *vory*—when you wish to disappear in this country, they are who you turn to. They say she made no attempt to contact them."

"And you believed them? Asimova has friends in those circles. They could be protecting her."

Valits smiled. It wasn't a warm smile. It wasn't a smirk. It was a smile of resignation. "Not at the top levels. It is a fact of my nation, a sad fact, that there is very little distance between our elected officials and the gangsters. They are all heavily invested in the Federation, and they would not protect her, not after we showed them the video you just saw. They have as much to lose as any of us."

Chapel nodded. "Okay. What about other politi-

cal groups? Other terrorist organizations. I'm sure
there are plenty that would love to help her give
Moscow a black eye." Valits looked confused by the
idiom. "To embarrass your government," Chapel
explained.

"Absolutely. But we have ways of getting information from those groups—we watch them very
closely—and we have heard nothing, not even chatter. She has not made alliance even with the other
Siberian nationalist and ethnic groups. She seems to
be working completely on her own."

Probably, Chapel thought, *because you've already
killed off everyone she could count on*—he doubted Bulgachenko was the only casualty of Nadia's mission.

"So that leaves us with nothing to go on," Chapel
said.

"Not quite. In our . . . desperation, we made one last
attempt to seek aid. We turned to your government."

Chapel's eyes went wide. For Russia to ask Washington for help with an internal political problem
was unheard of. Moscow must be even more frightened than he'd thought.

"We contacted your superior, Rupert Hollingshead. We wished to know if Asimova had said anything to him, given away any clue as to her plans.
He was not useful on that front. However, he did
discover one thing that could aid us. While he could
not track the signal she is using, he did recognize its
signature. I believe your friend on the telephone can
tell you what I mean."

Angel chirped in on cue. "That's right, sweetie.
I'm the one who recognized the signature, of course."

"Yeah?" Chapel asked her. "How?"

"Easy. Because it was the same kind of signal I use."

"I beg your pardon?"

Angel sounded sheepish as she answered. "I didn't believe it at first. I use a cutting-edge signal profile that lets me contact you anywhere on earth and make sure nobody can listen in to what I'm saying. It's all pretty technical, but basically I use packet switching and channel hopping algorithms to spread my frequency out over a broad band of—"

"Still too technical," Chapel told her.

"Probably best if I don't explain over this line, anyway. I was confused when I saw she was using the same technology. I was especially confused when I looked back over my notes for this mission. Remember when you asked me if I could listen in to Bogdan's computer?"

"Sure," Chapel said. That was on the train to Vobkent. Just after he'd realized that Bogdan even *had* a computer.

"I said I couldn't hack in directly, but maybe there was something I could do. I started building up a profile of the signal he was using. It's a match, Chapel. It's exactly the same. The message she sent, and the launch signal, came from Bogdan's computer. Or one using the same signal tech. The same tech I use."

"You're saying he just figured out your tech on his own?" Chapel asked, confused.

Angel snorted in derision. "Hardly. He stole it. Or rather, she did. It took me a long time to realize how. She would need access to my hardware to even begin to reverse engineer my tech. And when did she have access like that?"

"I'm afraid you're about to tell me."

"Yeah." The sheepish tone came back. "You remember Donny's yacht? When you came back up to the surface too fast? You remember anything unusual about that?"

Chapel cast his mind back. He had come up at speed, and he'd been unable to reach Angel during the ascent. When he broke the surface, the first thing he did was contact her again. He should have been able to reach her just by touching the anchor cable, because of the transponder he'd clipped to it, but—

The transponder had been missing.

He'd been too concerned with decompression sickness to think about what that meant. Somebody had unclipped it while he'd been surfacing, he knew that much. But he hadn't thought to look for it later. Even after he'd been taken to Miami, and the hyperbaric chamber there, his major concern had been for the one-time pad. When he found that Nadia could have stolen it, but hadn't . . . well, that was when he'd begun to trust her.

"Your transponder," he said to Angel. "She had it the whole time?"

"And she gave it to Bogdan, who adopted the tech for his ingenious little computer. You got it, sweetie."

"Okay, yet another way I screwed up," Chapel said. "But it might turn out in our favor. I'm guessing you can trace the signal, right? You can trace your own signal?"

"Uh," Angel said. "Well. Kind of."

"What does that mean?"

"My signal is designed to be untraceable. But—look, I'll skip the technical stuff this time. If you could triangulate the signal, if both you and I were looking for it at the same time, we could find it. But one of us would need to be pretty close, say, within fifty miles of the originating source."

"So we already need to know roughly where she is before we can hope to find her."

"I'm afraid you've got it."

Chapel nodded slowly to himself. With the best technology in the world, with the best computers and data analysis, it was going to come down to him. He was the one who was going to have to guess where Nadia had gone.

He thought back, trying to remember any clue she'd given him. Any idea at all.

This time, he didn't miss what was right under his nose. Or under hers, anyway. Assuming, of course, that anything she'd told him was the truth.

He turned to Valits, and he could hear the steel in his own voice. "How soon can we leave?"

Valits's eyes opened very wide. "You know where she is?"

"I can find her." He could take her down. He could get back at her for everything she'd done to him, all the lies she'd told him. He could get revenge.

"If you do this, if you lead us to her—I will make sure you go home. That you will be allowed to return to America, safely," Valits promised.

Oh, right. He hadn't thought of that. But it was nice, too.

As long as he made Nadia pay, first.

MAGNITOGORSK, RUSSIA: JULY 27, 10:14

They sent a helicopter down from the nearest air base to pick Chapel up. His clothes from the desert were long gone—no one had expected him to need real clothing ever again, so they'd burned what he had on when he was captured. Colonel Valits offered him an army uniform with no insignia, but it was the wrong army. Chapel had been a soldier too long to ever wear the uniform of another nation. In the end, one of the orderlies had to run into town and buy Chapel civilian clothes.

The helicopter came down in the courtyard of the hospital. Chapel watched it land through doubly sealed windows. He couldn't hear the rotors, just see the vast plume of dust the helicopter kicked up. It was an unarmed little machine, but that didn't matter; it was just there to take him back to the air base so he could get on a plane.

He had a very long way to go. Lots of time zones to cross.

"You truly think she is in Siberia?" Colonel Valits asked, coming up behind him.

"If it was anyone else . . . I might doubt it." It was the first place they would look for her. But Nadia was running out of time—assuming she hadn't lied about that, too. He had to believe that she really was dying, that she had only months left, maybe less, and that she would want to die where she'd been born.

Of course, if he was wrong, he would end up right back here with Kalin. So she *had* to be in Siberia. "She's sentimental. She wants to go home."

Valits shook his head. "I've already had troops turn the city of Yakutsk upside down looking for her. Not a single person has entered that place in the last week that I don't know about. And it's the only municipality large enough to have the kind of Internet connection and signal technology she needs."

Chapel knew better. Angel had told him that the necessary tech could fit inside a smartphone. At least, a brand-new, state-of-the-art smartphone. Nadia didn't need to be in Yakutsk—and the city wasn't where she wanted to be.

"I'll find her," he told Valits.

They shook hands and then Chapel headed down to the courtyard, toward the helicopter. A couple of Valits's soldiers followed him at a discreet distance. He wasn't going to ever be out of their sight, he knew, until this was over.

"Chapel," Angel said, when he had stepped outside and the noise of the rotors made it almost impossible to hear her. That might be the point— maybe she didn't want anyone listening in.

"Go ahead," he told her, as the dust blew past him in the artificial windstorm, as his empty sleeve snapped and fluttered behind him like a flag.

"The director has been briefed on what you're doing. He had one message to give you. Quote, 'Remember how Hercules defeated the hydra,' unquote. Does that mean anything to you?"

"Yeah," Chapel said, but he wouldn't explain, not to Angel. "Message received."

If you cut the head off a hydra, it just grew another one. Hollingshead had described Perimeter as being like that. Now he was talking about this mission. The objective kept changing, every time Chapel thought he'd gotten close to being done.

Hercules had figured out you didn't just need to cut the hydra's head off. You had to burn it at the stump. Make it impossible for the head to grow back.

Hollingshead was telling him to make sure Nadia never stung them again. He was telling Chapel to make sure she really was dead this time.

He was giving Chapel an order to execute her.

IN TRANSIT: JULY 27, 11:33

Chapel and the soldiers who made up his guard detail transferred to a transport plane at the nearest airport. It was a military jet, with little in the way of accommodations—even the seats were simply bolted to rails on the cabin floor, designed so they could be removed quickly in case the plane needed to haul cargo instead of people. Chapel picked a window seat, and his soldiers took the row behind him. He strapped himself in and let his head fall back against the seat. Closed his eyes. Sleep wasn't an option—he could do nothing but review his own thoughts, over and over.

They were dark thoughts and barely coherent. Mostly he just kept thinking how he'd been manipulated, how Nadia had used him, and how badly he wanted to make her pay for that.

But there was one small voice in the back of his head, one little pleading thought that just wouldn't go away. It kept telling him there was something wrong here. Not so much an argument, not even really a doubt. Just a memory—a memory of Nadia in the tent in the desert, lying there next to him. He remembered how he'd leaned over and kissed her and the look on her face, the surprise and the hope, then the confusion and frustration. She had seduced him, of course. She had known he was hurt and vulnerable after what happened with Julia and she had used that. Preyed on it.

But that look—it hadn't been the expression of a con artist whose game wasn't proceeding fast enough. She had looked genuinely hurt, like she had held something out to him, something real, and he was toying with *her* heart, not the other way around . . .

Of course, a good actress could fake that look. If that were the case, Nadia should have been up for an Academy Award.

It didn't matter. It couldn't matter. He had his orders. He knew where things stood, finally. It was time to end this mission, and there was only one way to conclude it. He was just going to have to push down that nagging little question in his head, push it down until it stopped popping back up.

He writhed in frustration against his seat. It was taking way too long for the plane to get moving. He needed to be airborne, headed toward his final meeting with her; he needed to—

Someone climbed in through the rear hatch of the plane and started walking up the aisle. Chapel didn't even bother to look to see who it was. This must be what was delaying them—they'd had to wait for some VIP of the Russian military who had insisted on being on this plane. Chapel sneered in frustration and turned his head to look out the window. When the newcomer dropped down into the seat next to him, Chapel tried to remember the Russian words for "occupied" and "go away."

He turned to face the newcomer and forgot all the Russian he knew. The VIP was, in fact, Senior Lieutenant Pavel Kalin. His erstwhile torturer.

"Good afternoon, Kapitan," the bastard said. His smile was broad and genuine. He was thrilled to see Chapel here.

"Get away from me," Chapel growled, in English.

"I don't think so. I think I will be staying very close to you now." Kalin leaned into the aisle and waved at someone. A moment later the plane's hatch closed and its engines started to drone. Clearly the plane had only been waiting for Kalin's arrival. "It took a great deal of persuasion to get myself assigned to this mission," he told Chapel.

"You had to torture somebody for your spot?"

Kalin's smile broadened. "Very droll. No, I called in some favors. But believe me, I would have moved heaven and earth."

Chapel clenched his teeth and looked away. This was the last thing he needed.

The plane lifted away from the airstrip with only a few jolts. Soon they were up in the sky, up where there was nothing to see through the window but clouds. Better, anyway, than looking at Kalin's face. It was taking pretty much all Chapel's resolve not to reach over and strangle the man in his seat. Of course, if he did, the plane would have to put down prematurely, and that would delay Chapel in the course of his revenge against Nadia. He supposed you had to pick your battles in this life.

"It looks like we'll be working together," Kalin said. "My orders are to keep a close watch on you but to follow your lead until I am told this is no longer appropriate."

"Let's get one thing straight, Kalin," Chapel said. "We are *not* partners. I'm not working with you. I'm working for Colonel Valits on behalf of my government. If you catch on fire during this operation, I won't spit on you to put you out."

"I could say much the same," Kalin told him. "I advised strongly against this madness—this foolish notion of sending you to catch her. This is an internal Russian matter, and bringing you in is folly. You should never have been briefed about what happened at Izhevsk. But Valits is a frightened man, just now. He thinks we need every resource available to catch Asimova."

"Maybe he's right. Considering that if we don't, she could start World War III any time she wanted to. And that she's got nothing to lose."

"There's no need to lecture me on her capabilities. I've been chasing the terrorist Asimova for longer than you knew she existed," Kalin explained. "I've gone to incredible lengths to find her and stop her. I will not waste all that time and effort."

Chapel found that he needed to know, more than he needed to get away from Kalin. "How long have you known what she was up to?"

Kalin studied his face for a while, as if trying to decide how much to tell him. Finally he shrugged and said, "It doesn't matter now. I'll tell you everything. It started as a matter of routine. Any agent of FSTEK working on recovering lost plutonium is, of course, carefully screened. There are so many temptations in that mission—one must consort with criminals and foreign agents, any of whom would gladly pay a king's ransom for even a small quantity of fissile material. Plutonium is, gram for gram, the most precious metal on earth. More than one of our agents has succumbed to making a deal with someone he should have arrested instead. So we keep a close eye on them. Asimova was especially worth watching, because she was a known political."

"You mean because of how she was arrested for attending a protest rally," Chapel said.

"Exactly," Kalin said, as if Chapel was finally getting the point. "Add to this that she had charmed Marshal Bulgachenko, the head of FSTEK. He would have given her the moon for a New Year's present had she asked for it."

"Did she—" Chapel hated to even ask, especially of an officious monster like Kalin, but he had to know. "Did they—"

"Fuck?" Kalin asked, turning the vulgarity over in his mouth like a candy. He left Chapel hanging for a long, cruel minute. Once a torturer, always a torturer, perhaps. "No," he said, finally. "The marshal had never had children, and he saw Asimova as a surrogate daughter. He was very proud of her, especially given her Siberian upbringing."

Chapel frowned. "You have a surprising amount of information on a dead man's inner thoughts and feelings."

"I was the man who killed him," Kalin said. His

smile didn't crack or even chip. "He was a traitor to the Fatherland. He deserved to die. But he was also a hero of our military, and I felt it was worth knowing why he had become corrupted."

Jesus, Chapel thought. How long had Kalin tortured the marshal before he killed him? The man might well have been a separatist—a terrorist, even—but nobody should ever be subject to the mercies of a man like Kalin. Nobody.

"I would have watched Bulgachenko even if he hadn't promoted Asimova so quickly. He was a known troublemaker, from even before my time. When the Soviet Union fell, there was some interest among the Sibiryaks in splitting off from the Federation. It was a short-lived political moment, but in that time Bulgachenko added his voice to the chorus. He even petitioned Yeltsin in person for self-determination for the Siberian republics. He believed he could form a government in Vladivostok, with, of course, himself as president. Yeltsin was a drunk, but he understood that Russia could not survive without Siberia—"

"Without its resources, you mean."

"Exactly," Kalin said. "Yeltsin grew angry and threw Bulgachenko out of his office. Before that day Bulgachenko was well on his way to being in control of the entire state security apparatus. Afterward he was relegated to FSTEK, which at the time meant he was put in charge of ordering around a few border guards. FSTEK was a kind of very well-paid gulag. Bulgachenko, of course, was an intelligent man, and he knew better than to protest. Instead he took this as an opportunity. When plutonium started disappearing from the stockpiles, he volunteered to go after it. He only needed a field agent, someone who could actually go out and recover the stuff.

"Asimova must have seemed like a gift from Jesus. She was capable, she was brilliant, and she was beautiful. A perfect symbol of the Siberia of his dreams. She would be a—ah, I know there is an American term, for a person who is the perfect image of—"

"A poster girl," Chapel suggested.

"Yes! That is it. She would be the poster girl for a new Siberia that was not beholden to Moscow. She doesn't even look Russian. So of course he confided everything in her. Told her all his plans. Told her that simple political pressure, even nonviolent protest of the kind she had tried, would be useless in creating an independent Siberia. By then they had both seen what happened to Chechnya and South Ossetia under Putin. The Federation has finished giving away territory. It will fight to hold on to what it has left. If Siberia was to gain independence, it must be able to fight back. But how? There is no military presence out east that is not staffed completely by those loyal to Moscow. A coup was out of the question. Bulgachenko's original plan was to use the confiscated plutonium to make dirty bombs. Put one in Moscow, one in St. Petersburg—perhaps a third in Nizhny Novgorod, just for good measure. Threaten to detonate them if demands were not met."

"That's—" Chapel shook his head. "That's—"

"Terrorism, yes," Kalin said. "The last resort of the politically deranged. It was Asimova who talked him out of it."

"Nadia?"

Kalin's eyes crept over Chapel's face until he felt like he was covered in bugs. "It would perhaps be better if you stop calling her by that name."

Chapel realized his mistake and shook his head. "I'll call her what I want to," he said. In his head the reply had been *I'll call her what I want to, asshole*, but he had some sense of decorum left.

Kalin shrugged. "Yes, Asimova convinced him his dirty bomb plan was folly. Which anyone but Bulgachenko could have seen. FSTEK is not some miraculous organization that can act unobserved. The plutonium it recovered was quite carefully logged and monitored by other agencies. If it went missing again, the theft would be discovered very quickly. And the response of my group—the Counter-Intelligence Division—would have been swift, decisive, and without qualm. Beyond this, dirty bombs are notoriously dangerous to build and deploy—and she already knew far too well the danger of handling plutonium."

"So it was her idea to hijack Perimeter?"

"They developed the plan together. But, yes, it was her brainchild. She knew, of course, that I would try to stop her. She knew that to get access to Perimeter she would need to become a rogue agent. She also knew she would be dead within the week if she did not find some protection somewhere. This, I believe, is why she went to the Americans. To you."

"You could have shut her down then with one phone call," Chapel pointed out. "You could have told us she was a terrorist. We would have arrested her in Washington and then held her for you."

Kalin's smile didn't change, but his eyes did. They

became weary suddenly, weary and resigned. "That would have meant sharing information with the Pentagon. Giving away secrets—telling you about Perimeter, for one thing. In Russia, some secrets are buried so deeply they can never be brought to light."

Chapel nodded. "We have a few of those in America, too."

"I was convinced," Kalin said, "that I could run her down myself. I did, in fact, call the authorities in Cuba and tell them she was violating their national waters. Unfortunately, the photographs I sent did not make it in time and she slipped through their fingers."

That explained the mysterious boarding of Donny's party yacht off Cay Sal Bank, Chapel thought—and why the Cubans hadn't arrested them then and there.

"Next I thought to catch her in Bucharest, and again in Uzbekistan, but both times you helped her get away," Kalin pointed out. "It seems she picked her protection very well."

"She convinced me that your agents were gangsters chasing Bogdan Vlaicu," Chapel admitted, since it seemed there was no point keeping that from Kalin now. He did not confess that after Vobkent he'd known she was being chased by the Russians, that they wanted her dead or alive. No need to give everything away.

"Indeed. She can be very persuasive." Kalin folded his hands in his lap. "Kapitan Chapel, I want to be clear on our roles in what is unfolding now. We need you to find her. That is all. Once we have a location, I will not permit you within earshot of the woman. I'd hate for her to charm you once more and have you switch coats again."

Chapel bit his lip. He could hardly complain or protest. After all, she had done just that—charmed him—once.

But he had his orders, and he knew what he needed, personally. Whatever Kalin thought was going to happen, however this was going to go down, Chapel planned on looking Nadia right in the eye at the last moment. If Kalin didn't like it, maybe he had to be taken out, too.

It wasn't the most unattractive prospect.

YAKUTSK, SAKHA REPUBLIC, RUSSIA: JULY 28, 05:37 (YAKST)

It was a clear night over Siberia, and as the plane swung north toward its destination, Chapel got to see the sun set, then peek back over the horizon and set again. Yakutsk was close enough to the Arctic Circle that its nights were only six hours long this time of year. When they landed, the sun was rising again and the first pink tinge of dawn was still lining one side of all the airport buildings.

It was enough to give his jet lag jet lag. Chapel hobbled out of the plane, his legs cramped from the flight and still sore, bruised, and lacerated from the beating he'd taken at Aralsk-30. He stepped down a short flight of stairs to the tarmac and thought he could feel the world turning under his feet.

His guard detail emerged behind him, weapons in their hands. Kalin came down last, looking fresh and ready for whatever happened next. If Chapel hadn't already hated the man with an undying passion, that would probably have been reason enough to start.

They were met by a Russian army officer in a long greatcoat with fur trim around the collar. He looked overdressed. Yakutsk was the coldest city of its size in the world, Chapel knew, but this was the height of summer and it couldn't be less than fifty-five degrees out. Windbreaker weather, as far as Chapel was concerned.

The officer looked confused as to whom he should salute. He finally settled on Kalin, who returned the gesture with a perfunctory touch of his forehead. The two of them spoke in Russian. Chapel could follow most of what Kalin said, but the officer's accent was so thick he might have been speaking ancient Etruscan.

They'd been expected, of course, and the officer had a car waiting to take them to an army base where they would be quartered. Kalin replied that wasn't necessary, that they needed to get to work right away. He ordered that the local troops ready a long-range helicopter at once.

The officer seemed a little put out that his offer of hospitality was rejected. He relayed the order, though, then waved for his troops to come over. There were about fifty of them, and they looked tired. Chapel gathered that they had been part of the detail that was turning the city of Yakutsk upside down looking for Nadia—for the terrorist Asimova. They had searched about a third of the entire city, going door-to-door and checking every house and place of business. They'd gone into cellars and up into attics and found no trace of her, but they were sure that with a little more time—

"She's not here," Chapel said, in Russian.

The officer turned to look at him with genuine curiosity. Chapel wasn't surprised. His presence here was a state secret, not the kind of thing Valits would have passed on to his low-ranking officers. Beyond that, a foreigner in civilian clothes with one arm was always going to stand out on an army base.

"She's not stupid enough to come to Yakutsk," Chapel went on, carefully sounding out the words in his head before he said them. "She knows you will look here first."

The officer opened his mouth to ask a question, but Kalin cut him off. He spoke slowly, perhaps for Chapel's benefit, but his words had the sound of true command. "This man is an American who specializes in advanced signal technology. His role is to help us find the terrorist Asimova. However, he does not possess a security clearance. Your men will not speak to him unless it is absolutely necessary, and under no circumstances are they to accept any order he tries to give."

The officer nodded in understanding. He looked distinctly relieved. Chapel had been a soldier long enough to understand why. No matter what rank you held in the military, someone was always your boss, and someone else probably took orders from you. You had to answer to the former for the mistakes of the latter. You always needed to know where everyone around you fit in, what category they belonged to. Now that Chapel was squared away, the officer could just write him off.

The officer led them to a nearby building where there was coffee and a simple meal of coarse bread and pickled fish. For about fifteen minutes they waited there until the helicopter was ready to receive them. Nobody spoke a word to him the whole time.

The helicopter turned out to be an Mi-8, recognizable by the twin turboprop power plants mounted over its canopy. It was a beast of a machine, a huge fuselage with the tail assembly sticking out the back like the tail of a tadpole. Drop tanks full of fuel studded its sides. Kalin led his troops onboard—twenty men in full body armor, each of them carrying a carbine and enough grenades to make them jangle as they jumped on board. He waved Chapel in last, putting him close to the hatch where he would at least get a good view of the ground. It occurred to Chapel that placing him there would make it convenient for Kalin to throw him out of the helicopter at altitude, if the need arose.

Kalin bellowed some orders over the noise of the screaming engines, but Chapel didn't bother translating in his head. He knew what his job was here.

IN TRANSIT: JULY 28, 06:14

From the air, from the crew compartment of the helicopter, Yakutsk was an island of concrete buildings huddling around the Lena River, surrounded on every side by close ranks of high pine trees that stretched away to the horizon. Here and there Chapel caught the reflection of moonlight on water glinting through the trees, but the pines were tall enough he couldn't ever figure out where the ponds and rivers were. He put his hand over his left ear and spoke to Angel through the hands-free unit in his right.

"Did you find it?" he asked.

"Sweetie, I'm a miracle worker, but some miracles are harder than others," she told him, sounding apologetic. His heart sank. If she hadn't found the information he needed, he was going to have a lot of explaining to do. "You asked me to find anything on Nadia's grandfather, but you couldn't even give me his name."

"He was a shaman who rode around on a reindeer," Chapel said. He forced himself to make a joke to cover how nervous he felt. "Did you try looking up Santa Claus?" He glanced north, over the endless landscape of trees. "I know *he* lives at the North Pole, and we're close here."

"Cute. But weirdly appropriate. Where you are now, they call Santa by the name Ded Moroz and he lives east of Finland. Believe it or not, his name basically means Grandfather Frost, and he's always accompanied by his granddaughter, the Snow Maiden."

"You're kidding me. You don't think she made the whole thing up—"

"I'd hardly put it past her," Angel said. "But at least this time, no, I don't think she was lying. I don't think she gave you a children's legend as her cover story. I looked back through her genealogical records. She had a grandfather on her father's side who was an accountant in Novosibirsk—there's lots of information on him; you have to love accountants for the way they keep such nice, tidy records. As far as her maternal grandfather goes, there's basically nothing. No national identification in the databases, no tax records, no death certificate, even. Not surprising if he really was a tribal shaman. Communications and transportation in Siberia were very spotty up until recently, and there's never been an accurate census for the more northern settlements. There are probably whole ethnic groups out there in the woods that don't even know that they're Russians yet, because nobody from Moscow has found them to tell them."

Chapel closed his eyes. "So you couldn't find what I need."

"I didn't say that. I did find something, but it's thin. I started poking around Nadia's parents' records. There was a lot more there. Her mother was a metallurgist, but she didn't start out that way. She was born in a village somewhere southwest of Yakutsk, an Evenk village where her stated occupation was 'herder.' She ran away from home when she was fourteen and ended up in Yakutsk—it's the only decent-sized city in a thousand square miles. That's where she got her training and where she met Nadia's father. She doesn't have a birth certificate, so I don't even know what the name of her village was—"

"That's starting to sound familiar."

Angel tsked him. "I'm working with obsolete database software in a language and even an alphabet I don't know. You're lucky I was able to find anything. Now, as I was saying, Nadia's mother doesn't have a birth certificate. But she does have a marriage certificate. And that certificate lists her father's name, Nadia's grandfather's name, and his place of residence."

"That's—that's amazing, Angel."

"Hold your applause. We know he was an itinerant shaman, that he moved around a lot. The village name on the marriage certificate might just be the last place he came from. But it's something. The name of the village was Gurangri. It's closest to a little town called Aldan, in the southernmost part of the Sakha Republic."

"Gurangri," Chapel repeated. He shouted over the noise of the helicopter's engines to Senior Lieutenant Kalin—the only person on board he was supposed to talk to directly. "We're headed for a village called Gurangri, near Aldan."

Kalin nodded and headed forward to tell the pilot.

Angel wasn't finished, though. "There is one problem. Gurangri isn't really there anymore."

"It's not?"

"In the nineties it was bulldozed, and then the land was strip-mined. It's a diamond mine, now. The native people were all relocated, a lot of them shipped south to Mongolia. Even if Gurangri was Nadia's grandfather's hometown, there won't be anything left there to connect her to him. No ancestral home, no relatives to visit, nothing."

Chapel shook his head. "That's not good. But you said that might just be the last place he came from."

He could almost hear Angel shrugging. "There are a bunch of other villages in the area. He could have been born in any of them, and anyway, when we talked about what to look for, we said that it might not be one specific place. You have some place to start, now, but that's the best I can do, I'm afraid."

"As usual," Chapel said, "you've been more helpful than I deserve."

"Just doing my job, sugar." Angel was quiet for a moment. "Chapel, if she's not there, if she's not within fifty miles when we triangulate her signal, you know this won't work, right? This is our only chance to find her."

"I know," he said.

"What makes you think she would go looking for her grandfather's village, anyway? She could carry out this blackmail plan from anywhere in the world."

"Sure. But she's a *Sibiryak*, a Siberian separatist. And when she told me she wanted to see her homeland again before she died, I think she was being sincere."

"You're saying she basically told you what her next move was, right before you were captured by her enemies," Angel pointed out. "We know she's lied about a lot of things."

"And maybe she *did* lie about this one," Chapel told her. "But I have to think otherwise. You didn't see the way her face lit up when she talked about her grandfather, about how he used to carry her with him on the back of his reindeer." Chapel shook his head. "I have to believe in this, Angel." He glanced around to make sure Kalin wasn't within earshot. "Because otherwise I'm all out of ideas."

GURANGRI, SAKHA REPUBLIC: JULY 28, 09:34

Midmorning, according to his watch. Chapel's body barely knew what day it was, much less whether it was natural that it should be morning now. He'd moved through so many time zones since leaving Washington that his internal clock had broken a spring.

"We should see the Gurangri facility soon," Kalin said, coming up behind his shoulder. Chapel had been glued to one of the helicopter's side viewports for hours, as if he was going to see Nadia down there in a clearing in the trees, waving up at him. As fast as they were moving and as thick as the tree cover was, he would have been lucky to see her if she had set out road flares to make an impromptu helipad.

They had followed a river for a while, a thin stripe of water the color of white wine that had twisted through the rough terrain of Siberia. After they'd left the river behind, the view hadn't changed much at all. Trees and more trees. Siberia seemed in some ways as desolate at the Kyzyl Kum, just more green. It didn't seem real; it couldn't be as big and as empty as it looked. He started to feel like he was flying over a miniature on a sound stage, as if those trees could be no bigger than ferns, and that Siberia was no bigger than a backyard garden.

Then he saw Gurangri, and the scale came back to him in a hurry. Angel had said the old village had been bulldozed and the land strip-mined. Chapel still hadn't expected this. Gurangri was a massive brown pit in the earth, easily two miles across. Its sides were terraced in concentric circles, the walls sharply rectilinear except where old mud slides had created meandering ramps down toward the bottom. Rusted digging machines stood on the various levels, dwarfed by the sheer size of the hole they'd gouged out of the earth. The lowest level was flooded and glared with an angry white light as the sun filled it.

It looked like a bruise on the side of the earth. Like a hole dug by a massive worm in a giant green fruit. It looked like Dante's Inferno, more than anything else. As the helicopter cut right across the middle of the pit, it was hard not to think that the pit was a giant maw about to swallow them whole. They wouldn't even make a fitting morsel for such a giant mouth.

All around the pit the excavators had cut short lengths of road, places where metal sheds and concrete buildings had once stood. Now these were all collapsed, their roofs fallen in and their walls crumbled down to debris.

"It looks like this place was saturation bombed," Chapel said.

He knew Angel would be able to see it even better than he could, through her eyes on the satellites. "It was abandoned around the turn of the century, when the diamonds ran out. The damage you see is just Siberia reclaiming its own—permafrost makes it impossible to build anything that lasts on this soil."

"Diamonds? They dug diamonds out of this hole?"

"There are diamond and gold deposits all over this forest," Angel told him. "Nadia wasn't kidding when she told you this was where Russia kept all its natural resources. There's probably oil and natural gas nearby as well—there's so much here, and so much land to cover they haven't even had a chance to survey it all."

Nadia would hate the pit mine, Chapel knew. It

would be yet another symbol of Moscow despoiling her homeland and taking all the profits. A village that might have meant something to her once had been completely wiped from the face of the earth to build this obscenity. She would never have come to a place like this. But beyond, on the other side of the pit, there were plenty more trees. Lots of forest to block your view of the gaping wound in your native soil.

"This is the place," Chapel shouted to Kalin. "This is where we start looking. Tell the pilot to take up station." It was time to lay the bait.

GURANGRI, SAKHA REPUBLIC: JULY 28, 10:13

The helicopter pinned itself to the air, hanging motionless over the center of the pit. Angel came on the line to tell Chapel she'd finished her satellite survey and there were three villages and over a hundred solitary houses within a fifty-mile radius of the pit. Nadia could be hiding in any of them.

The plan was to send a message over Angel's special frequency band, the same one Nadia had used to make her demands after firing the missile at Izhevsk. That signal couldn't be traced by normal means—it would be bounced around several satellites before it reached the Kremlin or Angel or anyone who could intercept it, and there was no way to trace it back through the electromagnetic labyrinth.

It had to be broadcast from the ground, though, beamed up to the satellites from somewhere. If Chapel was close enough to Nadia when she transmitted, his equipment could pick up the signal direct from the source. The signal would be faint when it came from the ground—it wasn't meant to be picked up by ground-based receivers—but it would be clear enough that it could be used to home in on her location.

Assuming, of course, that Chapel had picked the right spot. He needed a very strong signal to make the plan work, which meant he had to be within fifty miles of Nadia when she broadcasted. If he'd chosen the wrong spot, if she was more than fifty miles away from Gurangri, she might as well be on the moon. They would never find her.

"You all set, Angel?" he asked, staring out at the trees to the west of the pit mine.

"Go ahead. The next thing you say will go out on my band."

Chapel licked his lips. He'd considered very carefully what he could say—what would make Nadia respond. He knew that just calling to say hello wouldn't make her break radio silence. He had to give her something she wanted to talk about.

"Nadia," he said, "this is Jim Chapel. I know you can hear me on this band. I'm calling on behalf of the United States government. We know what you have, and the threat it represents. We'd like to discuss how we can help you. Please respond."

Chapel closed his eyes and waited to hear what came next.

Nadia had no way of knowing whether the Russian government would agree to her demands. The weapon she possessed—the Perimeter launch codes—made her incredibly dangerous to Moscow.

But the danger was even greater for America, since all those missiles were pointed at American cities.

If Nadia did launch, if she pushed the button, the death toll in America would mount to the tens of millions. Maybe the hundreds of millions. There was no way for America or Russia to stop all those missiles once they were in the air.

It was not out of the realm of possibility that the president might reach out to her, to try to find some way to defuse this situation. Hollingshead had actually gone to the White House to brief the president and see what he chose to do.

The president had responded that America refused to negotiate with terrorists. Judging by what Hollingshead had told Chapel, the commander in chief didn't believe that Nadia would actually launch. And he was willing to call her bluff.

So Chapel couldn't really offer Nadia anything of value. But he didn't need to negotiate with her, not really. He just needed to get her talking.

Chapel waited five minutes. The chop of the helicopter rotor sounded like an echo of his own heartbeat as the time ticked away.

When nothing happened after five minutes, Chapel nodded to himself. Then he repeated his message. "Nadia," he said, "this is Jim Chapel—"

The reply came before he could finish.

"Jim? Is that really you? You woke me up. If it is you, I don't mind. But I need to know it is you. I was certain you were dead. Tell me," Nadia said, "what was the worst part of our journey through the Kyzyl Kum?"

Chapel's eyes went wide.

He heard a click on the line. That, he knew, would be Angel shutting down the signal. She came back on a different frequency—he could hear the difference in audio quality. "Okay, sugar—give me a minute to crunch the numbers. It's better if you don't respond to her, just in case she has some way of tracking where *you* are."

"Understood," Chapel said.

He turned around and saw Senior Lieutenant Kalin staring at him. The man looked as patient but as insidious as a spider. As the seconds went by and Chapel said nothing, Kalin slowly raised one eyebrow.

He was ready, Chapel knew. There was no doubt in Kalin's mind what to do when word came in with Nadia's location. Chapel glanced around at the soldiers crouching in the helicopter's troop compartment. They'd been briefed. They knew what to do as well.

Just as soon as that location came in.

Chapel fought the urge to ask Angel how it was going. When she had something, she would let him know.

Maybe a minute passed. Maybe two.

When Angel came back on the line, Chapel nearly jumped out of his seat.

"Sweetie," she said, and he could hear it in the tone of her voice. He didn't need to hear what came next.

"Sweetie, I'm sorry. You're not close enough. I've got nothing."

GURANGRI, SAKHA REPUBLIC: JULY 28, 10:29

No.

No.

"No!" Chapel howled. He beat on the metal fuselage of the helicopter with his hand. He couldn't believe it—he'd been so sure. He'd been certain.

No. He'd wanted to be certain. He'd had one chance, and he'd convinced himself he knew how to finish this. But it had always been a crapshoot.

And now Nadia was going to get away. She had betrayed him, used him—seduced him—and now he would never get to her, never be able to look her in the eye and tell her—

"I take it," Kalin said, "that you were unsuccessful."

Chapel looked up at the man with burning eyes. "We weren't able to get a location on the signal, no," he said.

A playful little smile crossed Kalin's face. The man was enjoying this—enjoying watching Chapel rage in his moment of failure. Kalin had once had Chapel in his clutches, had been completely in control of Chapel, body and soul. Then Colonel Valits had come in and taken that away.

Now, that smile on Kalin's face said, things would return to their natural order. Chapel would be taken back to the hospital in Magnitogorsk. Kalin would use every method available to him to find out what Chapel knew. To break him down completely.

Chapel didn't care about that, though he knew he should. He knew what was in store for him. But his rage, his need for revenge, towered over any mere concern for his survival, any fear of what Kalin could do.

He'd been so close. He had screwed up, royally, by trusting Nadia, but he'd been given one chance at turning that around and now . . . now . . .

"Honey," Angel said in his ear, "maybe we can still get something out of this. I was able to track the signal enough to know that you were kind of right."

Chapel barely heard her. Kalin was barking orders at the pilots of the helicopter, telling them to turn around, to head back to Yakutsk.

"I picked up . . . something. Just an echo, really. But I can track her to an area of about a couple of thousand square miles, just based on that," Angel went on, whether anyone was listening or not. "I know she's no farther away from you than that."

Chapel looked down at his hand. It was balled into a fist. Maybe he could push open the side door of the helicopter. Maybe he could use that hand to grab Kalin, throw him down into the pit mine below—

"Sugar, did you hear me?" Angel asked. "She is in Siberia. I can verify that much."

The soldiers would open fire the second he grabbed Kalin. They would tear him to shreds with high velocity rounds. But if he was quick, if he moved now—

Wait.

"Angel? Say again?"

"She's definitely in Siberia. Somewhere near you, though near is kind of a relative term—"

"She's here?" he asked.

"Somewhere there, yes," Angel confirmed.

"Kalin!" Chapel shouted.

The torturer turned around to face him. "Yes?"

"She's here. Asimova is here, in Siberia. We just weren't quite close enough. But maybe—we can move the helicopter, and try for a second fix."

Kalin pursed his lips. He looked like he was weighing something in his head. Maybe the relative merits of avoiding nuclear war versus the pleasure he would take in turning Chapel into a sniveling, broken wreck of a man.

"You have failed us once," Kalin said. "Why should I think you would succeed a second time?"

Chapel shook his head. "We can find her. Still. We just need to get closer."

"And in which direction does this 'closer' lie?" Kalin asked.

It was a good question. A very good question. If Nadia was to the south, and Chapel ordered the helicopter to the north, he would waste this second chance. He needed more information. He needed to know roughly where she was, before he could find exactly where she was. Just like before, except this time he needed to be absolutely right.

"We are already nearing the operational range of the aircraft," Kalin pointed out. "We cannot stay airborne for more than an hour more."

"Then give me that hour," Chapel said. He couldn't bring himself to beg the man, but maybe logic would work. "One hour so we can save both our countries from burning up in nuclear fire. Do you really want to go down in history as the man who threw away the world just because he hated the man who could have saved it?"

"Please," Kalin said, sneering. "Such melodrama."

"If I'm wrong, one hour more won't make a difference. I'll be just as wrong then. I'll lose the protection of Colonel Valits, and you'll have me. But if I'm right—"

Kalin lifted his hands in resignation. "*Konyechno*. One hour."

GURANGRI, SAKHA REPUBLIC: JULY 28, 10:41

One hour to figure it out.

Less than that. A lot less. An hour in which to figure out the puzzle, get to the right location, and convince Nadia to come back on the line.

There wasn't enough time to get clever. He had to go back to his original intuition, the guess that had brought him this far. Nadia had returned to Siberia because she wanted to see it again before she died. She wasn't looking for pit mines or overcrowded cities, though. She would be looking for the land where she'd spent summers with her grandfather, riding around on the back of his reindeer.

He'd been an Evenk, one of the traditional ethnic groups of Siberia. Chapel turned to Kalin. "Where do the Evenks live?" he asked. "Do they have their own territory?"

"They do," Kalin said, lifting his shoulders. "The Evenkiysky District. It's west of here, over the border of Sakha."

Chapel nodded and touched the hands-free unit in his ear. "Angel, are there any villages in the Evenkiysky District? Any places that might have been there thirty years ago, where Nadia's grandfather might have been born?"

"More than a few, but they're spread pretty thin. That's an area of three hundred thousand square miles and less than twenty thousand people live there."

Talk about finding a needle in a haystack. "We know he lived in Gurangri once, back when it was an actual village. He can't have gotten very far from there if his chief method of transport was riding on a reindeer."

"You're probably right," Angel told him. He could hear her clacking away at a keyboard and imagined her fingers flying along as her screens showed one database after another, as she zoomed in on maps and then clicked away, zoomed in further on satellite pictures . . .

"Head west by southwest," she said, finally. "There's a cluster of villages about sixty miles that way—most of them just collections of tents, though some have permanent buildings. It's a little more densely populated there, north of Lake Baikal. But Chapel—even if she's somewhere in that cluster, you still need to get within fifty miles of her actual location. The cluster's spread over hundreds of square miles of terrain. She could be there and you still might miss her."

"Damn," Chapel said. He was running out of time and out of options at an alarming rate. "Angel," he said, "do we need to be stationary for you to get a fix on her transmission?"

"No," Angel said, and he could hear breathless excitement in her voice. "No—even if your helicopter was moving at top speed, I could still capture the signal. All I need is one packet of the direct transmission."

"So if we fly over this area, if we cover it from end to end and I can keep her talking long enough—"

"It might work," Angel confirmed. "It just might."

Chapel relayed his plan to Senior Lieutenant Kalin. The torturer didn't like it—already the helicopter was in danger of not having enough fuel to make it back to base, and flying at high speed would only drain the tanks faster. But he seemed to have accepted that this was the only way he would ever find Nadia.

The aircraft lurched as the pilot leaned on the throttle, and Chapel had to grab on to a stanchion or be thrown from his seat. Below he could see the forest hurtling by, just a green blur. After a few minutes, he had Angel set him up on Nadia's frequency again.

He took a couple of deep breaths. Forced himself to get into character. If his voice betrayed how much he wanted to catch Nadia, to avenge himself, she might shut down the broadcast immediately. He had to sound like he had the last time they'd spoken, in Aralsk-30. Like a man talking to his lover.

"Nadia," he said into his microphone, "you asked me a question. You asked me what was the worst part of crossing the Kyzyl Kum. I don't know what the worst part for you was," he said, "but for me it was probably having a giant lizard chomp my arm."

He heard a click and knew that Angel had muted his microphone. The helicopter's engines were screaming now—if Nadia heard that sound on the line, there was a small chance she might guess where Chapel was, and that he was close enough to be a threat.

Still, even with the mike muted, he made no sound. He held his breath while he waited for her to reply. Maybe he had waited too long before answering her. Maybe she already suspected this was a trap. If she was smart, she wouldn't transmit more than she absolutely needed to.

But no, he thought. She would think she was safe. Having stolen Angel's special frequency-hopping packet-switching whatever-it-was signal technology, she would know the Russians had no way of tracing her. She would know that only Angel, out of everyone in the world, had even the slightest clue how she was communicating.

Still, she took her time about it. Chapel had to let go of his trapped breath. He sagged against the fuselage of the helicopter, suddenly feeling very, very tired.

Then there was a click in his ear, and he heard Nadia speak.

Or laugh, rather. He remembered that laugh—it had always come to her so easily. "Jim, it is you," she said. "I'm so very glad you're still alive."

"That makes two of us," he told her.

IN TRANSIT: JULY 28, 10:59

"Jim," Nadia said, "how did you get out of there? The last time I saw you, you were down on the ground, and a Russian soldier was standing over you with a shotgun." She laughed again. He used to like that laugh. "I wept for you, because I was certain you were dead."

"They had orders to take us alive," Chapel told her. He tried to think of a cunning lie, something close enough to the truth she might actually believe it. "That shotgun was loaded with Taser rounds. One of them hit me in my artificial arm, and the silicone flesh protected me from the worst of the shock. I dropped to the ground and the soldier thought I was down, that he'd incapacitated me. I let him believe that. Once I took him down, there wasn't much left of the Russians to deal with."

"You're saying if Bogdan and I had come back for you—if we had doubled back—but instead we left you there, stranded . . ."

"Don't worry about that," Chapel told her. "Angel was able to get me some transport to the submarine." Maybe it could have gone down that way, if the Taser had hit him in his artificial arm instead of his chest. "But what about you—how did you get out of Kazakhstan?"

"Bogdan and I drove north, away from Aralsk-30. We were panicked. We thought that if you were not with us, your friends wouldn't pick us up. So we drove to a little oasis not far away and ditched the truck. I called Varvara and she had some of her friends come and get us and help us cross the Russian border—on camels, of all things. It was a frightening voyage but we made it."

"I would ask where you are now, but maybe it's better I don't know," he told her.

"I only wish you could be here with me," she told him.

He was dumbstruck by the idea. Did she have no idea how badly she'd betrayed him? No idea how he must feel about being used like this? He wanted to shout at her, to scream with frustrated rage, but he forced himself to control his voice. "Maybe we should talk some business," he told her.

"Yes, you said your president wants to help me," she replied. "I am a little surprised. I would have thought the alliance of your country with Russia would be too much damaged by such a thing."

She was right there. Though it could have gone a different way. He tried to imagine that alternative history, the one where he was actually negotiating with her. Making it up on the fly was tricky, but it had to be done. "Our top people considered that. They also considered the fact that if you launch those missiles, they're headed straight for American cities. We want to avoid that any way we can. Talk to me, Nadia. Tell me how we can get out of this with nobody pressing any big red buttons."

She must have wanted that, and badly. She must have been desperate for any kind of international recognition she could get—anything to put pressure on Moscow and make them bow to her demands. He could hear in her voice how relieved she was to think she had friends in Washington, even if she had to hold a gun to their heads to make them smile.

"Marshal Bulgachenko and I had this all planned out," she said. "We must obtain a United Nations resolution recognizing the sovereignty of the Siberian republics and their right to self-determination. The main barrier to this will be Russia's seat on the

Security Council, but if they can be swayed by diplomatic means . . ."

She droned on and on about politics. Chapel tuned most of it out—it meant little to him. He'd always been a good soldier, and good soldiers didn't worry about how the civilians brokered peace agreements. Good soldiers just prepared themselves for when those talks inevitably broke down. The main thing was that he'd gotten Nadia talking, and every second she went on was another chance to get a fix on her location.

Not paying attention to her, though, meant he was stuck inside his own head. Lost in there with his anger at her. *God, listen to her,* he thought. *She thinks this is all so reasonable. So possible. She betrayed me! She betrayed my country's faith! She used us, manipulated us, and now she thinks we'll help her finish what she started—*

"Jim? Did you hear that last part?" she asked. "It's crucial to building a lasting constitutional entity that recognizes the civil rights of all the disparate ethnic groups. Moscow won't like it because—"

"I've got to admit, Nadia, this is all a little over my head," he told her. "But keep going. This is all being recorded, of course, and I'll pass it on to people in the State Department who will understand it much better than me. In fact—"

There was a click on the line. Angel's voice cut in, stopping him in midsentence.

"Chapel," she said.

He froze, unsure if Nadia could hear him or not, unsure what Angel was going to tell him.

"I've got her," Angel said, her voice thick with emotion.

IN TRANSIT: JULY 28, 11:14

For a second Chapel refused to believe it.

"You have her location?" he asked. "Really?"

"Down to a resolution of about ten square yards," Angel told him. "You must have flown right past her. The signal was incredibly strong."

Chapel closed his eyes and said a little prayer of thanks.

"I've suspended your transmission to her," Angel said, "so she can't hear us talking. But I have her audio and she's asking if you're still there, if you're going to finish that thought. Do you want me to patch you back in?"

Chapel considered it. Nadia might get spooked if their conversation just stopped there. Then again, if he had to keep talking to her, chances were he would eventually lose his cool and start telling her what he really thought.

"No. And don't give her any sign why," Chapel told Angel. "Let her just think we got cut off by some technical glitch or something."

"Okay," Angel told him.

"Give me her coordinates," he said. "Tell me where she is, Angel. So we can finish this once and for all."

Angel relayed the latitude and longitude, minutes and seconds down to three decimal places. Chapel read the numbers off to Kalin, who relayed them to the pilot. The helicopter slowed way down and then banked into a wide turn—they had already passed Nadia's location, and they needed to double back.

"She's outside of a little village called Venaya, about seventy miles northeast of Lake Baikal. The village has about sixty people total, but the house she's at is far enough away that none of them have any reason to be out there. I'm guessing she's alone in the house, but I can't guarantee that. I *can* see smoke coming from its chimney. There's also a small single-prop airplane nearby, sitting on an improvised landing strip."

"A plane?"

"It's not surprising. There are no real roads anywhere near her—which isn't uncommon for Siberia. The permafrost devours anything less robust than a metaled highway every winter. For a lot of these villages the only way in or out is by air—or on the back of a reindeer."

There were places in Alaska that could only be reached by aircraft, Chapel knew, and probably for the same reason. No wonder this country was so sparsely populated. How long, he wondered, would it have taken the Russians to find Nadia, just searching door-to-door throughout Siberia? Nadia must have thought she had plenty of time—time to spin out her blackmail scheme, time to make the Russians do what she wanted.

Well, she was about to find out just how little time she had left.

Kalin ordered the helicopter to set down half a kilometer away from Nadia's location. Within another minute they were on the ground, and the soldiers started jumping out of the side hatch.

Time to go.

VENAYA, RUSSIA: JULY 28, 11:19

Chapel grabbed a stanchion and started pulling himself out through the hatch. Before he could touch his feet to the ground, though, Kalin turned and put a hand on his chest. "What do you think you are doing?" the torturer asked.

Chapel knocked Kalin's hand away. "I'm going in with your soldiers. I'm going to find her and make things right."

"I hardly think so. Do you honestly think I trust you around Asimova?" Kalin asked. "She has fooled you so many times already into betraying yourself. Why risk such shameful behavior again?"

"This time's going to be different," Chapel promised.

Kalin laughed. "You'll stay here, with the helicopter. We will not be gone for very long."

Chapel glanced at the soldiers already moving away through the trees. They were keeping low and staying silent, so they wouldn't alert Nadia to their approach.

He looked back at Kalin. Then he head-butted the torturer, hard enough to knock him right out of the helicopter.

In a moment Chapel was out, too, his feet making soft thuds as he ran across a carpet of pine needles as soft as a mattress.

He was pretty sure Kalin wouldn't shoot him. Not, at least, until Nadia was dead. Even afterward Kalin would want him alive just so he could torture him again. Nor would Kalin order his men to seize

Chapel—that would be too noisy, now when quiet was an absolute necessity.

He had no doubt that Kalin would find a way to make his life hell, but that was in the future. Right now Chapel had his orders from the director, and the only way to carry them out was to keep moving, to run as fast as he could—and get to Nadia first. Kalin would want to take her alive, for questioning. He'd want to make sure he got every last bit if information squeezed out of her before he let her die. Chapel's orders, on the other hand, were to kill her as quickly and as neatly as possible.

That would be tricky without a firearm, but he had learned long ago how to improvise.

He caught a look at the face of one of the soldiers as he sprinted past. The Russian looked more confused than anything else—Chapel passed him by too quickly for the man to register anger or curiosity. Chapel didn't slow down to learn how the soldier felt about an American spy running past him toward their shared target.

Soon he was past all the soldiers. They were taking their time, watching their backs. Chapel just wanted to get to the damned house. Before long he could see it up ahead, or at least one corner of it. It looked like it had been made of logs that didn't quite fit together, the gaps between the logs filled in with mortar. Its roof was high and peaked and covered in pieces of bark cut down to the size of shingles. He saw the smoke coming from the chimney. He saw it only had one window on the side that faced him, one narrow pane of glass.

He ducked lower until he was almost crawling,

then dashed up to the corner of the house and slid along its side until he found the door. Angel hadn't said if there was more than one door—most likely she couldn't tell just from satellite imagery. If there were two doors and Chapel came running through the front, he would need to move very fast before Nadia could escape out the back.

Well, he'd planned on getting this over with as quickly as possible, anyway.

He got his good shoulder into the door and burst through it, shattering the cheap lock that had held it shut. Immediately he dropped his head in case Nadia was armed, in case she started shooting as soon as she saw him.

As it turned out, she had something better than a gun.

VENAYA, RUSSIA: JULY 28, 11:22

"Jim," Nadia said. Her eyes were very wide.

Chapel took in every detail at once and had to sort through them. The house comprised a single room, with a cot on one side and a table on the other. Nadia was lying belly down on the cot, her feet up in the air behind her. She held her phone in both hands as if she'd been trying to make it reconnect to Angel's frequency. A short-barreled submachine gun lay on the cot next to her.

On the table was a laptop computer. Bogdan sat behind the laptop, clacking away furiously at the keys.

Chapel hadn't expected to find the Romanian

here. He'd assumed the two of them would have parted ways after Aralsk-30, that Bogdan's work was done. But of course it made sense. Nadia had been busy since then, setting up a secure line of communication and the ability to hack into the Russian nuclear arsenal. She would have needed some technical help for that.

Not that it mattered. Not in the slightest.

"Jim, I didn't think I would see you here," Nadia said, twisting around until she was sitting up and facing him. It was warm in the little house, and she wore nothing but a halter top and a pair of jeans. Her feet were bare. She looked good. She looked so good . . .

"You betrayed me," Chapel growled. "You used my country."

"Jim," she said, very carefully.

"You convinced me we were doing good. That we were going to make the world a safer place. When what you really wanted was to drive us to the brink of war," Chapel went on. He was on a roll now. "You—"

"Jim, stop," Nadia said.

"You've had your chance to talk. Now's my turn," Chapel said.

"No, I mean, stop moving." She carefully set down her phone and picked up the submachine gun. She didn't point it at him, but her meaning was clear. "I think you came here to kill me. Yes?"

"You betrayed me," he said.

"I lied to you, it's true. And now you want to kill me for it. But right now I have the gun. So let's all be calm."

He grunted in inarticulate rage and took another step toward her. Let her go ahead and shoot. It would only take him a second to get close enough, to get right up next to her and—

"If you're not afraid of this," she said, hefting the weapon, "then maybe I can stop you by telling you that Bogdan has the Perimeter software booted up and ready to launch."

That part of Chapel's brain which hadn't been overwritten by pure anger started to speak very loudly in the back of his mind, just then. It forced him to stop, for a second anyway, and turn to look at Bogdan.

"Is true, yes," the hacker said. He shrugged. "I can send the bombs. So be chill, man, yes?"

"He's got them on that laptop?" Chapel asked. "The codes you stole from Aralsk-30?"

"That's right," Nadia said. "So please, just stay calm. And don't move."

Chapel nodded and licked his lips.

He glanced around the room, seeing for the first time the rest of its contents. A pyramid of canned food in one corner. A wood-burning stove. A gasoline generator, its exhaust vented through the chimney, chugged away in one corner, providing power for the laptop. A thick cable ran from the generator to the laptop. If he could get close enough to pull that plug—but no, it would have battery power, still. Pulling the plug wouldn't shut down Bogdan's link to the missiles.

Chapel must have taken a step in that direction anyway, because Nadia jumped up and pointed the SMG at him again. "Please, Jim. Just don't move. Don't make me shoot you—I don't want to."

Through the anger that distorted his vision, Chapel could see that she meant it. She didn't want to kill him—she still thought there was something between them. Just how deluded was she?

Deluded enough, maybe, to launch a nuclear attack if he didn't do exactly as she said? He nodded and stepped back to the middle of the room, between her and Bogdan.

She must have caught a flash of movement outside the windows, then, because she jumped up and ran over to one and peered out. "Russian soldiers," she said, her breath catching in her throat. "You brought them here?"

"They've probably surrounded this place by now," he told her.

"Shit!"

Chapel nodded. "How exactly do you think this is supposed to end?" he asked her. "How long do you think they'll wait before they start shooting?"

"A very long time, if they know what they're risking," she said, ducking below the windowsill. She moved quickly around the room, to another window, and peeked out through that one. What she saw made her bite her lip in frustration.

Maybe it was just that—frustration—that caused her not to notice that Chapel had taken a step back, toward Bogdan.

"It wasn't supposed to be like this," she said.

"No, I can see that."

She looked deeply into his eyes, as if searching for something. Some sign that he could help her. Fix this somehow. She was still trying to use him. The thought made Chapel seethe.

She gave him a sad little smile. "If you call out to them, tell them I will launch if they do not fall back, perhaps—"

"Maybe," Chapel said. "Or—"

He had no intention of finishing that thought. He had just been talking until he saw the barrel of her SMG move away from his chest. The second it did, he swung around and brought his fist down hard on the screen of the laptop, smashing it down on top of Bogdan's hands.

The hacker screamed and pulled his hands back but too late. When he held them up, Chapel saw at least two of his long thin fingers were bent at unnatural angles. Another one twitched spasmodically. It looked like they were all broken.

Bogdan wasn't going to be typing with those hands anytime soon. He definitely wasn't going to launch any missiles.

"*Ogon'!*" Chapel shouted, to the soldiers outside— the command to open fire.

VENAYA, RUSSIA: JULY 28, 11:29

He had believed, when he ordered the Russians to attack the house, that he was willing to die in the cross fire as long as they took Nadia down as well. That he would give his life to make sure he got his revenge.

It appeared that some part of him disagreed with that calculation. He dropped to the floor, throwing his arm over his head, bracing himself for the noise and the chaos of a fusillade.

Just before he hit the floorboards, he saw Nadia staring down at him, a look of horror distorting her features. Horror and something else—disappointment?

Maybe she really had thought he would try to help her.

The cross fire he'd expected didn't come—but all hell did break loose.

Someone smashed a window and shoved a rifle barrel through. The door swung back hard enough to crack against its frame as soldiers rushed inside, weapons up and pointing in every direction. They were all shouting at once, and as Chapel peeled his arm back from his face he saw one of them grab Bogdan and throw him to the floor while another pair advanced on Nadia, weapons up, barrels pointed right at her face.

Kalin came rushing in, looking a little out of breath. He pointed at Nadia and barked out a rasping command Chapel couldn't follow. Nadia dropped her SMG, and one of the soldiers snatched it up.

"The codes," Kalin said. "Where are the codes?"

It took Chapel a second to realize that the torturer had spoken in English, that the question was directed at him. "On the laptop," he said. "It's all there."

Kalin nodded at one of the soldiers, and he grabbed the laptop off the table, yanking out its power cord. Bogdan moaned something in what Chapel thought was Romanian.

A smile appeared on Kalin's face. Chapel was surprised the man didn't start laughing maniacally.

"You," he said, in Russian now. "Asimova. You will come with me. I have some questions I'd like you to answer."

Chapel, still down on the floor, looked up at her face.

He could tell that she knew what Kalin was, and how he questioned people. A nasty pang of guilt cut right through Chapel—he had just delivered her into a fate worse than death.

She was a terrorist. She had betrayed him. Lied to him.

But nobody deserved what Kalin was going to do to her.

She must have decided she would rather go down in a hail of bullets, because before any of the soldiers could touch her, she spun around on one foot and delivered a perfect high kick to the chimney of the woodstove.

It came apart in pieces and sprayed soot all over the room. Smoke from the stove and the generator billowed out right in Kalin's direction and the torturer flinched. The soldiers all drew back, maybe thinking she'd set off a grenade.

The smoke filled the tiny room in an instant, making the soldiers choke and cough. Down on the floor Chapel had better air, but he couldn't see anything for a second as the powdery soot fell all around him. He heard the unmistakable sound of glass shattering and then, from outside, the staccato noise of assault rifles firing.

Even if he couldn't see anything, Chapel knew—she had made a break for it.

VENAYA, RUSSIA: JULY 28, 11:38

Chapel scrambled forward on his hand and knees and got over to the cot. The window above it had been smashed out of its frame, just as he'd expected. He put his hand on the cot and levered himself back up to his feet, even as the dust cleared and Kalin came storming across the room, waving one hand in front of his face. Chapel started to reach for the windowsill, intending to chase after her, but then he thought of something and looked down again.

The cell phone was gone. He remembered clearly how she'd set it down, very carefully, before picking up the submachine gun.

The gun was gone, too—she must have scooped it up before she burst through the window. That made sense—she knew there would be more soldiers outside, that she would have to fight her way clear. But the phone—she had had only a fraction of a second to escape. Why had she wasted time picking up the phone?

Something nagged at him, some memory that wouldn't quite rise to the surface. Maybe she had wanted the phone so she could contact Varvara and beg for help, for some means of escape. But she must have known that even Varvara wouldn't help a wanted terrorist—Valits had told him as much, that the top level *vory* in Moscow had turned their backs on Nadia. She didn't have a friend left in the world—so who did she want to call?

It wasn't like she'd felt some desperate need to play Angry Birds on her smartphone, or something—

Kalin peered out the window. "She won't get far," he said, in English. "And we have the codes on the laptop. The world is safe, yes? But until she is captured, this is still an embarrassment. And it is your fault, you know. Had you not attacked me and come running in here without—"

"Quiet!" Chapel said. He was too busy thinking to deal with Kalin.

Smartphone.

The world's most dangerous smartphone. He had it now. She'd told him, once, that all the data in Perimeter's tape banks, every bit of it, would fit in one small corner of a smartphone's memory.

You could put all the launch codes on a phone, and—

And Bogdan could easily have built an app that would let her launch the missiles with just a few swipes on her touchscreen.

"Shit," Chapel said. "Shit!"

"What is it?" Kalin demanded.

Chapel shook his head and pushed himself through the window. He caught himself with his hand on the far side, then pulled himself up to his feet and started running.

Much as he'd expected, there were wounded soldiers everywhere. Nadia might be a terrible shot, but with an SMG you could just spray bullets in a wide arc—you didn't need to aim. He saw one man lying on the ground, clutching his side, and without even being asked, the soldier pointed into the woods. Chapel dashed in that direction—just in time to hear a whirring noise like an angry lawn mower.

"No," he said, "no—Kalin, you didn't even bother to secure the—"

He stopped wasting breath on words, then, because he had staggered out into a clearing in the trees, a narrow lane cut through the woods that ran straight for about two hundred yards.

At the far end of that strip, Nadia was already lifting into the air in her little airplane. He saw the wings glimmer as she crested the trees and shot into the clear air, and then she was gone, out of sight.

Behind him Kalin came pushing through the trees, a look of utter annoyance on his face. "I think you have failed," the senior lieutenant said. "I think your mission, as Colonel Valits described it, was to capture her. And you did not. Now, you will return with me—to Magnitogorsk. To our hospital."

Chapel whirled on him, and every watt of frustrated, pent-up rage he'd ever felt burned from his eyes. "You fucking idiot," he said. "She has her phone."

"I fail to understand—"

"The codes are on that phone, and the means to launch the missiles. She still has the codes—and she's getting away!"

IN TRANSIT: JULY 28, 11:49

The helicopter swung by to pick them up from Nadia's airstrip, its wheels not even touching the grass as they jumped in through the side hatch. Kalin ordered the wounded to stay behind and wait for medical evac. He seemed annoyed that he even had to waste the time it took to let his uninjured soldiers on board. He stared at Chapel for a very long time before permitting him to climb in.

"It would be wise, I think, to leave you here," the torturer told him. "But I am afraid you would find some way past my injured men so you could run off. No, I will keep you with me, Kapitan, but only so I can watch your every move."

From the belly of the helicopter Chapel looked back at the wounded soldiers on the ground below. Those who could were standing, holding their weapons still so they could guard Bogdan. The hacker looked up, and for a moment Chapel met his eye. There was no rancor there, no accusation, even if Chapel had nearly crippled him. Bogdan looked like he'd expected things to end this way.

Chapel pulled the side hatch shut, and the helicopter lifted into the air without wasting another moment. "Neither of us is going anywhere until this is done," Chapel told Kalin. "What direction did she head?"

"South. I imagine she is attempting to flee to Mongolia," Kalin said. "There are Evenks there, a few of them, and they would certainly take her in. She knows we will not be able to send a major force after her there, for fear of angering the Chinese."

Chapel couldn't worry about the politics or what Nadia had planned. He just wanted to know how they were going to reach her. "Is this helicopter fast enough to catch up with her?"

Kalin sneered. "That old crate she is flying? We can spin circles around it," Kalin told him.

"Good—then this won't take long," Chapel said.

"It had better not. Thanks to how long it took you to find her, we are running low on fuel. Already we are down to our reserves. We can force her down, then fly to Irkutsk to refuel, but only if we catch her in, say, the next hour."

Chapel shook her head. "We can't afford to antagonize her. We have to talk to her, get her to surrender peacefully. Don't forget what she's capable of. She could start World War III at any moment. If she feels she has nothing left to lose—"

Kalin inhaled sharply. "I wish to bring her in alive, if possible. But this situation is straining the bounds of possibility. We will attempt to negotiate a surrender. If she does not agree, I fully intend to shoot her down. This craft carries a heavy machine gun that could shred her plane in less than a second."

"That might be all the time she needs to launch."

"A risk I'm willing to accept. I have specific orders—she is not, under any circumstances, to be allowed to leave Russian territory. No matter the cost."

Chapel stared at the man. "If she does launch," Chapel said, "if all those missiles fire at my country—you really think America won't shoot back?"

"*Konyechno,*" Kalin said. "But it will not come to that. She is bluffing."

Chapel turned away in frustration. "You're crazy," he said.

"I wonder, Kapitan . . . I have been chasing Asimova for many months. You knew her a few weeks. Which of us came to know her better? The real woman?"

"It doesn't matter what either of us knows. The risk is just too great."

"That is not your decision to make. Your part in this is already done. You brought me to her—now I will determine her fate."

Chapel moved to one of the round viewports on the other side of the fuselage. He couldn't get a good look forward, not without barging his way into the cockpit, and he doubted Kalin would stand for that. He desperately wanted to look where they were going, but . . . maybe he could get the next best thing. "Angel," he said, "I need some intel."

"Go ahead, sugar."

"Nadia just took off in a small civilian plane, a six-seater, it looked like. She's headed south. Toward Mongolia, we think. Can you pick her up on the satellites?"

"Give me a sec . . . something that small's going to be hard to zoom in on while it's moving . . . okay, I see her. And there you are, in your helicopter. She's got a good head start on you, but you're gaining quickly."

"How long before we catch up?"

"I'd estimate nine minutes," Angel said. "Sweetie, you said she's headed for Mongolia? If she is, she's got a long flight ahead of her. The border's about five hundred miles away."

"She has nowhere else to go."

"I get that. But it'll take her hours to reach the border, and that gives the Russians a lot of time to bring her down."

Chapel frowned. "The problem is, we're running low on fuel. She might still get away from us if we're not careful."

"You're not the only aircraft in Siberia," Angel told him. "Let me check something. Okay, sure. There's an air force base at Irkutsk, not that far from your location. There are three fighter jets being wheeled out onto a runway right now. Sweetie, the Russians are not going to let her get away. Those jets are designed to take down heavy bombers. They'll have no trouble shooting down a little plane like hers."

Chapel knew she was trying to be helpful. She was telling him that he could just sit back and let the Russians take care of his problem—finish his mission for him. She didn't know. "Angel—she has the codes. On her smartphone. She could launch at any time."

"Oh, boy."

"Yeah," Chapel said. "I'm willing to bet we hear from her very soon. I think she'll threaten to launch if they don't let her cross the border. And I know for a fact that my partner Kalin here won't give his bosses time to negotiate. We need to find a way to contact her, to start talking to her, right now."

"You don't think—I mean," Angel said. "If." He couldn't remember the last time he'd heard her at a loss for words. Finally she asked him, in a very small voice, "You think she'll do it?"

"I have no idea," Chapel said. She had lied to him about so many things. Lied about who she was, what she wanted. He had no way of knowing what she might actually do, when the time came.

He had to find a way to make sure she didn't have to make that choice.

IN TRANSIT: JULY 28, 11:56

"You're about a minute from catching up to her," Angel reported.

"And she still isn't answering her phone?" Chapel had asked Angel to open a line to Nadia, but so far without success.

"She might be too busy flying the plane to pick up," Angel pointed out.

Chapel shook his head. Across the helicopter's cabin, Kalin looked at him and raised an eyebrow.

"Her only chance is to talk . . . come on, Nadia. Come on!" He struck the fuselage with his hand. "She's got to have a plan."

"Are you sure? She wasn't expecting you to find her at that house in the woods. She wasn't expecting you to break Bogdan's hands. You seem pretty good at wrecking her schemes, now that you're not on her side."

"What are you saying, Angel? That I've betrayed her, like she did me?"

"Not at all," Angel said. "I was just pointing out that she had a plan, a solid one, but now it's messed up. Maybe she just panicked and ran."

Chapel almost started to say that this was Nadia, that she would always have a plan, but hadn't he just said a few minutes earlier he had no idea what she was capable of?

But he did know her, at least a little. He'd known where she would go to hide out and hatch her master plan. And he knew now that she would improvise something, come up with some wild, final scheme to achieve something before she died.

A sharp point of guilt stabbed him right through the chest. He thought of Bogdan, standing sullen and unsurprised amid his guards. What had he delivered Bogdan into? Kalin would take him back to Magnitogorsk, when this was done. The Romanian was hardly innocent, but he didn't deserve that.

And what of Nadia? She deserved something, some punishment for betraying Chapel, for holding the world hostage. But was it right to shoot her down just hours from the border, from freedom? At the very least she should be given a trial, a chance to speak for herself. Kalin was going to make sure that didn't happen.

Chapel couldn't let guilt get in the way of his mission. Director Hollingshead had ordered him to kill Nadia, to make sure this was truly over, with no loose ends.

Kalin cleared his throat. "We will begin negotiations," he said. "If she does not wish to speak, so be it." He picked up a microphone handset and nodded at the helicopter's copilot. There was a painfully loud squawk as the helicopter's loudspeaker system switched on.

"Asimova," Kalin said, and the name echoed like a thunderclap from the helicopter's undercarriage. "Set down immediately," the torturer said, in Russian. "This is your only chance for survival."

"That's your idea of negotiation?" Chapel demanded. "What about the launch codes on her phone?"

Kalin gave him a look of utter disdain, but then

he spoke into the microphone again. "If you have demands, they will be passed on to the authorities, but only after you set down at the nearest landing strip." He switched off the microphone. "Kapitan, you know nothing of dealing with terrorists. It is my entire line of work. Perhaps you will let the expert perform, now?" When Chapel started to protest, Kalin added, "I will not put ideas into her head. If she intends to threaten her way across the border, she must be the one to say so."

Chapel shook his head and looked down at the floor. He counted to a hundred in his head. Only when he'd finished did he speak to Angel.

"Any reply?" he asked her.

"None," Angel said, just as he'd known she would.

Chapel nodded. Then he stood up and went to the viewport in the side hatch. He couldn't see anything but trees, far below. He wrestled with the handle—it wasn't easy with only one arm—and shoved open the hatch, letting cold air rush inside the cabin. Some of the soldiers protested, but Chapel was already sticking his head out—he needed to see. He needed to see Nadia, or at least her plane, one more time before they shot her down.

Looking straight ahead he saw her tail assembly instantly. The helicopter pilot had moved up behind Nadia so close he felt like he could almost reach out and touch the plane. Neither aircraft seemed to be moving—it was like they were both hanging motionless in the sky, separated by just a short gap of air, while the world moved beneath them.

Chapel had a sudden idea. It was crazy, of course. No, more than that. It was stupid. But maybe it was better than just sitting in the helicopter and waiting for Kalin to open fire.

IN TRANSIT: JULY 28, 12:03

The copilot shouted something back at Kalin, and the torturer nodded. "We have enough fuel for another twenty minutes of flight. After that we must set down at Irkutsk," he told Chapel. "To be safe I will give her another fifteen minutes before I open fire. Though I think we both know already that she will not set down or speak to us. She must think I do not have the will to kill her."

"I guess she doesn't know you that well," Chapel said.

It was now or never, then.

"Kalin," he said, "does this helicopter have any rappelling equipment on board? Even just a hoist I can hang a line from so I could hot rope?"

Kalin almost smiled. "Nothing of the sort."

Damn. That would make things a lot harder. Still . . .

"Tell me you are not thinking—" Kalin began.

"If I can get on her plane, if I can get inside, I can talk to her. I can talk her down, I'm sure of it," Chapel said, even though he wasn't sure of anything. Expressing his doubts wouldn't help him make his case. "Look, if we could just get above her, get as close as possible, I could jump over."

"Utter folly," Kalin said. "You would fall."

"Maybe," Chapel admitted.

"You will fall and die for nothing."

"Or maybe I stop her from launching."

"Moving closer to her aircraft might be seen as an aggressive move," Kalin pointed out. His smile was getting wider by the second. Apparently Chapel's idea amused him. "She might launch if we approached like that."

"Yeah, well, that's a risk I'm going to have to take. Not to mention the risk of jumping out of this helicopter. I don't suppose you have any parachutes?"

Kalin laughed. It was not a pleasant sound. "Oh, Kapitan, you are not just a fool, you're a maniac as well. I admit I am impressed that you refuse to give up, even now."

Too dumb to just give up. Maybe they would write that on Chapel's tombstone. After he fell a couple of hundred feet into all those pine trees down there.

"It's a chance. It's worth doing. It—"

Kalin raised a hand for peace. "I will allow you to try," he said. Of course, that had been the real obstacle all along. Chapel was more or less Kalin's prisoner, and he couldn't take any action now without Kalin's say-so. Chapel was a little surprised Kalin had agreed to his plan. "I will allow it because it would amuse me to see you die. Either falling through the air, or on board the plane when I shoot it down."

Chapel glanced around at the soldiers in the cabin—but of course, none of them spoke English. "Just get me as close as you can," he said.

Kalin gave the pilot an order. He had to confirm it—the pilot didn't refuse, but clearly he thought the idea was insane. But eventually the helicopter started moving closer to the plane and lifted above it. Chapel watched the plane get bigger. When he'd come up with this idea, the plane had looked motionless in the sky, as if it were just hanging there. As they drew near, however, he saw it was moving quite a bit, side to side, up and down. It didn't matter how good a pilot Nadia might be, currents in the air would keep the plane from holding to a smooth course.

He tried not to look at the ground, at the endless expanse of trees. That wasn't where he was headed, he told himself. Looking forward, he could see the blue stretch of Lake Baikal, and then the plane came close enough it blocked out the view.

He studied the top of the plane as they approached. The wings were mounted high up on the fuselage, above the cabin, which gave him a good, broad surface to land on, but they were also made of metal smoothed down to reduce wind resistance. There was a radio antenna he might grab onto, though he wasn't sure it would hold his weight. He was just going to have to get lucky.

The helicopter pilot brought them closer, and closer still, until they were right on top of the plane, maybe ten feet above it. Chapel could have just stepped out of the side hatch and fallen onto Nadia's wings. If he slipped, though, it wasn't like he would get a second chance. "Closer," he called out. "As close as you can get!"

The helicopter sank a few feet in the air.

Kalin leaned out the side hatch to look down with Chapel. It occurred to Chapel that he could just grab the torturer and toss him out in that moment.

But doing that, as satisfying as it might be, wouldn't help him convince Nadia not to launch.

"Twelve minutes, Kapitan," Kalin said. "Best to go now, and not hesitate."

IN TRANSIT: JULY 28, 12:06

The wind that buffeted Chapel was cold enough to freeze the water in his eyes, if he didn't keep blinking. He would have to jump forward, ahead of the plane, or the wind would tear him off into empty space.

He went through all the motions in his head, all the different ways this could go wrong and how to avoid them. There was a lot he couldn't account for, though, plenty of variables he couldn't know in advance.

He braced his legs against the fuselage of the helicopter. Took a deep breath. Released his grip and—

Jumped.

The free fall seemed to last far too long, time stretching out as adrenaline flooded his veins, every neuron in his brain firing at once with one single message: what the hell did you just do? He hung there in the air with his legs and arm outstretched and the wing surface of the plane came looming toward him, a white cross like the X that marked the spot where he was going to die, the spot where he pushed his luck just a little too hard—

And then he hit, much harder than he'd thought he would, his whole body slamming against the top of the plane, his chin striking a rivet in the white metal that made him feel like he'd loosened his teeth. The hands-free unit in his ear popped loose and disappeared behind him, torn away by the wind. All the breath exploded out of him in a single burst, and spots swam before his eyes.

And then, over the whirr of the plane's propeller and the rhythmic thumping of the helicopter's rotor he heard a horrible, soul-crushing sound, a squeaking, squealing noise of rubber being dragged across metal.

His feet were sliding across the wing top, the soles of his shoes trying desperately to grip as the wind tried to push them off.

Chapel shot his hand out, trying to grab for the radio antenna.

It was too far away. He couldn't reach.

Desperately he tried to extend his fingers, to get even the slightest grip on the thing, but even as he strained and pushed he was sliding backward, his belt buckle grinding against the wing. He was going to slip off, he was going to fall—

Forgetting about the radio antenna, he looked desperately around him for anything else he could grab. One of his feet slipped over the back of the wing and there was nothing there—he brought his knee up, tried to get his shoe back on the wing, tried to push himself forward but only managed to speed up his slide, and then both his legs were hanging off the back of the wing. He splayed his fingers out, tried to hold on to the wing with just friction, knowing it was a losing battle, knowing—

He swiveled himself around, trying to get more of his body up onto the wing, and his hand went underneath, under the back of the wing surface. And touched something—yes, there! On either side of the plane a diagonal strut stuck up at an angle to support the weight of the wings, a thick bar of steel exactly the right diameter to be used as a hand-hold. He could just brush it with his fingertips, but if he shoved himself backward a little more, gave up a little more of his hold on the wing . . . yes! He grabbed it solidly in his hand, just as his body started to slip over the edge, faster and faster. If he fell from the wing, he knew his own momentum would tear him from the strut, so he rolled off carefully, getting his legs down, swinging them toward the plane. He couldn't see the landing gear but he kicked around until he got one foot on the wheel and pushed himself against the side of the plane.

His hand couldn't hold on to the strut for much longer. It was holding up almost all of his weight—his foot on the landing wheel couldn't get a stable hold. He brought his other foot up and wrapped his leg around the strut. That would hold a lot better than his hand. It gave him a chance to breathe, a chance to think of what to do next.

Looking around, he found the hatch on the side of the plane that would let him inside. It looked like it was miles away, but maybe, if he really extended his arm he could just reach it . . .

His fingertips brushed the latch, and the hatch popped open, torn backward by the wind. It bounced back and forth on its hinges, threatening to slam closed again. He was going to have to jump for the hatch, and there was nothing beneath him this time, nothing to catch him if he fell.

He knew there was no other option. He pushed himself off the strut, launching himself toward the hatch just as it flapped open again. His hand shot out and found something to grab onto and he pulled himself inside the plane, just as the hatch flapped shut and latched itself behind him.

He lay on the carpeted floor of the plane, in the leg well between two rows of seats, and just focused on breathing. It was quiet and warm there, so quiet and warm after the freezing sky of Siberia. He would just give himself a second, just rest for half a second before—

"Jim?" Nadia asked.

IN TRANSIT: JULY 28, 12:08

Chapel scrambled up onto his feet. He lifted his hand to show it was empty, then took a step forward between the two rows of seats.

Up ahead of him, Nadia sat strapped into the pilot's seat, looking at him over her shoulder. One of her hands was on the steering yoke. The other held her phone.

"Please," he said. "Don't do anything rash. I just came to talk."

"You jumped out of a helicopter and onto my plane to talk? Jim, that was . . . that was insane."

"That's my job. Doing stupid things for America."

She gave him a smile. It wasn't a match for the warm, excited smiles she used to give him, back when . . . before she . . .

He fought down his anger, his need for revenge.

There were bigger things at stake here than getting back at her. "Nadia, you've really painted yourself into a corner here. The Russians are going to shoot you down in about ten minutes if you don't start talking to them. You have to give them something."

"Do I?" she asked. She glanced back through the windscreen. "They seem to be backing off. I thought for a moment they intended to ram this plane."

"They're holding back right now. But they don't need to ram you. They've got a machine gun that can cut the wings off this thing."

She sighed. "Come forward. I can't talk to you over my shoulder like this and fly at the same time."

He made his way to the front of the plane and sat down next to her. There was no copilot's position, no controls in front of him. He wouldn't be able to fight her over who got to fly. Not that he even knew how, though he supposed Angel could talk him through it . . . damn. He'd lost his hands-free unit when he jumped. He could still call Angel on the phone in his pocket, but for all practical purposes he was on his own.

"Just—just put down the phone, for now," he told her. "Please? I know what you can do with that thing."

"If I put down the phone, you'll have no reason not to kill me."

"The thought had occurred to me," he said, before he could stop himself. "But I won't. I plan on living through this. If I tried something, you would lose control of the plane, and then we'd both die."

"Perhaps you think it would be worth it, after everything I did."

He closed his eyes and rubbed his face with his hand. Then he looked over at her and met her eyes. And realized he had no idea what to say next.

She kept the phone in her hand.

"Anyway," he said, "I've seen you fight. You could probably take me."

That made her smile again. There was a little more light in her smile this time. "Count on it." But still she didn't put down the phone.

"Okay," he said, trying to keep his voice calm. He had to think of this like a hostage negotiation— with three hundred and fifty million people, the population of America, as the hostages. "All right. You don't want to put down the phone. So tell me what you do want. Tell me where we go from here."

"You know what I want." She glanced through the windscreen at the helicopter, which was keeping station just clear of her wing tip. "It looks like I'm not going to get it."

"So what's your plan?" he asked.

"My plan?"

"You have one, don't you?" he said, as gently as he could.

"Oh, certainly." She laughed. "I did. But as usual, you came along and made it impossible."

"I—what? As far as I can tell I've just been along for the ride this whole time. I was there to help you make things this desperate."

"Come now," she said. "I won't believe that. You knew right away when you met me—you knew I was up to something. That's why you spied on me, isn't it? That's why you kept looking for the gaps in my story. It's why you seduced me."

"I didn't—wait, what?" Chapel asked, blinking rapidly. "I did what?"

IN TRANSIT: JULY 28, 12:12

"I didn't seduce you—you seduced me," Chapel said, very slowly, as if he was working out a complicated math problem. "You led me on, you used the fact that Julia had just dumped me—you knew I was weak, vulnerable—"

"You knew I was attracted to you," she said, "and you played hard to get, driving me crazy."

"You made the first move!"

"Only after you made me want you. And what about in the desert, in the tent, when you woke me to kiss me, then turned away?" She shook her head. "You were trying to weaken my resolve, and it worked."

"It . . . did?"

She looked over at him. "I would have told you everything. I would have brought you in on my scheme, even if it meant wrecking everything the marshal and I had worked to attain. Back in Aralsk-30, just before the soldiers arrived—I was going to tell you about Siberian independence, and stealing the launch codes. I was going to give you a chance to join me—or stop me."

Chapel's eyes went wide.

"I thought," she said, and clearly it took some effort to dredge up the words, "that I could go it alone. When I left Marshal Bulgachenko for the last time, when I went rogue, I thought I could live the rest of my life without any human comfort or warmth. It wasn't going to be very long, was it? But I had no idea what people need when they must face up to their own mortality. The loneliness was incredible. It was like winter had come and I knew the sun would never rise again. And then you came along. Jim, we were never going to be happy marrieds. We were never going to have children or a nice little house with a lawn you would mow every weekend. I knew that. But the thought of just having someone there, someone to stand beside me, someone to be with me at the very end . . . I suppose it is easiest just to say that I did not want to die alone."

Chapel forced himself to blink his eyes. It made him realize he'd been staring at her, unable to believe what he heard.

"When you called me, when you told me America wished to help me," she said, softly, "I knew it was a ruse." She shook her head. "It was just so good to hear your voice."

"Seriously?" he asked.

"When I thought you were dead . . . it was almost too much to bear."

Chapel couldn't believe it. Her feelings for him had been real? He'd been running on rage for so long, convinced she had seduced him to keep him in line, to keep him moving in the direction she wanted to go. But this changed everything—

He shook his head.

She had still betrayed him. Lied to him. Used him to forward her political cause. That hadn't changed.

"No. No. You lied to me from the start," he said. "You used me."

"I know you hate me, Jim. I understand why."

"Because you used me and my country to steal a weapon of mass destruction?"

"Yes," she said. "I won't deny it. I will say I did it for the best of reasons. To free my people from Moscow."

"Through an act of terror," he insisted.

"After all we've been through, you can't even call me a freedom fighter?"

"That's just semantics. What you did was wrong, Nadia. You put my entire country in jeopardy. And if you launch those missiles, the United States will be forced to retaliate—it's just the way things are. You'll destroy Russia as well. Some of our missiles are aimed at Siberia, you know."

"It's that clear, is it? There is no moral quandary in your mind. I'm one of the bad guys."

"As long as you're holding that phone, yes," he said.

She turned to face him. Looked deeply into his eyes. What would she find there? He didn't even know himself, anymore. Despite what he'd said, this situation was anything but clear. Would she find hatred still burning in him, or something else? Maybe just a wish that things could have been different?

She pursed her lips and looked back through the windscreen. Lake Baikal filled most of the view, now, as big as a sea, an ocean. Mongolia lay just a few dozen miles from its southern shore.

"I wanted to see this," she said. "This lake—it's the heart of Siberia. It is the deepest lake in the world, did you know that?"

"No," he said.

"Perhaps the oldest lake, as well. We—the

Sibiryak—we sing folk songs about the 'glorious Baikal sea.' We tell the story of a fugitive from the gulags who rowed across Baikal in a lard barrel, to return to his family."

"It's beautiful," Chapel said.

"Moscow wants to build a nuclear plant here. They'll have to relocate all the Buryat people, who have lived a traditional life along the shore for ten thousand years. Moving them is a small price to pay for development of the region, Moscow says."

"Nadia," he sighed, "we don't have time for—"

She reached over and handed him the phone.

IN TRANSIT: JULY 28, 12:16

Chapel closed his eyes and clutched the phone in his hand. For a second he just breathed deeply, releasing some of his pent-up tension. Then he ejected the SIM card from the phone and shoved it in his pocket. He took the battery out for good measure.

Only then did he consider the fact this wasn't over.

He took out his own phone and lifted it to his ear.

"What are you doing?" Nadia asked, staring at him.

"I'm going to tell Kalin that he doesn't need to shoot us down," he told her.

"Don't."

"Look, Nadia—we have to figure out some way to end this where nobody gets hurt."

"Unlikely," she pointed out. "Even if I were to put down at Irkutsk and surrender myself, do you think they would just let me go?"

He knew perfectly well that if Kalin took her alive, he would ship her to Magnitogorsk and make every day she had left a new kind of hell. He couldn't let that happen to her, not now . . . no. He wouldn't do that to his worst enemy.

Director Hollingshead had ordered him to kill Nadia. That would be cleaner than what would happen if she lived.

But he was still Jim Chapel. He was still too dumb to just give up. "There has to be a way—there has to be some way we can get you out of the country— you were headed for Mongolia, right? To the Evenk community there?"

She laughed. "That's an interesting idea. I wish I'd thought of it."

He stared at her with wide eyes. "That wasn't your plan? But then what did you think you were going to do?"

"Fly until they stopped me," she told him.

He shook his head. "No. No, I won't let you kill yourself." He switched on his phone. "Angel, do you hear me?"

"Loud and clear, sugar," the sexy voice said.

"I have the phone," he told her. "It's over—this can end now."

Nadia looked over at him with an expression of pure regret. He knew what he was doing to her— taking away her last, romantic gesture—but he refused to accept that she had to die. Not now, knowing what he knew.

"I'll connect you to the helicopter," Angel said.

He waited while she routed the call. In the silence he looked over at Nadia and wondered what he could have done differently. How this could have worked out, in a more perfect world. But what would that even mean? If she had come to the Pentagon, back at the beginning, and asked for his help, asked him to help her free her people—he would have declined. He would have said it wasn't in America's interest. That it wasn't his job.

Maybe, back in Uzbekistan, when she had told him she was a rogue agent, when he had tried to abort the mission—maybe if he'd stuck to his guns, he could have gotten her out of there, taken her to the States and gotten her asylum.

But she wouldn't have accepted that. She would have pressed on toward Aralsk-30 without him. She would have walked into the desert on foot if she had to.

Maybe if they hadn't gotten separated after they shut down Perimeter—

"Kapitan?"

On the phone Kalin sounded annoyed. As if Chapel was distracting him from important work.

"Senior Lieutenant," Chapel said, "I've recovered the phone. Asimova is no longer a threat. I want to talk about—"

"I'm sorry, Kapitan," Kalin interrupted, "this line is not very clear. I can't understand what you're saying."

"Kalin, don't be an ass," Chapel said. "I have the codes! This doesn't have to end badly for any of us!"

"Perhaps you should call back later," Kalin told him.

And then the connection went dead.

Nadia looked over at him with frightened eyes. "What did he say?" she asked. "What is he going to—"

Chapel jumped out of his seat, grabbing her to pull her down to the floor of the plane, as if that would make any difference.

At that same moment, the helicopter opened fire.

IN TRANSIT: JULY 28, 12:18

The Russian PKT machine gun could fire eight hundred rounds of 7.62 x 54 mm R ammunition every minute. Each of those bullets, which were as big as Chapel's index finger, left the barrel traveling 2,700 feet per second and carried more than 3,500 joules of energy. The PKT had been designed to chew through armored vehicles at a range of nearly half a mile.

Nadia's airplane, which was a civilian model made mostly of wood and very thin sheets of aluminum, had no armor whatsoever.

Kalin fired an entire belt of ammunition into the plane—two hundred fifty rounds—over the course of roughly nineteen seconds. The gunner was a soldier trained in airborne fighting, and the range was very short. All but a handful of the rounds struck the plane.

The majority of them struck the tail assembly, which was deformed by the impacts. Parts of it fell away completely as debris. Some of the bullets struck the wings, boring deep holes through the aluminum and breaching the plane's fuel tanks. Others entered the engine compartment and destroyed delicate and vital components.

One bullet struck the propeller, which was a carefully constructed piece of laminated strips of wood, hand carved and painstakingly shaped by a master craftsman in a factory in Volgograd. The propeller cracked and disintegrated instantly.

Seventy-three rounds found their way inside the cabin of the aircraft. These were able to smash out every piece of glass in the cockpit and destroy some of the plane's instrumentation. Other rounds lodged in the three rows of seats, which were actually some of the sturdiest components of the plane. Others were absorbed by the walls, floor, and ceiling of the cabin, and some passed through the plane and out its front end without meeting serious resistance.

Six rounds entered the volume of space where Nadia and Chapel lay in a heap in the leg well of the front row of seats.

Three passed close enough to Chapel that he felt them pass him by and heard them buzz like bees. One of them grazed his back, digging a trench through his skin and muscle tissue and causing blood to trickle down his side. One passed directly through the place where his artificial arm would have been, if Kalin hadn't taken it away.

One bullet entered Nadia's left side just above her navel, passed through her chest cavity and emerged from her right shoulder, at a substantially slower rate than when it had emerged from the machine gun's barrel.

The bullet went through one of her lungs. It missed her heart by a fraction of an inch, instead nicking her aorta, the main vessel that brings blood to the heart. Blood immediately began to leak into her chest cavity and found its way through the hole in her lung. There was additional trauma from hydrostatic shock and from broken fragments of her ribs, which moved around inside her chest like shrapnel.

It was not the kind of injury the human body was designed to survive.

IN TRANSIT: JULY 28, 12:19

The wind howled through holes in the fuselage. The temperature in the cabin had dropped twenty degrees. Chapel opened his eyes.

He saw Nadia's face, her eyes looking into his.

Blood speckled her lips.

"Nadia," he said. "Nadia, are you hit?"

"I think so," she said. Her voice was very small.

"Hold on," Chapel begged. "You're going to be okay—just stay with me."

There was blood on Nadia's face, but her eyes were still clear. They looked around at the devastation of the plane, then up at Chapel.

"Help me up," she coughed. Her breathing didn't sound good, but her voice was firm and strong.

"We shouldn't move you—there could be damage to—"

"Jim," she said, "we are falling out of the sky."

He got his arm around her and helped her slide back into the pilot's seat, not without a few screams of agony. Red bubbles popped inside her shirt and he knew that couldn't be good, but when she was sitting up, she gave him a smile.

Chapel forced himself to look forward, through

the void where the windscreen had been. He could see nothing but blue water. It was impossible to tell how quickly it was coming toward him, but he imagined it would be faster than he might wish.

Nadia reached out and tapped some of the controls—those that hadn't been smashed to pieces. She grabbed the steering yoke. "No power," she said. "No response from the rudder. I think the ailerons still work, but the elevators . . ." She pulled back on the yoke. The effort made her scream again. "Jim— help me."

He moved behind her, then reached around and grabbed the yoke in the middle, pulling it toward her. "You think you can still land this thing?"

Laughing clearly caused her pain, but she couldn't help herself.

"What I can do," she said, pausing now and again to cough up blood, "is allow us to crash at a slightly more shallow angle than nature had planned." She looked up at him. "Jim, you know how to swim, don't you?" She closed her eyes. "What am I saying? When I met you, you were about to go diving."

"You're going to try a crash landing on the lake?"

"There is no choice in that," she told him.

"But this isn't a seaplane—it'll sink like a rock."

"Yes."

Chapel shook his head. "There has to be—there must be another—"

"Jim, you should learn a little Slavic fatalism. What goes up must come down, yes? *Konyechno*."

She wrestled with the yoke in silence for a while. A band of sky appeared over the water ahead of them, but only the merest line of light blue.

"The water will be very cold," she told him. "You must be careful of hypothermia."

"We'll hold on to each other, to share our body heat," Chapel promised her.

"I wonder," she said, "if in a hundred years, will the Sibiryak sing folk songs about the woman who flew into Baikal? I wonder if they will be free, then."

"Nadia, I'm going to get you to shore, we'll find a doctor—"

"Jim," she said, "this is what I wanted from you. Not professions of love, not poems and flowers. Just that you would be with me at the end. Holding my hand. You must strap yourself in—the landing will be very rough."

He started to protest, but he knew she was right. He strapped himself into the seat beside her. Then he reached over and took her hand.

They hit the water fast enough that the wings tore off the plane. Water flooded in through the broken windscreen, a great wave of it smashing over Chapel, almost cold enough to stop his heart. It filled his mouth, crushed him back in his seat. Water filled the cabin almost instantly, and he clamped his mouth shut to hold on to a desperate breath. His hand was yanked free of hers by the wave. He wrestled with his straps, got loose somehow. He reached for her, found her face.

There was nothing left in her eyes.

He waited—almost too long. But in the end he kicked his way out through the windscreen, kicked his way to the surface until his mouth and nose crested the water and he could suck in another breath.

Lake Baikal is one of the world's clearest lakes. He could look down and see what remained of the airplane, slowly shrinking below him, for a very long time. He watched it go—until the very end, her *svidetel*. Her witness.

UST-BARGUZIN, RUSSIA: JULY 28, 13:17 (IRKT)

The crew of a fishing boat dragged the one-armed American out of the water and took him back to shore. There the fishermen wrapped him in a blanket and left him sitting on the dock, because he said he wanted to stay by the water. He was shaking with cold and bleeding from several wounds. The fishermen called in the local policeman to talk reason to this American stranger. But the policeman just threw up his hands. Of course the American did not have to go to the hospital, if he did not want to. "*Konyechno*," he said.

The American looked up at him with a gaze so piercing it made the policeman flinch. "You are Siberian?" he asked, in a deplorable accent.

"*Ya Russkiy*," the policeman replied, *I am a Russian*.

The man from the lake said nothing. He just went back to looking over the water.

Most of the people who had come to take a look at the stranger went back to work. A few children stayed down by the docks, playing on the cold shore, shooting each other with finger guns, swooping around with their arms out like the wings of airplanes.

The policeman came back a while later with

a mug full of some yeasty-smelling yellow liquid. "*Kvass*," he said.

"What's it made of?" the man from the lake asked.

"Fermented bread. I put raisins and lemon in it," the policeman told him. "It will help you regain your strength."

The man from the lake grimaced—clearly he was no Russian—but he drank down the contents of the mug. Then he ate the raisins from the bottom. The policeman smiled. He took off his hat and ran a hand over his close-cut hair. "I have called the pertinent authorities, I thought you should know. They are sending someone."

The man from the lake just nodded. "It will be a man in a black suit, who comes here to kill me," he said.

The policeman started to protest—it was his job to protect people from being killed, not help the killers, but the man from the lake held up his hand in protest.

"You have done the correct thing," he told the policeman. "I am an enemy spy. The man in the black suit is FSB."

The policemen nodded sagely. "Ah, I see. You are crazy." That explained a great deal. Though not, perhaps, how the man got in the lake in the first place. "You . . . you are a madman, yes?"

"*Konyechno*," the man from the lake said, and he gave the policeman a weak smile.

But a little while later a helicopter landed on the rocky beach. It drove the children away like frightened gulls, though they did not go far—mostly they ran for the shelter of the pilings under the dock.

The helicopter took its time setting down. The

pilot could not seem to find a flat surface to put his wheels to. Eventually, though, he did find the right patch of rocky ground, and the rotors spun down with a sad whine. The side hatch opened and a man stepped out, then started walking smartly toward the dock and the man from the lake. The policeman watched with his hands laced across his stomach, unsure of what he should do.

He was especially confused because the man who jumped out of the helicopter was not wearing a black suit. Instead he had on a very grand military uniform, with many medals and golden insignia, some of which identified him as being a colonel in the Strategic Rocket Forces.

Maybe, the policeman thought, the man from the lake really was a foreign spy.

The colonel took the man from the lake away. Together they boarded the helicopter and flew off. Eventually the children came out from under the dock and started to play again.

The policeman wondered if he would ever know what that had all been about. In the end, he shrugged, because he knew the answer. "*Konyechno, nyet,*" he said to himself. Of course not. That wasn't how things worked.

THE PENTAGON: AUGUST 13, 14:06 (EST)

Director Hollingshead fiddled with a loose bit of thread on one of his sleeve buttons. "My apologies, son, for, well. For your having to take the long way home."

Chapel said nothing. There had been a lot of paperwork and rooms full of arguing people, back in Russia, before he was finally allowed to leave. Bureaucracy was the same everywhere, it seemed. Colonel Valits had made sure he didn't slip through the cracks. He'd been a man of his word—once Nadia was dead, he made sure Chapel got to go home.

The mission was over.

"Not, altogether, ah, a glorious success," Hollingshead said. "Would you agree?"

Chapel stood at attention, just inside the door of the converted fallout shelter that Hollingshead used as his office. The old man was sitting in a leather-covered armchair across the room. He had not, so far, ordered Chapel to be at ease, nor asked him to come any farther into the room.

"Sir, yes, sir," Chapel said. He was back in uniform, which always made him feel a little better. One sleeve of his tunic was pinned up at his side, because he had yet to be issued a new prosthetic arm.

"The Russians, of course, won't speak of what happened. Ever, well, again," Hollingshead went on. "I don't think diplomatic relations will be affected, but . . . you know. How these things . . . well."

Rupert Hollingshead had a cast-iron spine—Chapel had seen him give orders that would make a normal man's blood run cold. He was one of the most powerful spymasters in the American intelligence community.

When he stammered, when he hemmed and hawed and put on this absentminded professor act, it was just that—an act. Designed to either put people at their ease or fool them into thinking he was as ineffectual as he looked. He looked like a jovial old Ivy League academic, but it had been a long time since he had acted like one when he was alone with Chapel. His performing like this now worried Chapel very much.

"Sir, if you would like my resignation, I will have it for you by—"

Hollingshead took off his glasses and stared openmouthed.

"Resignation?" he asked. "Son, what exactly are you suggesting?"

"I failed you, sir," Chapel said. He was speaking a little too candidly for protocol, but he supposed there were times when you had to be honest. "I allowed myself to be emotionally compromised by Asimova. I put my country at risk as a result."

Hollingshead shook his head. He dropped one arm over the side of his chair and let his glasses dangle there. He cleared his throat noisily.

Only then did he speak.

"Son, if she fooled you, well . . . she fooled me first."

Chapel said nothing.

"Oh, for Pete's sake," Hollingshead said, jumping up from his chair. "Come inside and sit down. I'm not a dragon you need to beard in its lair. Let me fix you a drink."

It was then that Chapel realized the jovial professor act hadn't been for his benefit at all. It had been Hollingshead's way of attempting to deal with his own guilt and doubt. Once the drinks were poured and handed out, Hollingshead put his glasses back on and studied the contents of a manila folder for a while. "You accomplished all the tasks I set for you.

You rendered Perimeter nonfunctional, and from all our chatter analysis it looks like they don't even know what you did—which means they won't know the damned thing is broken, so they won't try to fix it. They think Asimova went to Aralsk-30 only to steal the codes, not to rejigger the computer."

"So the system is really down?" Chapel had wondered about that. He only had Bogdan's word that Perimeter had been sabotaged—the Romanian might have spent all that time at the terminal just playing *Minesweeper* or something.

"There's really no way to tell, of course," Hollingshead replied. "Ah, well, there is one way. We could nuke Moscow and see if their missiles all launch automatically."

"Sir, with all due respect, I think that kind of testing would be counterproductive," Chapel said.

It had been meant as a joke. Hollingshead laughed, though not very convincingly. "Asimova is also dead. I ordered that, as well, didn't I?"

"Yes, sir."

Hollingshead nodded. "I'll have to live with that for the rest of my life. That I ordered the execution of that charming young girl. Of course, they never found her body. Baikal is the world's deepest lake. It would take them years to search the bottom, to find her bones. I doubt they'll make the effort." He glanced at Chapel out of one eye, as if trying to catch him in some compromising facial expression.

There was nothing there for him to find.

"I watched the plane go down. I nearly drowned myself. There was no way for her to survive—even before the crash, she was dead, I think."

Hollingshead nodded agreeably. "Case closed, then. The Russians don't wish to talk about it—I suppose we do the same."

"Very good, sir."

"There are a couple of loose ends, of course, but we'll just get those out of the way. There was a bit of a media to-do in Russia. A couple of Siberian journalists saw a military helicopter shoot down an unarmed civilian plane. There have been . . . inquiries. A man named Pavel Kalin, formerly a senior lieutenant of the FSB, has been stripped of his rank and forced to resign. He hasn't been seen in nine days."

"Is he dead, sir?" Chapel asked.

"No way to know. They may just be keeping him out of sight until the media flap blows over." Hollingshead turned to a new page of his dossier. "Then there's Bogdan Vlaicu, a Romanian national. He was detained by the authorities on July the twenty-eighth. Officially, he's never mentioned again in any documents."

Chapel closed his eyes. Bogdan hadn't deserved what he got. Broken fingers—and the promise of a lot worse. Even if Kalin was out of the picture, somebody would have Bogdan now. Someone would be torturing him, trying to figure out what he'd done at Aralsk-30. He could still unravel the entire mission.

"We did, however, pick up a rather strange transmission from the Russian department of prisons," Hollingshead said. "It appears a prisoner matching Vlaicu's description was being transferred to a high-security facility outside of Magnitogorsk, under heavily armed guard. But when his transport arrived in that city . . . there was no one in the back."

Chapel couldn't help himself. He flinched in surprise.

"Apparently there was a computer error involved. The prisoner was put on the wrong vehicle or something . . . it's unclear. What is known is that he's now missing and presumed at large. Both Russia and Interpol have him on their most wanted lists, but no one's reported a single clue as to his whereabouts. You couldn't be any help in that investigation, could you, son?"

"Sir, I can honestly say I have no idea where he might go," Chapel said. And for once in his life it was pure, unvarnished truth.

Go, Bogdan, go.

Hollingshead closed the folder. "Good enough. Finish your drink, then be on your way. I'll have a new assignment for you soon—Angel will give you the details."

Just like that.

Neat, clean, tied up in a ribbon.

Done.

Chapel finished his drink and turned to go. From behind him, before he could open the door, Hollingshead made a little noise of surprise, as if he'd just remembered something.

"Oh, son," he said, "one thing—when Asimova handed you her phone, on the plane."

"Sir?"

"You had all the Russian nuclear launch codes in your hand. That must have been a frightening prospect."

"Yes, sir," Chapel admitted.

"You know, if we had those codes now . . . well. There are a number of things we could do with them, you see. We could learn a bit from them, and in the case of an emergency they might come in handy."

Chapel stood very still and thought for a moment. Thought about what he should say next. He had, of course, known the value of that smartphone. He'd known how much the Pentagon would like to have had it. He had known it was his duty as an officer of military intelligence to smuggle it out of Russia.

But nobody should have that power.

Nobody.

The smartphone—and its crucial SIM card—were at the bottom of Lake Baikal. The deepest lake in the world. They would stay there forever.

"When you fight a hydra, sir," he told Hollingshead, "it may be tempting to let one of the heads grow back. But you can't, can you?"

"No, son, no," Hollingshead said. He shook his head and smiled, a little smile of self-deprecation. "No, you burn it down to the stump."

"Exactly, sir," Chapel said. And then he did leave.

EPILOGUE

Julia Taggart closed up her office after her last consultation—a poodle whose nails had been clipped too short—and headed out the front door, intending to go home and . . . do something. Maybe there would be dinner involved. There would certainly be a television there. She watched a lot of TV these days, mostly just so her apartment wouldn't sound so empty.

Before she could take a dozen steps toward the subway station, though, a man came walking up the street, waving and calling her name.

Her heart sank when she saw him. She knew him—they had met one time before.

"You'd better come inside," she said, because she didn't want anyone to see her talking to him in the street.

He was very tall and very thin, with short hair that managed to look messy. He wore a sweater vest and tie, even in the oppressive heat of August in New York City. He always smiled, even when it was ridiculously inappropriate.

He'd never given her his name. She knew perfectly well what that meant.

"I did what you said," Julia told him. "I broke up with him. Why can't you leave me alone, now? I haven't even spoken to him in months."

"Yeah, sure," he said, showing lots of teeth. "And your country appreciates that."

He had said he would out Chapel. Reveal his identity to the media, release all the details of his missions to any reporter who wanted to listen.

For someone with as many enemies as Jim Chapel, that would be a death sentence.

He'd said the only way to make sure that didn't happen was if Julia cut all ties with Chapel—refused to ever see him again.

She had demanded to know why. The little man said that her relationship with Chapel was a liability and could compromise his effectiveness. It was an obvious lie, but Julia had never gotten any more out of him.

She had wrestled with whether or not to do what he said. In the end she'd decided she loved Jim enough to make the sacrifice. To keep him safe. She had walked away.

Done exactly what this man had asked.

"Well, then, what the hell do you want now?" Julia demanded, back in the office that was starting to warm up already since she'd turned off the air-conditioning. A bead of sweat started rolling down the back of her blouse. She didn't want to be here. She wanted to be free of it all. Even before he'd come to her, she had wanted to be free, away from the web of secrets, the uncertainty, the never knowing. She might have broken up with Chapel on her own. It was the main reason she hadn't told this little creep to go fuck himself.

She had to admit, though, she'd been scared. The kind of people Chapel worked for could do things to you. They could make you disappear, if you didn't do what they said.

"Did Rupert Hollingshead send you?" she demanded now.

The little man's smile just grew. "That's kind of funny, actually. That you would think that. No, I'm with a different agency. I'm a civilian."

"CIA?"

The little man just smiled. She wasn't going to get an answer there.

"Listen, I just came by to show you something." The little man took a piece of paper out of his pocket. It was folded untidily into a little, thick square. He unwrapped it fold by fold and then handed it to her. She saw it was a printout of a photograph. It was black and white and the resolution wasn't very good, but she could make out what it showed all right.

It showed two people standing on what looked like a hotel balcony. One of them was Chapel, definitely. She didn't know the other one—a woman with black hair, wearing a very skimpy nightgown.

In the picture Chapel was . . . touching her.

He had his hand in her panties.

Julia put a hand over her mouth, because she didn't want the little man to see her reaction to the image.

"That was right after you dumped him," the little man said. "Can you imagine? He couldn't even wait for a decent interval."

She threw the piece of paper back at him. "What the hell is your problem? Why would you show me this?"

"I just wanted you to know you made the right decision," the little man said. Her anger seemed to surprise him. "I wanted you to see what kind of man Jim Chapel is."

"Get out," she said. "Get out! And never come back!"

The little man ducked his head—it wasn't quite a nod—and headed for the door. "I'm sure I'll be seeing you again," he told her.

She just stared at him, her emotions so large they threatened to turn her inside out.

"I'll be looking forward to it," he said.

Turn the page for an early look at
the next heart-pounding Jim Chapel
mission from David Wellington

THE CYCLOPS INITIATIVE

Coming soon from William Morrow!

PROLOGUE

There was no sound.

Not that there was anything to hear, 10,000 feet up, except the faint scratching hiss of the wind as it spilled across carbon fiber control surfaces. Riding high on a column of warm air the old predator's engine barely ticked over. It was very good at conserving its energy. It was very good at waiting patiently. Waiting and watching with its single, unblinking eye.

Chuck Mitchell was asleep at his post.

He had the best of all possible excuses. His wife had given birth to a beautiful little girl three weeks ago. Mitchell hadn't slept more than a couple of hours a night since—he'd been far too busy sitting up at night next to the crib, watching her squirm and wriggle, counting her ten perfect fingers, her ten perfect toes.

But if anyone needed to be awake at his job, it was Mitchell. He worked at the busiest port in America, scanning cargo containers as they passed through on their way to grocery stores and warehouses and schools across the country. It was his job to oversee the PVT gamma ray monitor. All day long cargo containers passed through his station, one every few seconds—more than sixty million a year. They went under a giant yellow metal arch and came out the other side and nine hundred and ninety-nine times out of a thousand, nothing happened.

That thousandth time Mitchell very much needed to be on top of his game. Because the PVT scanner checked those boxes for signs of radioactivity. The yellow arch was essentially a giant Geiger counter.

So Mitchell did his best to fight the tide of sleep that kept washing over him. He mainlined coffee. When that wasn't enough he would jab himself in the leg with a pen—anything to make him wake up.

It was a losing battle.

The cargo containers were all the same. They didn't stay in front of him long enough for him to even know what was inside them. The noise of the giant rolling belt that carried the boxes was a droning, repetitive sound that lulled him to sleep. Staying awake was just about impossible.

There was only one thing that could possibly yank him back, one sound.

A steady, persistent ticking. The sound he heard in his nightmares. The sound the detector made when it picked up stray gamma radiation.

Mitchell's eyes shot open. He nearly fell off his chair. Without even thinking about it he slammed his palm down on the big red button in front of him, stopping the belt, freezing the cargo container in place under the arch.

The ticking sound didn't stop.

The old predator could see in color, though the early light made everything the same three drab shades of gray. Below, in the sprawling yard, the boxes stood in endless ranks, bluish-gray and reddish-gray and yellowish-gray. The predator's eye swiveled back and forth in its socket as it read the numbers printed on the top of each box. This took longer than it should have.

The drone was an old model, one of the first wave of UAVs to see real action. It was obsolete now, and it had been declawed—stripped of its weaponry and most of its fancier software. It should have been decommissioned a year ago.

But it could still fly. It could still loiter up there, so high up it looked like just another bird, a speck against the blue sky. It could still see—its camera eye had not grown near-sighted over the years.

It still had one more mission in it.

Mitchell's hands shook as he pulled a lead-lined vest over his shoulders. The same kind dentists wore when they took x-rays of your jaw. He jumped down from his station and took a hesitant step toward the cargo container.

The PVT equipment kept ticking away.

Mitchell knew that most likely this was a false positive. There were all kinds of things that gave off gamma rays—everything from fertilizer to kitty litter to bananas. The chances that this box was full of, say, weapons-grade plutonium were vanishingly small.

He waved his hand-held scanner over the box's bar codes. If the bill of lading said it was full of kitty litter he would have a little laugh and go back to his chair and fall asleep again. It had to be kitty litter, right?

The box's forms all claimed it was full of plastic water bottles.

Someone had shipped this box with counterfeit paperwork. Somebody had wanted to make sure nobody knew what was really inside.

Mitchell closed his eyes and tried hard not to panic. Was this the moment he'd trained for? He'd never actually seen radiological cargo come through his post before. It had just never happened. But when he took this job he had known it might.

His duties at this point were clear. He was supposed to alert his superiors and then open the box and make a visual inspection of its contents.

Mitchell licked his lips because they were suddenly very dry.

If he did what his job required, if he popped the seals on that box, he might expose himself to the radiation inside. Most likely it wouldn't be enough to actually hurt him. Most likely it would be like getting a single chest x-ray, nothing that would have long-term effects on his health.

Most likely.

There. The number the drone had been sent to find. It was printed on the top of a cargo container near the docks where the big ships came in, a box sitting underneath a yellow arch.

The drone shifted its control surfaces a few degrees, turned about on its circling course. Then it put its nose down and opened up its throttle, launching itself into a powered dive.

"I can't," Mitchell said, aloud. "I just can't. Not with the baby . . ."

He stared at the box, knowing what he was supposed to do. Knowing he would probably get fired if he didn't do it.

Knowing he couldn't.

If he got sick now, if he couldn't work, who would take care of his perfect little girl? His wife had quit her own job to look after the baby. If he got sick—

He would go and find his supervisor, go and explain. He turned on his heel and started to walk away from the box, away from—

He didn't get very far.

The drone weighed nearly five thousand pounds. It had a top speed of three hundred miles an hour. Dropping out of the sky like a javelin it was moving even faster than that when it struck the cargo container.

Its eye hit the steel side of the container and shattered in a million shards of glass. Its nose, made of carbon fiber and Kevlar, disintegrated on impact.

But its wings were edged with pure titanium. They smashed into the container with enough force to tear through the box's metal walls, to pulverize its contents and send them flying, a thick roiling column of powdered metal that hung glittering in the air until the wind caught it.

The noise of the impact could be heard five miles away.

"Oh God, no, please," Mitchell whimpered.

He couldn't hear his own voice. His ears weren't working.

He was down on the concrete and he felt like half

his face had been scraped off. There was blood on his cheek, wet and hot. He struggled to get up and saw pools of burning jet fuel all around him, saw chunks of dull gray metal strewn everywhere.

That wasn't the worst of it. Something had hit him in the back. Something hard and sharp. His first thought had been that he'd been struck by a bullet, but it had been much bigger than that and it had knocked him down like a giant hand pressing him against the floor.

Whatever it was, it was still back there. He was— he was impaled on it.

Blood was pouring from his stomach. From where the piece of debris had punched right through him—and the lead vest he wore. He'd been so worried about radiation. That didn't seem so terrifying anymore.

In the distance he heard the sirens of emergency vehicles, coming closer.

He wondered if they would make it in time.

He wondered if he would ever see his little baby girl again.

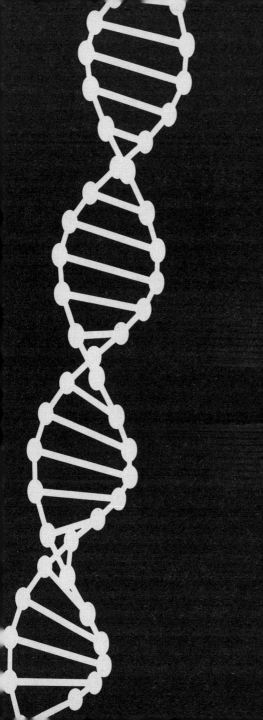

PART I

"If I were you," the marine said, "I'd think real careful about my next move. There's a lot riding on this."

Jim Chapel stared the man right in the eye. As usual, there was nothing there. Years of clandestine missions in the Middle East had given Marine Sergeant Brent Wilkes total control over his facial expressions. The man just didn't have a tell as far as Chapel could see.

And he was right—there was a lot at stake. Chapel glanced down at the table and did a mental calculation. Two sixes showing, and Chapel only had queen high. If Wilkes wasn't bluffing, the game could be over right here.

Chapel sighed and threw his cards down on the table. He found that he couldn't care less. "Fold," he said.

Wilkes' mouth bent in a fraction of a grin and he grabbed for the pot—nearly a full bag of potato chips. He stuffed them in his mouth one after another with the precision that marked everything he did.

Chapel had spent three months in the smelly motel room with Wilkes, as much as sixteen hours out of every day, and he still couldn't get a read on his partner. Wilkes didn't seem to care about anything except poker—but playing cards and thinking about cards seemed to be plenty to sustain him. After the first week Chapel had realized how outclassed he was, and had refused to play for money any more. They didn't have anything else to wager with so they'd played with potato chips instead. It didn't seem to matter to Wilkes. He played the game to win, not to make money.

The floor around the marine's chair was littered with a drift of empty potato chip bags. He ate each little crumb that he won, scouring the table bare, but then he just dropped the empty bags on the floor, completely uninterested in keeping the room clean. At the end of each day Chapel picked up the bags and threw them out, knowing he would get to do it again the next day.

And meanwhile nothing whatsoever changed with the case.

They were holed up in the motel because it was supposed to be the meeting place for a high profile black marketeer, a place where he could meet and make deals with military personnel from the nearby Aberdeen Proving Ground. A lot of very expensive military hardware had gone missing from Aberdeen, and intelligence suggested it all came through this motel. Chapel had identified one Harris Contorni as the buyer, a former army corporal who had been dishonorably discharged. He'd gathered enough evidence to show that Contorni had connections to the east coast mafia. He'd thought that once he identified the culprit his involvement with this case would be finished. After all, chasing low-level crooks like Contorni was way below his pay grade.

Instead he'd been ordered to see the case through. Which meant a semi-permanent stakeout of the motel where Contorni lived. Chapel had planted listening devices all through Contorni's room and phone and car and then he'd moved in to a room three doors down and then Wilkes had shown up and Chapel had gotten the worst sinking feeling of his life.

His boss had given him scutwork to do. And then he'd assigned Chapel a babysitter just in case.

It was a pretty clear vote of no confidence.

And one he'd earned, he supposed. He'd screwed up badly the year before on a mission in Siberia. Put a lot of people in danger. Even though he'd fixed things, even though he'd completed his mission, he knew his boss, Director Hollingshead, must have lost a lot of faith in him.

"Wanna play again?" Wilkes asked.

"Not now," Chapel said. He looked at the cards scattered across the table and realized he didn't even care enough to pick them up and put them away. This case was turning him into a slob—breaking his lifetime habit of cleaning up after himself.

Months had passed with no sign whatsoever that Contorni was putting together another deal. Months of doing nothing but breathing in Wilkes' air. He was losing his edge. Getting rusty.

"Alright," Wilkes said. "You mind if I run down to the store, get some soda? All these chips I keep winning make me so dry I don't even piss anymore. I just fart salt."

Chapel waved one hand in the air, not even bothering to be disgusted. Wilkes left without another word.

When he was gone Chapel checked the laptop on the nightstand, but there was nothing there. Contorni hadn't made a call in six hours, and though he'd driven approximately twenty-five miles in his car over the last twenty-four hours, he had gone nowhere near the Proving Ground. Nothing. As usual.

Chapel sat down hard on the bed. He considered doing some calisthenics but the room already smelled like sweat and dirty laundry. Maybe later. Instead he reached into his pocket and took out his hands-free device. He stared at it for a while, knowing he was probably making a mistake, but then he shoved it in his ear and pressed the power button.

"Angel," he said. "Are you there?"

"Always, Sugar," she replied.

He closed his eyes and let himself smile a little. That voice . . . it was like having someone breathe softly on the back of his neck. It made him feel good like nothing else did anymore.

He hadn't spoken to Angel in weeks. He'd missed it.

He had never met her. He had no idea what she looked like, or where she was located. He didn't even know her real name—he'd started calling her Angel and it just stuck, and now even his boss referred to her that way. He'd chosen the name because when he was in the field she worked as his guardian angel. If he needed to look up the criminal record of a deadly assassin, or just find the best route through traffic during a car chase, she was the one with the answers he needed. More than that she had walked him through some very tricky missions. She'd saved his life so often he didn't even keep track anymore.

She had become more than just a colleague to him. Among other things, she was the only woman in his life, now that his girlfriend had dumped him.

But now that he was working the stakeout, he barely got to talk to Angel at all. There was no need for her special skills on this mission, no need to occupy her valuable time with the running tally of how many poker hands Chapel lost or how many days had passed without new intelligence.

"Anything to report?" she asked, now. "Or are you just checking in?"

"Nothing," he told her. He wondered what he sounded like to her. There'd been a time she respected him, even admired what he'd achieved in the field. Had her esteem for him dropped as she listened to him grow more and more dejected? "Any word from the director? Any new instructions, any hint of reassignment?"

"You know I would call if there was," she told him. There was something in her voice, a cautious little hesitation. She was waiting to hear why he'd called.

It was too bad he didn't have a good answer. He couldn't very well tell her that he'd called because he was lonely. Every time the two of them spoke cost taxpayer money. Maybe something more than that, too. He knew she worked with other field agents as well—even Wilkes knew who she was, though he said he'd only worked with her once, and briefly. Maybe when he'd called she'd been in the middle of saving somebody else's life. Most likely she would have told him so, however, or just not answered her phone.

"What about that other thing I asked you about? Did you turn up anything more on Wilkes?"

"I'm still not sure what you're hoping to find," she said.

594 / DAVID WELLINGTON

"I just want a better idea of who I'm working with here. I need to be able to trust this guy when push comes to shove."

Angel sighed. "You know I can't tell you much. He's a Raider, as I'm sure you've already figured out."

Chapel didn't need any great detective skills for that. Wilkes had a Marine Corps logo tattooed on his arm and the distinctive haircut of a jarhead. If he was working for Hollingshead's directorate that meant he was special ops—specifically the United States Marine Corps Special Operations Command, MARSOC, the Raiders, the newest branch of secret warriors in SOCOM. He would be what the service called a Critical Skills Operator, which meant he would be trained in everything from unarmed combat to language skills to psychological warfare.

All well and good. But there was something about Wilkes that bothered Chapel. Call it a gut feeling, or intuition, or just keen observation. But he suspected the marine was holding something back. That he had some dark secret he didn't want Chapel—or Hollingshead—to know about.

"And you say his record is clean. No red flags anywhere in his file."

"None," Angel replied. "He served a bunch of tours with military intelligence in Afghanistan and Iraq. When he got home, about three years ago, he was recruited by Director Hollingshead personally. He checks out—I vetted him myself."

"And you worked with him, too, on a mission," Chapel said.

There must have been a certain tone in his voice. "Are you getting jealous?"

Chapel forced a laugh. "Hardly."

"You know I'm yours, first and last," Angel said. "You were just on mandatory vacation at the time; a mission came up, and he and I were just free at the right time. Don't worry, Chapel. Nobody's replacing you in *my* heart."

It felt damned good to hear that.

He just wished he was sure Director Hollingshead felt the same way.

Chapel respected and trusted his boss implicitly. He would even admit to loving the man, the way a soldier loves a worthy commanding officer. Hollingshead was fair-minded and he took good care of his people. But he was also a pragmatist.

If he was going to replace Chapel, then Wilkes was a perfect choice. Chapel was rushing toward his mid-forties, way older than any field agent should be, while Wilkes still had good years in him before he hit thirty. Chapel had been badly wounded in combat and he had screwed up a vital mission by misjudging a foreign asset. Wilkes was tough as nails, smart as a whip, and had no bad marks on his record at all. It would just make sense to put Wilkes on the most vital missions and have Chapel make a more or less graceful descent into, say, an analyst position or have him work as a consultant or, God forbid, run stakeouts for the rest of his career.

If Chapel had been in Hollingshead's place he would make the same decision.

It didn't mean he had to like it.

"Chapel, are you okay?" Angel asked. "You went quiet there."

He shook himself back to attention. He realized he'd been sitting there ruminating while Angel was on the line. He was so comfortable with her, so utterly at home talking to her that he'd let his brain shut down.

"I'm . . . fine. I . . ."

Maybe it was time to lay his cards on the table.

His mouth was suddenly dry. He swallowed thickly and said, "I'm fine, Angel. I just need to know something. You and I have been through so much, I'm hoping I can count on you to tell me something even if you have orders not to."

Angel didn't respond. Maybe she was waiting to hear what he said next.

"I need to know—is my career over? Because it's pretty much all I have left." He shook his head, even though she couldn't see him. "When Julia left, when . . . when Nadia died, I . . . I guess I started to wonder about what I'm doing. About what kind of life I can have, now. I took my time and weighed things and I think, well, I think if I can keep working, if I can keep going on real missions, then it'll be okay. All the sacrifices I've made don't matter. Not if I can still be of some use. But if I'm being put out to pasture I'm not sure I can keep—"

He stopped because there was a click on the line. A soft mechanical sound that could have meant anything. Maybe somebody else was listening in, or maybe Angel had just changed the frequency of her signal, or—

Three annoying beeps sounded in his ear. The tones that indicated a dropped call.

"Angel?" he said. "Angel, are you there?"

Angel's equipment was the best in the world. There was no way she could get cut off like that, not just because of a bad cellular link or rain fade or anything like that.

"Angel?" he said again.

There was no reply.

TOWSON, MD: MARCH 21, 07:36

When Wilkes got back Chapel was still trying to raise Angel. He had a phone number for her, one he'd never written down, only memorized. There was no answer on that line. It didn't even go to voicemail, it just rang and rang. He tried to get in touch with Director Hollingshead next, calling a number for a pet store in Bethesda that was a front for the Defense Intelligence Agency. The woman on the other end of the line listened to his access code, then told him to hold the line while she connected him.

At least he got an answer this time—a very polite, very serious-sounding man who told him the Director was not available to take his call. Chapel knew better than to ask if he could leave a message. His access code had been logged and Hollingshead would know Chapel had called—if he could, he would call Chapel back as soon as possible.

Wilkes had returned with a two liter bottle of soda and with his own phone in his hand. He kept trying to get Chapel's attention but Chapel just waved him away. If something had happened to

Angel, if she was in trouble, he would move heaven and earth to help her. Nothing else mattered. Even his mission was less important. If Harris Contorni was in the middle of selling backpack nukes to Iran in his motel room three doors down, well, that would just have to wait.

Wilkes finally did get his attention by grabbing Chapel's phone out of his hand.

"What the hell do you think you're doing?" Chapel demanded.

Wilkes didn't reply. He just tapped Chapel's phone screen a couple of times with one finger while unscrewing the top of his soda bottle with his other hand. Then he handed the phone back and took a long slug of cola.

Chapel looked down at his phone. Wilkes had opened an app that decrypted incoming messages from the Pentagon. What he read there made him swear under his breath.

ABORT CURRENT MISSION.
W AND C TO REPORT NGA HQ
FOR BRIEFING 0900.
AUTHORIZED POSEIDON.

"Poseidon" was Director Hollingshead's code-name for the month, which meant he'd sent for the two of them personally. The headquarters of the National Geospatial-Intelligence Agency were in Fort Belvoir in Virginia, less than an hour away. The two of them just had time to clean up and get their uniforms on before they had to leave.

All of which was fine—but the first line of the

message was what made Chapel's eyes go wide. They were being told to abandon their stakeout, just for a briefing? Something truly serious must have happened.

"When did this come in?" Chapel asked.

"Five minutes ago. Looks like you were too busy to notice," Wilkes told him. He took another long pull on his soda, then capped the bottle and threw it on the bed. "What were you up to?"

Chapel tried to decide how much he trusted Wilkes. "Something's going on with Angel," he said, finally. "Her signal cut out and I can't get her back on the line."

"Maybe it's something to do with this briefing."

Chapel could only shrug. "You take first shower. I'm going to keep trying to reach her."

FORT BELVOIR, VA: MARCH 21, 08:51

Chapel had an office at Fort Belvoir—as did half the intelligence staffers in America. It was an enormous, sprawling facility packed with the headquarters of dozens of agencies and offices and directorates large and small. He'd worked there for ten years, back before his reactivation as a field agent, but that had been in the southern area. NGA headquarters was in the north area, a region of the fort he'd rarely visited. He'd never even seen the NGA building before.

He had no idea whatsoever why he was being summoned there. Normally he would have called Angel to ask her—to get some idea of what he was walking into before the briefing began. But she still wasn't answering her phone.

Wilkes played with the radio the whole way there, trying to find some news broadcast that might give them an idea what had happened. There was nothing. Some freak wildfires in Colorado caused by a massive lightning strike. The governor of New Jersey was in trouble again for reasons so boring Chapel just tuned them out. That was no reason to cancel a six month investigation just so two operatives could attend a briefing.

When they arrived at their destination Chapel just took a second to look at the place. What he knew about the NGA was limited. The National Geospatial-Intelligence Agency was responsible for SIGINT and imaging, he knew that much—it was a clearing house for all kinds of intelligence ranging from satellite data to radio broadcast intercepts to actual maps of sensitive areas. Its mission was just to collect information that might be useful to other agencies, and as far as he knew it didn't carry out operations on its own, it just provided support. He knew that it was supposed to have been vital in locating Bin Laden in Abbottabad.

Apparently that kind of support paid off.

The NGA building was the third largest federal building in the DC area—only the Pentagon and the Ronald Reagan Building were bigger. Much of its size came from its unusual shape. From above— say, from a satellite view—the structure looked like two enormous concrete parentheses framing a central atrium like the world's biggest greenhouse. The atrium was five hundred feet long and more than a hundred feet wide. It was big enough to have its own weather system. As the two of them headed inside, Chapel couldn't help but look up at the massive span of arching trusses overhead that screened the sky.

The atrium was full of people headed from one side of the headquarters to the other, some in military uniforms, some in civilian clothes. None of them looked particularly scared or tense, but maybe they didn't know what was going on either.

Wilkes was already moving ahead toward a security station that blocked the main entrance to the complex. Chapel rushed to catch up—then slowed down when he saw there was a metal detector station.

"Just step through, sir," the attendant said. She was a middle-aged woman with that look security professionals get, like they've seen literally everything and none of it was particularly interesting. "There's a line behind you."

He gave the woman a smile. This was always tricky. "I'm afraid I'm about to make your day more complicated," he told her. "I—"

"No firearms are allowed inside," she told him, running a practiced eye up and down his uniform. "No weapons of any kind. If you're worried about your belt buckle you can take your belt off."

"It's not that," Chapel said. "I have a prosthesis."

Her world-weary stare didn't change. "You'll have to remove it."

He considered arguing but knew there was no point. So while everyone in the NGA stared he unbuttoned his uniform tunic and then stripped out of his shirt until he was naked from the waist up. In a government office building.

Anyone seeing Chapel like that would take a second to realize what was different about him. His left arm, after all, looked exactly like his right one. It was the same skin tone and there was the same amount of hair on the knuckles and the forearm.

That appearance ended at his shoulder. There his left arm flared out in a pair of clamps that were snug against the place his real arm used to be. He reached over with his right hand and released the catches that held the arm in place, then pulled the whole thing off and put it in a plastic bin so it could be scanned.

As it ran through the machine, the attendant didn't even look at him. She studied her screen making sure there were no bombs or weapons hidden inside the prosthetic. The fingers of the artificial hand ducked in and out of her x-ray scanner, as if reaching out of the guts of the machine for help.

At least a hundred people, most of them in civvies, had stopped to watch. Some of them pointed at him while others whispered to each other with shocked expressions on their faces.

Chapel had been through this before. He tried not to let it bother him. On the other side of the security barrier, Wilkes watched with a sly smile. He knew about the arm, of course—they'd been living together for months now. Most likely he just wanted to watch Chapel squirm. Well, Chapel did his best not to give his partner what he wanted.

When the scan was done and Chapel, sans arm, had passed through the metal detector, the attendant picked up the artificial limb and handed it back to Chapel. He started to take it from her but she held on a second too long.

"Sir," she asked. She looked like she was having trouble finding the right words. Finally, she just said, "Iraq?"

"Afghanistan," he told her.

She nodded. "I have a cousin. Had . . . had a cousin. He died in Iraq. Sir—do you think it was worth it?"

Chapel wanted to sigh. He wished he knew the answer to that one himself, sometimes. It wasn't the first time anyone had asked him the question, though, and he knew what to say. "I'm sure he thought it was. I'm sure he went over there to serve his country, even knowing what that could mean."

The woman didn't look at him. She just nodded and gave him his arm back.

By the time he put the arm and his uniform back on, Wilkes was nearly jumping up and down in impatience. "Come on," he said. "We're going to be late."

FORT BELVOIR, VA: MARCH 21, 09:03

They were given guest badges and instructions on how to find the briefing room, but nobody arrived to take them there. The two of them hurried through a series of windowless hallways and down several flights of stairs because they had no time to wait for an elevator. When they arrived at their destination Chapel estimated they were at least one floor underground. He knew what that meant—he'd been in enough secure facilities in his time to know you put the really important rooms in the basement, where anyone inside would be safe from an attack on the surface.

Chapel pushed open the door and found himself in the largest, most high-tech briefing room he'd ever seen. Every wall was lined with giant LCD screens, some ten feet across, some the size of computer monitors. Currently they were all showing the same thing: a murky picture of a stack of shipping containers, with a deep fog or maybe a cloud of dust swirling between them. The view didn't give him any new information he could work with so instead he looked at the people gathered in the room.

There were a lot of them. Maybe fifty. Half were dressed in military uniforms from every branch of service—even the Coast Guard and the National Guard were represented. Judging by the insignia they wore, Chapel, a Captain in the US Army, was the lowest ranking man in the place except for Wilkes, who was a First Lieutenant. He recognized some of the faces because they belonged to generals and admirals.

The other half of the crowd wore civilian clothes—conservative suits and flag pins. He recognized far fewer of them because he rarely dealt with civilian agencies, but he could tell right away they were all intelligence people by the way they kept glancing at each other as if they expected to be stabbed in the back at any minute.

Chapel definitely recognized one man in the room, a man in an immaculate navy blue suit with perfect white hair and deep blue eyes that could have drilled holes in armor plate. That was Patrick Norton, the Secretary of Defense. The boss of Chapel's boss, and the leader of the entire military intelligence community of the United States. The boss, in other words, of almost every person in the room.

"Shit just got real," Wilkes muttered.

The two of them moved to the back wall of the room and stood at attention, waiting to be put at their ease.

It didn't take long. Rupert Hollingshead came out of the crowd and shook both their hands.

The director—their boss—didn't look like he belonged in either camp. He wore a tweed suit with a vest and a pocket watch and unlike everybody else he had facial hair—a pair of mutton chop sideburns that stuck out from either side of his wide face. He didn't look like an intelligence professional at all, but more like a genial old professor from an Ivy League university. It was rare when Chapel didn't see him smiling and nodding quietly to himself as if he were lost in thought.

Today was one of those rare days. He'd never seen the director look so serious. The tweed, the smiles, even the pocket watch—those were all part of a costume, very carefully designed to put people at their ease and make them think he was no kind of threat. Today, though, it looked like he'd had to hurry over here so fast he didn't have time to put on his proper uniform, which would have marked him as a rear admiral. His face looked, for once, like it belonged to the man Chapel knew—the spymaster, the head of a secret Defense Intelligence Agency directorate. A man who was capable of sending field agents to their deaths, a man who could handle even the most grim situation report.

"Stand down, boys," he said, in a voice that was not quite a whisper but which was unlikely to carry across the room. "I'm sure you're wondering why you're here."

"Yes, sir," Chapel said. Wilkes just watched the director's face.

"You two are here because I might need to send you on a new mission right away. Stand back here and keep quiet, alright? We'll talk when this is done."

Chapel very much wanted to tell the director about Angel's dropped call and the fact that she'd been incommunicado for hours now. But this was neither the time nor the place. Even as Hollingshead stepped away from them, back into the muttering crowd, the briefing began.

FORT BELVOIR, VA: MARCH 21, 09:13

A woman wearing a pantsuit—a civilian—stepped up to a podium on the far side of the room and asked everyone to take their seats.

"Thank you for coming, everyone," she said. "I'm Melinda Foster, and I work for the NGA. We brought you all here to our offices as a kind of neutral territory. The NGA provides imaging product for both civilian and department of defense organizations, and the current situation is going to involve both sides of the intelligence community. My job isn't to make policy decisions, though. I'm just here to give you the facts as we know them. Then we'll open the floor to discussion."

She picked up a remote control and clicked a few buttons. Behind her, on one of the big screens, a map of Louisiana appeared with a red star superimposed on the Mississippi delta. "This morning, just before six AM, the United States suffered a radiological attack."

This wasn't the kind of crowd that would easily erupt into chaos. Nobody jumped to their feet or shouted for more information. But Chapel could feel all the oxygen draining from the room as the crowd drew a deep and collective breath.

On the screen a map of the Port of New Orleans appeared. "The night before a cargo container came into this, our busiest port. It came with counterfeit paperwork, and it was full of low-level radioactive waste. I need to stress that does not mean weapons-grade radiologicals. Instead, we're talking about the stuff that gets discarded all the time by workers in nuclear power plants. Everything from scrapped computer components to contaminated safety equipment down to the gloves and protective clothing the workers used. All that stuff is considered as hazardous material and is normally processed along with spent nuclear fuel."

A slide came up on the screen showing a pile of garbage that looked harmless enough, just as she'd described it.

"Radioactive particles can adhere to this material, so it needs to be disposed of carefully. But apparently some nuclear plant somewhere didn't feel like paying to do that. So instead they just stuffed it in a cargo container and sent it overseas. Most likely it was being shipped to a developing country where it would end up in a landfill. Along its journey, however, it passed through our port. This is, of course, illegal—hence the counterfeit paperwork. Just before six AM, this cargo container entered an inspection station in the Port of New Orleans. It went under a PVT gamma ray detection arch, a piece of technology we've installed in all of our shipping hubs specifically to catch this kind of event. We know that we did, in fact, log a gamma ray detection event. Normally the cargo container would have been isolated in a quarantine facility and traced back to its origin. Today, however, we never got the chance."

Foster clicked her remote again. The image on the screen changed to show a Predator UAV—an aircraft everyone in the room would instantly recognize.

"At the same time an MQ-1 drone was passing overhead. It was an old, demilitarized model, one of the first generation drones. Civilian agencies and even law enforcement are using these now for basic surveillance functions. Local air traffic control was aware of the Predator but nobody seems to have raised any red flags—they assumed it was a routine sweep. The port is monitored at all times by a variety of systems, including drones, and while this one didn't have an official flight plan everyone seems to have assumed that was just an oversight. Now, these drones don't just fly themselves. Somebody has to actively control them from another location. So we know what happened next was not just a glitch.

"The drone descended at speed toward the port facility just as the cargo container passed under the PVT arch. It impacted the container with a considerable amount of force. The drone wasn't carrying any weaponry but simple physics was enough to catastrophically damage the cargo container. Its structural integrity was compromised and its contents were dispersed over a wide area. Some of the non-metallic components inside, like those rubber gloves, were aerosolized in the impact.

"What that means is that a large quantity of radioactive material was dispersed across the port facility, in some cases traveling a quarter mile before it came to a stop. Dust from the gloves and clothing may have been carried much further. Preliminary analysis shows that a significant area of the port has been affected."

She clicked a button and a new picture came up, this showing an overhead view of the enormous port facility. A red stain indicating the spread of radiation covered almost half of the view, looking like a spray of blood from a cut artery.

"The port was evacuated just after the event. There was only one direct injury—a Charles Mitchell, the operator of the PVT arch, was hit by flying debris. He was found dead on the scene. Meanwhile, we have HAZMAT crews all over the port trying to collect as much of the debris as possible. Though the overall levels of radiation are very low, it just isn't safe to let workers back inside the facility until we can complete our clean-up."

She clicked her remote and the view returned

to the video Chapel had seen before—the dust-shrouded pile of cargo containers.

"Ladies and gentleman," Foster said, "Mr. Secretary. The impact—the crash—of this drone was intentional. It was very well planned. What it boils down to is that terrorists have just exploded a dirty bomb on American soil."

ELECTRIFYING THRILLERS BY
MATTHEW DUNN

SPYCATCHER
978-0-06-203786-2

Will Cochrane is the CIA's and MI6's most prized asset, and now his controllers have a new assignment: neutralize one of the world's most wanted terrorists, believed to be a general in the Islamic Revolutionary Guards. But on a breakneck race through the capitals of Europe and into America's northeast, the spycatcher will discover that his prey knows the game all too well . . . and his agenda is more terrifying than anyone could have imagined.

SENTINEL
978-0-06-203794-7

CIA headquarters receives a cryptic message from an agent operating deep undercover in Russia: *"He has betrayed us and wants to go to war."* Unable to make contact, the director turns to Will Cochrane. His mission: infiltrate a remote submarine base in eastern Russia, locate the agent, and decode his message—or die trying.

SLINGSHOT
978-0-06-203805-0

On the streets of Gdansk, Poland, Will Cochrane waits for a Russian defector bearing a document about a super-secret pact between Russia and the U.S. Under a hail of gunfire, a van snatches the defector away from both Will and a recovery team from the Russian foreign intelligence service. Now, it's up to Will and his CIA/MI6 team to find the defector before the Russians do.